"YOU'RE GOING TO CATCH
YOUR DEATH OF COLD."

Jonathan stepped free of the ladder and planted an expensively booted foot on the roof.

Regina gasped, letting go of the telescope and twisting around on the stool so fast, she almost turned it and herself over. "What are you doing here?"

"Joining you," Jonathan said with a smile.

She turned back to the telescope resolutely.

Jonathan repressed his smile. She was still angry at him. The thought amused because he actually liked her angry, at least a little. When Regina's temper was on the rise, her eyes sparkled, and she said things that gave him insight into her character. A character he was getting impatient to know more about. He was a healthy, virile man, and the small taste of Regina he'd had since meeting her wasn't nearly enough to quench his appetite. Since the weather had kept her in the house, he'd been content to leave her alone, out of respect for her feelings for Hazel, and because he'd been too busy at the mill to give her the attention she deserved. But now that Ferguson had taken over the day-to-day operations, Jonathan was determined to give Miss Van Buren just what she needed.

A lesson in kissing.

BOOK YOUR PLACE ON OUR WEBSITE AND MAKE THE READING CONNECTION!

We've created a customized website just for our very special readers, where you can get the inside scoop on everything that's going on with Zebra, Pinnacle and Kensington books.

When you come online, you'll have the exciting opportunity to:

- View covers of upcoming books
- Read sample chapters
- Learn about our future publishing schedule (listed by publication month *and author*)
- Find out when your favorite authors will be visiting a city near you
- Search for and order backlist books from our online catalog
- Check out author bios and background information
- Send e-mail to your favorite authors
- Meet the Kensington staff online
- Join us in weekly chats with authors, readers and other guests
- Get writing guidelines
- AND MUCH MORE!

**Visit our website at
http://www.kensingtonbooks.com**

A
STYLISH
MARRIAGE

Patricia Waddell

ZEBRA BOOKS
Kensington Publishing Corp.
http://www.kensingtonbooks.com

ZEBRA BOOKS are published by

Kensington Publishing Corp.
850 Third Avenue
New York, NY 10022

All Kensington titles, imprints and distributed lines are available at special quantity discounts for bulk purchases for sales promotion, premiums, fund-raising, educational or institutional use.

Special book excerpts or customized printings can also be created to fit specific needs. For details, write or phone the office of the Kensington Special Sales Manager: Kensington Publishing Corp., 850 Third Avenue, New York, NY 10022. Attn. Special Sales Department, Phone: 1-800-221-2647.

Zebra and the Z logo Reg. U.S. Pat. & TM Off.

First Printing: June 2002
10 9 8 7 6 5 4 3 2 1

Printed in the United States of America

One

New York State
Winter 1889

It was late afternoon when Regina Van Buren opened the door to find a stranger standing on her front porch. A threatening winter wind was blowing off the Hudson River, rattling the shutters of the large boardinghouse while snow swirled and danced through the air.

"Miss Van Buren?" the man inquired in a deep but pleasant voice. With the collar of his coat pulled up to protect him from the wind, and the brim of a snow-speckled hat pulled low over his eyes, she couldn't make out his features.

"Yes," Regina replied, shivering as a blast of arctic air swept into the foyer. She glanced past the stranger's wide shoulders toward the street. There was no carriage waiting, and she wondered if he'd walked from the train station at the south end of town. Surely not, considering the weather. Thinking that perhaps he'd come from the large brownstone across the street, she wondered if she was finally about to meet the mysterious Mr. Parker.

"May I come in?" he asked, stomping his feet to rid his boots of snow. "It's freezing out here."

"Oh . . . of course," Regina said, stepping back. Since she wasn't alone in the house, she wasn't fearful that she might be opening her door to the devil. Mrs. Chalmers was in the kitchen, baking yeast rolls for supper. The stout cook could brandish a rolling pin better than most men could wield a sword. Besides, it wasn't in Regina's nature to be fearful of the unknown. Those who knew her could attest to her adventurous spirit.

Jonathan stepped into the house. Beneath the brim of his hat, his silvery eyes studied the young woman who had invited him in from the cold. He'd seen Regina Van Buren before, albeit from a distance, and he was pleased to discover that her complexion was flawless and her features as classical as the profile etched into the cameo brooch pinned to the neckline of her lacy blouse. Her chestnut hair was swept away from her face and piled on top of her head in an artful array of curls. Jonathan's gaze moved over her, taking in the lush curves of her young breasts, lowering slowly to a narrow waist that he was willing to bet had nothing to do with a tightly laced corset, then lower still, to where a blue wool skirt flared over womanly hips. She barely reached his breastbone, but she stood tall and proud, her sapphire eyes bright and clear.

"I hope I'm not inconveniencing you," he said.

Regina caught her breath when the man removed his hat, revealing hair as black as Pennsylvania coal. He was tall with a military posture to his shoulders. His eyes were pale, a flashing silver-gray, cast into a ruggedly handsome face. His cheekbones were high, his nose straight, but it was the eyes that captured Regina's attention. They possessed a volatile quality that warned the world to keep its distance.

"It's no inconvenience, Mr. Parker," she replied, knowing that her visitor had to be the enigmatic man who had recently purchased the textile mill. When he didn't correct her, Regina knew she was standing face-to-face with the man the small hamlet of Merriam Falls had been gossiping about for several weeks.

She frowned as she turned to close the door. Normally, she didn't notice men, having little use for their arrogant ways and antiquated attitudes. But she couldn't help noticing this one. There was a compelling aura about him, an almost grim intensity, and she wondered if all the rumors she'd heard were true. The man was obviously wealthy. His clothing was well tailored, and his boots were made from expensive leather. He spoke like a gentleman and dressed liked a gentleman, but underneath the deceiving elegance of his attire, Regina sensed a dark side to his character.

She'd heard, as had most of Merriam Falls, that Jonathan Belmont Parker was a man whose wrath was to be avoided at all cost. It was said that he ran his businesses like a sea captain did his ship, demanding unwavering loyalty from those he employed. Seeing him now, standing tall and rigid before her, Regina suspected the rumors were more fact than fiction. The man exuded a predatory air of self-confidence.

"I was just about to have tea," she announced, smiling in spite of the fluttery sensation that had overtaken her stomach. "Would you care to join me?"

"Thank you," Jonathan replied, placing his hat and gloves on the marble-topped table just inside the foyer entrance. He didn't bother asking Regina how she knew his name. His reputation had apparently preceded him.

He followed her into the parlor, wondering how the vibrant young lady would react to a proposal of marriage.

Jonathan's decision to marry had been made with the same methodical precision he used in managing his numerous businesses. A few months shy of his thirty-sixth birthday, and bored with his bachelor life, he'd arrived at the conclusion that it was time to take a wife and begin a family.

Being a meticulous man, and having parted with a great deal of money to buy the textile mill, he'd had his manager make inquiries into the citizenry of Merriam Falls. To his amazement, Jonathan had discovered that the small town had one very respectable, very interesting young lady. *Regina Van Buren.*

Miss Van Buren had been born in Merriam Falls and raised in a manner befitting a lady. Her father had died in an accident on the Hudson River. Necessity had dictated that Sylvia Van Buren, Regina's mother, take in boarders. After her mother's death, Regina assumed responsibility for the boardinghouse on Whitley Street. She attended church regularly and paid her bills on time. Considered dependable and trustworthy, she was a straightforward young woman whose support of the suffrage movement was tolerated by the town's male hierarchy because she was soft-spoken and pleasing to the eye.

But it wasn't her political ideology that intrigued Jonathan. A lot of women supported the cause fostered by Susan B. Anthony, Elizabeth Cady Stanton, and Lucy Stone. What made Regina Van Buren intriguing was her hobby. The young lady was infatuated with astronomy.

Jonathan's private investigation had revealed that fact along with several others. Regina possessed an intensive scientific library, centered around the works of Sir Isaac Newton, Sir William Herschel, John Couch Adams, and the French astronomer Urbain Jean Joseph Leverrier.

It was said on a clear night, winter cold or summer warm, Regina Van Buren could be found atop her flat-roofed carriage house, gazing at stars through the lenses of an eight-foot telescope that had come all the way from Germany.

Regina poured tea while Jonathan sat down in a wing chair that faced the fireplace.

"Who is this?" he asked as a pair of emerald eyes surveyed him. The large tabby cat stretched leisurely before leaving the cozy comfort of the tiled hearth to rub against Jonathan's trouser leg.

"Bramwell," Regina introduced the resident feline. "He's extremely spoiled, terribly fussy about his diet, and utterly adorable only when he wants to be."

Jonathan's head was bent as he stroked Bramwell. The light from the fireplace made his hair take on the sheen of wet ink. He was a handsome man. Handsome indeed, and an uncontrollable shiver raced up and down Regina's spine. When he looked up, catching her gaze, she felt the shiver turn into an earthquake of sensations, starting in the center of her body and moving outward like ripples on a pond.

The man's presence was having a debilitating effect on her nervous system. Her hands were trembling, and she could feel her heart pounding. For a tense moment the only sound in the room was Bramwell's contented purring and the metallic ticking of the mantel clock. Giving herself a mental shake, Regina remembered her manners and the fact that Mr. Parker had arrived unannounced on her doorstep. Assuming that he'd come for a logical reason, she handed him a cup of tea.

"Since you recently purchased the house across the street, Mr. Parker, may I inquire as to what prompted this visit? Or may I assume that someone in your employ requires a room?"

Jonathan smiled, turning his handsome face into an irresistible one. "You may," he said with a light smile. "My manager will be needing a place to sleep and take his meals. Your establishment came highly recommended."

"I have a small suite on the second floor," Regina

told him, delighted by the possibility of renting out the rooms. "A small parlor and a bedroom," she explained. "The rooms are available now, if your manager's need is an urgent one."

"I expect him by the end of the week," Jonathan told her. "His name is Richard Ferguson. He'll be overseeing the daily operation of the mill. I'm sure the rooms will be more than adequate. I'll have my secretary send over a check for the first month's rent."

"That isn't necessary," Regina replied. Most of her boarders paid on a weekly basis. "A week's rent in advance is all I require."

"A month's rent in advance," he countered in a voice laced with authority. "I insist."

Regina caught her breath, then smiled. She could certainly use the money. She'd just ordered a new tripod for her telescope. The advance rent would more than pay for the carpenter's work. "If you insist," she replied, coming to her feet. "I'll show you the rooms."

"That won't be necessary." Jonathan waved her offer aside. "My manager isn't hard to please."

Resuming her seat, Regina got the distinctive impression that the man's employer was just the opposite. It was easy to tell that Jonathan Belmont Parker was a gentleman accustomed to having his way. Especially with the ladies. Without glancing at him, she could feel his gaze. The room had become quiet again, while outside, the wind whistled through the trees, promising that the worst of the weather was still to come.

Jonathan sipped his tea, content for the moment to simply sit and observe Regina Van Buren. He wasn't sure what he'd expected when he finally met the young lady face-to-face, but it definitely wasn't an uncontrollable urge to pull her into his arms and kiss her until she lay limp in his embrace. But that's just what the lady provoked in him, an animalistic need to dominate, to govern her, body, mind, and soul.

Jonathan assumed his aroused body was reacting to the simple fact that he'd been too busy to visit his mistress in New York City. That and the presence of a pretty woman were no doubt the cause for his unexpected reaction to Miss Van Buren. She was by far the prettiest young lady in Merriam Falls, but he wasn't a stranger to beautiful women. Her virginity interested him because he was considering her for the position of his wife. Normally, he avoided virgins. They were a troublesome inconvenience, at best.

Of course, he expected his bride to be virginal. He looked over the rim of his cup. On the surface, Miss Van Buren appeared to meet all his requirements. She was pretty, intelligent, and graceful. Her defense of suffrage said that she was independent-minded and strong-willed. Her fascination with astronomy indicated that she had a well-educated but romantic mind. All in all, she had just enough spice to make the relationship interesting.

He glanced around the room, taking note of the suffrage flyers lying on the desk near the window. Deciding it would be as good a time as any to test her stubbornness on the issue, he used the pretense of the weather as a reason for leaving his chair and moving to the window. He glanced outside before commenting on the heavy snow clouds that were gathering to the north. Regina agreed that anyone venturing out in the morning would find themselves requiring the services of a sleigh rather than a carriage.

He picked up one of the pamphlets, eyeing it casually before turning to look at her again. "Do you support Wyoming's admission to the Union?" Jonathan asked, holding the leaflet in his hand.

Regina leveled her sapphire gaze in his direction. It

was no secret that she did more than support Wyoming's entry, she'd written countless letters supporting the progressive thinking of the territory's current legislature. Wyoming's women had voted since 1870 under a bill passed by the first legislative council in the territory, and there was a desperate fear that the politicians in the nation's capital would require the right to be withdrawn before allowing Wyoming's request for admission to become a reality.

"Yes," Regina told him in a firm but polite voice. "I support Wyoming's admission with its current state constitution intact. Of course, I'm sure Senator Vest of Missouri would disagree with me. He's made it perfectly clear that he will never vote to admit any state into the Union that adopts woman suffrage. He considers suffrage not only a calamity but an absolute crime against the institutions of the people of this country," she finished, quoting the senator almost verbatim. She kept her gaze fixed on Jonathan, studying him closely as she asked, "Do you support Wyoming's admission, Mr. Parker?"

Jonathan looked up from the pamphlet. His gaze ran over Regina, taking particular interest in the way her silk blouse fit snugly across her young breasts, and the unconscious but telling habit she had of moistening her lips with the tip of her pink tongue. "I don't oppose Wyoming's entry into the Union," he said honestly. "As for suffrage, I'm not totally apathetic to the plight of women, Miss Van Buren."

"Then you agree that we should have a voice? A vote?" she prompted him, knowing men frequently hedged on committing themselves publicly to the cause of fairness.

She'd lost count of the number of men who had tried to woo her by seeming to believe in the legal and political equality of women. Time, however, revealed their true character, and Regina quickly let it be known that she could never hold real affection for a man who thought her nothing more than a female chattel.

Jonathan gave her a dark little smile. "I agree that women are intelligent and capable," he remarked. "However, I don't agree that they are, or ever will be, a man's equal."

She wasn't surprised by his response, having already gauged him to be an arrogant man. It was a pity, since she had to admit a certain attraction to the gentleman. Actually it was more than an attraction. Something about the man touched something *inside* her. It was more than the intimidating quality of his masculinity. When he looked at her, Regina *felt* his gaze the same way she could feel the heat of the fire warming her skin. It was an elusive touch, but that didn't make it any less real. Looking into his silvery eyes was very much like looking through the lens of her telescope. The sensation made her light-headed, as if she'd just discovered an unknown corner of heaven.

Taking a quick breath to calm her reaction, Regina gave her guest a brilliant smile. "I'm sure the majority of men agree with you, Mr. Parker, although I admit a reluctance in understanding why. Surely the male gender isn't insecure enough to believe that women want to become men. I assure you, we do not. Suffrage isn't a personal issue, it's a legal issue. Since this country's very beginning, women have been counted in matters of taxation and census, yet we become noncitizens on election day. A contradiction that demands correction."

The lady had a quick mind and a quick tongue, he'd give her that. Jonathan put down the printed leaflet that was being distributed throughout the eastern states, and moved toward the fire, closer to the woman who was the real issue. "Men have their insecurities," he confessed with a devilish smile. "We are, after all, human.

I think our main difference is a philosophical one, Miss Van Buren. Even you can't argue the fact that men are bigger and stronger. While the disparity is a physical one, it creates a cultural gap between the genders that has existed since the beginning of time. Men are instinctively protective, while women are gifted with, shall we say, softer inclinations."

"You mean God created us to be wives and mothers," she countered without hesitation.

"I believe there is a biblical verse or two that supports the theory," he said, pleased by her personal convictions even if he didn't agree with them. Yes, she'd do nicely as his wife. If there was one thing Jonathan hated, it was complacency. Miss Van Buren might not be the most willing bride in history, but she'd certainly be a challenging one.

Regina scowled. "You sound like Reverend Hayes. He's a pious man who thinks suffrage is a spiritual abomination. He prefers women who appreciate the sphere to which God and the Bible have assigned them. Needless to say, I am not one of those women."

Jonathan smiled in spite of himself. The expression lasted for a brief moment. Then his eyes grew dark, and the intensity Regina had noticed earlier returned. When he spoke, his voice was almost a whisper. "If Reverend Hayes considers you an abomination, the man needs spectacles."

The fire crackled, sending a tiny flurry of sparks up the chimney. Jonathan watched as Regina's vibrant blue eyes opened wide and a blush of color reddened her cheeks. Her reaction made the urge to kiss her almost uncontrollable. Knowing women and appreciating their many talents, Jonathan realized his first taste of Regina wouldn't be enough to quench his appetite. In fact, he was almost certain he wouldn't be satisfied until their wedding night, when he could strip her naked and enjoy every inch of her luscious little body.

Regina was no coward, and she'd had some experience in dissuading a man's attention, but she was helplessly out of her league when it came to this man. If any other man had been so bold in his remark, she would have whittled him down with a sassy retort, but this man made her mind go numb. She stared at him, speechless for the moment.

"Tell me, Miss Van Buren," he inquired in a soft voice, "what other causes do you support?"

Regina blinked, clearing her mind's eye of the image of Jonathan Parker's mouth coming down over hers. She couldn't be entirely sure that the offhand compliment he'd given her had been anything more than that—a compliment. Always enthusiastic to debate with someone who didn't begrudge her the right to speak her mind, she quickly regained her composure. "I support any cause that gives people the right to determine their own destiny," she replied candidly. "Men and women alike. The suffrage movement isn't limited to the female gender. It's a petition for the rights of the individual. We have children working in factories, Mr. Parker. Children who are being denied an education because the money they earn for their families is more important than their minds. And what of our cities? New York is becoming a hodgepodge of nationalities. If the people who flock to our shores are to become productive, dedicated citizens, they must be educated. Their children must be embraced, not ignored."

"You have a compassionate heart," Jonathan said, admiring her sincerity.

It was refreshing to find a young lady who didn't think of herself first and everyone else later. She'd make a good mother. The image made Jonathan's body go taut. The lady was having more than a mild effect on him.

Acknowledging just how much of an effect forced Jonathan to reevaluate his initial intentions. He'd originally planned a six-month engagement, with a wedding in late summer, followed by a European honeymoon. Judging his current state of arousal in the short amount of time he'd been with the lady, he knew he'd be lucky to last a month. Which meant he'd have to accelerate the time schedule. It was the eighteenth of January. They would marry before February reached an end.

Jonathan never considered the possibility that there wouldn't be a wedding, because he'd never failed to achieve what he set out to accomplish. He didn't believe in fate or chance or blind luck. A man's destiny was controlled by determination and common sense.

"You must think me seditious," Regina said, knowing she was considered that by others, especially by the men of Merriam Falls. Were it not for her parents' honored memory, she knew she would be labeled a radical female, one who thrived on disrupting the community's harmonious existence.

"There's no rebellion in speaking your mind, Miss Van Buren. I find myself agreeing with you more than disagreeing."

"Ahhh," she mused. "But of those matters upon which we disagree, we disagree wholeheartedly. Am I correct?"

"I am a man," Jonathan replied, spreading his hands wide to show her that what she saw was all there was to see. "Being a man, my view of the world is somewhat different from yours. A man's upbringing encourages him to be supportive and protective of those placed in his care. Nature and history support that role. The male of the species is normally larger, stronger, and more aggressive than the female."

"There are exceptions to that rule," Regina pointed out.

"There are always exceptions, Miss Van Buren," he replied, amused by her willingness to argue with him. "But, as I said, history has few queens and thousands of kings. Physical strength is an asset, and the need to dominate is as innate in men as it is in any other animal."

Regina wasn't sure how a conversation about the political rights of women had turned into a seductive discussion, but it had. She knew the basic differences to which he was referring, the primal contrast between male and female. If she were the kind of lady the godly Reverend Hayes wished her to be, she'd be blushing to the tips of her toes. But the heat inside her wasn't caused by embarrassment. For the first time in her life, Regina wanted to experience those differences. She wanted to feel a man embracing her, kissing her, wanting her. She yearned to discover the secrets of passion and desire. The realization disturbed her more than Mr. Parker's artfully delivered innuendo.

"I've kept you too long," he said, taking a step closer to the chair where she was sitting. He looked down at her, liking the rich color of her hair and the sparkle that never seemed to leave her eyes.

All of Regina's womanly instincts came into play as she met his gaze. It was one thing to be attracted to the man, and something else to be in thrall of him. Yet, at that moment, her mind was having very little control over her body.

"I will expect your manager on Friday," she said, feigning a nonchalance she didn't feel. "Are you certain you don't want to inspect the rooms? I wouldn't want Mr. Ferguson to be uncomfortable."

"I'm sure he'll be pleased with the rooms." His mouth softened somewhat and his features relaxed, but his gaze was still guarded. "May I call upon you again?"

The request surprised Regina almost as much as the

silky texture of his voice. She met his eyes and found herself trapped by them, held hostage by their luminous power while his mouth curved into a smile that would tempt an angel. If she had any sense, she'd put the man in his place. He was arrogant, albeit in a charming way, and certainly more experienced with women than she was with men. He had a way of making his presence felt without saying a word. As well educated and independent of mind as she was, Regina wasn't certain she could handle a man like Jonathan Belmont Parker.

She was about to tell him that she wasn't inclined to pursue a personal relationship with any man, when he reached down and lifted her hand from the arm of the chair where it had been resting. He raised it to his mouth, never taking his eyes off her face. His touch was warm and strong, and somewhere in the part of her mind that was still functioning properly she wondered what it would feel like to have him touch more than her hand. For a brief moment his gaze wandered from the neckline of her lacy blouse to where her skirt flared over her lap and onto the floor, covering the tops of her high-buttoned shoes.

She was drowning in the depths of his silver eyes, when he lowered his head and placed a soft kiss on the top of her hand. Regina looked at his bowed head, at the thick waves of raven hair, and forgot that she was supposed to be a gentle-bred young lady. She wanted to reach out with her free hand and touch him. She wanted to feel the texture of his hair, his skin, as keenly as she was feeling the brush of his lips over the flesh of her hand.

A moment later her hand was being released, and Jonathan was looking down at her again. "You are delightful, Miss Van Buren. Don't disappoint me by saying that my company is unwanted."

"It's not unwanted," she heard herself reply.

Her body was hot and cold at the same time. Her heart was racing while her brain was numb. Thankful that she was sitting down, because her knees had gone weak, she managed a cordial smile. "I enjoy discussing politics," she said, reaching for any excuse she could find to explain her acceptance. "Please, sir, do call again. Perhaps we can debate Mr. Green's campaign to expand the geographic boundaries of the City of New York."

Jonathan smiled. Andrew H. Green had urged the development of Central Park. The gentleman was currently encouraging the expansion of New York City proper by including the municipalities of Throgs Neck, Unionport, Olinville, Williamsbridge, and Brooklyn. The results, if they were achieved, would add over seventeen thousand citizens to the city.

"I'm not sure Green will get what he wants the first time he steps in front of the legislature," Jonathan said. "Brooklynites are fiercely loyal. They won't part with their independence easily."

"Neither will women, once we gain it," Regina announced with a hint of sass.

It was Jonathan's turn to smile. "I look forward to our next stimulating conversation."

Regina wasn't sure she wanted another stimulating conversation with this man. He was part sorcerer, part wolf. Standing in the firelight, his hair gleaming like a gypsy's, his eyes ablaze with life, she wondered if she dare accept the challenge he represented.

"Good day, Regina," Jonathan said, taking his leave.

It wasn't until several minutes later, still sitting in the chair, still staring at nothing in particular, and still feeling the touch of his mouth on her skin that Regina realized he had used her given name. She knew then that Mr. Parker had deliberately touched her, and by touching her, he had somehow laid claim to her future.

Two

After leaving the warmth of Regina's parlor, Jonathan walked across the street to his elegant three-story house. The wind was unrelenting as it wrapped a swirling blanket of sleet and snow around him. Overhead, the clouds had grown dark and gray. Mindless of the weather, Jonathan was whistling as his boots crunched into the half frozen snow covering the threshold of his home.

"I'm in the mood for a brandy," he announced as he handed his coat to Bisbee, a slender, gray-haired man with the face of a scholar.

"Does your mood indicate that your search for a wife is over?" the servant inquired, giving the coat a firm shake before hanging it on the rack by the door to dry.

The butler had been in Jonathan's employ for almost ten years, but unlike most servants, Bisbee hadn't been groomed to serve the elite upper class. He'd been trained to steal from them. His hand had been in Jonathan's pocket, about to pilfer a gold watch, when the young American had pulled a pistol and threatened to end the Englishman's life right then and there. Fortunately for Bisbee, Jonathan was an excellent judge of character, so instead of shooting a thief, he'd gained a skilled employee, one who had a keen sense of things that didn't always fall on the right side of the law. Over the years Bisbee had proved invaluable in obtaining certain types of information, little-known details that kept Jonathan one step ahead of his competitors.

"Miss Van Buren is captivating," Jonathan replied. His smile was triumphant as he headed for the library. "Take notice, Bisbee, there'll be no more quiet evenings once the lady takes up residence. She's a zealous suffragette."

"From your expression, I gather that her zeal hasn't dissuaded you from your decided course," Bisbee remarked, smiling behind his employer's back. The Englishman had a great deal of respect for the man who paid his wages. Having that respect, and enjoying the personal bond they had established over the years, Bisbee wanted to see Jonathan content.

Pouring himself a generous drink, Jonathan turned and grinned at the servant, who had followed him into the room. "Shall I say that the lady's zest for the more adventurous things in life leads me to believe that she will make an amicable partner. I dread the thought of spending the remainder of my days bored by a prim woman whose interests are limited to social gossip and Paris fashions." He smiled as he walked to the hearth, where a fire was blazing. "My first meeting with Miss Van Buren went better than I had anticipated. She's the one, Bisbee."

"I look forward to meeting the young lady," the butler replied. "Until then, I have placed the day's mail on your desk, along with the mill reports you requested."

Bisbee turned toward the door, trusting Jonathan's instincts. The younger man's ability to discern a person's true character was one of his greatest assets. The butler had helped in this instance, using his position as the head servant of the Parker household to gather whatever information he could about the young woman who maintained the boardinghouse. Like his employer, Bisbee found himself intrigued by what he'd learned. If Regina

Van Buren was half the woman she presented herself to be, the future couple would be well matched.

As Bisbee left the room, Jonathan settled into a chair, gazed at the fire, and thought about the young suffragette who lived across the street.

Regina was very pleasing to the eye, but he found himself contemplating her other qualities as well. She was headstrong, independent, and committed to her personal beliefs. Unusual traits in a young woman, but ones that appealed to Jonathan's nature the way the scent of a flower attracted the attention of a bee. He wasn't surprised that Regina hadn't married. She was far too outspoken for most men. Her thirst for knowledge, displayed by her interest in astronomy, spoke to her spirit as well as to her mind.

He wondered if the lovely young lady had ever been kissed in the moonlight. His male instincts told him she hadn't. At least not the way she should be. He smiled at the thought and made a mental note to correct the oversight as soon as possible, hoping the weather would accommodate him. The storm brewing outside would get worse before it got better, which meant Regina would be confined until the skies cleared.

Thoughts of kissing his future wife turned Jonathan's mind away from Regina's intellectual qualities and back to her physical ones. He glanced toward the windows of the library, splattered with a slick mixture of snow and sleet, and thought about the fiery depths of her sapphire eyes. Tempting eyes. Deep and clear, like pools of spring water, beckoning a man to come drown in them. Honest eyes. Eyes that announced what she was thinking, eyes that proclaimed her potential for passion.

There was a challenging quality to her, he decided, one that called to him in a strange, enticing kind of way. He found her enthralling in an inexplicable fashion that bothered him as much as it pleased him. She was a woman of the times, determined to venture beyond the restrictions that had been placed on her gender for generations, yet she possessed a wholesome quality that had him convinced she'd be a giving wife and caring mother. The qualities were a contradiction. The paradox had captured his attention immediately.

He'd wanted her from the moment she'd opened the door and looked up at him, her blue eyes unable to hide the mixture of curiosity and fear that shone in them. The demure cut of her clothing hadn't kept him from seeing the lush curves of her body. Once again Jonathan let his mind envision what she would look like naked, stretched out on the double bed upstairs, her bottomless eyes watching him, her lips parted in moist anticipation of the kisses he would press upon them, her richly colored hair spread over the pillow.

His body, still aroused by his first encounter with her, was humming, his blood still warm despite the chilling weather he'd stepped into when he'd departed her home. The act of making Regina his wife would be one of delicate passion, a slow-building desire that would culminate in a blissful surrender of sweaty bodies and rumpled linens.

When Regina wasn't in his bed, she'd be a delightful dinner partner, debating and arguing whatever issues had been displayed in the daily newspaper. She'd be an entertaining and charming hostess, although he didn't intend that taking a wife would change his lifestyle completely. He savored his privacy, and invitations to his home were a rarity. When they were issued, they were motivated by business, not a personal interest in his guests. He'd discovered since becoming a successful financier of textile mills, railroads, and steamships that listening to those he did business with was far more fruitful than talking to them.

Listening was a trait he sincerely regretted not learning sooner in life.

The disturbing thought drove Jonathan from his chair in front of the fire to the coldness of the sleet-drenched windows. On his way across the room, he glanced at the portrait of a young girl displayed over the mantel. He'd painted the portrait himself, from memory. The painting showed a little girl at play. Her face was lifted toward the sky, her mouth smiling as a colorful kite reached for the clouds.

It was the only image Jonathan had of his younger sister, except the one that haunted his mind day and night.

The heavy cloak of regret weighed down his shoulders as he watched the approaching storm. He'd been twelve, a boy on his way to manhood, but still child enough for his head to be filled with the mindless enchantment of life. Unlike the men he did business with, Jonathan hadn't been born to the elite circles of Manhattan society that now clamored for his attention. He'd been born the son of a butcher-shop owner and a common woman who had loved both her children without restraint or restriction. The grief that had taken his mother's smile still lingered on his own face, if anyone was keen enough to search for it.

It had been a common enough day on the east side of Manhattan, with vendors rolling their carts up and down the streets, shouting for the people milling in the narrow thoroughfares to spend their money on tin pots and fresh-baked loaves of Italian bread. He'd worked that morning in his father's shop, trimming fat from slabs of beef. He'd had to complete the work before being allowed outside to play. His mother had come downstairs, leading Abigail by the hand. Jonathan had been instructed to watch his younger sibling. Being more boy than man, he'd resented the burden of the blue-eyed little girl.

An hour later, playing in the alley behind his father's shop, engrossed in a game of hide-and-seek, he'd completely forgotten about Abigail, confident that she would obey his brotherly command not to wander too far. But Abigail had been only six, too young to know better, and too intrigued by the sights and sounds of the bustling immigrant community to linger very long on the doorstep while her brother played with his friends.

The terrible scream had penetrated the alley. He'd raced into the street to find his little sister crushed under the wheels of a beer wagon. Abigail's eyes had stared lifelessly up at him. In the middle of the night, he could still hear his mother's unbelieving scream and see the life drain from her eyes as surely as it had drained from those of her daughter.

No one had blamed him, at least not with words, but Jonathan knew if he had *listened* to his mother and his father, if he had obeyed them and accepted his responsibility, Abigail would still be alive. The guilt had come close to killing him. He'd worked tirelessly in the butcher shop, slashing thick slabs of meat with a razor-sharp cleaver, wanting to make his father's burden easier and by doing so to somehow lighten his own.

But no amount of work could take away the pain. His mother rarely smiled after Abby's death, and Jonathan couldn't lift the fault from his own young shoulders. It stayed with him as he grew, making him acutely aware that he'd failed his parents. He had most certainly failed his sister.

Despite the long hours he worked in the butcher shop, Jonathan was still smart enough to make an impression on his teachers. He'd excelled at math and literature, and with the money he'd made working for his father, he went on to college. The guilt and grief that motivated him had lessened, but it had never disappeared. He carried it still, buried deep inside him, a constant reminder to use his ears as well as his mind.

The lesson had its benefits, he supposed. By listening to people he acquired an insight into their lives; what they liked and disliked could be discerned by their tone of voice or the subtle way their expressions changed. He'd listened to Regina Van Buren. The words she'd used to describe her political sympathies were as important as the way she'd spoken them.

The words had been heartfelt and filled with conviction, and Jonathan had no doubt that Regina truly believed women were due the same rights under the law as men. His argument with suffrage wasn't a political one, and he didn't begrudge the vote to women in general. What he did begrudge them was the idea that they were the same as men. Women were as different from men as a rose was from an oak tree.

A smile tempted the corners of his mouth as he thought of teaching Regina about those differences, but his fantasy was interrupted when Bisbee announced that the constable of Merriam Falls was waiting to see the town's newest citizen.

A few moments later the butler showed Frank Fowler into the library.

"I apologize for bothering you at home, Mr. Parker," the constable said. His eyes gleamed with approval when Jonathan offered him a stout whiskey to warm his insides. "But seeing you own the mill, and seeing that the girl worked for you, I thought it best you find out from me instead of reading the news in the paper."

"What news?" Jonathan asked, handing him the glass. "And what girl?"

"Hazel Glum," Fowler said without preamble. "We found her body this morning, inside the old storage shed at the north entrance to the mill."

"What happened?"

"She was strangled," the constable told him. "Her body's frozen solid, but there are bruises around her throat."

Jonathan motioned for Bisbee to come completely inside the room before shutting the library door. If there was trouble on the horizon, he wanted the butler to know as much about it as he did.

"You say this young lady worked for me," Jonathan said, looking at the constable. "I don't mean to appear insensitive, Mr. Fowler, but the mill employs dozens of young women. I've yet to meet any of them."

"Understandable," the constable said after taking a sip of the finest Irish whiskey he'd ever tasted. "Hazel lives across the street at Miss Van Buren's boarding-house. Or, should I say, she did live there. From what I've been able to gather so far, she was supposed to be in Buffalo, visiting her cousin."

"Then Miss Van Buren wasn't the one who alerted you to the fact that the girl was missing," Jonathan remarked, confident that if Regina had been upset about something as important as a missing boarder, he would have sensed her distress.

"No. Telling Regina isn't going to be easy. Hazel was a regular boarder. Lived there for years."

"I'm sure it won't be a pleasant task," Jonathan replied, meaning to be present when the bad news was passed on. His future bride might think she didn't need a man's influence in her life, but she was going to need a strong shoulder to cry on, and Jonathan meant for it to be his. "Tell me what happened, or, rather, what you think happened."

Fowler combed thick, pale fingers through his graying hair. "I'll be damned if I know," he mumbled. "Pete Bryson found the body. He works for you too. He was making his usual delivery of coal for the heating stoves.

Opened the shed door and there she was, lying on the ground like she'd just curled up and gone to sleep."

"Are you saying the young lady's person wasn't assaulted?"

"Dr. Rumley said she wasn't touched," Fowler assured him. "Except for the bruises around her neck, of course." His face took on a pensive look. "Hazel wasn't much to look at. Plump in all the wrong places, if you get my meaning."

"How old was she?" Jonathan asked.

"Twenty-five or twenty-six," the constable told him. "Worked at the mill since she got out of school. Her mother moved to Buffalo after Hazel's father died. There's an older brother. I sent him a telegram as soon as I left Dr. Rumley's office. Hazel sent her mother money regularly. I saw her at the post office every Wednesday, just like clockwork."

The mill distributed wages to its workers on Tuesday, so the regularity of Miss Glum's visits made sense. Knowing the rates Regina charged her boarders, and assuming by what the constable had told him, that Hazel didn't spend her money on fripperies and fandangos to impress a beau, it seemed logical that she had enough funds to help support her widowed mother.

Jonathan sat down at his desk, opening the ledger that detailed the mill's production on a daily basis, along with the wages paid to each of its workers. He found Hazel Glum's name among the list of women laborers who worked on the second floor of the massive factory.

"Why would anyone want to strangle a young lady who seemingly led a boring life?"

"That's got me puzzled," Fowler admitted. "Hazel never gave anyone any trouble, unless you count that article in the paper."

"What article?" Jonathan arched a dark brow.

The constable put down his empty glass, grimacing

at the topic he was about to discuss. "Hazel did more than share Miss Van Buren's house," Fowler informed the two men in the room. "She read those suffrage pamphlets too. It gave her some strange ideas. She was always ranting and raving about getting a union started at the mill, and how men couldn't see one inch farther than their own noses. That sort of thing."

"I see," Jonathan said in a low voice. He cast Bisbee a quick glance. The butler shook his head, silently agreeing that the news didn't sit well with him. Neither man liked the idea of Regina being so closely connected to a young woman who had just been found murdered. "Then I'm correct in assuming that the good citizens of Merriam Falls aren't inclined to support such aggressive thinking."

Fowler hesitated, then grunted. "If you hadn't bought the mill, Mr. Rutherford would have fired Hazel on the spot. The only thing that saved her job was his not being the boss any longer. He gave her a stinging lecture about minding her own business, then warned her to keep her silly notions to herself."

"Did she?" Jonathan asked.

Fowler shrugged his thick shoulders. "As far as I know, she did."

"Apparently the young lady left a lasting impression on someone, or do you think her death was the result of someone passing through our modest community with murder on his mind?"

Since there was no reason for anyone to pass through Merriam Falls in the dead of winter, the question made as much sense as Hazel Glum's untimely death.

Jonathan's expectations that Regina might have need of his shoulder didn't prove true. She did, however, re-

quest his company when she announced that she wanted
to see Hazel's body.

"I'm not sure that's a good idea," Jonathan said,
knowing that Hazel's remains had had time to thaw. The
results wouldn't be pretty.

"I want to see her," Regina insisted, shattered by the
news of her friend's death, although she didn't show it.
She was in shock. Why in the name of God would anyone want to hurt Hazel? Murders occurred in the dark
alleys of cities and in garishly decorated brothels.
Crimes of passion and greed. Murder wasn't something
that happened in Merriam Falls. The small town was as
boring as day-old toast.

Realizing that fact was no longer true, Regina stood
up and walked into the foyer, where her cloak was hanging by the front door. Hazel had lived in the boardinghouse and eaten her meals in the dining room like a
member of the family She'd shared her dreams with Regina, talking about her innermost wants and desires, admitting that she was too plain and too plump to harbor
the hopes of ever finding a husband. So instead of dwelling on an imaginary knight in shining armor, Hazel
turned her attention to suffrage. She'd been even more
zealous than Regina in her support of gaining women
the right to vote. Regina was the only one who knew
that besides sending money to her mother in Buffalo,
Hazel had been a regular contributor to the coffers of
suffrage. Once a month the mill worker had sent money
to New York City to support a small newspaper that
printed political news about suffrage legislature that was
being proposed all across the country. Hazel's monthly
donations had helped to print the pamphlet Jonathan
found in the parlor.

"Where is she?" Regina asked, looking past the handsome mill owner to where the constable was standing,
his hands tucked into the pockets of his winter coat.

"At Dr. Rumley's office," Fowler told her.

"You don't need to identify the body," Jonathan reminded her as he watched her drape the cloak around her shoulders. "According to Mr. Fowler, everyone in town was familiar with the young lady."

"She was my friend," Regina replied stiffly, fighting the tears brimming against her dark lashes. She gave Jonathan a fierce look, one that said she was going to do what she was going to do and he could either come along or not.

Knowing a stubborn woman when he saw one, Jonathan told the constable he would follow in the carriage with Miss Van Buren. Relieved to know that he wouldn't have to be the one to undrape Hazel's body for Regina's mournful gaze, the constable nodded and left the boardinghouse. He had a few inquires to make. After all, he was the town's only law officer. It was up to him to solve the mystery of Hazel Glum's murder. In the meantime, he wanted to make sure the other women in town weren't scared out of their wits. The new mill owner didn't seem to think the crime had been caused by the hands of a stranger, but Frank couldn't think of anything else that made sense. He knew every breathing soul who lived in Merriam Falls, and there weren't any murderers among them.

A short time later, while darkness enveloped the tiny hamlet next to the Hudson River and snow blanketed the rooftops, Jonathan watched Regina fight to control her emotions. She sat across from him in the carriage. The hood of her cloak concealed her hair and most of her face. Jonathan couldn't see her eyes, but he knew they were clouded with tears. Her chin was trembling, and her gloved hands were tightly folded. Her body was as rigid as the frozen fences that lined the main street of Merriam Falls.

Jonathan wanted to reach across the carriage and draw

her close. He wanted to cradle her on his lap while she cried out her grief, to shelter her with his arms and comfort her with the warmth of his body. But he couldn't touch her. Not yet. For all intents and purposes, they were still strangers. She'd been surprised to find him standing on her doorstep twice in one day, but the surprise had been replaced by the shocking news the constable had delivered.

"Tell me about Hazel," Jonathan said.

Regina looked up at the sound of his voice, deep and strangely soothing inside the cold confines of the carriage. She concentrated on the image of the Hazel she had known, not on the corpse she was about to view in Dr. Rumley's office.

"Hazel was a very nice person," she finally replied. "She played the piano and she loved to read."

"I understand she had been boarding with you for several years."

Regina nodded, the lump in her throat making it almost impossible to speak. "After her husband died, Hazel's mother moved to Buffalo. Hazel's brother owns a small haberdashery there and his wife was expecting their first child. Hazel didn't want to go. She and her brother never got along. She didn't want to burden him with another mouth to feed, so she got a job at the mill and rented a room from me."

Jonathan wanted to ask Regina about the dead woman's interest in suffrage. Just how enthusiastic had Hazel Glum been? Knowing it wasn't the right time, he remained silent.

The carriage came to a stop in front of a small cottage. The amber glow of the gaslights inside the house outlined the icicles that had formed on the slanted roof. The bitter wind lashed at Jonathan's back as he helped Regina out of the carriage.

"Are you sure you want to do this?"

"I'm sure," she said, her voice shaky and her hands trembling, but not from the cold. She couldn't feel the weather. Her body and mind felt numb, and Regina prayed that the numbness would last until she was alone again.

"Very well," Jonathan replied, taking her arm.

The ground was frozen and slick, but his surefootedness got them to the porch. He rapped on the front door, glancing briefly at the small shingle that proclaimed Dr. Rumley's services to the town. When the door was opened by a roly-poly man with bright amber eyes, wearing a black coat and boasting spectacles on the wide rim of his nose, Jonathan ushered Regina inside. The good doctor led them to the back of the house, through a clean, efficient-looking examination area and into a smaller rectangular room. There was just enough light to see the body of Hazel Glum, draped with a white sheet, lying on the table.

"There isn't much to see," Dr. Rumley said as politely as he could.

"I'd like a few minutes alone," Regina said, turning to look at the doctor, who had treated her for a rash when she was still wearing bows in her hair and pinafores.

Dr. Rumley nodded, leaving the room.

Jonathan didn't budge.

"I'll be fine," Regina assured him, surprised by his protective attitude. Silently, she was grateful that Jonathan had joined Constable Fowler, and that he was with her now. Having him at her side gave her the strength to be with Hazel one last time, to assure herself that the murderer who had taken her friend's life hadn't abused her in any other way.

Jonathan didn't say anything as he moved to the table, lifting the sheet away from Hazel Glum's face. The dim light softened the gruesome swelling that was taking over her features, but it was easy to see she'd never been a woman of great beauty. Dark, limp hair framed her face, and beneath her double chin Jonathan could see the dark bruises left by the man who had crushed her throat. The bodice of her dress was stained, but her clothing didn't appear to be ripped or torn. There were no bruises on her face or arms, no sign that she'd been struck before being strangled.

"People saw only the old maid she was going to be one day," Regina whispered. "They never looked below the surface to the person she was on the inside." A silent tear marred her pale cheek as she looked at Jonathan. "She always had the most adorable laugh."

Jonathan dropped the sheet, only to watch a smaller, more delicate hand raise it again. He looked at Regina as she stared down at her friend. She bit her bottom lip to keep from crying out, and he knew the demon she was fighting. He'd fought the power of death as a young boy, hating it almost as much as he'd hated himself for not being there when his sister needed him.

Hesitantly, Regina reached out and touched the small silver cross lying on Hazel's chest. "This didn't help her," she said in an angry whisper. She was angry. Angry at the man who had stolen Hazel's life and angry at God for allowing the crime to take place.

"Don't try to understand it," Jonathan told her. "Whether we like it or not, death has a way of invading all our lives."

She looked up and saw the pain in his eyes. He'd lost someone the same way she'd lost Hazel. Unexpectedly, without warning. She watched as he reached out and undid the clasp holding the fragile silver chain. When Jonathan pressed the delicate cross into her hand, Regina's fingers closed around it, letting her body's natural heat warm the cold metal.

"There's nothing we can do for her now," he said.

Gently urging Regina toward the doorway, he waited until they were once again standing in the soft glow of the hallway lights before he looked down at her. "Was Miss Glum seeing anyone? Secretly meeting them at the mill?"

"No," Regina answered, shaking her head as she spoke. "There wasn't anything clandestine about Hazel. And she wouldn't meet a man in the dark. She wasn't like that."

The doctor joined them, insisting that Jonathan take Regina straight home. He also recommended a sip of brandy before the young lady retired.

By the time Jonathan got Regina home, the house was buzzing with the news of Hazel's death. The cook, Mrs. Chalmers, met them at the front door, her eyes swollen with freshly shed tears, her comforting arms reaching out to embrace Regina the moment she was inside. Jonathan removed his hat and coat, determined to stay and see that his future bride was resting peacefully before he returned to his own home and the unanswered questions that surrounded Hazel Glum's death.

Regina didn't resist Jonathan's attention. Instead, she let him take her cloak, then lead her into the parlor, where she immediately burst into tears. She wasn't sure how she ended up in his arms, she knew only that his long, lean body felt warm and strong, and that his hands rubbing gently up and down her back felt wonderful. He felt alive, and she wanted to absorb that life, to use it as a shield against the cold fingers of death that were now holding Hazel Glum.

Jonathan held her close. Her hands gripped the lapels of his jacket as sobs escaped her throat. He hadn't been wrong about what it would feel like to hold her. Even in grief, her body was warm and soft, molding against him in an intimacy she was too upset to notice.

He hugged her closer, reassuring her in the most fundamental way a man could reassure a woman.

Under the cold ache of grief, Regina felt the warmth of Jonathan's embrace. Slowly the shock of Hazel's death relented, and the tears subsided, leaving her face stained. She looked up at him through wet, spiky lashes.

"I'm sorry," she whispered.

"Don't be."

He released Regina just before Mrs. Chalmers carried in a pot of tea. The cook gave him an approving smile before she exited the room, leaving the door slightly ajar.

Ignoring the tea, Jonathan walked to a cabinet in the corner of the room and found what he was looking for. He poured a small amount of brandy into one of the teacups.

"Here, drink this."

Regina accepted the cup.

"Slowly," Jonathan cautioned her.

She obeyed him, taking a tiny sip of the mellow liquor, then grimacing. She'd never drank spirits before. Mrs. Chalmers kept the brandy because one of their boarders, a stump-shouldered but pleasant-mannered man, insisted that it helped his arthritis.

The warming effect of the brandy soothed her nerves, and Regina began to relax. She looked up from the cup to find Jonathan staring at her, his silver eyes reflecting the firelight that danced on the hearth. His dark hair was damp from the snow, and she remembered the way she'd held on to him. She should be embarrassed, since she barely knew the man, but she wasn't.

She didn't flinch when he reached out and lightly touched her hair, pushing a wayward strand behind her ear.

"I'll make sure someone meets Hazel's brother when

he arrives," Jonathan told her, taking charge the way he always did when someone depended on him. "Drink the rest of the brandy. Then get some sleep."

"I'm not sure I can," Regina said weakly, her hands still trembling. "I can't stop asking myself why."

"We're all asking ourselves that question," Jonathan replied. "The next few days are going to be demanding ones. You need to rest."

"I'll try."

The tears she'd cried on the man's suit had been natural ones, but she couldn't allow herself to become dependent upon his company. Sooner or later she was going to have to face the fact that Hazel was dead. As for any other dependency, her friend's death hadn't changed the fact that she had no interest in pursuing a relationship with the enigmatic Mr. Parker. He was much too domineering to suit her.

"I'll visit you in the morning," Jonathan said.

"That isn't necessary," she told him. "Thank you again. Your company this evening has been appreciated."

"Appreciated?" He smiled a slow, lazy smile that made the blood in Regina's head rush to her feet. "I find I enjoy being appreciated," he replied. "At least, by you."

Regina wasn't sure what to say, so she didn't say anything at all. Instead, she found herself staring at his mouth, wondering shamefully what it would be like to kiss him.

It didn't take her long to find out. His hand reached out and touched her cheek, then slowly moved down her tearstained face until his fingertips were pressing ever so gently against her lower lip. Her eyes drifted shut under the featherlike caress while her heart raced inside her chest. When the kiss finally happened, it was soft and caring, the sweetest thing she'd ever felt.

Jonathan used every ounce of control he possessed

to keep the kiss from becoming what he wanted, forcing it to be what Regina needed instead, a gentle reassurance that she wasn't alone. Knowing his limitations, he lifted his mouth. "Sleep well," he whispered. "Dream of me."

Three

Regina awoke the next morning to discover that she'd done exactly as Jonathan had asked. She had dreamed of him. Dreamed of his arms holding her again, his mouth brushing over hers, his hands making her body burn. She sat up in bed, stretching her arms over her head, blinking against the brilliant sunshine that was streaming through the window. Donning a thick robe, she walked to the window, smiling at the fairy-tale images before her. Icicles sparkled like rows of diamonds decorating the bare tree limbs. The Hudson lay gleaming between its snow-covered banks, an impassable silver ribbon of frozen water. The snow had ceased and the wind was no longer howling like a lost soul. The day was crisp and bright, the sun reflecting off the landscape like a candle flame off a glass mirror.

Remembering Jonathan's decree that he would call upon her again that morning, Regina hurried into her dressing room. The small heating stove next to the porcelain tub was still warm, although the wood Mrs. Chalmers had put into it the previous night was little more than orange embers. Regina carefully lifted the large kettle of water that had been left for her morning toilet and filled a porcelain basin. Once she'd washed her face and hands, she brushed her hair, coiling it into a stylish chignon at the nape of her neck. She chose a dark blue dress from her wardrobe, ignoring the black one she would be expected to wear to Hazel's funeral. The blue dress was severely plain, meeting the current circumstances. Without adding a scarf or lace to the collar and leaving her favorite cameo brooch on the dressing table, Regina descended the staircase.

As expected, Mrs. Chalmers was in the kitchen, preparing breakfast for the boarders who worked in the shops of Merriam Falls rather than the mill, which began work an hour before the shops opened. Regina offered everyone seated at the large dining room table a brief smile before she joined Mrs. Chalmers in the kitchen. There was little to say; everyone who lived in the house had known Hazel and was as baffled by her murder as Regina.

Hastily Regina reached for an apron. She tied it around her waist, then reached for a pot holder to open the oven door. Withdrawing a tray that held thick slices of toast, she placed it on top of the stove before speaking to the cook. "The storm has passed," Regina said.

"Thank God," Mrs. Chalmers replied before scooping up coffee beans and adding them to the coffee mill on the counter. She began cranking, knowing a second pot of coffee was always required with breakfast. "I asked Avery to pull the sleigh out of the carriage house. I need to go into town this morning. Do you still need some embroidery thread?"

"Yes. I'll give you a sample so you can match the color," Regina replied, gingerly picking up the hot toast and placing it in a small basket lined with a checkered towel.

Neither woman spoke of the previous day's events or the upcoming funeral. There would be time for that once the boarders had been fed and the dishes done. Then, as was their custom, Regina and Lucy Chalmers would sit down at the small table in the kitchen and relax with a second cup of coffee.

Breakfast was a stiff-lipped affair with everyone intentionally avoiding the sorrowful topic of Hazel's death. The faces of the other women at the table showed the stress of their previous night's sleep; their eyes were swollen, their complexions pale. Seeing them, Regina felt a twinge of guilt. She'd drifted off to sleep with the memory of Jonathan's kiss keeping her warm. Her friend's death hadn't penetrated her dreams at all, and she wondered if perhaps that had been the real motivation behind Jonathan's unexpected kiss and the bold command to think of him during the night. Had he known that it would keep the nightmares away?

If so, Regina was thankful. It was hard enough to go about the day's business with the image of her friend filling her mind. She didn't want to fall asleep thinking about poor Hazel's body being frozen solid in a rickety old woodshed because everyone had assumed that she was in Buffalo and therefore hadn't missed her. But she couldn't help wondering why. Hazel had never done a malicious thing in her life. There was no reason whatsoever for anyone to want to kill her. Dr. Rumley had assured the constable that the young woman hadn't been abused in a sexual way, and there hadn't been any evidence on her body to contradict the physician, which meant the man hadn't had rape on his mind. Nothing made any sense.

Regina was still trying to sort out everything that had happened in the last twenty-four hours, when a curt knock on the front door made her heart skip several beats. She hurried to the door, then paused, taking a moment to smooth her hands over the full skirt of her dress. She'd never been vain, so she explained the hasty movements by telling herself that she was a bag of nerves and needed a second to catch her breath. When she opened the door, she felt her heart begin to melt. Jonathan stood on the porch, looking strikingly male.

He was so tall, she had to tilt her head back to meet his gaze. The cozy warmth of the foyer was suddenly filled by a rush of cold air as his concerned gaze swept over her, taking in the somber mood of her dress and the shadows under her eyes.

Without a word he stepped inside, taking off his hat to reveal a mass of damp, wavy black hair. He kept his eyes trained on Regina as he closed the door.

"Good morning," she said, feeling a vivid rush of color overtake her pale cheeks. The man was entirely too handsome to ignore, she decided silently. There was no way she could maintain a discreet indifference to him.

"Good morning," he replied in a deep, rich voice. "How are you?"

The question had a thousand answers. Regina wanted to blurt them all out; she was happy to see him, upset over Hazel's death, confused by the butterflies that had started fluttering in the pit of her stomach, and frightened that the murderer hadn't left Merriam Falls. Instead, she offered Jonathan a weak smile and replied, "I'm fine."

He didn't believe her.

"Did you sleep well?" he asked.

His sultry whispered words came back to her. *Dream of me.* Regina looked toward the dining room door, where Mrs. Chalmers was standing, wiping her hands on the corner of her apron. "We were just about to have a cup of coffee. Would you care for one?"

"No, thank you," Jonathan said. "I'm on my way to the mill. I just wanted to make sure that you—"

"I'm fine," Regina repeated. "But thank you for taking the time to ask."

"I'll always have time for you," Jonathan stated, uninhibited by Mrs. Chalmers's presence. He'd forsaken all thoughts of a time schedule. After the events of last night and the possibility that Regina could be in danger, he intended to marry her as soon as possible. "I consider you a friend, and I hope you consider me the same."

At that instant Regina knew that Jonathan was talking about more than friendship. It was burning in the depths of his silver-gray eyes. His tone was possessive, his expression intense, the same way it had been the night before. The world quivered under Regina's feet as the realization hit home. Jonathan Belmont Parker was proclaiming his intentions. He wanted to court her. The kiss he'd given her the previous night had been as deliberate as his unspoken declaration was now.

Regina felt a sensual excitement uncoil inside her, consuming her senses the way thoughts of the tall, handsome man had consumed her dreams. She licked her lips, unaware that the movement made Jonathan's body tighten in response.

The sound of a door being opened and closed somewhere in the house broke the silence between them, and Regina found her voice. "I could use a friend," she heard herself say.

Jonathan gave her a quick, flashing smile as he reached for the doorknob. "Make sure you lock the door behind me," he instructed her. Her surprise at being told what to do in her own home showed on her upturned face, and he fought the urge to kiss her again. "I'll call for you this evening. Dinner at eight," he informed her as he opened the door and stepped outside.

Regina gave Mrs. Chalmers a sideways glance, blushing all the while. "The man's very smug, isn't he?"

Mrs. Chalmers smiled from ear to ear, then chuckled. "He's a man, make no mistake about that."

"What do you mean?"

"I mean he isn't one to sip tea in the parlor and wait patiently for you to come to your senses," the cook explained candidly. "That man gets what he wants, and he wants you."

Regina smoothed her perfectly combed hair, then frowned. "He's a complete stranger."

"Most men are until you're married to them," Mrs. Chalmers replied matter-of-factly.

"Well, then he will remain a stranger." Regina bristled. "I'm not interested in marriage, and you know it. A wedding ring won't replace the freedom I have running my own house and determining my own fate."

"Maybe not," the cook agreed good-naturedly, "but if a wedding ring would get me that kind of man, I'd put one on my finger in less time that it takes to shoo Bramwell out of the kitchen."

Regina rebuked the cook with a firm scowl. "A man's good looks, or lack of them, is no way to judge his character. Mr. Parker is far too dictatorial for my tastes. I prefer men who don't think they rule supreme."

Mrs. Chalmers didn't argue. She laughed out loud. "When you find one, let me know."

While Regina pondered just exactly what Jonathan had in mind, he watched as the gray-black outline of the mill came into view. The huge three-story factory rested on the southern bank of the Hudson River like a hibernating bear. Its stark angles stood out against the snow, its chimneys pumping thick smoke into the clear winter sky. Seated inside a sleigh, Jonathan surveyed the mill and its adjacent buildings. The woodshed where Hazel Glum's body had been found was hidden from view by the eastern wing of the mill, but Jonathan meant to inspect the site before day's end. He also meant to meet with each of the mill's various supervisors. Before he shared a candlelight dinner with Regina, he was determined to discover as much as he could about the young woman who had worked for him before her murder.

The sleigh stopped in front of the mill's office and Jonathan got out, knowing his arrival was expected. Bisbee had sent a messenger that morning announcing his employer's intention to review the mill's operation. The manager, soon to be replaced by Richard Ferguson, was waiting inside. Jonathan had met Stanley Randolph during his initial inspection of the premises and disliked the man on sight. Tall, and so thin he appeared undernourished, Stanley hadn't impressed Jonathan with his knowledge or his ability to oversee the complicated machinery that made the mill a noisy, unpleasant place to work.

"Mr. Parker," Stanley said, acknowledging Jonathan with a pair of weak brown eyes.

"I want all the supervisors in my office immediately," Jonathan ordered. He had always managed his businesses the way he managed his personal life. Methodically and without fringes. If a man did his job and did it well, he was rewarded. If he didn't, he was replaced. As harsh as it sounded at the beginning, the people who worked for Parker & Company quickly realized that Jonathan never expected more from them than he was willing to give of himself.

"I'll gather them up," Stanley replied, his tone making it clear he had expected to be given an exclusive interview with the mill's new owner.

Jonathan walked across the cold slab floor and into an office with dull paneled walls and a desk that looked like it had been salvaged from a sinking ship. The office was only slightly warmer than the main lobby at the mill's entrance. Several clerks were all busy working, still wearing the thick winter jackets they had put on before leaving their homes.

"Get some stoves in here." Jonathan snapped out the

order as one of the clerks came his way. "And enough wood to keep us from freezing to death. Is the rest of the place this damn cold?"

The clerk hesitated for a moment, wide-eyed and clearly shocked that he'd been spoken to under any circumstances. He sorted through the commands and questions, then nodded.

"Then make sure I don't find it this way tomorrow," Jonathan told him. "People can't work with frostbite."

"Yes, sir," the clerk said, coming to attention like a military cadet. "We'll have to get the stoves from the general store."

"I don't care where they come from," Jonathan said as he opened the door of the office that had been used by his predecessor. "Just get them. And don't be slow about it."

Another "yes, sir," and the young clerk was running for the door. If the new man in charge cared enough to keep the place warm, he couldn't be all that bad, no matter how much Stanley had complained about him stealing the mill out from underneath old man Rutherford's nose.

Jonathan unbuttoned his coat, then thought better of it, and buttoned it back up again. The thick walls of the mill kept the wind out, but they absorbed the cold like a sponge. He sat down at the desk, thinking half his workers had to be regular patients at Dr. Rumley's office. It was a wonder they didn't all have pneumonia.

The sky was a dull gray by the time he left the mill. He'd met with anyone of any authority, asking questions directly or indirectly that might offer him some insight into how much Hazel Glum had been liked or disliked by her coworkers. He'd reviewed her employment records, lacking as they were, to discover that she had been both diligent and productive. He'd spoken with the young man who had stumbled upon her body, as well as the women who had worked with her the last day she'd been at the factory. If Pete Bryson had been a suspect in Jonathan's mind that morning, the suspicion was put to rest the moment Jonathan met the young man face-to-face. Little more than a boy, Pete Bryson didn't have the strength to hold a willing female in his arms, which meant it was highly improbable that he could have overpowered a woman of Hazel Glum's substantial size.

When the long, frustrating day reached an end, all Jonathan had been able to discern was that Hazel had been a good-natured, hardworking young woman who frequently spoke her mind when it came to the issue of suffrage and unions to protect the rights of workers. In spite of her rhetoric, she had been liked by the majority of people in Merriam Falls, and they joined Regina Van Buren in mourning her loss.

After issuing a firm order that no woman, regardless of her size or marital status, was to be allowed to walk home alone, Jonathan called it a day and finally allowed himself to think about the night to come. There was an anxious quality to his step as he left the mill.

As the sleigh made the turn off the main road that ran the length of Merriam Falls and on to Whitley Street, Jonathan glanced toward Regina's house. A smile broke over his face when he spied a petite young lady wearing a heavy coat, woolen mittens, and a red wool hat, standing on the roof of the carriage house.

Regina tucked the wool muffler more snugly around her neck, then bent over and looked through the lens of the telescope to focus it. She was unaware that anyone was watching, nor did she care. She'd been confined to the house long enough. She'd paced the floor of the parlor until her feet hurt. Cold or no cold, she needed the freedom of the outdoors to clear her mind. Braving the brisk wind, she was determined to spend some time enjoying the heavenly view. Darkness had come as quickly as the sun had vanished behind the horizon, and the winter sky was just beginning to flicker with stars.

Regina often used the telescope as a diversion. Looking at the moon, and watching the stars sparkle like angel tears, took her mind off the mundane day-to-day things that went along with running a boardinghouse. On the roof she was as free as a nighthawk, bound to nothing but an infinite sky.

Like so many women of her day, Regina accepted the restrictions of her lifestyle without liking them. She supported suffrage, but she also had to support herself. That's why the Merriam Falls Literary Circle was disguised as a reading club and met behind the closed doors of her front parlor. She'd been born in a small town, and knowing small-town mentality, she accepted the boundaries it created. Of course, she could sell her home and move to the city, but she loved the banks of the Hudson, and what would she do if she did leave? She didn't have the patience to be a schoolteacher, and although New York City offered a tempting variety of gilt and glitter, she didn't like its crowded conditions and noisy tenement buildings.

Regina supposed that's why she loved stargazing. Looking through the lens of her telescope, she could almost imagine dancing on the white surface of the moon. It was a romantic notion that had nothing to do with anything, but it made her smile.

Jonathan stepped down from the sleigh, turning to look at the carriage house again. He waved, then called out, "Remember, Miss Van Buren, dinner at eight."

Regina stood up sharply. The man was bellowing like a street vendor. What would the neighbors think? "I'm not sure—"

She didn't have time to finish before he called out again. "Eight o'clock," he repeated. "I'll send someone to escort you across the street."

"That isn't necessary," Regina called back, knowing good and well everyone as far south as the train station and as far north as McKinley's tavern could hear them conversing.

"It *is* necessary," Jonathan contradicted her. "Be ready."

His words left a feverish promise echoing in Regina's ears as he walked up the front steps of the home he'd purchased only a few weeks before. With her cheeks burning as brightly as the stars shining overhead, Regina mumbled under her breath. *The man is no gentleman.*

Gentlemen were boring, and Jonathan Belmont Parker was the most exciting man she'd ever encountered. Her infatuation with him made her furious, but she couldn't deny that she was feeling a great deal warmer than when she'd first climbed the ladder that led to the roof.

Turning her attention back to the telescope, she aimed it at the western sky, savoring the drifting shades of twilight as they struggled against the invading blackness of the night. In spite of her intentions to keep the man at a distance, Regina found herself lowering the lens until she was looking into the front window of the house across the street. She'd never used her telescope to spy on anyone, but then, she'd never had a neighbor like Jonathan Belmont Parker.

She could see through the clear glass of the windows into the library. The shelved walls were filled with books, and she wondered if they had come with the house or if the new owner had brought them with him. The telescope's power was apparent as Regina began to read the titles in the library. Among a classical selection of the world's best literature, there were volumes that dealt with machinery, law, and exotic religions. Her handsome neighbor was becoming more mysterious by the moment. Suddenly, the man appeared in front of her. The telescope made it seem as if Jonathan were standing on the roof beside her, the view was so unimpaired, and for a moment Regina felt very much like a spy.

A moment later her natural curiosity overruled her common sense, and she continued gazing through the lens, absorbing the sight of Jonathan Parker and liking it far too much for her own good. Unable to force her eyes away, she watched as he helped himself to a drink, then walked to the desk, where he casually browsed through a stack of mail. When the butler came into the room, Regina wished the telescope had the power to hear as well as to see. She wasn't very good at reading lips, so she didn't have any idea what the two men were conversing about, but it was apparent that Jonathan was doing more than discussing the dinner menu.

Mindless of the increasing cold, Regina kept the lens of the telescope focused on the first-floor library. It was several minutes later before Jonathan set his drink aside and came to his feet. He walked out of the room, and Regina felt his absence as keenly as she'd felt it the previous night when he'd strolled out of her parlor.

A light flickered, then softened to a constant glow on the second floor. Regina responded by moving the lens an inch or two higher. Within moments she knew she was looking into the master bedroom of the grand house. The suite was decorated in rich tones of chocolate brown and ivory. The butler went about his business, turning up the gaslights until the corners of the room were rid of shadows before pushing open two pocket doors to reveal a huge French porcelain tub with brass spigots.

As if thinking of him made him appear, Jonathan walked into the room. Regina held her breath as more words were exchanged. The butler stepped out of view. With her eyes riveted to the telescope like an ancient mariner eagerly seeking land on the horizon, she watched as Jonathan shed his jacket, then began loosening his tie. Within minutes his naked chest was revealed to Regina's curious eyes. Her mouth went dry as she studied him, uninhibited by anything but her own morals.

The male beauty of bronze skin, lean muscles, and a thick carpet of black hair covering his chest made the intimacy of what Regina was doing almost fearful. She had no right to spy on the man. He was in the privacy of his own home, standing in the middle of his bedroom. She ought to be ashamed. She was, but not enough to turn the telescope away from the male glory of his bare chest and toward the huge vanilla moon that was decorating the night sky.

Regina swallowed the lump in her throat and continued looking at the man who had intrigued her for the last two days. She moved the lens just enough to see that the butler was filling the tub. Water gushed from the brass spigots with a fury as steam curled lazily toward the ceiling.

He's going to take a bath!

The realization hit Regina like a whirlwind, almost knocking her off her feet. She clutched the telescope like a lifeline, while a heated excitement flooded her body. She was well read and well educated, and not entirely naive when it came to men, but she'd never seen a man without his shirt, and she'd certainly never seen one bathing naked in a porcelain tub.

Jonathan glanced at the small clock sitting on the dresser. Soon it would be time to send Bisbee across the street to escort Regina to dinner. The cook had been told to prepare roasted lamb, glazed carrots, and a delicate French dessert that Jonathan had taken a liking to on one of his many trips to Paris. When his eyes lifted from the dresser's marble top to the window, Jonathan froze for a brief second. The hair on his neck stood up and his body went taut. He wasn't sure how he knew it, but he'd bet the mill and half the railroad he'd just purchased that Miss Regina Van Buren was gazing at him instead of at the stars.

A small flitter of refracted light confirmed his suspicions, and Jonathan almost laughed out loud. *The little lady's more adventurous than I imagined,* he told himself. *In that case, I'll make sure she gets an eyeful.*

"That won't be necessary," Jonathan said, turning away from the window to speak to Bisbee. "I can manage. Go downstairs and make sure dinner is coming along. I want Miss Van Buren properly entertained tonight."

"As you wish," Bisbee replied, unaware that Regina was about to be thoroughly entertained by his employer.

Smiling to himself, Jonathan took his time. He unbuckled his belt, then slowly slid the leather through the loops of his trousers with practiced ease. Making sure he was sitting in plain view of the window, he perched on the edge of the double bed and removed his shoes and socks. When he reached for the buttons on his trousers, he had seduction on his mind.

If Regina wanted an anatomy lesson, he'd be pleased to give her one, but being experienced and knowing that a little was sometimes more pleasing than a lot, he reached for the silk robe Bisbee had left lying at the foot of the bed. He'd never stripped for a woman's pleasure before, nor had he ever thought to enjoy it so much. Making each move a prelude to what they would one day share as husband and wife, Jonathan slipped his arms into the robe, then sashed it loosely around his waist.

His next movements were slow and seductive as he reached inside the flaps of the robe and pushed his trousers and underwear over his hips, then down his legs. When he stepped away, he wasn't wearing anything but the loosely sashed robe. Making sure to keep his face averted so the sassy little spy on the rooftop couldn't see his satisfied smile, Jonathan walked to the tub. The robe parted as he moved, revealing the muscular length of his bare legs.

Across the street, Regina sucked in her breath and held it until her face started to turn blue. When Jonathan slipped out of the silk robe and tossed it to the floor, she almost swooned. His lean body was statuesque. Hard and strong and powerful. The tremor that went through her left her feeling weak. With a husky moan, she held on to the telescope to keep from falling flat on her face.

Jonathan sank into the warm luxury of the bath. He'd given his greedy-eyed little bride-to-be just enough of a look to sharpen her curiosity. Leaning back against the warming porcelain, Jonathan leisurely soaped his arms and chest. He knew Regina was watching as the cloth moved over and around his upper body. He took his time, growing hard and tight under the shield of water that covered him from the waist down.

He was torturing himself, but it was worth it, knowing that she was watching. He also knew that women could be as easily enticed as men. Every move he made was a promise, every swipe of the wet cloth a silent pledge that one day he would do the same thing to her. He thought about bathing her while she sat in the tub with him, her hips wedged snugly between his outstretched legs. While he dreamed of rubbing his hands all over her soapy body, Jonathan hummed a risqué little tune.

Regina had never imagined that a man could be so beautiful. She had gazed at the moon and the stars and privately praised God for his creativity, but what she saw before her now was pure perfection. This wasn't a stone statue, carved by an artist's hand; it was flesh and blood, alive and breathing, and all man. Remembering Mrs. Chalmers's remark that morning, Regina felt herself blushing in spite of the cold.

The more she looked at Jonathan, the more she

wanted to find some miraculous way to reach out and touch him. She wanted to feel the heat of his skin mixed with the steamy dampness of the bath. She longed to run her fingers through the wet mat of hair that covered his chest. The need to feel his mouth on hers became a burning pain in the pit of her stomach. Shivers raked her body, but they had nothing to do with the cold wind blowing over the rooftop. She began to ache in a way she'd never ached before. Her muscles felt tight, her joints stiff, but her insides were like honey, soft and liquid and growing warmer by the minute.

If this was passion, it was no wonder women warned their daughters against it. Regina felt the intangible lure drawing her closer and closer to the flame. Like a giant cat's, Jonathan's movements intrigued her, firing her imagination until her lack of experience left her wondering what came next.

When Jonathan stood up, letting the water cascade down his naked body, Regina jumped back from the telescope so quickly, she almost ended up on her backside. She covered the telescope, then hurried toward the ladder. Knowing she'd fall and break her brazen neck if she wasn't careful, she took several long breaths before she left the roof. The bitter air made her lungs ache, but it had no power over the heat that had claimed her senses.

On her way down the ladder, all Regina could think about was that she was supposed to have dinner with Jonathan Parker in less than an hour. How in heaven's name was she going to look the man in the face after she'd spent the last few minutes staring at his . . .

Four

The colorless shades of twilight had been replaced by a cold darkness as Regina slipped into a royal blue dress. Her hands were shaking as she fastened the tiny jet buttons that ran from her wrists to her elbows. The dress wasn't new, but its color complemented her eyes. Thinking it sinful to have dinner with a man while her friend lay dead in the undertaker's building at the far end of town, she was tempted to send Mrs. Chalmers across the way to offer her apologies. Instead, she kept getting dressed, blushing as she stood in front of the large oval mirror to survey the final results. Even with her eyes wide open, she could still see the image of Jonathan Parker's naked body rising from the porcelain tub like a male Venus rising from the sea.

The blush of embarrassment had left Regina's face by the time she opened the door. This time she found on her threshold a gangly man dressed in a black coat and wearing a top hat. He introduced himself as Bisbee, Mr. Parker's butler, and Regina forced herself to act as if she were seeing him for the first time. The smile on Regina's face faded when she stepped outside and felt as if she were taking the first step into the proverbial lion's den.

Her heart raced as they walked across the street. The heels of Bisbee's perfectly polished shoes crunched into the frozen snow, and the sound echoed, blending with the frantic beating of Regina's heart. When they reached the door of the imposing residence, the butler opened it and ushered her inside.

The foyer was much more impressive when it wasn't viewed through Irish lace and the lens of a telescope. The dark wooden floors gleamed, reflecting the light of the large chandelier suspended from the vaulted ceiling. Regina's gaze swept the entryway, then moved upward, stopping on the wide landing of the staircase. Jonathan was staring back at her. He was almost as impressive dressed in dark evening clothes as he was standing naked in a tub with water dripping down his body.

"Good evening," he said, his voice low, his gaze seductive as he came down the stairway and joined her in the large open vestibule.

Regina found her voice, but she couldn't think of anything to say except to offer him a gracious hello and silently pray that she didn't make a fool of herself before the evening came to an end. Every time she looked at him, she thought of how his body had gleamed in the lamplight, how his muscles had rippled under his skin, and how much she'd wanted to reach out and touch the thick mat of dark hair covering his upper chest. When he offered her his arm, she found herself looking at the pearl studs on the front of his shirt, just above his black vest, and her heart skipped beats. For the life of her, Regina couldn't block the image of what he looked like naked from her mind. It was going to be a very long evening.

"Would you care for something to drink before we dine?" he asked, guessing where her thoughts were. There was the slightest blush of color to her cheeks, and she'd just licked her lips in a nervous little gesture that made the urge to take her into his arms almost unbearable.

"No, thank you," she replied, wishing she could undo

the damage she'd done to her nervous system by spying on the man. Her stomach was in knots, her palms were sweaty, and her feet were as cold as the snow covering every roof in Merriam Falls.

Jonathan smiled to himself as he escorted Regina through the large double doors that led to the formal dining room. Tall, graceful white candles flickered in the center of the table, adding an intimate charm to the tastefully decorated room. The table was elegantly set with bone china and Waterford's best crystal. Bisbee took his place near the serving board while Jonathan pulled out a chair and seated Regina.

"I'm glad you came," he whispered in her ear.

"I shouldn't be here," she replied, feeling a new bout of nervousness overtake her as his breath brushed across her skin. He was standing so close, she could smell the soap he'd used to bathe. "It isn't proper."

He smiled then, and Regina's heart stopped. "Something tells me that you don't always do what's proper, Miss Van Buren. Am I wrong?"

Jonathan saw the color rise in her cheeks again and felt a twinge of guilt, but the guilt lasted only a second. If the daring Miss Van Buren was bold enough to watch a man bathing, then she had the courage to endure a few well-placed remarks.

"I'm not sure I understand you, sir," she responded, feeling a wave of shame wash through her. Confident that the man didn't know she'd been spying on him, she squared her shoulders and forced herself to meet his gaze.

His eyes were like silver fire, and Regina felt her insides start to melt.

"I'm referring to your personal convictions, of course. Your enthusiasm for suffrage," he clarified the remark. "Most young ladies talk about fashion or the next town social."

"I'm not most young ladies," Regina replied, grateful to discuss a topic she knew something about. Whenever she thought about Jonathan Parker, her mind seemed incapable of holding a single rational thought. "And, yes. I'm committed to suffrage. But I'm not the only woman who embraces the idea of equality, Mr. Parker. There are thousands of us."

"But I'm having dinner with only one," he reminded her. His smile was slightly teasing as he poured the wine. "Perhaps while we dine you can enlighten me as to why women insist on being accepted as equals. One has only to look at us to know we're different."

Regina swallowed hard. She looked away from the handsome man filling her wineglass and concentrated instead on unfolding her ivory linen napkin. She reminded herself that she wasn't alone in the house. Bisbee was beginning to serve the meal, and there were other servants about in the kitchen, and probably even more on the third floor, resting after a day of polishing and cleaning the large house.

Once the napkin was unfolded, Regina realized she was going to have to brave her way through the evening. There was nothing else she could do. She met Jonathan's gaze and forced a smile to her face. "Our differences are more than physical ones, Mr. Parker. But so are the things we have in common. Men and women are both blessed with brains, and we both have the ability to use them to our betterment. Don't you agree?"

"I agree that we're both human," he replied. "Male and female. Distinctively different in more ways than one."

She held his gaze while a feeling of inadequacy engulfed her. There was definitely something intimidating, almost threatening, about the man. Sitting so close she could see the shadow of his dark lashes on his high cheekbones, Regina was surprised to find herself wish-

ing him even closer. She felt frozen in time, as if he
were touching her again the way he'd touched her the
night before, his arms warm and strong around her,
blocking out the fearful sight of Hazel's lifeless body.
She'd needed his arms then, but she didn't need them
now. She was strong enough to stand on her own two
feet, strong enough to make her own living, and more
than strong enough to resist the temptation this man presented. All she had to do was keep her mind focused
on getting though the evening.

"Just because men are bigger and stronger doesn't
make them better," she countered with her usual forthrightness. "Women have just as much to offer the world
as men."

"I'm sure they do," Jonathan replied, amused by the
way her blue eyes sparked when her temper was on the
rise. "I didn't invite you to dinner to argue, Regina."

The way he said her name made her suck in her
breath. It wasn't the first time he'd used it, but this time
there was a possessive quality to his voice, as if he'd
earned the right to address her so casually. She gave
him a hard glance, but it bounced off.

The food was delicious. The asparagus soup was rich
and creamy and the lamb was roasted to perfection.
When Regina asked about the meat's distinctive flavor,
Jonathan told her it was spiced with herbs he'd brought
back from India. She wasn't surprised that he'd traveled
around the world. His demeanor was far more sophisticated than that of any man she'd met before.

"I've read that women have even less value in India
than they do in this country," she remarked, continuing
their conversation about women's rights.

His eyes caught hers and held them for a long, ten-
sion-filled moment before his features relaxed and he
gave her another dazzling smile. "India has a unique
class structure. If you're at the bottom, it makes little

difference if you're a man or a woman. Life is extremely difficult for everyone."

"Where else have you been?" Regina found herself asking.

"China, Europe, Africa, everywhere in between." He shrugged his shoulders. "I prefer to meet the people I'm doing business with. My favorite city is Copenhagen. It's unique."

Her eyes went over his face, taking in the angular features that could be harsh or handsome, depending upon his mood. There was an intelligence in his silver eyes that alarmed her. He'd seen a lot in his relatively short lifetime. Good and bad. Happiness and pain. Yet, when he smiled at her there was a quality of sensuality that made her spine tingle.

Wherever he'd traveled, he'd experienced life at its fullest. For a moment she envied him. What would it be like to be a man, to have the freedom to go anywhere you wanted, do anything you wanted.

"Why Merriam Falls?" she queried him. "It's a dull little town."

"Don't underestimate what a small town has to offer," he said as he lifted the wineglass to his mouth. He hesitated for a moment, and she noticed the strength of his hands.

His fingers were long, his nails well manicured, and the back of his hands were dusted with the same dark hair that covered his head and chest. Regina refused to think about the other hair on his body and what it looked like wet and sleek against his skin.

Once again Jonathan knew the direction her thoughts had taken. It delighted him to know that he'd made an impression on her. The lace at the throat of her dress was fluttering, and he could see her pulse racing. She'd been shocked by what she'd seen, yet she was attracted to him. He didn't have any doubt about it, and he didn't have any hesitation in using it to get what he wanted.

"I enjoy traveling," he continued. "I'm sure I'll see Paris and the Orient again. But I felt a need to settle down, so to speak. Merriam Falls seemed as good a place as any."

Regina sensed there was more to his decision than that, but she didn't argue the issue. After all, it was none of her business. Yes, he was experienced and well traveled. And yes, he enticed her in ways she couldn't explain. But they were still strangers, and she dared not give him the impression that she wanted to be anything more. If he had reached the point where he was considering "settling down," it meant he was thinking about marriage, and she had no interest in a legal union that would take away what little freedom she had as a single woman.

"When did you become interested in astronomy?" Jonathan asked as Bisbee served a delicate pound cake dessert, crowned with a rich caramel sauce and chopped nuts.

Regina flinched slightly. "My father enjoyed the hobby," she told him. "Mother wanted to pack his telescope away with the rest of his things, but I wouldn't let her."

"Did you know several ancient cultures believed that celestial bodies influenced their lives?"

"Of course," she replied, pleased that she'd found someone who didn't scoff at her unusual pastime. "Astrology encourages the belief that the stars and moon have a direct effect on our destiny."

"But you're not a student of astrology," Jonathan said.

"No. I don't believe that something as distant as a star can determine my success or failure as a person," she told him. "Astronomy is much more scientific."

"You prefer facts to assumptions, then," he remarked

with a touch of humor in his voice. "Finally. Something upon which we can agree. I've always been one to trust what I see with my own eyes. It's much more reliable than depending upon the interpretation of others. Don't you agree?"

Regina wasn't sure how to respond. No matter what they were discussing, she felt as if Jonathan was talking about her. Realizing that he was waiting for an answer, she nodded.

The iciness left his silver eyes for a moment. She watched, mesmerized, as he lifted the wineglass to his mouth and took a drink. She felt a strange kind of pressure begin to build in her body, as if she'd somehow grown too big for her skin and it was threatening to burst.

"Tell me about Copenhagen," she said, needing something to distract her before she embarrassed herself and swooned right there at the table. "Why is it your favorite city? Most people talk about London or Paris or Rome."

"Copenhagen is a beautiful city. Charlottenborg Palace is one of the most striking buildings I've ever seen. Attending the Royal Theater is like attending a coronation. I've invested a great deal of money in Denmark. It gives me an excuse to visit as often as possible. The people are friendly, the food is delicious, and the view from the eastern shore of Sjaelland Island is spectacular. The color of your eyes reminds me of the Baltic Sea in summer. The water is deep and blue and mysterious."

Regina blushed to the roots of her hair. She couldn't help it. No one ever had said anything so blatantly seductive to her before. But it was more than the words Jonathan had used, it was the way he'd used them. His voice was as smooth as the French wine she'd been sipping with her meal.

"Don't be embarrassed," he said, reaching out to take her hand. "You are a very beautiful woman, Regina."

His touch was disturbing. It wasn't like the previous night, when he offered her comfort. She could feel the strength and heat of his hand even though he was barely touching her. It was uncanny how much she could sense from him. She knew then and there that she wasn't imagining his desire for her. It was burning in the depths of his gaze, summoning her like the distant beam of a lighthouse beckoned ships to the safety of a harbor. As instinctively as Regina recognized the passion, she also realized that there was little safety in the arms of a man bent on seduction.

"Why did you invite me here?" she asked in a breathless whisper that told Jonathan just how much his touch affected her. "If you're in the market for a mistress, then you've wasted your time, Mr. Parker."

"What if I'm in the market for a wife," he replied, smiling.

Regina sucked in her breath. "Then you're most certainly wasting your time, sir. I have no inclination to marry. Ever."

He laughed under his breath, undaunted by her rejection. "You have a quick tongue," he said, still amused. "And a sharp mind. I think we're going to get along very well."

The man was as stubborn as a frozen carriage wheel. Regina came to her feet, tossing her linen napkin to the table. "I think I should leave," she declared, realizing that Bisbee had exited the room after serving dessert. At least the butler hadn't witnessed her embarrassment when Jonathan had told her he considered her beautiful. "It's getting late and poor Hazel—"

"Hazel is dead. I'm not insensitive to your loss, but I didn't invite you here to mourn," Jonathan said, standing as well. He moved toward Regina, making her feel small and helpless.

She wanted to run, but her feet seemed glued to the

carpet. She wanted to admonish him, to scream that he was being rude and unfeeling, but she couldn't seem to get enough air into her lungs to form the words.

"You're alive, Regina. And I'm alive." His eyes sparkled with life, reinforcing his words. "I invited you here tonight because I want to get to know you. And you came because you want to know me. Admit it."

He reached out and took her arm. Once again his touch seemed electrifying, as if she needed his strength, his energy, to keep on living. He led her out of the dining room and across the hall into a lushly decorated parlor. The sound of Bisbee quietly closing the pocket doors behind them didn't register. All Regina could hear was the drumming of her heart. When Jonathan released her and moved toward the large gramophone standing in the corner, she didn't think about escaping. She couldn't think at all. The man had taken over her mind the same way he seemed to be taking over her life.

She watched as he cranked the gramophone. Music began to fill the room. When he turned to face her, Regina felt the world melting away. He moved toward her. She felt his hand slide around her waist, his touch burning through the layers of clothing that separated her skin from his. She raised her head and looked into his eyes. Her heart stopped completely, and when it started beating again, the fear was gone.

For a moment there was only the gleaming gaze of his silver eyes and the beating of Regina's heart to fill the world. There was no yesterday, no tomorrow. There was only the here and now, and the enticing, unspoken possibilities that filled the air between them.

Regina had never felt this way before. Suspended in time, as if she were living every moment of her life in one sensual instant.

"Dance with me," he said in a husky whisper. "I want to feel you in my arms again."

They began to dance, their eyes locked, their bodies moving as one.

"Close your eyes," he whispered as his mouth pressed lightly against her temple. "Don't think of all the reasons you shouldn't be here. Think of all the reasons you don't want to be anywhere else."

It was a shocking thing to say, but Regina couldn't rebuke him.

He didn't hesitate, but pulled her close against him, letting her feel the hard length of his body moving in rhythm with her softer one. His mouth was poised at her temple, his breath teasing her skin. Her feet followed his every move while the music surrounded them and the fire danced on the hearth. She could smell his cologne and the faint scent of soap that clung to his skin. Images of what she'd seen earlier came rushing back into her mind, no longer blocked by her stubborn resolve to make it through the evening. She remembered the way he had moved, his body unrestricted by clothing, like some pagan god.

The way he made her feel was pagan too. Wild and uninhibited. Her head lifted and she searched his face, looking for something, but she wasn't sure what. He smiled and she felt herself drowning again, going under for the last time.

As the music ended, Jonathan stared down at her. God, she was beautiful! And she fit his arms as if she'd been made to waltz in them. Still holding her by the waist, he lowered his head until their lips were almost touching. Her nails bit into the shoulders of his jacket, and he smiled.

"I'm going to kiss you, Miss Van Buren."

It wasn't a request. It was a statement.

Time stopped again for one long, sweet moment, and Regina felt her lips parting in anticipation of the kiss she wanted so much, she was dying inside.

Jonathan made the waiting enjoyable as he slowly traced her lower lip with the tip of his index finger, feeling it tremble. "The French have a very special way of kissing," he told her. "Don't be afraid. Trust me."

She let out a short breath just before his mouth claimed hers. Her hands clenched into tiny fists, then relaxed as she discovered what he meant by special. His tongue was gentle but persistent, tasting her in slow strokes that made her insides quiver and her knees go weak. She clung to him because there wasn't anything else she could hold on to. The world was whirling underneath her feet. Her hands slid from his shoulders until they were pressed against his chest. She could feel his satin vest and the cool silk of his shirt that covered the hard male planes of his chest. And she could feel the heat of his body through the cloth, the same way she could feel the heat boiling up inside her, turning her bones to jelly.

Then the ground seemed to vanish completely. Her feet weren't touching the thick Persian carpet. She was lost in the steely strength of his embrace, but she still wasn't close enough. His mouth was hot and hard and persistent, making her feel things she didn't want to feel yet couldn't deny.

Jonathan couldn't resist taking Regina's soft, willing mouth as completely, as thoroughly, as he wanted to take her body. He thrust his tongue between her moist, parted lips again and again, craving a deeper taste of her the way a thirsty man craved water. The catch of her breath told him she liked the intimacy they were sharing, and it spurred him on, making his arms tighten around her until she was clinging to him, until he could feel every sweet curve of her body.

He forced himself to go slowly, to tease and tantalize her while he tormented himself. She was young and innocent, while he was experienced. He knew the pleasure waiting for them; she didn't. But she would, he vowed to himself as he moved his mouth to the delicate curve of her throat and licked at the pulse racing there. She'd know much sooner than she realized. But not soon enough for him to be satisfied tonight.

"We shouldn't." She managed a weak protest as his tongue teased her skin, promising things she couldn't even imagine, yet making her want them so desperately, she didn't have the will or the strength to push him away.

Each fleeting brush of his body against hers was a fire burning out of control. Each breath she breathed was scented with him, each lick of his tongue was a siren's song in her mind. His teeth closed ever so gently on the soft flesh of her throat, and she gasped.

"You like my touch," he chided her in a seductive whisper that said he knew her better than she knew herself. "And my kisses."

Regina trembled. She was light-headed. And he was right. She did like his kisses. She liked everything he was doing to her.

"Please," she moaned, not sure it was a plea to be let go or held tighter.

Jonathan relaxed his hold, slowly lowering her until her feet were once again standing on solid ground. But he didn't let her go. Instead, he placed light butterfly kisses on her closed eyes, her brows, the tip of her upturned nose. His hands flexed on her hips, savoring what little he could feel of her through the royal blue gown. "You're sweet to kiss. Too sweet for me to stop."

Regina slumped against him. Her body wasn't her own. His kisses had stolen it the same way his whispered words were stealing her common sense. She wanted more of his embrace, not less. She wanted to stay in his arms forever, to savor the strength of his maleness, to feel loved.

But he didn't love her.

The realization was enough to bring her determination back. She pushed against his chest, and his arms dropped away.

"You're much too bold, sir," she said, wishing her words had the same fire as the kisses they'd just shared. "My only excuse is that I thought you a gentleman."

Jonathan laughed, a deep male laugh that said he didn't give a hoot about being a gentleman. "You're a woman, Regina. Fire and ice, and everything in between. And I'm a man. We don't need excuses. We need each other."

Regina started to speak, but she didn't know the kind of words she wanted to fling in his face. She felt insulted, and rightfully so. The man was arrogant, insufferable, and she never wanted to see him again. She turned and headed for the door, but he stopped her.

His fingers wrapped around her wrist as he swirled her back around, forcing her to meet his gaze. "You're a feisty little cat, Miss Van Buren. But I like that. In fact, I like it so much, I'm making my intentions perfectly clear. I'm going to marry you."

"You're—"

"Proposing marriage," he said. "And if the way you allowed me to kiss you is any indication, you'll accept." He smiled, then arched a devilish brow. "Sooner or later."

"As soon as hell freezes over," Regina snapped, so angry she wanted to bash him over the head with the expensive Tiffany lamp. Unfortunately, he was still holding her wrist, and the lamp was across the room. "Let me go!"

His hold lessened, but it didn't disappear. His hand moved until his fingers were laced through her own. "I'll have Bisbee walk you home," he said, moving toward the door.

She followed, but only because it was her one means of escape. Realizing that she had indeed stepped into a lion's den made Regina even more angry. She was fuming as Jonathan jerked the braided cord to summon the butler.

"I won't marry you," she said, reaffirming her first refusal. "I don't want or need a husband."

"You might not want a husband, but you *want* me," Jonathan said arrogantly. His eyes were as piercing as a winter wind as he looked at her. "Deny it if you can."

Regina jerked her hand free. She was about to slap her host silly, when the pocket doors slid open, revealing Bisbee, looking totally dignified and only mildly curious as to why Regina was blushing from head to toe.

Her hand dropped to her side.

"Miss Van Buren is leaving," Jonathan said as calmly as he'd tell the butler that he was ready for his morning coffee and paper. "Please see her home."

Bisbee nodded, then stepped back, giving Regina room to exit the parlor. She marched toward the front door like a soldier, her shoulders squared, her head held high. She didn't say a word until Bisbee turned the knob on her own front door, then tipped his hat as he told her good night.

"Tell Mr. Parker . . ." Her words drifted into nothingness. She couldn't have a servant deliver the stinging lecture his employer deserved. Jonathan might not have any manners, but she did. "Good night," she finally said, then closed the door.

Bisbee walked across the street, smiling all the way.

Five

For the next two days Regina stayed inside her house. She told herself it was out of respect for Hazel's memory, but she knew it was a lie. She couldn't risk seeing Jonathan again so soon after he'd kissed her senseless, then arrogantly proposed marriage.

She moved from the chair in front of the window, where she'd been reading, and began to pace the room. In truth, she was more to blame than Jonathan for her current feelings. She'd been wrong to spy on him and wrong to accept his dinner invitation. Allowing him to kiss her so intimately had been the worst possible mistake. Her body still ached from the things he'd made her feel, and the ache wasn't going away. It had become a part of her, a slow, sweet feeling that had invaded her senses.

Mrs. Chalmers was in the kitchen, baking pies and cakes for the guests who would overflow the boarding-house after Hazel's funeral. The weather was still bitterly cold, but the snow had stopped, and the roads had been cleared enough for carriages to once again assume their way through the streets of Merriam Falls.

Regina longed to take a walk, but she was afraid of what she'd say or do if she confronted Jonathan on the street or in one of the small shops in the center of town. She returned to her chair, thinking to finish the book she'd been trying to read for the past forty-eight hours, but the words blurred in front of her face as silent tears escaped her. Regina wasn't sure if she was crying for her lost friend or because she simply needed to cry, to cleanse herself of what she was feeling, and in the cleansing to hope that the strange feelings Jonathan evoked could be replaced with the old, familiar thoughts that had always been her foundation.

Unfortunately, ever since Jonathan had kissed her in that very special way, she'd been unable to think of anything but being kissed again. She felt like she was tumbling head over heels down a steep hill, unable to stop. The avalanche of emotions that had taken hold of her had her head pounding and her nerves on edge. Even Mrs. Chalmers had commented on her unusual restlessness. Regina had blamed it on the uncertainty that had invaded the town since Hazel's death, but deep inside she knew it was much more than that.

She was a practical, rational-thinking woman, or at least she had been until the evening she'd been pressed against Jonathan's body, returning his kisses. Now Regina wasn't sure who she was. Or what. Her body seemed to be on fire, her thoughts smoldering like embers on a hearth, her spirit as restless as the wind that was shaking the last of the snow from the leafless branches of the trees outside the window.

She'd read about passion and desire and love. The words had been elegant, the prose magical, but the reality of actually feeling those emotions was an elemental whirlwind that blew away the fairy-tale images, replacing them with the power of the experience. Wanting Jonathan—and she had wanted him—was the strongest sensation she'd ever experienced.

Admitting that much to herself, Regina was also forced to admit that she wanted to experience those sensations again. She wanted to feel the heat of his hands and the demanding pressure of his mouth. She wanted to dance with him again, in the middle of a ballroom, where she could be the envy of every woman watching, and in the dim light of the parlor, where there was no one to hear the music but the two of them. The thoughts that had taken hold of her were inflaming, but she couldn't quench them with common sense.

Jonathan Parker wanted to marry her.

The idea was preposterous. They were total strangers. Yet . . .

Regina leaped out of the chair, slamming the book shut with so much force, Bramwell flipped his tail, letting her know she'd disrupted his nap. Knowing she had to get outside or go insane, she walked into the foyer and reached for her cloak. Within minutes she was trekking through the ankle-deep snow that lined the edges of the street. The air was brisk and clean and refreshing. She blinked as she looked toward the winter sun. The wind stung her cheeks, but she didn't care. It was a welcome distraction.

What wasn't welcome was the sudden appearance of Bisbee, Jonathan's butler. The slender man came racing after her, one hand holding his top hat in place while he struggled to button his long winter coat with the other. "I say, Miss Van Buren," he called out. "Mr. Parker wants—"

"I could care less what Mr. Parker wants," she replied once the servant caught up to her. He was much closer to her own height than was his employer, which pleased Regina no end. She didn't like looking up to men, especially a man who thought she was going to get married at the drop of a hat. The more she thought about Jonathan's supercilious proposal, the madder she got. The man was entirely too smug for his own good.

Well, he had a few things to learn about her. First of all, she wasn't going to swoon at his feet, no matter how much she liked his kisses.

"Mr. Parker insists that you have an escort," Bisbee finished as he fell into step beside her. "It isn't safe, what with Miss Glum being murdered and all."

Regina gave him a fierce scowl. "It isn't dark, and I'm not sneaking about the woods, sir. It's broad daylight, and I'm going into town to do some shopping. There's no danger in that."

If Bisbee agreed or disagreed, he didn't say. Instead, he continued walking by Regina's side, plodding through the snow as if his life depended upon it.

"I don't wish or need a companion," she said stiffly, hoping he would relay the message to the arrogant man who paid his wages. "Please, do go about your business."

"You are my business, miss," Bisbee said, pulling on the gloves he'd hastily tucked into his pockets when Jonathan had ordered him not to let Regina out of his sight. "I'm to see that you get into town safely, then back home again, once you're done with your shopping."

Regina came to an abrupt stop. The hem of her dove-gray dress was covered with snow, but she didn't care. She was seething inside. "I don't mean to be rude," she said, turning to face Bisbee. "But I don't belong to Mr. Parker. Thus, he has no control over what I do or when I do it. In other words, I don't want a butler tagging along behind me like a lost puppy. No offense meant, of course."

"None taken," Bisbee said in a crisp English tone. "Nevertheless, I'll be following you into town and back again. I have my orders."

"And Mr. Parker expects them to be obeyed," Regina said tightly. "Tell me, Bisbee, does your employer always get what he wants?"

"Never known him not to." A smile flashed on the

butler's face. He turned his collar up against the wind and continued matching Regina step for step.

By the time they reached the post office, Regina was beginning to wonder why Jonathan wanted her. She wasn't looking for a husband, so she wasn't inclined to "settle down," as he'd so aptly put it. Her appearance was only passably pretty compared to the women she'd seen in New York City, and she certainly didn't have the exotic beauty of the women in the far-off lands he'd visited. So why her? It didn't make sense.

She waited as Bisbee reached out to open the door of the post office, then stepped inside. A small potbellied stove was doing its best to keep the rectangular room warm, while the clerk, a young man by the name of Henry Overly, stuffed letters into the pigeonholes on the far wall. Not expecting any mail but seeing a small envelope in her designated slot, Regina gave Henry a pleasant smile. A few moments later the letter was placed in her outstretched hand.

"I'm sorry about Hazel," Henry said, putting down the stack of newspapers the train had delivered that morning. "She always had a kind word to say about everyone."

"Yes, she did," Regina replied, knowing the mail clerk would miss Hazel more than most. The two had become friends since Hazel had taken up the weekly routine of sending funds to her mother in Buffalo, and she knew that the gingerbread cookies her friend had baked faithfully each Tuesday usually ended up being eaten by Henry. "It's tragic."

"Constable Fowler doesn't have a clue who did it," Henry blurted out, repeating the frustrated words he'd overheard that morning when the law officer had picked up his own mail.

"I'm sure he'll uncover something," Regina said hopefully. "We can't let this crime go unpunished."

Henry nodded in agreement. "I gave you Mr. Parker's mail this morning," he said, turning his attention to the English butler. "Do you want to post a letter?"

"No," Bisbee replied, tipping his hat. "I'm merely keeping the lady company."

If Henry thought it strange for Regina to have an Englishman in a top hat escorting her about town, he didn't say anything. Instead, he picked up a small knife, sliced through the string holding the newspapers, and handed one across the counter to Regina. "It's two day's old," he said apologetically. "The weather."

"I know," she replied. "But spring will be here soon. All we have to do is be patient."

She left the small post office hoping that patience wasn't one of Frank Fowler's virtues. The constable needed to find Hazel's murderer, and soon.

"Mr. Parker is making some inquires," Bisbee said as he shut the post office door with a firm click. "Since the young lady worked at the mill, he thought it prudent. Don't fear. He'll get to the bottom of things. He always does."

"I see," Regina replied, wondering what kind of questions Jonathan was asking. She'd already told him that Hazel wasn't the type of woman to meet a man in the dark. Still, she was relieved that someone was taking the murder seriously. Frank Fowler didn't seem to be doing anything more than complaining that it didn't make sense.

Turning to her left, Regina walked down the swept sidewalk, past the barbershop, where Reverend Hayes was having his beard trimmed, and into the mercantile that supplied most of the town's necessities.

The tiny bell over the door chimed and the scent of waxed candles and maple syrup assaulted her nose. Regina smiled as she noticed a tall jar of candy sitting on the counter. Whenever she'd followed her father into town, tagging along behind him in much the same way Bisbee was trailing her, he'd treated her to a piece of hard candy or a peppermint stick. It was one of her fondest memories. That and sitting on his lap while he looked through his telescope. He'd turned learning about the stars into a romantic adventure, telling her stories, and drawing out the constellations so she could understand the names ancient people had given them.

"Good day, Miss Van Buren," the proprietor called out as he put down the case of canned peaches he was unpacking. "What can I do for you?"

"Nothing in particular," Regina replied, knowing Mrs. Chalmers had already picked up the things the boardinghouse needed. "I want to look at some yard goods," she said, pointing toward a large table. "I'll let you know if I want some cloth cut."

The storekeeper returned to his duties while Bisbee made himself comfortable on a bench near the front door. Regina strolled to the yard goods counter. She idly fingered a bolt of rose-colored silk. The color would go well with the dark blue suit she'd recently sewn from a Paris pattern. Deciding that Bisbee might as well earn his keep, she waved Mr. Corwin away from the case of canned peaches and asked him to measure out what she needed. He obliged with a smile while she moved away from the yard goods table and to a small rack lined with scented soaps and toilet water.

By the time she left the store, Regina had spent the month's advance rent that Jonathan had paid for his manager. It wasn't like her to be impulsive, but she couldn't resist loading down Bisbee's arms with packages. Maybe the next time she stepped outside, the servant wouldn't be so quick to follow. But the British butler was as undaunted as his employer. In fact, his step seemed slightly more spry on the return trip than when he'd followed her into town.

Once the packages were unloaded in the parlor, Bisbee tipped his hat, gave Regina a sharp wink of his eye, and marched out the front door.

"That's an unusual man," Lucy Chalmers remarked, pulling back the lace curtain that covered the glass panel of the front door to give him a second look.

"Not as unusual as the man he works for," Regina mumbled under her breath. She tossed her muff on the chair and stretched her hands toward the fire. "How about a cup of tea?"

"I just put the water on to boil," Lucy said, tucking the curtain neatly back into place. "Sit down and rest. If I had known you wanted to go into town, I would have had one of the men bring the sleigh out of the carriage house."

"I didn't plan on going into town," Regina explained, then sighed wearily. "I got restless."

"Try not to think about it," Lucy said. "The only thing we can do for poor Hazel now is pray that Frank Fowler finds the man. The girls are scared out of their wits."

"They should be." Regina shuddered at the thought of another woman being attacked.

"Mr. Parker gave instructions that no woman, married or not, was to be walking home on her own," the cook said. "He called the men together yesterday, or so I heard, and made it clear that he's holding them responsible for the welfare of the women at the mill."

"I'm not surprised," Regina told her. "Mr. Parker is a man who takes his responsibilities very seriously."

"That's not the only thing he's taking seriously," Mrs. Chalmers replied with a hint of humor to her voice. "He's courting you, you know."

"He's doing no such thing," Regina gasped.

Mrs. Chalmers laughed. "I think he is. And so does half the town. At least the half that heard him invite you to dinner last night. He's got a nice rich voice. It carries a long way."

Regina blushed as she recalled the way Jonathan had shouted up to her when she'd been on the roof of the carriage house. "He's much too arrogant for me to take seriously," she said, fumbling over the words. "Besides, I don't want to be courted."

The cook shrugged her shoulders as if to say that it wasn't going to make much difference what Regina wanted.

The next day Regina was forced to agree.

Wearing a black wool dress with jet buttons and a high collar, she stepped outside the front door, dreading the short walk to where Hazel's funeral would take place. The front door across the street closed in unison, drawing her attention. Jonathan strolled down the steps, dressed in formal black, and looking sinfully handsome considering he was on his way to church.

He didn't hesitate at the curb but stepped into the street and marched right up to Regina. "I ordered the carriage brought around," he said, acting perfectly natural about the whole thing.

"I prefer to walk," Regina said, forcing herself to be polite.

A short second later the carriage, drawn by two sleek-muscled bays, came to stop at the end of the short walk that separated the boardinghouse from Whitley Street. Regina glared up at him through the black lace of her hat.

"Shall we?" he said, taking her arm.

In respect for Hazel and the church service she was about to attend, Regina maintained her composure while Jonathan led her down the walk. The carriage driver held the door open until they were both seated comfortably, then closed it with a soft click and resumed his seat atop the expensive carriage that was more suited to the streets of New York than the snowy lanes of a Hudson River hamlet.

"You're still angry," Jonathan stated.

"I'm not angry. I'm furious," Regina corrected him. "And you're being presumptuous if you think you can simply waltz into my life and turn everything upside down. While I may admit a certain attraction for you, Mr. Parker, I'm certainly not foolish enough to marry a man who thinks women are little than more female toys created for a man's amusement."

He smiled but stopped short of laughing. "Is that the impression I gave you, Miss Van Buren? If so, I apologize most profusely. Believe me, I wasn't thinking of toys when I kissed you."

As an apology went, it was a poor one. Regina could see the laughter in his eyes. "What were you thinking of, sir? Marriage? I can't believe you're serious. We hardly know each other well enough to consider a lifetime together. And even if we did, I assure you, it wouldn't be a pleasant relationship. We have nothing in common."

"On the contrary," Jonathan replied, wishing he had more time. The church was only a few blocks away, and he wanted to kiss her again. Unfortunately, by the time he got her into his lap, her veil pushed aside, and his hands where he wanted them to hold her in place, they'd be at the church. "We have several things in common," he continued. "We are both honest, hardworking people who aren't restrained by the limited imaginations of others."

"I know several men who meet those parameters," she told him sharply. "I don't want to marry them. And I certainly don't want to marry you. I have no desire to enter into a stylish marriage."

"A stylish marriage?"

"You know perfectly well what I'm talking about. You

don't want a wife, Mr. Parker, you want a parlor decoration. A woman who will sit stylishly by your side, saying nothing, thinking nothing, doing nothing without your permission, while you go about the daily business of enjoying life in the manner to which you've become accustomed, and she lives her life through and around you, her husband. A mundane, dull existence for any woman, I assure you."

"You have a rather dim view of men, don't you?"

"I have a realistic view," Regina corrected him. "I'm flattered by your proposal, but as I've said, I'm not interested in marriage. To anyone."

"What if I insist?"

"Are you threatening me, sir?"

This time he did laugh. "No, Regina. I'm warning you. I'm a patient man, to a point, but I always get what I want. And I want you."

She shivered at the sensuous tone in his deep voice. Her fingers dug into the folds of her black dress as she tried to keep her temper under control. She could see the church steeple through the carriage window. There wasn't time to rebuke his arrogance.

They entered the church, carefully observed by the majority of the people in Merriam Falls. Regina wished she could explain the circumstances, that she hadn't meant to enter the church with Jonathan Parker at her side, but she knew no one was interested. The gossip that Mrs. Chalmers had warned her about had already taken over the town, so her appearance with Jonathan was being taken as a confirmation. Denying that she cared for the man would be a waste of breath.

With a firm hand Jonathan guided her to one of the front pews, where Mrs. Chalmers was waiting. The boardinghouse cook didn't seem the least bit surprised to see Regina being escorted by the handsome mill owner. Turning her gaze toward the casket draped in black and sitting in front of the altar, Regina blinked back a tear and sat down.

Jonathan sat beside her, close enough for her to be reassured by his presence, but far enough away to keep the boundaries of respectability intact.

When the minister stepped to the pulpit, a worn leather Bible in his right hand, Regina prayed that whoever was responsible for Hazel's death paid for it dearly. It wasn't a forgiving prayer, the kind she'd been taught to offer to God's ears, but she couldn't help what she was feeling. She glanced across the church to where Hazel's brother was sitting. He seemed in shock, his face expressionless, his eyes staring blankly at the casket that housed his sister's body. Regina said another silent prayer, asking God to give Hazel's family the strength they needed to recover from their loss.

Reverend Hayes began his eulogy in a firm, quiet voice. The middle-aged minister was a small, round-bellied man with graying brown hair and dark shoe-button eyes. David Quinlan stood next to him. The younger man was a seminary student who was serving a winter semester as assistant pastor in the small parish. Regina had never warmed to the staunch young man with wavy brown hair and pale amber eyes, who seemed to take life much too seriously. Although his eyes held a quality of strength, she rarely saw the ability for kindness or good-fellowship reflected in their tawny depths. But then, perhaps she was misjudging the young man, since Emily Fowler, the constable's daughter, seemed taken with the aspiring minister.

Regina listened attentively as Reverend Hayes listed Hazel's Christian qualities, asking the Almighty to accept her soul into heaven. When the minister began to warn the husbands and fathers in the church to look out for the women God had put into their keeping, Regina bristled.

"God has bestowed upon you the responsibility of seeing that the women under your care are shown a straight path," Reverend Hayes said in a solemn voice. "There is an evil among us, enthusiastically recruiting our young women, leading them down a road that will become their ruination. I solicit you to recognize this abomination, to cast it out of your homes and hearts. It is the thesis of the devil, this thing called suffrage. It will destroy our families. Drive it out from among us. It is a spiritual abnormality that cannot be allowed to take root and live."

Regina was halfway to her feet, when she felt a firm hand pull her back.

"This isn't the time or place," Jonathan whispered.

Regina stiffened, but she sat back down. Reverend Hayes was glaring at her from the pulpit, and David Quinlan looked like he wanted to toss her out of God's house on her ear. By the time Reverend Hayes was done blaming Hazel's death on the unspiritual path she had chosen to follow, Regina was boiling underneath the black crepe of her dress. As the congregation stood to sing a final hymn, it was all she could do to keep still. How dare the man turn Hazel's life and death into a political sermon meant to frighten and intimidate.

Jonathan stepped out of the pew and effectively blocked Regina's exit. "Not in a church," he whispered, giving her a look that said he knew exactly what she was thinking.

"I want to—"

"Not in a church," he repeated himself. "You can offer your condolences to the brother later. I'm taking you home."

Before Regina could protest, his hand was firmly gripping her elbow and she was being led outside. By the time Jonathan ushered her into the waiting carriage, she was mumbling under her breath and digging her heels into the snow. Neither one did her any good. Within seconds the carriage was on its way to the boardinghouse.

"How dare he!" she fumed.

"Take a deep breath and calm down," Jonathan said. "You won't accomplish anything by bashing the good reverend over the head with his own Bible."

Two deep breaths later, Regina was still so angry she was shaking inside and out. "You can't possibly think he was right in saying all those things," she snapped. "Hazel was one of the most giving, caring people I have ever known. The suffrage movement didn't murder her."

Before Jonathan could reply, the carriage came to a stop in front of the boardinghouse. Knowing he had only a few minutes before the house was filled with mourners, he helped Regina out and dismissed the driver. Once they were inside, he prepared himself for another fit of female temper.

Regina tossed her gloves on the table on her way into the parlor. Bramwell took one look at her and vacated his favorite chair, strolling past Jonathan with a loud meow that hinted the gentleman might want to follow his example and find a nice, safe place to hide.

"I'm surprised Hazel's brother just sat there and listened," Regina fumed as she unpinned her hat with enough fury to dislodge several chestnut curls.

Jonathan let her rant and rave as he removed his hat, coat, and gloves. By the time he joined Regina in the parlor, she was pacing like a caged lioness. Although he had to agree that Reverend Hayes had been overly harsh in his condemnation of women's rights, he did have to agree that Hazel's suffrage sympathies could have had something to do with her demise. The last three days hadn't revealed a single clue that might solve the young woman's murder. The only thing she'd ever done to upset anyone was plead zealously for suffrage. Which meant that Regina could be in danger. Jonathan had no intention of letting anything happen to the blue-eyed little vixen he'd decided to marry.

Regina stopped pacing when Jonathan came into the room. With tear-brimmed eyes she looked at him. When he opened his arms, she walked straight into them.

"I'm crying because I can't do anything else," she mumbled into his chest.

He smiled as he held her close. "Cry," he told her. "It's better than having two funerals in one day."

"I want to . . ." A sniffle disguised what she wanted to do to the town's aging minister.

She looked up at Jonathan through eyes blurred with tears of grief and outrage. With the exception of her father, she'd never had a man be protective and caring. Regina knew she should step away from him, but she didn't want to leave the steely comfort of his embrace.

Jonathan wiped a tear away as he tipped her sad face up to his. He didn't like seeing her like this. It gnawed at his insides. He bent his head slowly and covered her quivering mouth with his own. The kiss was meant to be comforting, but he heard her breath catch, and the sound brought the hunger he'd kept contained for the last two days to the surface.

Regina felt his arms sliding around her, bringing her close, and she allowed him to hold her intimately, until she could feel the strength of his body pushing away the emotional weakness she felt because there was nothing she could do for her friend but mourn.

The kiss was deep and possessive, as if there were nothing else on earth that demanded his attention. His mouth was warm, and the kiss heated her body until she felt dizzy. When it finally ended, Regina slumped against his chest.

"You need to go get ready for your guests," Jonathan said, wishing he could bolt the door against the upcoming intruders and keep Regina all to himself. He wasn't feeling very solemn at the moment.

Realizing that half the town was due to come walking through the door, Regina stepped back and blinked away the sensual fog that always seem to engulf her whenever she was in Jonathan's arms. "You have to stop kissing me," she mumbled. She knew her face was tearstained and her hair was coming undone. If anyone saw her like this, they'd think she'd been doing exactly what she'd been doing.

"That's very unlikely." Jonathan chuckled lightly.

"I'm not interested in marrying you," Regina said halfheartedly.

"Maybe not today," he whispered as he brushed a kiss over her forehead. "But there's always tomorrow."

Six

The guests overflowed the parlor. Jonathan walked among them, introducing himself to those who had yet to make his acquaintance, while Regina shared memories of Hazel with her friends. The majority of people, young and old, male and female, worked at the mill, and they all had something special to recall about the young woman whose body had been found earlier that week.

An hour after Jonathan had calmed her down with an unexpected kiss, Regina was still struggling between anger and remorse. Angry over the funeral sermon that had labeled suffrage a murderer and remorseful because *there were none so blind as those who would not see.*

She knew it was hopeless to try to convince a man like Reverend Hayes that the suffrage movement wasn't an attempt to emasculate the male gender. He was set in his ways, as were most men. But yet, younger men like Jonathan and David Quinlan seemed just as opposed to opening their minds. As Susan B. Anthony had once said, suffrage was a political cause being won one person at a time, a slow war that required diligence and patience. Regina was quickly running out of both.

While she helped Mrs. Chalmers serve tea and slices of cake, Regina was fighting another battle, one that grew more difficult each time she glanced Jonathan's way. She felt anything but composed with him close by. Every one of her senses knew he was there. There was

no escaping his gaze or his imposing presence. Whenever he found an opportunity to walk by, she could smell
the seductive scent of his bay rum cologne. Even more,
she could still taste his kiss, hot and lingering in her
memory.

It was almost torturous to know that she was unable
to do anything about it. As angry as she was that he'd
knocked on her front door one day and taken over her
life the next, she couldn't ignore the pulsating sensations
he created within her. A part of her was eager to learn
about passion. It was a shameful thought, but it was
there, tempting her at every turn.

She hated Jonathan's arrogance, his surety that she'd
eventually relent to his well-planned seduction, yet Regina couldn't argue that he was winning. The more she
told herself marriage to the man would be the end of
her independence, the more she thought about sharing
every hour of his life. What would it be like to wake
up beside him in the morning, to feel the heat of his
body warming hers?

The question was fresh in her mind when she looked
up to find Jonathan staring at her. Their eyes met, and
a wave of anticipation swept through her. She wished
she could hold on to the hostility that had captured her
when he'd led her out of the church, but it was impossible when his gaze moved over her so intimately, she
could almost feel his hands caressing her body. She
stood motionless, helplessly trapped by his sorcerer eyes.
An arrogant gleam began to shine in their silvery depths,
and she ached to slap it away.

When he moved toward her, she wanted to run, but
there was no place to go. The parlor was crowded with
people, grouped together here and there, talking in
muted whispers about how the constable hadn't been
able to find anyone who might be responsible for Hazel's

death, and dreading that another murder might take place before the criminal was apprehended.

"Are you okay?" Jonathan asked, coming to stand by her.

"I'm fine," Regina assured him, although she wasn't.

"Hazel's brother is getting ready to leave. He wants a word with you."

Regina had learned from Mrs. Chalmers that Randall Glum had arranged to take Hazel's body to Buffalo for burial. Another funeral service would be held there for Mrs. Glum's sake. Regina did her best to smile as she approached the gruff-looking man with a thick brown mustache and wide sideburns. Like Hazel, he was stout and unattractive, but Regina knew he was hardworking and was providing the best home he could for his mother and his own family.

She wondered if he had accepted the reverend's explanation for Hazel's death, that a young woman left alone had come under the influence of a sinful cause and that that cause had brought about her death. Seeing the pain in his eyes, she knew Randall had taken the minister's sermon to heart.

"Miss Van Buren," he said, setting his teacup on the mantel. "It's been a few years."

"Yes, it has," Regina replied, barely remembering the young man who had left Merriam Falls to work as a store clerk in his uncle's shop in Buffalo. Randall Glum was at least twelve years her senior. "Please give your mother my deepest sympathies."

"I will," Randall said. He reached inside his coat pocket and pulled out a small velvet pouch. "I thought you might like to have this."

Sensing what was inside, Regina's hands trembled as she opened the tiny blue velvet bag that held Hazel's silver cross. Tears pooled in her eyes as she nodded, unable to express what she was feeling. She had asked

Mrs. Chalmers to give the cross to Hazel's brother, thinking he might want to keep it as a memento. To have it returned to her was humbling.

"Every letter she wrote had your name in it," Randall said. "You were her best friend."

"And she was mine," Regina said, realizing that was why the pain cut so deeply. She'd always been able to talk to Hazel, to express her feelings, good or bad, without being rebuked or ridiculed. Now she was alone. There was no one else who understood her the way Hazel had understood her. She looked up at Randall, saddened by the guilt she saw on his face. "Don't blame yourself," she said. "Whoever did this is to blame, not you, not Hazel, and certainly not her belief in a woman's right to choose her own path."

"I keep telling myself that," Randall replied in a voice shaken by grief. "But I was her brother. The head of the family. I should have insisted that she come live with us."

"She wanted to be independent. Make her own way," Regina replied, holding the delicate cross in the palm of her hand. "It was her choice."

Although she couldn't be sure that her words had eased some of the guilt weighing down Randall's broad shoulders, he did appear to relax a little. "Thank you," he said, then held out his hand. Regina shook it, smiling and crying at the same time.

A moment later she felt Jonathan's arm around her waist, pulling her away from her guests. "You're exhausted," he said. "Go upstairs and get some rest. I'll stay down here with Mrs. Chalmers."

Regina shook her head, but once again it did little good. Jonathan steered her toward the staircase. When she put her hand on the wide mahogany banister to resist being ushered upstairs like a sleepy child, he chuckled lightly before looking down at her. "You're a stubborn woman, Miss Van Buren. I'm only trying to help."

"You're being bossy," she replied, although she kept her voice low so only his ears could hear her. "I'm quite capable of deciding when I need to retire from *my* guests."

This time the smile reached Jonathan's eyes, making their wintry depths sparkle like sun on a frozen lake. "You're going to fight me all the way, aren't you?"

"I'm not fighting," she said, "I'm simply telling you that I've been managing my own life for quite some time now, and I intend to go on managing it."

"I could toss you over my shoulder and carry you upstairs," he teased, half meaning it. He would have liked nothing better than to watch Regina's sweet little bottom bounce off the mattress before he came down after her, pinning her underneath him. After that he'd kiss her until all thoughts of fighting vanished.

"And I could have Constable Fowler toss you into a snowbank," she replied, calling his bluff. "Now let me go. We need another pot of tea, and Mrs. Chalmers is busy."

His hand dropped away, but not before his eyes warned her that sooner or later they would be alone again, and when they were, she was going to pay a price for refusing him now.

Jonathan was about to follow Regina into the kitchen to help her make tea, when they were interrupted by the appearance of David Quinlan and Emily Fowler. Blond with blue eyes and a cherub complexion, Emily Fowler didn't impress Jonathan with her little-girl smile and debutante ways. In fact, she was the kind of young woman he avoided at all cost. Thankfully, she seemed well matched to the man who was escorting her.

David Quinlan looked the standard seminary article in his black wool suit with its square pockets and a conservative tie. His face was all angles and straight lines, his nose long, his mouth narrow, and his shoulders so square it made people wonder if he had a poker welded to his spine.

"Miss Van Buren," Quinlan said, speaking in a nasal tone that irritated Regina almost as much as his holier-than-thou attitude. "May I offer my condolences."

"Thank you," she replied before greeting Emily with a warm smile. Although she had little in common with the constable's daughter, Regina didn't dislike her. In many ways, she felt sorry for Emily. Her father was a domineering man and her mother had the disposition of a wilted flower. If David Quinlan could make her happy, then Regina wished her happiness.

"I couldn't help but notice that you were upset during the funeral service, Miss Van Buren," David Quinlan remarked. "May I assure you that Reverend Hayes is sincere in offering the advice he gave this afternoon. As minister of this parish, it is his obligation to remind us of our duty to God and to each other."

Regina changed her mind. She wouldn't wish David Quinlan on anyone. Keeping her temper under control more for Emily's sake than for her own, Regina gave the assistant pastor a brief smile. "I'm sure Reverend Hayes believes what he said," she replied. "However, I don't believe it. In fact, I couldn't disagree more. Suffrage is a noble cause, Mr. Quinlan, and Hazel Glum was a noble woman. Her epitaph will be the kindness and courage she displayed for everyone in Merriam Falls to see."

An awkward silence followed Regina's remarks. Giving Jonathan what appeared to be a sympathetic smile, David Quinlan took Emily by the arm and escorted her into the parlor, leaving Regina the momentary victor.

* * *

A week later Regina was still feeling guilty about being so blatantly rude to David Quinlan, although her temper was still smoldering over the way the town's holy fathers had explained Hazel's unnecessary death. The temperature had warmed just enough for the snow to turn to sleet at night and rain during the gray daylight hours that had embraced Merriam Falls since the day after the funeral service.

Curled up in a chair in the parlor with an unread book of poetry on her lap, Regina looked out the window, wondering if spring would ever come, and if it did, would she be able to step outside her house without stumbling over Bisbee or one of the other servants Jonathan Parker employed in the ostentatious house that sat directly across the street. Sighing, Regina doubted it. Jonathan was definitely making his presence known. Especially since the new mill manager had arrived and taken up residence on the second floor of the boardinghouse.

Richard Ferguson was a middle-aged man with dark auburn hair and friendly brown eyes. He was a lean, thoughtful gentleman with a raspy voice and a hefty appetite that made Lucy Chalmers smile. He'd cleaned his plate the first time he'd sat down at the table, then asked for seconds. When it came to dessert, he remarked that he'd never tasted a finer apple pie. The remark had won him Lucy's heart. The older woman was in the kitchen now, kneading out dough for a peach cobbler, something Regina was sure they wouldn't be having on a normal Tuesday evening if Mr. Ferguson weren't in residence.

Amazed that women were so gullible when it came to male compliments, Regina frowned at her own vulnerability. She couldn't blame Lucy for being smitten with the new boarder. Richard Ferguson was a nice man. Regina wished she could say the same about his employer. Jonathan had gone from mildly irritating to totally insufferable in the space of a week. He'd even had the audacity to tell Richard Ferguson that he and Regina were unofficially engaged, and that he'd appreciate the man keeping on an eye on things at the boardinghouse. When Regina had marched across the street to inform the brash Mr. Parker that they weren't anywhere near *unofficially* engaged to do anything, he'd simply smiled one of his irresistibly wicked smiles, kissed her on the tip of her nose, and announced that he was late for an appointment.

The worst part was that Mr. Ferguson had repeated the unofficial announcement to several men at the mill, who had repeated it to any worker who would listen, who had then repeated it to everyone in the town of Merriam Falls. Within a matter of hours, the unofficial engagement had become officially known.

Regina had gone into the village the following day, escorted by the reliable Bisbee, to find herself the recipient of congratulations. She'd tried denying the gossip, but it had been a waste of time. As far as the people of Merriam Falls were concerned, she was all but married to Jonathan Belmont Parker.

Regina's mouth tightened into a grim smile as she picked up Bramwell and stroked the large tabby cat from ear to tail. With the cat tucked under her arm she stared out the window. The rain was abating and the clouds seemed less formidable than they had for the past two days. If the sky was clear that evening, she'd use her telescope, making sure it was firmly pointed away from Jonathan's house. If she never saw the man again, it would be too soon.

Knowing she was lying to herself, Regina squeezed her eyes shut against the truth. She had to face the fact that she was more enamored of Jonathan Parker than she cared to admit. At first she'd told herself it was infatuation, the excitement of discovering a handsome, exhilarating man on her doorstep. Then she'd told herself it was curiosity. A strange, sensual curiosity that had gotten the better of her common sense. But now, feeling the ache inside her body grow with each thought of him, Regina knew that she'd stepped beyond the boundaries of curiosity and into the realm of love. Somehow in the last two weeks she'd fallen in love with Jonathan, and she wasn't sure what she should, or could, do about it.

It seemed simple enough, considering he'd proposed marriage in the most forthright way a man could go about it. Yet, it wasn't simple at all. Jonathan had made it very clear that he wanted a wife. But wanting a wife and wanting the person Regina prided herself on being were two different things. Added to that complicated set of circumstances was the fact that Jonathan was overbearing, arrogant, and much too sure of his ability to manipulate her for Regina to feel comfortable with the relationship.

The man could make her toes curl and her heart stop with one kiss, but marriage was much more than kisses. It was a lifetime commitment. People who married needed to be friends and confidants. They needed to share common interests. Passion was all well and good, but it had its limitations.

Or, at least, she suspected it did. The only passion she'd ever felt had been in Jonathan's arms. If she let him continue with his campaign to persuade her into becoming his wife, she would certainly discover the limits to which passion could satisfy a man, because that was all their relationship would be. He had never claimed to hold any real affection for her. Nor did she expect him to. They were still acquaintances, people who barely knew each other. Marriage meant sharing a bed, and meals, and hours in each other's company. It meant creating children and a long-term partnership that would last until one of them was dead and gone.

Gazing out the rain-splattered window, Regina saw her life stretching out before her. Like the colorless haze that was clinging to the damp ground, her future had neither form nor substance. She supposed that next winter she'd still be running the boardinghouse, attending suffrage meetings, and reading in the late afternoon to fill the empty hours. She'd still be respected in the small town she called home, because in spite of her personal convictions, she didn't wear bloomers when she rode a bicycle, and she didn't display a suffragette pin on her lapel. But despite her social acceptability, she'd still be alone.

"Would you like poached carrots or creamed potatoes for dinner?" Mrs. Chalmers asked, walking into the room and interrupting Regina's soul searching.

"Potatoes," Regina replied without thinking. She sat Bramwell on the carpet before she turned around. "Unless, of course, Mr. Ferguson prefers carrots."

"Don't be teasing me," Lucy said, flushing slightly. "I enjoy cooking for a man who likes to eat."

"I think it's wonderful," Regina said honestly. "There's no reason you shouldn't enjoy Mr. Ferguson's company. You've been a widow for ten years now."

"I could say the same thing about you," Lucy replied. "You could do a lot worse than Mr. Parker, especially here in Merriam Falls."

Regina ignored the remark the same way she'd been ignoring every other comment Lucy had directed her way when Jonathan was the object of the sentence. Instead of retaliating with words, Regina yawned.

"You're not fooling me," Lucy Chalmers said as she shooed Bramwell off the settee. "You're smitten with the man."

"I am *not* smitten," Regina said defensively. "I dislike him, and I dislike his dictatorial ways."

"I don't think so," Lucy remarked before she returned

to the kitchen, where the peach cobbler was baking in the oven.

Regina wished she could storm after the cook and argue that she hated Jonathan Parker and his high-handed ways, but having been honest with herself before Lucy came into the room, she was forced to continue to be honest. She didn't hate Jonathan at all. In fact, she was becoming more *smitten* by the day. Which meant, for the first time in her orderly, routine life, she didn't know which way to turn.

A temporary solution came shortly after dinner. Mr. Ferguson was on his third helping of cobbler, when Regina excused herself from the dining room. It hadn't rained for hours and a quick survey from the front porch told her that the sky was clear.

Pushing her arms through the sleeves of a drab brown coat, she sat down on the bench in the foyer and pulled on her boots. The rain had turned the previous week's snow into slush. Without the boots, her shoes would be filled with icy water before she reached the carriage house and the wooden ladder that led to the roof and her canvas-draped telescope.

From atop the carriage house, Regina looked over the small town of Merriam Falls. Here and there, light flickered from parlor windows as the people inside the houses settled down to read or embroider or to talk about the day that had faded away with the setting sun. Just beyond the crested roofs of the town shops, she could see the mill. Beyond that was the Hudson, its bluish-black water weaving its way between the snowy banks that would blaze with wildflowers come spring.

Regina stared steadily into the darkness until the last muted coloring of twilight vanished completely, and she was surrounded by the thick winter night. Keeping her back to the house that sat directly across Whitley Street, she loosened the canvas tarp that protected the telescope from the weather. Once it was folded back, she unbuckled the leather straps that kept the eight-foot tube from twirling like a weather vane when the wind was blowing and turned the sophisticated instrument toward the crescent moon.

Once the telescope was focused to her satisfaction, Regina retrieved the small stool she kept for lengthy viewings, brushed off what was left of last's week snow, and sat down. She peered through the crystal lens of the telescope, adjusting it by small increments, until the distant image of the moon clarified before her eyes. She could see the pearly aura that it wore like a silver halo. Concentrating on the celestial body with its strange shadows, Regina felt her worries ease away.

As always, they were replaced with romantic imaginings. The moon she was staring at now was the same moon that was casting its silvery light on the ancient pyramids of Egypt and the Tower of London. It was the same moon Josephine had seen from her Paris balcony, and the stars that flittered and flickered like tiny diamonds were the same stars that the Vikings had used to guide them on their courageous journeys into the northern seas. She supposed that was why the heavens fascinated her so. Gazing at the stars, she could imagine herself anywhere, doing anything, she could be . . .

"You're going to catch your death of cold," Jonathan said as he stepped free of the ladder and planted an expensively booted foot on the roof.

Regina gasped, letting go of the telescope and twisting around on the stool so fast, she almost turned it and herself over. She gave him a fierce scowl. "What are you doing here?"

"Joining you," he replied with a smile.

Regina turned back to the telescope, refusing to let Jonathan's unexpected appearance bedazzle her more than the heavenly lights she had been observing.

Jonathan repressed a smile. She was still angry at him. The thought amused him because he actually liked her being angry, at least a little. When Regina's temper was on the rise, her eyes sparkled, and she said things that gave him an insight into her character, a character he was getting impatient to know more and more about. He was a healthy, virile, man and the small taste of Regina he'd had since meeting her wasn't nearly enough to satiate his appetite. Since the weather had kept her inside the house, he'd been content to leave her alone out of respect for her feelings for Hazel, and because he'd been too busy at the mill to give her the attention she deserved. But now that Richard Ferguson had taken over the day-to-day operations, Jonathan was determined to give Miss Van Buren just what she needed.

A lesson in kissing.

Regina readjusted the telescope, refusing to acknowledge Jonathan's presence more than she already had. What woman in her right mind would provoke a man she didn't like, and at the moment Regina didn't like Jonathan enough to give him the time of day.

"I'm not going away," he said in a smug voice, "so you might as well unglue your eye from that lens and look at me."

"The moon is much more interesting," she said blandly. The tone belied the emotions that were swirling around inside her. Tiny prickly sensations were running up and down her spine, and her breathing was much too fast for anyone who knew her to think that she was bored.

"Regina, I want you to put that telescope aside and come here," Jonathan said, slipping off his gloves and tucking them into a coat pocket.

"I want you to go away," she said, fulfilling half his request when she turned to look at him. "In fact, I'd very much like you to go away and stay away."

"No, you wouldn't," Jonathan countered just as smugly.

His gaze moved over her, trailing from her irritated expression to the curves that he knew lay underneath her heavy coat. His hands were itching to unbutton the woolen garment and get underneath to the warm, willing woman he knew Regina could be once he got past her stubbornness.

When Regina finally looked at his face, illuminated by the pale moonlight, she saw her future in the wintry depths of his silver eyes. She sat still for a moment, instinctively knowing that the rooftop of the carriage house had somehow turned into a crossroads. She could stand her ground and contine being who she was, or she could step into Jonathan's arms and be the woman she wanted to be.

The trees rustled around her, their naked branches scratching and scraping against the sides of the building. The night air grew heavy, as if it were weighted down by the burden of the decision she was about to make.

"Come here," Jonathan said in a low voice. "I've missed you."

The words were Regina's undoing.

Jonathan didn't feel the slightest twinge of guilt about his plan to eventually seduce Regina into marriage. After the evening he'd invited her to dinner and kissed her, he'd known that she wasn't going to be a willing bride. Since she was much too proud to forfeit her suffrage ideology for a wedding ring, he'd have to do things the old-fashioned way. By mid-February he'd have Regina in his bed. A discreet ceremony and a large donation to the Merriam Falls Methodist Church would take care of the rest.

As Regina took another step, the doubtfulness that had filled her mind for the last three days returned with a vengeance. If she let Jonathan kiss her, and the look on his face said that he was most definitely going to kiss her, she'd lose rather than win. As much as she wanted to be in his arms, she had to make him realize that she wasn't going to be coerced into a marriage she didn't want.

She stopped in her tracks. The toe of her boot made a ripple in a small rooftop puddle as she slid her gloved hands into the pockets of her old coat. When she looked up at Jonathan, her eyes were as clear as the moonlight shining down on the silent currents of the Hudson River.

"I don't appreciate your giving Mr. Ferguson the impression that there is some sort of commitment between us. And I certainly don't appreciate the gossip that's overtaken the town as a result of your deliberate remarks. I can't post a letter without being congratulated on our recent engagement."

Jonathan wasn't surprised by her defiance. Instead of apologizing, he smiled down at her. "I can't be held responsible for what other people say."

"You most certainly can," Regina told him. "You started the gossip when you told Mr. Ferguson to keep an eye on me. I don't need watching, Mr. Parker. I've been taking care of myself for several years, and I've grown quite proficient at it."

"Things aren't like they used to be," Jonathan replied. "Hazel was murdered, and the constable hasn't a clue as to who killed her. I will not allow you to put yourself in danger."

"Being engaged isn't going to keep me out of danger," she argued. "You're using the circumstances to justify your actions. Well, they aren't justified. I want you to leave me alone."

"Am I bothering you?" he asked in a suggestive whisper.

She looked past him to the second floor of the boardinghouse. The windows facing the carriage house were dim panes of glass that reflected the pale moonlight. The lone streetlamp at the junction of Whitley and Beecher Streets cast a yellowish circle of light that extended a few yards into the darkness. Beyond that, the street was an empty avenue of wintry shapes and shadows. The northern end of the carriage house was protected by a row of thick evergreens decorated with dripping icicles and clumps of damp snow. For all practical purposes, the roof was obscured from view, giving them the privacy that was normally offered by a closed door.

"I said, do I bother you?"

His insistence irritated Regina. "The last thing I need is an arrogant man who proposes marriage to a woman he doesn't know anything about. Believe me, I will not be the kind of wife you expect me to be."

"What kind of wife will you be?"

Regina tilted her chin a little more stubbornly. "The kind that expects marriage to be a partnership, a giving and taking of ideas and emotions. The kind of wife who will refuse to have her personal beliefs stuffed in a closet while her husband rules supreme. If I had my way, the word *obedience* would be removed from the wedding ceremony. It's archaic and degrading."

"Is it the word *obedience* or the word *marriage* that frightens you the most?" Jonathan asked, taking a step in her direction.

"I'm not frightened," Regina said, wishing there were a way to leave the roof without going past Jonathan. He was blocking the ladder. Feeling trapped by his gaze and the sensually asked question, she glanced around for an exit that didn't exist. Finding no way to avoid what had to be said between them, she met his gaze once again. "I'm not against marriage if the people speaking the vows love and respect each other," she said. "I'm against men thinking that a wedding ring is a title of ownership."

"In most countries it is," Jonathan said in a low but matter-of-fact voice. "The way I see it, marriage is whatever the two people getting married want it to be."

Regina gave him a disbelieving look. "I'm sure you're not the first man to say one thing and eventually do another."

"But I am the first man who has ever asked you to marry him."

"That's beside the point. And you didn't ask me. You handed down a decree."

"On the contrary," Jonathan said with a strange, wistful tone to his voice. "I think it's precisely the point. I'm the first man who hasn't played at being your lover."

"We are *not* lovers," she corrected him. "We're neighbors. Nothing more."

Jonathan laughed. "Neighbors don't kiss the way we've kissed."

Regina wasn't in the mood to be reminded how many times Jonathan had kissed her or how disturbing his kisses had been. "Men say whatever they think is necessary to get what they want, then change their tune once a woman's legally bound to them."

"And you're upset because I want to bind you to me," Jonathan said, closing the gap between them with one well-measured step. "I'm guilty," he confessed in a deep whisper. "I want you, Miss Van Buren. Any way I can get you."

Seven

It was one thing for a man to kiss a woman, then propose marriage. It was another thing altogether for him to look her straight in the eye and say he *wanted* her.

Having never been directly propositioned before, Regina tried to think of words sharp enough to put Jonathan in his place, but there weren't any words in her mind. All she could think about was touching him again. It was maddening, and her temper began to boil, but this time it was frustration fueling her mood.

Jonathan knew exactly how she felt. If he didn't get his hands on her soon, he was going to explode. Using the lull in their conversation to his advantage, he reached out and touched the cool skin of her cheek.

Regina flinched. "Don't," she said. The word sounded more like a plea than a rebuttal.

"I have to," Jonathan whispered, repeating the light caress with his ungloved fingertips. "Touching you has suddenly become the most important thing in my life."

Regina's resolve melted instantly. She looked up at him with eyes that revealed all her secret dreams and desires. In that one moment Jonathan saw right into her soul, and he knew he hadn't made a mistake in choosing Regina to be his wife. She was a beautiful, vibrant woman filled with hidden passions, and he held the key to them in his hand.

The feelings that rose up inside Regina at Jonathan's touch left no room for anything else. When his fingertips outlined her mouth like an artist sketching out the design he would soon bring to life with brush and paint, she parted her lips.

Jonathan lowered his head and claimed her mouth in a gentle kiss that took every ounce of control he possessed to keep gentle. He wanted her with a fury that was making his blood boil, but he couldn't let her know how much. As sophisticated as Regina thought herself to be, she was nowhere near experienced enough to understand the kind of passion Jonathan was keeping bottled up inside him.

Throwing caution to the wind, Regina returned the kiss, hesitantly at first, then with more exuberance as Jonathan's arms folded around her. She curled her fingers into the hair at the nape of his neck and sighed a tiny female sound that made Jonathan dare to hold her even tighter.

Restricted by the bulky clothing they were wearing, Jonathan silently cursed the winter climate that kept them garbed in thick wools and cumbersome coats. In spite of her previous words, Regina didn't protest when he slowly turned them around so he was near the wooden stool and she was standing with her back to the edge of the carriage house roof.

With the patience of a man who wasn't easily defeated once he'd made up his mind to have something, Jonathan kissed her again and again as he took small, insignificant steps that brought them closer and closer to the stool. Once he could feel the stool pressing against the backs of his legs, he lifted his mouth away from Regina's, gave her a quick smile, and sat down.

Regina blinked wide-eyed when she went from being kissed to being perched on Jonathan's lap like a puppy. When she braced her hands against his shoulders in an attempt to free herself, Jonathan shook his head, then covered her mouth again. This time he wasn't timid about it. His tongue probed between her parted lips, teasing and tasting, while her hands went from pushing him away to holding on to him for dear life.

Her breath left her lungs in a gasp of surprise. She yearned for the promise he was giving as she yielded to the tormenting sensations he kindled so easily within her. Regina knew she was being scandalous and wanton in allowing him to touch her so boldly, but she couldn't think clearly enough to stop the feverish need that was claiming her body.

The stool was small and Jonathan's legs were long, but he managed to keep Regina on his lap despite the awkward circumstances. He felt a rush of pleasure and a strange sort of tenderness as he kissed her. The kiss was slow and deep and unbearably sweet. She trembled in his arms, and he smiled on the inside. The coldness of the evening was forgotten as he placed his hands inside the folds of her woolen muffler and cradled her face, letting his thumbs rub against the pulse that was fluttering just beneath her sensitive skin.

When he had to let her mouth go or die from lack of air, he buried his face in the curve of her throat and breathed in deeply. The womanly scent of her mixed with the crisp night air and the subtle fragrance of evergreens.

Regina opened her eyes and looked up at the stars. They seemed to be shining more brightly than they'd been a few minutes earlier. She moaned softly as Jonathan's tongue licked at a small patch of skin.

"You taste so good," he said, his breath warming her flesh. "Put your arms around my neck."

She did as he requested. He uttered a soft groan as she moved on his lap, making herself more comfortable.

It was strange to be held in a man's arms like a child, but she liked it.

He planted tiny kisses along the curve of her face. Then his hands were moving too. They went to the front of her coat, releasing the frog fastenings with agile speed.

"Let me," he said when she moved to stop him. "I only want to touch you."

Once again Regina did as he requested. Despite the warning bells going off in her head, the night seemed to belong to Jonathan, and she belonged to the night. The hunger she had tasted in his kiss was answered by her own hunger. Above her, the stars and moon were shining, and in a romantic corner of her mind, she was everything she'd longed to be. A real woman. Her hands returned to circle Jonathan's neck while her coat opened to reveal a green cashmere dress with ecru lace and tiny pearl buttons.

Jonathan slid his hands inside the opening he created. He moved them over Regina's ribs, holding her gently but firmly. "You feel warm," he whispered in her ear.

Regina closed her eyes and bit back the words she wanted to say. She wasn't warm, she was hot. The fire inside her was making her bones melt, and her blood was running as fast as a newly thawed stream. She made a soft purring sound as his hands stopped underneath her breasts, framing them with his thumbs. She'd never allowed a man to hold her so intimately, yet she didn't protest. There was a rightness about how she was feeling, a rightness about the way his hands seemed to fit her body so perfectly. The whirlwind of emotions she'd been feeling since she'd first seen Jonathan suddenly became one emotion. The solitary feeling simultaneously invaded her heart and mind and body, and she knew that what she felt wasn't infatuation or curiosity. It was love. Strong and powerful and frightening.

The potency of the moment stole her breath. Jonathan's eyes gleamed with passion and possession, and she felt more vulnerable than ever. She could feel the power of his gaze the same way she'd felt it the day she'd opened her front door and found him standing on her porch. She felt his hand tighten around her waist.

"Whether you like it or not, you belong to me," Jonathan said, unaware of what she was feeling but seeing the turmoil on her face.

He didn't give her time to argue. His mouth covered hers again. Regina was so absorbed by the kiss, she didn't feel one of his hands leave her long enough to unfasten his own coat. All she could feel was the pressure of his mouth claiming hers and the heat of his body as he pushed aside cold wool until the soft cashmere covering her breasts was pressed against the starched linen of his shirt. She strained to get closer to the masculine warmth that had turned a cold winter night into a sultry dream.

Despite the sweet pressure that was making his trousers feel too small, Jonathan kept himself under control. A rooftop with icy puddles wasn't the place to make love to a virgin. When he finally had Regina under him, her body willing to accept his, he wanted her stretched out on a feather bed. But that didn't mean he couldn't use the starlight and the velvety darkness to his benefit. Although it was blatant seduction, Jonathan justified it by reminding himself that he had every intention of marrying Regina. Once his conscience was appeased, there was no reason for him *not* to touch her.

His hands moved again and Regina tightened her arms around his neck. She was acutely aware of the male power she felt underneath his clothing, and her mind raced back to the night she'd looked at that power. She could recall seeing the sinewy strength of his muscles, covered in nothing but soapy water. The image of the way he'd looked standing in the tub, tall and sleek and graceful, filled her mind. She held him tight, feeling their heartbeats merge into one.

His lips found hers again, and she was caught in a tempest. He kissed her over and over, small, quick kisses that made her pulse race, followed by long, full kisses that made her feel like she was floating.

His hands cupped her breasts as his thumbs rubbed over their aroused tips, making the ache inside her intensify until Regina thought she was going to go up in flames. His warm breath feathered over her face and throat as he continued tormenting her with kisses. She squirmed in his lap, and he groaned out loud.

His hands moved again, completely covering her breasts, and Regina wanted to pull back, but she couldn't. He'd been right when he'd declared that she belonged to him. Her body was his. It no longer responded to logic. With a desperation she wasn't able to understand at the moment, she yearned for more of his touch, not less.

As his thumbs brushed over and around the hard tips of her breasts, shielded from a more thorough exploration by layers of fabric, Regina moaned. No amount of clothing could keep her from feeling the abrasive caress, and her nipples became hard little crowns. She was shocked, but she'd never felt anything half as wonderful. Feeling Jonathan's hot, demanding mouth take hers again, Regina's only thought was that she never wanted the moment to end.

Jonathan nibbled at Regina's lower lip, then eased his tongue inside her mouth. His hands moved from her breasts to the small pearl buttons at the throat of her dress. One by one, he unfastened them, until he could ease his hand under the sheer cotton of her chemisette and touch the warm skin of the woman who was sitting on his lap.

Her fingers dug into the thick wool coat that covered his shoulders. Every muscle in her body tightened as his fingers explored the soft skin he'd just exposed. Regina didn't feel the coldness of the night air. She was too busy feeling Jonathan's touch and the urgent need that was building inside her. She couldn't protest the shocking caress of his lean hands. The pleasure she felt was overwhelming. The small part of her brain that was still working said she shouldn't permit him the scandalous intimacy, but it felt so good.

The sweet heat of his fingertips tracing her nipple excited her, and she groaned softly as she buried her face against the front of his shirt. "You shouldn't."

"Shhh," he whispered as he continued teasing the small, hard nubs he'd discovered.

The shocking sweetness washed over her again, and Regina shut her eyes against the shame she was going to feel in the light of day. When the moist heat of his mouth replaced his hands, she stiffened, shocked to the core of her being. A weak attempt at pushing him away ended with another female moan as his mouth grew more greedy.

Regina's breath left her in a long sigh that was part protest, part surrender. Her arms still laced around his neck, she yielded to the pleasure.

Jonathan felt her capitulation and recognized it for what it was. His lean hand slipped around her breast, cradling it against his palm as he increased the assault on her senses. He felt her nipple swell even tighter against his tongue as he sucked her harder and harder. When she moved on his lap in an attempt to get closer, he groaned deep in his throat.

"If you don't stop squirming, I'm going to forget I'm a gentleman," he warned.

His head lifted and he looked into her face. This wasn't the first time he'd held a woman in his arms or caressed her breasts, but it was the first time he'd seen passion flare in the eyes of a virgin. Regina's face was flushed, and her mouth was slightly swollen from their ardent kisses. His glance darted from her well-kissed mouth to the rosy tip of her breast. She was the most beautiful thing he'd ever seen.

"We shouldn't," Regina said, knowing she sounded as breathless as she felt.

"Do you want me to stop?" he asked as his thumb and forefinger gently stroked the hard crown of her right breast.

"No." Regina breathed out the word, knowing it was the most foolish thing she'd ever said. She should demand that he stop. She should be clawing at his eyes and cursing him, but all she was capable of doing was wanting more of the exotic pleasure that came with the slight touch of his hand.

She was too naive to understand that the control he was maintaining came with a price. But Jonathan was willing to tolerate the sweet torment in exchange for the pleasure he was giving her. He wanted every moment Regina spent in his arms to be well remembered. He wanted her to long for his touch as much as he longed to touch her. He wanted her tossing and turning in her bed, dreaming of him and the earthly pleasures he was just beginning to teach her.

He felt the violent beating of her heart under his mouth as he lowered his head and kissed the ivory perfection of her skin. Her breasts were full and flushed with heat, their milky slopes revealed in the pale moonlight. Jonathan looked down at her, wishing he could strip every inch of cloth away, wishing he didn't have to go slowly.

"Don't be afraid," he whispered as he undid another button, then one more. He had to see all of her that he could see, touch all of her he could touch. "Your skin feels like warm silk."

He felt her stiffen, then relax, and he knew he could do whatever he wanted with her for as long as the moonlight lasted. It was seduction pure and simple, but Jonathan didn't care. He was powerless to keep his hands off her, and knowing that he intended to marry her made the small amount of conscience he had at the moment evaporate. Even though she was innocent, she was passionate, and the combination went to his head like whiskey on a hot day.

He shifted his legs, easing them out in front of him, forgetting he and Regina were sitting on a rooftop in the middle of winter. He moved Regina until she was reclining in his arms, her face buried inside his coat, her cheek resting against his chest. He tilted her face up, then covered her mouth with his own, stilling her last words of protest. He knew just how to touch her, how to calm her fears and coax her into accepting his hands as they eased more and more of her clothing aside. When he began to suck her again, she instinctively arched her back.

He savored her like a fine wine, licking and teasing her nipples, stroking her breasts with his fingertips while the heat of his body kept the cold at bay. Regina was at the mercy of his expertise, unable to fight what he was making her feel, unable to calm the storm that was brewing inside her. She'd never imagined that a man's touch could be so gentle—or so demanding.

Jonathan continued seducing her senses, mindless to anything but the moment, wanting more of her with each brush of his mouth across her velvety nipples. He forced himself to be patient, while his body coiled tighter and tighter. When he knew he couldn't handle another moment of sensual torture, he reversed the seduction, kissing her with less demand, while his hands soothed rather than enticed.

Regina's sanity returned when Jonathan began buttoning her dress, slowly covering what he'd uncovered, lightly caressing what he'd boldly touched moments before. She shivered inside the circle of his arms, finally feeling the coldness of the winter night, finally realizing that she'd come close to letting this man have his way with her. She blinked, then searched his face in a feverish silence as he eased her coat back in place. Her breasts were aching and her nipples were still hard. She was burning on the inside, but the fire had eased to embers instead of sensual flames, and she blushed as he gave her a tender smile.

"I could kiss you until the sun comes up," he said, brushing a light kiss over her swollen lips. He held her on his lap when she tried to stand. "Look at me."

Feeling shy, embarrassed, and angry that she'd been so easily led down the path of temptation, Regina forced herself to look at him. He was a sorcerer. He'd almost tricked her into forgetting that she wasn't interested in marriage. She didn't want to look at him, so she looked at the night sky instead.

"Please, let me up," she said raggedly.

"You're going to be my wife," Jonathan said, ignoring her request to be released.

She felt his fingertips again, brushing back a wayward strand of hair, idly stroking her cheek as he reaffirmed his attentions. The light caress brought the magical feelings back to life, and Regina fought them again. This time she won, meeting his gaze with a new determination.

"I have no desire to marry," she said firmly, thinking that if she repeated herself often enough, he'd have no choice but to listen.

"What about desire, then? Are you saying I didn't just make you tremble with it?"

"You're being intentionally rude!" she spat out.

"I'm being truthful, and you know it. If we weren't on a rooftop in the middle of winter, I wouldn't have stopped kissing you, and you wouldn't have wanted me to stop," he pointed out. "Deny it if you can."

Regina wished she could. She wished she could call him a liar, rant and rave, and toss him off the roof. But she couldn't. She had longed for his touch before he had placed a hand on her, and she despised herself for being so weak. "I will not be seduced to the altar," she told him, knowing that was his plan. "And I won't be bullied."

"Have I bullied you?" He arched a dark brow and spread his hands wide to show that he wasn't hiding anything from her.

Regina stood up, putting as much distance between them as she could on the small roof.

"You've told everyone that we're engaged," she challenged. "Your actions are as inexcusable as your methods."

Jonathan offered her an encouraging smile rather than a discouraging one, and she wanted to scream at the top of her lungs.

"I didn't do anything you didn't want me to do," he pointed out.

Regina blushed in the darkness. "You're being rude again."

"My actions are the actions of any man who is extremely attracted to a woman," he explained. "You claim to be an intelligent, freethinking woman, Regina. Do you honestly think that men marry women they *don't* want?"

Regina knew when she was on the losing side of an argument, and there was no way she could win this one. A few moments earlier she'd been a willing partner, a helpless victim of passion. She wondered what it was about him that made her say and do things she'd never say or do with anyone else. Despite her wildest dreams, she'd never imagined what had taken place tonight. She'd let this man kiss her and touch her in ways no decent woman would allow, and she'd enjoyed it. She should be ashamed of herself, yet they both knew that it had been his control, not hers, that had brought their love-making to an end.

"It's late and it's cold. Good night, Mr. Parker."

Instead of making his way to the ladder, Jonathan straightened the telescope and began securing the leather straps that held it in place. Once that was done, he covered the imported instrument with the canvas tarp, then secured the tarp with four bricks that Regina kept on the roof for just that purpose.

"You're absolutely right," he said, turning to face her once he was satisfied that the telescope was protected from the weather. "It's cold. It's time we went inside."

Assuming that he meant they were to return to their separate houses, Regina descended the ladder. She waited until Jonathan had both feet on solid ground before she bid him a curt good evening and turned toward the small porch at the rear of the house. Mrs. Chalmers would be in the front parlor this time of night, so Regina could go up to her room without anyone seeing her. She needed time to herself, time to recover from the effects of Jonathan's rooftop visit.

She opened the back door and stepped inside, blinking as she confronted the light and a flash of conscience. Telling herself what was done was done, she turned to latch the door behind her, but Jonathan was in the way.

"It's late," Regina said nervously. In the light she could see the effect she'd had on him. His eyes were a dark, steely gray, his mouth slightly swollen from the kisses they'd shared.

"I want to talk to you about something," he announced.

His tone was serious, and Regina sensed that the man she'd kissed on the rooftop was gone. In his place was the businessman who was rumored to have the instincts of a hungry wolf.

She allowed him to follow her into the kitchen. A pot of tea was sitting on the warming plate of the stove. Regina poured two cups while Jonathan removed his coat and hung it on the rack beside hers. He was looking at her with concern as she placed the cups on the table and motioned for him to have a seat.

Before Jonathan sat down, he reached into the inner pocket of his jacket and removed a small envelope. "Did you help Hazel write this?"

Regina took the envelope from his hand and withdrew the folded newspaper article. She didn't have to read it. The article Hazel had penned several months before her death was an artful attack on the bigoted political views that had kept women trapped under male thumbs since the beginning of time.

Regina gave the faded piece of newspaper a quick but mournful glance, then sat down. "No. I didn't help Hazel write it. But I agreed with her. I still agree with her," Regina added, wondering if Jonathan had any idea just how seriously she believed in gaining women the right to vote. She reminisced silently for a moment, then returned the article to the envelope. "So you think Reverend Hayes was right. You think Hazel was a victim of suffrage."

"No," Jonathan said, shaking his head. "I don't think suffrage killed Hazel. I think someone who hates suffrage killed her."

"Who?" she asked, realizing her hands were trembling as she reached for her teacup. She'd been too shocked by her friend's murder to think about the motive behind the crime. All she'd been able to see was that Hazel's death had been cruel and senseless.

"I don't know," Jonathan told her. "Suffrage may be blessed by women. Some more silently than others," he added, giving her a quick smile. "Men, on the other hand, have varied opinions. Some, like Reverend Hayes, think it more sinful than Eve's first transgression. Others laugh about it. The majority of men will do whatever they can to keep the vote out of women's hands. While others—"

"Hate it and the women who support it," Regina finished for him.

"That's just it," Jonathan replied. "Disliking suffrage is one thing. Hating it enough to kill—it's too extreme for a normal man to consider."

Regina sat back, fingering the rim of her teacup as she stared blankly into the brownish liquid. Jonathan was right. Most men hated the idea of suffrage, but they didn't hate the women campaigning for the cause enough to kill them. They ranted and raved against giving the vote to their female counterparts. They lectured against it when their wives and daughters embraced the cause, but they didn't kill over it.

"I don't want you writing an editorial," Jonathan said, returning the envelope to the inside pocket of his jacket. "And I don't want you debating with men who don't agree that women should be elevated to the status of equal citizens. Not until the constable has Hazel's murderer behind bars."

Regina closed her eyes as the ramifications of what had actually happened in Merriam Falls sank into her mind. It was difficult to believe that someone in the small town was housing that much hatred inside them.

"Promise me," Jonathan said in a commanding voice.

Regina opened her eyes. Her gaze lingered on his handsome face, then lowered to his broad shoulders. He spoke with the authority of a man who was used to having his way in the world. For the first time since meeting him, Regina was not offended by Jonathan's domineering ways.

"Promise me," he demanded, reaching for the hand that was resting on the tabletop. "Until all this is sorted out and the man is found, I don't want to have to worry about you."

"I'll be careful," she said. The feel of his hand circling hers was far more than comforting. She couldn't let him know that his slightest touch affected her so strongly.

She'd be careful, but she wasn't about to give Jonathan an excuse to hover any closer than he was already hovering. "Does Constable Fowler agree with you?"

Jonathan let out a frustrated breath. "The constable insists that whoever killed Hazel must have been a stranger. He refuses to consider my explanation without further evidence."

"And there isn't any evidence."

"Just my instincts," Jonathan said.

Instincts that had made him a small fortune, Regina reminded herself. "It's hard to imagine," she said, removing her hand from Jonathan's gentle grasp. She took a sip of tea before she spoke again. "You're new to Merriam Falls. I was born here. The people may be limited in their thinking, but they aren't malicious or meanspirited."

"No one ever completely knows another person's heart," Jonathan told her. His gaze was still determined, but his voice had softened. "Whoever killed Hazel can't be measured by normal standards. They don't apply to this kind of hate."

Regina found herself silently agreeing. She wasn't totally naive. The world could be a dangerous place.

The clock in the parlor chimed the hour, and its soft echo reminded them both how late it was. Jonathan came to his feet. "Be sure to keep the doors locked, and don't try to evade Bisbee when he accompanies you into town."

His haughty words pricked at Regina's temper, but she didn't argue.

"Good night," Jonathan said before his dark head swooped down and his mouth claimed hers for a hard, quick kiss. "I have to go to Philadelphia for a few days. Until then, behave yourself."

Before Regina could say anything, he was gone. She sat at the table for a long while, thinking how complicated her life had become in just a few short weeks.

Eight

Jonathan was forced to remain in Philadelphia much longer than a few days. The business deal he was negotiating was one of the most complex ventures he'd ever undertaken, and his fellow investors didn't have his flair for adventure. Nevertheless, he returned to Merriam Falls confident that the money he'd put into developing new mining equipment would one day reward him several times over. As he departed the train and waited for the porter to retrieve his valise, Jonathan pondered the idea of taking Regina for an unconventional honeymoon. The land he'd recently purchased in the Yukon Territory was as wild as the young lady he planned to marry. As much as the idea intrigued him, the weather made it impractical. It was early February. A few weeks in New York City would serve his purposes just as well. He wasn't overly concerned about where he and Regina spent their honeymoon as long as they had one.

Jonathan got into a hired carriage, eager to see his reluctant fiancée. The northern horizon was piled high with slate-gray clouds straining to unload another furious blanket of snow over the Hudson Valley. The weather made everything seem gray, and he wondered what kind of mood Regina would be in when he greeted her.

Telling himself she had to have missed him as much as he missed her, he discarded his misgivings and greeted Bisbee with a smile. "How are things?" he asked as he handed his coat to the butler.

"Quiet," Bisbee told him, sounding somewhat bored. "And Philadelphia?"

"Noisy at first," Jonathan replied. "No one seems to appreciate the possibilities of an unexplored frontier as much as I do. It took some doing, but I convinced the gentlemen to go along with me. The Yukon is a ripe mistress waiting to be wooed. I think I'll take Regina to the Northwest this summer. A second honeymoon, so to speak."

"I'm sure the lady will enjoy it," Bisbee replied with his customary noncommittal smile. Having experienced several doses of the young lady's temper, he wasn't entirely sure the first honeymoon would take place.

"Speaking of my intended bride," Jonathan said as he walked into the library and helped himself to a drink. "Has she been behaving herself?"

"If you are inquiring into the lady's state of health, she is well," Bisbee informed him. "If you're inquiring into her state of mind, the answer is somewhat different."

Jonathan turned intense gray eyes toward the servant. "What did she do?"

"She was on her way to visit the constable," the butler told him, "when I pointed out that you had acquired a promise of sorts, that promise being that she was to refrain from engaging in activities that might draw her unwanted attention. She threatened to bash me over the head with the closest thing at hand. Fortunately, the constable wasn't in his office. I then escorted Miss Van Buren home, ignoring her request that she never set eyes upon my ugly face again."

Laughing with relief, Jonathan sank into the chair in front of the fireplace and stretched out his legs. The urgent need that he felt to hold Regina in his arms again wiped the humor from his face. He felt his body shiver in anticipation of the pleasure she could give him. Unlike on his previous business trips, Jonathan hadn't availed himself of female company while he'd been in Philadelphia. He wasn't used to going without a woman for weeks at a time and his body was protesting his self-induced abstinence.

But he didn't want just any woman, he wanted Regina Van Buren, and the wanting was making him impatient.

"Take your ugly face across the street and deliver an invitation to dinner," Jonathan instructed Bisbee. "It's time I put an engagement ring on the finger of our lovely little suffragette."

"She'll decline the invitation," Bisbee informed him. "It's the last Wednesday of the month."

"What's that got to do with anything?"

"The Merriam Falls Literary Circle meets the last Wednesday of every month. Miss Van Buren is the founder of the academic endeavor."

Jonathan didn't like the idea of having his plans postponed. While Bisbee went about his business, Jonathan sat in the library realizing that he'd already come to think of Regina as his wife, his property. The term would infuriate her, but he couldn't help his possessive attitude. It had nothing to do with women and their campaign to gain political equity and everything to do with wanting to keep the lovely lady at his side. She was bright and beautiful and she made him feel at peace. The emotion was foreign to him, since he'd spent most of his life enjoying the freedom his bachelorhood and wealth provided.

Sipping his drink, Jonathan supposed he was settling down to the idea of taking a wife and siring a family. That must be why he was grateful to be home instead of attending the parties that came part and parcel with wooing investors into letting go of their cash. He'd always enjoyed traveling, and the insight he'd gained into human nature was a benefit whenever he walked into a business meeting. It also had it advantages where women were concerned.

He'd spent a great deal of his adult life in foreign countries, learning their cultures and experiencing their pleasures. As the fire crackled in the hearth, Jonathan thought of all the exotic things he had to teach Regina. But first he had to convince her to marry him.

He'd stopped questioning why his original intentions had turned into an obsession. It was enough for him to admit that he wanted Regina more than he'd ever wanted another woman. Admitting that, Jonathan set his drink aside and went upstairs to change.

Across the street, Regina was putting the finishing touches on a tray of shortbread cookies that would be served with tea once the members of the literary circle were gathered in the parlor. It was the first meeting since Hazel's death, and Regina was looking forward to the company of her fellow suffragettes. No one outside the small group of eight women and Mrs. Chalmers knew that the literary circle was actually an educational meeting that kept the isolated females of Merriam Falls in touch with what was happening elsewhere in the country.

Regina gathered news from the correspondence she maintained with other groups in New York and as far away as St. Louis and Charleston. It wasn't much, but it kept the idea of suffrage alive when the majority of the town's citizens would gladly see it fade into oblivion.

The group had stacks of diary entries, letters, and other personal accounts from the women who believed as they did, that suffrage was possible. If women banded together, they would eventually be heard, and once their voice became loud enough, they couldn't be ignored.

* * *

"I almost didn't come," Elisa Emerson announced as she unbuttoned the dove-gray coat that had kept her warm during her short walk from Hanover Street. Elisa's father was the president of the local bank, a stern man who had little use for the nonsense known as suffrage. "Every time I think about poor Hazel . . ."

"She believed in what we're doing," Regina said firmly. "And we're friends. We need each other now more than ever."

"You're right," Elisa agreed as she pressed her cheek against Regina's. "Forgive me."

"There's no need for forgiveness," Regina told her. "The others should be here soon. Why don't you help me in the kitchen. Mrs. Chalmers has been so busy baking peach cobblers and apple pies, she forgot about our meeting tonight. I have a tray of cookies cooling."

Elisa followed her into the kitchen. The room was large and warm and smelled like vanilla. "I was in town this afternoon, shopping. I saw Mr. Parker at the train station."

Regina's heart jumped to life at the news, but her expression remained unchanged. "I understand he was out of town on business."

"And I understand that the man has all but begged you to marry him," Elisa replied, making the gossip sound romantic. "He's very handsome."

"He's old-fashioned and arrogant," Regina replied stiffly. She began removing the cookies from the baking sheet. As she arranged them on an oval platter, she ignored the spark of interest that was lighting up Elisa's eyes. Of all her friends, Elisa was the most naive. Regina was certain that the girl had never been kissed, and she'd certainly never allowed a man to take the liberties Regina had allowed Jonathan to take the last time they'd been together.

Wanting to push the embarrassing experience out of

her mind, Regina concentrated on making the cookie platter into a work of art. She hadn't uncovered her telescope since the night Jonathan had kissed her so shamefully. The very thought of going up to the roof of the carriage house brought a rush of heat to her body, making it ache and throb. She felt that way whenever she thought of Jonathan, hot and achy and sluggish, as if she were running a fever.

"I wonder if he bought you a ring?" Elisa went on, mindless of the disapproving look Regina gave her. "My father said Mr. Parker is the wealthiest man ever to live in Merriam Falls. Perhaps he will give you pearls. Or diamonds! It's perfectly acceptable if you're engaged."

"Mr. Parker and I are *not* engaged," Regina said for what must have been the hundredth time. "I have no intention of marrying anyone."

"I know you believe in suffrage," Elisa said wistfully. "I do too. But I want to get married. Someday." She sighed longingly. "That is, if I can ever find a man who meets with Father's approval. You stole Mr. Parker before my parents could invite him to dinner."

"I didn't steal anyone," Regina said, aghast that her friend might be interested in Jonathan. "By all means," she added, hating the jealousy that came out of nowhere, "invite Mr. Parker to dinner. I hope he and your father become the best of friends."

Elisa laughed. "You do like him," she teased. "It shows."

"The only thing showing is my temper," Regina corrected her. "The man makes me furious. He has no right to give anyone the impression that we are more than neighbors."

"He seems to think he does," Elisa told her, glancing over her shoulder. "I think it's very romantic. And so does Melinda Pratt. She bet me that you'd be married before the Fourth of July." Elisa smiled. "I said it would be a June wedding. It's the newest rage, you know, getting married in June, then going off to Europe for a summer honeymoon."

"I'm not going to Europe," Regina snapped. If Melinda Pratt was spreading the gossip, it had reached the boroughs of New York City. The schoolteacher wasn't a member of the literary circle mostly because she couldn't be trusted to keep a secret.

"Is that someone knocking on the door? I'll go see while you finish with the cookies."

Regina watched her friend exit the kitchen. Frowning at the cookies displayed on the platter in front of her, she wondered how many times she'd have to deny that she and Jonathan were engaged before anyone took her seriously. Even Mrs. Chalmers wasn't convinced. Instead, she'd taken to crocheting in the evenings, insisting that a bride needed lace.

Regina had teased her back, hinting that the ivory lace taking shape could be used on any wedding dress. Mr. Ferguson had taken to escorting the widow to church, and everyone knew that was the sign of a serious relationship.

The thought of Lucy Chalmers marrying brought another frown to Regina's face. It wasn't that she didn't wish the woman happiness. She did. It was just that she thought of Lucy as family, and if she remarried, she'd move out and into a house with Richard Ferguson. Refusing to think about marriage in any capacity, Regina wiped her hands on a towel, smoothed an invisible wrinkle from her black wool skirt, then picked up the platter and left the kitchen.

The meeting went well, but it lacked the exuberance Hazel Glum had always brought to the monthly gathering. They discussed the recent petition that Elizabeth Cady Stanton had placed in front of the state legislature, demanding that the State of New York take women seriously and adopt an amendment that would give them the right to vote. As the meeting came to an end, Regina suggested that they establish a fund in Hazel's memory. The money could be used to further the cause of suffrage. Every member of the literary circle agreed, pledging a portion of their monthly income to establish the fund.

As Regina bid them good night, she made each of her friends promise to be careful. It was dark outside, and although they might not want to believe it, they could be in danger. The farewell put a damper on what had been an otherwise enjoyable evening.

"I'll walk with you," Regina insisted as Elisa buttoned her coat.

"Then you'll be alone on your way back," Elisa pointed out. "My house isn't that far. I'll be fine."

"I'm going with you," Regina said, reaching for her cloak. She draped it over her shoulders, knowing she and Elisa wouldn't reach the corner before Bisbee joined them. "I enjoy cold nights."

Since it wasn't all that rare for Regina to sit on the roof of the carriage house and look at the moon for hours on end, Elisa didn't argue. Regina chatted with her friend, but she also noticed the gentleman walking directly across the street, keeping perfect pace with the ladies he was escorting.

She didn't have to see the man under the glow of a street lamp to know that it wasn't Bisbee strolling down Whitley Street. It was Jonathan Parker himself. A tingle of excitement raced through Regina's body. She hadn't seen him for days, but the time hadn't softened her thoughts of him. The memory of his kisses burned as brightly as ever.

As she walked alongside her friend, Regina began to understand how dependency could take over a person's mind and body. How it could overwhelm their better judgment until it became the center of their universe. Is that how the murderer was feeling? Was he constantly dwelling on the freedom men would lose if women gained the right to vote? Had he become obsessed with silencing their voices? Is that why he had strangled Hazel instead of putting a knife through her heart?

Regina shivered under the woolen warmth of her cloak. She tried to listen to what Elisa was saying, but she couldn't focus on the younger woman's idle chatter. She could feel the stark coldness of the winter night and hear the crunch of snow under her feet, but those were physical things. Her mind was reliving the night Jonathan had joined her on the roof, his voice low and soothing as he whispered how much he enjoyed touching her, his lips warm and hard and demanding as he taught her how emotional a kiss could be. The feelings gripping her mind were more real than the world around her. She couldn't shut herself away from them the way she could retreat into the parlor and chase away the coldness of the winter night.

"I'll see you on Sunday," Elisa announced, bringing an end to Regina's reverie.

"At church," Regina mumbled, realizing she'd been in another place and time. "Yes. I'll see you on Sunday."

Regina waited until Elisa was pushing open the front door of her home and stepping inside before she turned away from the gate. Jonathan was standing directly across the street, his tall body outlined by the amber glow of the street lamp at the corner of Whitley and Hanover. His hands were tucked into the pockets of his coat, but his shoulders were straight and wide. Regina fancied that she could see the smug smile on his face, but he was too far away for her to be certain he was smiling at all. In spite of the distance, she could feel his gaze. Time and space didn't seem to be a barrier between them. The realization made her shiver again. What was she going to do about the man?

Jonathan waited until she was halfway home before he crossed the street and joined her. He fell into step as though they were taking a leisurely afternoon walk. "I understand you've been giving Bisbee a difficult time."

Regina stopped. The darkness engulfed her, denying Jonathan the look at her face he'd been longing for. The distant chiming of the courthouse clock told them the hour, reaffirming that she should indeed be inside her home. For a brief moment she wanted to run back to the boardinghouse and slam the door against the feelings Jonathan evoked, but she didn't move. Instead, she looked up at him, his features shadowed by the lack of light.

"I hope you had a successful trip," she said with cold politeness.

"I missed you," he replied.

The simple words crumbled Regina's defenses before she could build them. She'd spent the last few days compiling all the reasons she couldn't allow Jonathan to pursue a marriage that would never take place. Her reasons were logical. But what she was feeling was pure insanity. Instead of replying to the declaration that he'd missed her, Regina started walking again. She didn't stop until she was standing on the front porch of the boardinghouse. "Good night," she said, deciding the fewer words she exchanged with the man, the better. He wasn't going to listen to them anyhow.

"Don't I get a good-night kiss?" he teased.

Her cheeks were flushed with color, but Jonathan couldn't be sure if it was the weather or his request that painted them such a pretty pink.

"I have nothing to give you, Mr. Parker. And I would prefer that this be our last conversation," Regina said, hoping the words hit home. She didn't have the strength to resist him much longer. "If you're a gentleman, you'll accept my wishes and act accordingly."

"I'm a gentleman only when it suits my purposes," Jonathan said as he reached around her and opened the door. He stepped back and waited for her to enter the house.

When she did, Regina wasn't sure if he'd follow her or not. She was doing battle with herself now, half of her hoping he would leave, the other half praying he wouldn't.

She stepped over the threshold and into the warmth of the foyer. Her hands were trembling as she began to unbutton her coat. She could hear him beside her, shutting the door with a soft click, then the sound of his boots on the floor as he moved up behind her. His hands wrapped around her waist, and he pulled her back against him.

"Stop fighting me, Regina," he whispered against her hair.

"I have to," she said, pulling away and swirling around to face him. She was angry again. Angry that he could vaporize out of the darkness and make her feel the most frightening things. Angry that she couldn't stop the feelings from materializing. "We're strangers. I don't know anything about you. Nothing of any consequence, that is. All I know is that you've decided to marry and that I've been selected to be the bride. It's ridiculous. And you're being impossible. Please, go away and leave me alone."

"No."

Short of screaming at the top of her lungs and bringing Mr. Ferguson downstairs to throw Jonathan out the front door, a feat that was unlikely considering the man paid his wages, Regina fisted her hands and watched as Jonathan removed his gloves, hat, and coat. When he was standing in front of her in a dark blue suit with a blue and white floral vest and a white shirt, looking very much the businessman, she released a frustrated sigh and marched into the parlor.

As expected, Jonathan followed her.

"I was born in New York City," he said, helping himself to one of the leftover cookies.

"I really don't care where you were born," she replied, gritting her teeth.

He smiled. "We're getting acquainted. Isn't that what you want? For us to know each other."

"What if I don't want to know you?" she snapped. "What if I find you rude, your behavior outrageous, and your motives—"

"As I said, I was born in New York City. My father owned a butcher shop. My mother was . . . a mother. She was tall and graceful and lovely. Like you, I have no sisters or brothers." He wasn't lying. Abigail was dead. "Do you mind if I pour myself a drink?"

"By all means," Regina retorted, throwing up her hands in defeat. "Would you like me to fluff up the cushions on the settee? Or should I call Mrs. Chalmers and have her set a pot of tea to boiling?"

"I prefer brandy," Jonathan said, laughing on the inside. God, she was beautiful. And he wasn't leaving the boardinghouse until he'd kissed her at least once. No, make that twice. He'd been away for almost two weeks. A man deserved a little something in payment for his abstinence.

Regina began clearing away the saucers and cups that had been used during the literary meeting. She was stacking them on a tray, determined to carry them into the kitchen, then take herself upstairs as quickly as possible. If Mr. Jonathan Parker wanted to sit in her parlor, sipping brandy, he was more than welcome to do so— alone!

"I met Bisbee in London," Jonathan said as he closed the liquor cabinet. "He was trying to pick my pocket."

That bit of news got Regina's attention. She set the last of the teacups on the tray, then looked at Jonathan. "Bisbee's a pickpocket?"

"A retired pickpocket," he informed her with a devastating smile. "I decided he was far more interesting than the majority of men in the House of Lords, so I hired him." He smiled at her. "Of course, his previous vocation is a secret I expect you to keep. Being a butler now, he has a certain image to maintain."

Regina was certainly surprised. She knew even less about Jonathan than she realized. It was hard to imagine him hiring a pickpocket, yet the relationship between the two men seemed a perfect match. They both went about getting whatever they wanted any way they could get it.

"There really isn't much to tell," Jonathan said, referring to his private life. "I'm a businessman who has traveled a great deal. I could bore you with stories about Paris and London and Hong Kong. Or would you prefer to hear about the Hawaiian Islands. You feel like you've stepped into paradise."

Paradise!

Regina had some idea of what he was talking about. She'd stepped into paradise that night on the roof. Jonathan had taken her there. No. He'd tempted her with the promise of paradise. A promise that scared her more than she wanted to admit. She turned away from him, afraid that her face might reveal what she didn't want him to know. That he made her feel things no lady should feel, want things no lady should want, yearn for things that had nothing to do with independence and suffrage.

Jonathan sipped his brandy. He could do one of two things. He could take Regina in his arms and kiss her until she forgot they were in the parlor. Then he could make love to her in front of the fire. Come morning, she'd be forced to marry him. Or he could claim the good-night kiss he'd asked for at the door and return to his own home, leaving her to dream about him again. Wanting the first so badly his body was beginning to ache but knowing that the second course of action was the wiser, he finished his brandy and set the glass on the mantel.

"Dine with me tomorrow evening," he requested.

His silvery gaze was covetous as he waited for her answer. Regina felt her heart begin to race. She should refuse the invitation. It would only reaffirm the gossip that was running rampant in town. But the curiosity was still there, making her tremble on the inside. The need to know more about this man was an illness for which the only cure was being with him.

Jonathan stepped away from the mantel. Regina was fighting herself more than she was fighting him, and it pleased him beyond words. When he gently took her by the shoulders, she flinched, but she didn't pull away. Smiling, he bent and covered her mouth with his own. The kiss was tender and hungry and shockingly pleasant.

"Tell me I'm not welcome here," he said in a daring whisper.

"I can't," Regina said breathlessly. She felt like she'd sunk to the bottom of a large abyss, only to be flung upward again. Every time the man touched her, she became disoriented.

He leaned down and kissed her again. Regina wasn't sure if she was flying or floating. When he released her, she slumped against him. "I hate you for this," she mumbled a weak, venomless protest.

Jonathan was all smiles as he picked her up and put her down in a large overstuffed chair near the fire. His lips brushed across her mouth in the lightest of kisses. "Dinner. Tomorrow night."

She was a woman who prided herself on being in control of her life, but Jonathan could strip that control away with nothing more than a glance from his wintry eyes. Tonight she'd come full circle, from hating him to loving him to hating him again for making her feel so spineless, so unable to resist him. Regina told herself that she'd not have dinner with the man, but she knew it was a lie. He'd gone beyond an obsession. She was addicted to his kisses. Addicted and totally lost.

"Good night, love."

Regina looked into his eyes. For a brief moment she could almost believe that he'd spoken the endearment with real affection. The illusion faded as he gave her an arrogant smile.

She watched as he walked out of the parlor, knowing that she'd reaffirmed his arrogance by allowing him to kiss her. Why couldn't she resist the man? She wasn't a weak woman, but when it came to Jonathan Parker, she didn't seem to have a backbone.

Doubting that she'd find the answer sitting in the parlor and staring at the fire, Regina picked up Bramwell and carried the big cat upstairs. Once she was in bed, she stared at the ceiling while her pet curled into a ball and promptly fell asleep. Disgusted with herself and her inability to put Jonathan out of her mind, it was hours before she finally slept.

Nine

The next twenty-four hours were the most stressful of Regina's life. By the time a lavender sunset graced the sky over Merriam Falls, bringing a chilly twilight, anxiety had taken over her mind and body. She paced the carpeted floor of her second-floor bedroom, dressed in a silk chemise, petticoats, and stockings. A coffee-colored evening dress lay on the bed.

The more she thought about being alone with Jonathan, the more Regina knew that this particular evening was of extreme importance. The man was probably sitting across the street, plotting all kinds of ways to compromise her. He'd come dangerously close to it the night he'd climbed the ladder to the top of the carriage house. More important, she'd come dangerously close to letting him.

"Are you ready?" Mrs. Chalmers called from the hallway. A light tap followed her words, and Regina opened the door.

"As ready as I'll ever be," she said, hiding her nervous hands in the folds of her petticoat. She walked to the bed and picked up the dress. It had been an impulsive purchase made two years before when she'd traveled to New York City to attend a dinner rally held by Elizabeth Cady Stanton. The dress had a tight-fitting waist with a skirt that flared to the floor in a graceful cut. The bodice was outlined in black piping and accented with tiny chenille balls that reminded Regina of golden tears. The neckline was much lower than anything she normally wore, but it was cut for evening.

With Mrs. Chalmers's help, Regina was buttoned into the elegant dress. Her hair was brushed and piled high on her head. Her only jewelry was a choker of pearls and matching earrings, inherited from her mother. The final result made Mrs. Chalmers smile with approval.

Regina looked in the mirror and frowned. She looked like a woman dressing to please a man.

"You're beautiful," Lucy whispered, giving her a quick hug. "Mr. Parker won't be able to take his eyes off you."

"That's what I'm afraid of," Regina mumbled under her breath.

"If you don't want the man courting you, then put the dress back in the wardrobe and pen him a note. Tell him that you're indisposed with a headache. Richard can deliver it."

"Richard?" Regina smiled. "I didn't realize you and Mr. Ferguson were on a first-name basis."

"Don't be changing the subject," Lucy retorted. "Are you having dinner with Mr. Parker or aren't you?"

With her eyes fixed on the mirror, Regina pinned a small black feather into her hair and smiled for her friend's sake. "I'm having dinner with the gentleman."

"Then put on your shoes." Lucy laughed, pointing at Regina's stocking-clad feet. "I'll fetch your cloak. You don't want to keep the *gentleman* waiting."

A few minutes later Regina took a deep breath and stepped into the foyer of Jonathan's home. Bisbee had escorted her across the street, something she considered a total waste of time, but she hadn't argued with the servant. She was saving her arguments for his employer.

When Jonathan appeared, his smile said he liked what he was seeing. His gaze flickered over her gown, return-

ing to its low-cut neckline. "You look lovely," he said,
stepping forward to take her hand. He raised it to his
mouth and placed the lightest of kisses just above her
knuckles. "Thank you for coming."

Instead of leading her into the formal dining room
across from the parlor, he escorted her down the hall,
past the library door, and into a smaller room. A round
table draped with an ivory linen tablecloth was set for
an intimate dinner. The centerpiece was a small cande-
labrum with its silver base rimmed by white and red
flowers. Gold-trimmed Limoges porcelain and European
crystal gleamed in the candlelight.

The room was as impressive as the table setting. The
walls were papered in a bold Chinese red. The windows
were draped in gold velvet with white lace panels. Two
exotically painted vases standing nearly five feet tall
framed a small settee that was overflowing with soft pillows. The fireplace was white Italian marble.

Regina was drawn toward the mantel, where a collection of tiny ivory and teak elephants was displayed.
She'd never seen their like before, and she couldn't resist
reaching out to touch them. Realizing their value at the
last moment, she hesitated.

"Go ahead, touch them," Jonathan said, coming up
behind her. "This is my favorite." He picked up one of
the largest figurines, carved out of teak. The elephant's
ceremonial headdress and draping was painted bright
yellow. Its tiny tusks were ivory, trimmed with small
gold bands. As he handed the unique artwork to Regina,
she realized the stones embedded in the animal's draped
saddle were emeralds. The gems sparkled in the firelight,
and the animal's exquisitely carved features made it
seem almost alive.

"You've been to India?"

"Several times," he told her. "The tusks on this one

are solid gold." He pointed to a small elephant with its trunk lifted high above its ivory head.

"It's beautiful."

"Not as beautiful as you," Jonathan whispered, taking the figurine from her hand and returning it to the mantel.

His smile didn't reassure Regina. She was about to move toward the table, when he stepped in front of her, gracefully blocking her escape. "Don't be afraid of me," he said. "And don't be afraid of yourself."

"I'm not afraid," she replied, wanting to end the evening before it had begun. The gall of it all was that the man was right. As usual, she was trapped between wanting him and not wanting him, falling in love and being terrified of the fall.

"Yes, you are." He looked down at her, his eyes gleaming as brightly as the rare jewels that adorned the parade of elephants behind her. "You're afraid of marrying me because you're afraid that you might like being my wife. You're afraid that you could actually enjoy *belonging* to me."

She glared at him. "I'm afraid that spending more than a few hours in your company will drive me insane," she snapped. "You're the most arrogant man I've ever had the misfortune to encounter."

Jonathan's laughter filled the elegant room as he moved to a small side table, where a bottle of champagne was resting in a silver bucket of ice. The sound of the cork popping free of the bottle reverberated like cannon fire as Regina watched him. While he filled two glasses, she tried to concentrate on the artwork over the mantel. The painting was as exotic as the miniature elephants.

A Turkish temple stood tall against a swirling desert sky. An open doorway allowed whoever was viewing the painting an artful glimpse inside the harem. Women clad in gauzy scarves gathered around a tiled pool, leisurely awaiting the sultan. Rather than revealing the secrecy of the harem, the painting intensified the viewer's curiosity. Realizing where her thoughts were taking her, Regina turned her attention away from the painting, but she wasn't fast enough to escape Jonathan's keen eyes.

"It's a rendering of the Top Kapi Sarayi," he told her. "The sultan's summer palace."

"A memento of your visit?"

"No. The palace was destroyed almost thirty years ago, long before I visited Marmara," he told her, delighted by the jealousy in her voice. "I bought the painting because I liked it."

"It isn't the kind of thing you usually see displayed in Merriam Falls," she said, looking around the room for a less sophisticated topic of conversation. There wasn't any. The entire room was furnished with souvenirs from Jonathan's exotic travels.

Fortunately, Bisbee chose that moment to serve dinner. Regina allowed herself to be seated at the table. When she lifted her gaze she found herself looking at the painting once again. From a suffragette's point of the view, the image was degrading and insulting. Women maintained only to please a man. Yet, looking at it from another perspective, a nameless point of view, Regina found the painting intriguing. The artist had captured the sensuality of the harem, not the sexuality. The colors were as soft as a lover's caress, the shadows beckoning rather than frightening. The women looked content, as if the pleasure they received from the sultan was well worth their captivity.

You're afraid that you could actually enjoy belonging to me. Regina closed her eyes against the words. She didn't want to think about belonging to Jonathan. But if she did, would her face show the same contentment as those of the women in the painting? Could she *enjoy* being a possession? Could she belong to Jonathan and still belong to herself, or would she have to sacrifice her soul to satisfy her body?

"You never answered my question," Jonathan said after Bisbee had finished serving a delicious meal and they were alone again. "What frightens you the most? Marriage or me?"

Had he learned some mystical way of getting inside her mind, Regina wondered as she reached for her water goblet. And why did he persist in trying to make her acknowledge her fear of him. Putting on a polite smile, she lied to the best of her ability. "I'm not frightened of either one."

"Then why won't you consider becoming my wife? I assure you, I'm not a tyrant. I won't censor your every move. Or restrict you from reading essays penned by the matrons of suffrage."

"You're already censoring my every move," Regina reminded him. "I can't step outside my own house without the faithful Bisbee at my heels. It's become an embarrassment."

"I'd rather have you embarrassed than endangered."

There was something about his tone that gave Regina pause. It was more than a statement, it was a declaration of intent. Like Jonathan, she was forced to admit that the danger hadn't disappeared. The constable was still looking for the man who had murdered Hazel.

"You're still avoiding the question. If you're not afraid of marriage, or me, then you must be afraid of yourself."

"It isn't a question, it's a puzzle," Regina said, feeling like a mouse caught in a well-concealed trap. "Why should I be afraid of myself?"

"Because I make you feel things you've never felt before," Jonathan said. "Because you want everyone, including yourself, to believe that you're immune to the power of passion."

"You're being rude," she said, feeling her face redden.

His candor was almost as upsetting as the realization that he was very close to the truth.

Passion was a man's adventure—and a woman's weakness.

Jonathan sipped his champagne. He'd decided earlier that day that he was approaching Regina from the wrong direction. Short of seducing her and forcing her to the altar, he could spend countless hours debating the pros and cons of marriage, or he could use her natural sensuality against her. After several hours of thoughtful evaluation, he'd come to the conclusion that Regina was using suffrage as a shield, a way to keep any man from getting too close. The best way to persuade her to marry him was to make marriage more appealing than the limited independence she now enjoyed. He had to convince her that she'd gain rather than lose by becoming his wife.

"Surely a well-educated woman like yourself is mature enough to discuss passion. People are passionate, Regina. Male and female alike. There's nothing shameful about it."

Mortified that they could be sitting at the dinner table discussing something as intimate as passion, Regina tried to look anywhere but at Jonathan. She'd expected him to try to seduce her, but with kisses, not with images that refused to leave her mind. He was silently taunting her with sensations that hadn't been forgotten, couldn't be forgotten.

"You like the painting of the sultan's palace," he said, daring her to deny it. "Would you like to know why you like it? Why it doesn't offend your innocent sensibilities?"

Regina remained mute. She knew she'd been a fool to come to dinner. She should have locked herself in her room, away from his sorcerer eyes and devilish smile. He'd been impossible to resist before. What had made her think that she could deny him tonight?

"You like the painting because you're a passionate woman," Jonathan told her. "I can see passion is in your eyes, and feel it when I touch you."

"Marriage isn't about passion. It's about respect," Regina replied stiffly, doing her best to ignore the effect he was having on her. He was a man with a purpose, but that purpose had nothing to do with love. "Why should I give up the liberty I have as a single woman to become the possession of a man who openly admits that he's more interested in acquiring a legal wife and a mother for his children than he is in acquiring a partner to share his life?"

"Marriage offers a woman more freedom than you can imagine," Jonathan said. His gaze moved from her face to the low-cut bodice of her dress. "A married woman isn't restricted by society's limited imagination. She isn't forced to wear a stoic mask when she's alone with her husband. She has the freedom to turn her fantasies into reality."

"I don't have any fantasies," Regina retorted. She'd lost count of the times she'd lied to him so far that evening.

"Everyone has fantasies," he told her. "Things they imagine in their minds, dreams that keep them awake at night. Tell me you don't stare at the moon and wonder what it would be like to reach up and touch it. Tell me you're not dreaming when you look at the stars." His eyes lifted to her face and held her prisoner. "Tell me you've forgotten our night on the roof."

Regina stood up so fast, she almost overturned the chair. "I'm leaving," she stammered. "I won't stay here and be seduced."

"I'm not seducing you," Jonathan said. "I'm being truthful with you. All I'm asking in return is that you be truthful with yourself."

Regina wanted to call him a liar. She wanted to march

out of the room, but she didn't move. She stood motionless, trapped by his words. Once again, he was right.
She yearned for him to touch her. She dreamed of what
it would be like to touch him in return, to feel the heat
of his body along every inch of hers, to cast off the
restraints society put upon women and let passion rule
completely. To enjoy the freedom men had enjoyed for
generations.

The truth was her undoing. She knew that everything
she was feeling, everything she wanted, everything she
dreamed about, was burning in her eyes for him to see.
At that moment, she felt as if her very soul were resting
in his hands.

"Tell me you don't feel the passion between us,"
Jonathan dared her once again. "Tell me that you don't
want what I want."

He stood up and walked around the table. His hand
was a gentle manacle around her wrist as he drew her
into the circle of his arms.

Desperate to fight what was happening to her, Regina
turned her face away. She didn't trust herself to speak.
Everything Jonathan had said was true. He seemed to
know her better than she knew herself.

"Don't fight it," he whispered. "We're a perfect
match."

"We're nothing alike," she told him. Her voice was
shaking. She wanted to run away, but Jonathan was still
holding her.

"You're wrong," Jonathan whispered against her lips.
"We're perfectly matched when it comes to this."

He kissed her, and Regina felt the passion explode.
It was deep and searing, burning through her body like
wildfire, melting her resistance.

His tongue delved into her mouth, teasing and withdrawing, tasting and tempting her until she was shuddering in his arms. His mouth moved to her throat, to

the pulse beat that proved he was right. She was a woman of passion. He placed fiery kisses over her collarbone and into the valley between her breasts. She writhed against him, arching her back, demanding more of his touch.

"Don't fight the passion, darling. Set it free," Jonathan whispered as his hands moved to the row of buttons at the back of her dress.

Before Regina could clear her mind, the gentle caress of Jonathan's hands made the passion flare again. Another wave of emotion washed through her as he kissed the corners of her mouth, teasing her lips with his tongue. Each kiss was deeper, more arousing, than the last.

Her hands crept up the front of his dinner jacket to rest on his shoulders, then around his neck as she tried to get closer to the fire. She was trembling inside and out as she felt him undo the buttons at the back of her dress.

The small, passionate sounds she was making set Jonathan's body on fire. His hands were hungry to caress more than her spine through the silk of her chemise. He wanted to feel the warmth of her skin, to feel her burning for him. He wanted to feel her moving under him, arching to meet his hips as he moved inside her. He made a ragged sound as his fingers freed the last button from its hole and Regina's bodice sagged. It took only an instant for his hands to push it the rest of way the down, freeing her to his touch. And touch her he did. His hands cupped her breasts while his thumbs traced their hard crowns. Her soft moan told Jonathan everything he needed to know. Regina could tell him no, but her body was saying yes.

Regina had just enough sanity left to hear someone knocking on the door. It took her another moment to realize that the knocking wasn't coming from the hallway but from outside the house. A few seconds later she heard Richard Ferguson's voice. They were on the verge of being caught in a most compromising situation. Regina struggled against Jonathan's embrace. "No," she said, pushing him away. "No."

Jonathan blinked, startled by the sound of voices. Realizing that they were about to be disturbed, he quickly turned Regina around and began fastening the buttons he'd just undone.

"Stop fidgeting," he said. "Bisbee has enough sense not to come into the room without knocking."

Regina certainly hoped so. If anyone saw them now, it would be the end of her reputation. "This can't happen again," she vowed.

Jonathan didn't respond. He wasn't above admitting a temporary defeat, because he knew it was only a matter of time until Regina surrendered completely. As aroused as he was, he had to admire the lady's determination. She was as challenging as she was beautiful.

When Bisbee tapped discreetly on the door, Jonathan replied that he'd be out in a minute. The sound of the butler's retreating footsteps joined the echo of Regina's pounding heart as she composed herself.

Half angry, half embarrassed, and totally unprepared for what she'd just experienced, Regina fought to control the irrational sensations that were rippling through her body.

"Mr. Ferguson is waiting," she said, her face taut with determination. "I'm sure it's important, or he wouldn't be calling on you this late in the evening."

Jonathan's mouth curved into a wicked smile. "I'll be back in a few minutes."

"It's late," she said, eager to flee the room and the things she was discovering about herself. "I should go."

"Not yet," he said.

He walked to the door, opened it, and stepped into

the foyer. He'd taken a risk tonight, confronting Regina so boldly, but he was certain he had won. He'd felt the tremor of her body when he'd held her in his arms. The decision he'd made to marry her was the right one. A woman with Regina's passion would be wasted on most men.

"What's wrong?" Jonathan asked the moment he saw Richard Ferguson's face.

"There's been another murder," the mill supervisor answered, exchanging his hat for the neat whiskey Bisbee has just poured him. "I've been with the constable for the last hour."

"Who?"

"Elisa Emerson. I found her body when I left the mill. She was strangled, just like the other one."

Jonathan felt his blood go cold.

The victims were getting closer and closer to Regina.

Ten

Regina cried until she didn't have any tears left. She couldn't stand to think of Elisa's beautiful face frozen by death. When Jonathan had told her of another young woman's murder, another friend found lying in the snow with bruises around her throat, Regina had gone numb inside.

She was still numb.

The church was as quiet as the grave awaiting the crepe-covered casket displayed in front of the altar. The impending funeral ceremony was more than a formal good-bye to an innocent young woman. It was a stark, heart-wrenching reminder that whoever had murdered Hazel Glum hadn't been passing through the small town. The killer was still among them.

Regina desperately wanted to understand why God would allow such a crime to take place. Even Reverend Hayes was somber as he stepped to the pulpit and asked the congregation to bow their heads in prayer. David Quinlan didn't join the minister. Instead, he sat in one of the pews, comforting Emily Fowler. The two young women had been close friends. Elisa's parents sat in the front pew, their eyes red and swollen from crying, their faces blank with disbelief that their beautiful child was gone. Everyone in the church carried the same disbelieving expression on their face. Another woman had been killed, murdered by a maniac who was masquerading as one of their own.

Constable Fowler looked more angry than mournful, and Regina wondered what he thought of Jonathan's assumption now. As soft, sorrowful music began to fill the church, Regina wiped her eyes with her already damp handkerchief.

Jonathan sat next to her. When he reached out to take her hand, she welcomed it, needing his strength in a moment of monumental sorrow. Thoughts of passion were forgotten, replaced by the agonizing truth that she'd lost another friend. The worst part was knowing that the loss wasn't due to disease or accident. Elisa's life had been taken from her, stolen by an unknown assailant with hatred in his heart.

Jonathan watched as Regina tried to contain her grief. When Richard Ferguson, enlightened by a conversation with Lucy Chalmers, had passed on the information that Regina's literary circle was little more than a costume event, a guise for a monthly meeting of young suffragettes, Jonathan had cursed long and hard. Despite his warning, Regina hadn't called off the meeting. He would have canceled it himself if he'd known that the young women weren't sitting in front of the fire critiquing poetry. But then again, he couldn't be sure the murderer wouldn't have killed Elisa anyway. If not Elisa, then another woman. Even Regina, if he'd been able to get to her.

Who was to say how deep the man's hatred was planted?

Like Frank Fowler, Jonathan was angry. Whoever was setting out to silence the suffragettes of Merriam Falls was doing a fine job of it. There had been no clues left with the body. No signs of struggle. Not even a footprint by which to judge the size of the man who had wrapped his hands around Elisa Emerson's throat.

As Reverend Hayes eulogized the fair young lady who had been taken from them, Jonathan thought about his sister. Abigail, if she had lived, would have been the same age as Elisa Fowler. Would his sister have become a female savior of suffrage determined to gain recognition for her gender, or would she have been like Emily Fowler, content to let a man's arms comfort and guide her? He'd never know.

Reminding himself that he couldn't undo the past, Jonathan glanced at Regina. Even with her face paled by grief and her eyes red-rimmed from tears, she was beautiful. Knowing that the danger he'd suspected was real, he was more determined than ever to keep her safe. The constable had enacted a curfew, insisting that no woman was allowed on the streets after dark. The fathers and husbands in town had taken it a step further, most of them forbidding their women to venture past their own thresholds, even during the day, unless a male member of the family was with them. The women weren't protesting. They were frightened, and with good cause.

When the final prayer was said, Jonathan was still holding Regina's hand. He wasn't going to let her out of his sight until the murderer was behind bars. A painful longing clutched at his heart, and Jonathan knew he couldn't allow death to rob him a second time. He'd do whatever he had to do to keep Regina safe.

"She's doing what!" Jonathan demanded.

"Miss Van Buren's up on the roof, spying on people." Richard Ferguson repeated himself. "Lucy said she got the idea this afternoon. She thinks that telescope of hers is going to find the killer."

"Of all the ridiculous ideas," Jonathan fumed. He was out the door and down the steps before Richard caught up with him. "What the hell does she think she's doing?"

It wasn't a real question, so Richard didn't bother answering it. In the space of a heartbeat Jonathan was climbing into the carriage the mill supervisor had left in front of the main entrance. It was well past sunset. The winter sky was a rich black dotted with iridescent stars and wispy pale clouds. The moon was full and bright and hanging low on the horizon. It was a perfect night for gazing at the heavens.

Richard told the carriage driver to take them back to town, then climbed inside and sat across from his employer. "She told Lucy that the constable wasn't doing enough," he explained to Jonathan. "Apparently Miss Van Buren has decided that if her telescope is powerful enough to look at the moon, it's powerful enough to watch the streets at night. She's sure she's going to see someone sneaking around in the dark."

Jonathan was too furious to reply. He should have known that Regina was too impatient to wait for the authorities to discover who had killed her friends. He hadn't seen her since the day of Elisa Emerson's funeral. She'd confined herself to the boardinghouse, but Jonathan knew it wasn't entirely out of grief. She was avoiding him.

"She's going to get herself killed," he said. "Of all the stubborn people I've ever met, she's the most stubborn—"

"And the prettiest," Richard Ferguson interrupted, flashing his employer a knowing smile. "Lucy's scared out of her wits. She had me put a double lock on the doors. Miss Van Buren didn't like it. She said it was giving in to things instead of standing up and doing something about them."

Jonathan was growing as impatient as Regina to find the killer, but he wasn't likely to become one of the

man's victims. After Elisa's body had been found and
Lucy had divulged that the monthly literary meetings
weren't literary at all, he'd become increasingly concerned about Regina's safety. The killer had to know that
the lovely Miss Van Buren was the nucleus of the Merriam Falls suffrage movement. He had to know that her
determination and dedication was the glue that held the
other young ladies together. What better way to stop the
expansion of the cause than to bring Regina's life to an
end.

The thought of her body being found behind a woodshed turned Jonathan's blood to ice.

The carriage stopped in front the boardinghouse.
Jonathan climbed out, unsure of what he was going to
do but determined to do something.

Regina knew who was climbing up the ladder. The
long days and nights since Elisa's death had made her
even more restless than usual. Jonathan's contribution to
her restlessness had been the challenge he'd issued over
the dinner table. *Marriage offers a woman more freedom
than you can imagine.*

The statement had been swirling around inside her
head for days. She'd always known that she was bolder
than most women, more outspoken, more willing to fight
for what she wanted, but she'd never labeled her actions
as passionate. Passion was something a proper lady
didn't feel, something that happened in the dark. Yet the
feelings she had for Jonathan were just as strong, just
as vibrant in the light of day as they were when she'd
sat on his lap on this very roof. She'd experienced the
same quickening in her body when he'd held her hand
coming out of the church that she'd felt the evening he'd
kissed her for the first time.

Tell me that you don't want what I want.

Was she really passionate? Did she possess the desire
Jonathan said he saw burning in her eyes? Was her lust

for freedom more than a willfulness to be independent? But more important, was she willing to risk her pride, and her heart, to test the theory?

The questions rolled around in Regina's head as she waited for Jonathan to reach the top of the carriage house. When he did, one glance at his face told her that he was furious. An emotion she couldn't define fluttered in her heart by just looking at him. She tried to ignore the sensation, the yearning that made her want to fling herself into his arms, to feel the warmth she felt whenever he stepped into her world. She felt like she was standing on a cliff instead of on the roof of a simple carriage house, and that a good puff of wind would send her tumbling to the ground. One way or another, she had to get her feelings for this man under control.

"Are you out of your mind?" Jonathan asked, stomping his feet to rid them of the snow his boots had accumulated marching across the yard and up the ladder. "I ought to have Constable Fowler arrest you for breaking the curfew. That might keep you safe."

"I'm perfectly safe," Regina replied, managing her temper just enough to keep from yelling back at him. "This is my rooftop. I'll do whatever I please on it."

Her defiance irritated Jonathan even more than the fact that she was putting herself in danger. The combination of anger and fear had his heart pounding as he stepped over the canvas telescope covering and reached for a woman who needed to be shook until her teeth rattled.

"You're going back inside," he said.

Regina sidestepped out of his reach, then put her hands on her hips. It wasn't a very effective stance, since she was bundled up in a thick winter coat with a muffler and gloves, but Jonathan got the point. She'd come up on the rooftop to use her telescope, and she wasn't budging until she'd done just that.

"Where did you get the idea that you could spy on people?" Jonathan asked. He was still going to get her off the roof, but he had to be careful. They didn't have a great deal of room, and he didn't want her to fall and break her neck while he was trying his best to make sure she didn't get strangled.

Regina blushed at the question, and she prayed the cold weather had already reddened her cheeks enough to hide her embarrassment. She couldn't tell Jonathan that she'd gotten the idea several weeks ago, the night she'd spied on him.

"The constable isn't doing anything," she told him, diverting the question. "He thinks keeping women off the streets is the answer. It isn't, and you know it. No one is safe until that madman is locked away."

Or hung, Jonathan added silently. "Frank Fowler is the law officer in Merriam Falls. Not you."

The moment he said the words, Jonathan knew Regina would take them the wrong way.

"What you really mean is that Frank Fowler is a big, brave man and I'm just a lowly, helpless female."

"That isn't what I said."

He hadn't taken the time to retrieve his long coat from the walnut rack in his office. The wind wasn't blowing that briskly, but it was still February, and the ground was blanketed in snow that had fallen in late December and grown in depth with each passing storm. He was freezing to death. He wanted to get Regina inside, where she was safe, then he wanted a drink. A strong drink, something that would drive the cold fear out of his body.

"Isn't it?" Regina challenged. "You're like every other man I've ever met. You think women don't have the sense to know up from down. You think we're incapable of doing more than keeping your beds warm and having babies. Well, I'm just as capable of discovering who's killing women in this town as Frank Fowler is.

And that's exactly what I'm going to do. I'm going to sit on this rooftop for as long as it takes and watch every *man* in Merriam Falls. I'm going to find out who's killing my friends!"

She was shaking inside and out by the time she finished delivering the speech. Tears stung her eyes, but she refused to let them defeat her. The thought of spending one more day pacing the parlor, or staring out the window wondering who had strangled Hazel and Elisa, was driving her closer and closer to madness. She had to do something.

Jonathan was just as motivated. He let her catch her breath while he gauged the distance between himself, Regina, and the edge of the roof. Since he wasn't encumbered by the same heavy clothing as she was, he knew he could reach her with one long step. But she couldn't see it coming.

"I'm not saying your idea doesn't have merit," he said in a lower, calmer voice. "What I'm saying is that the man is killing women, women who support suffrage, and you're the one who brought the idea to town. Don't you think sitting on top of this roof is a little like opening the door and inviting him in for tea and cookies?"

Regina wasn't in the mood to be logical. She was vibrating with an anger that had started to build weeks before, when Hazel Glum had been killed. She was angry at Reverend Hayes for preaching against suffrage. She was angry at the men in town for agreeing with him. She was angry at Frank Fowler because he didn't have the slightest idea who was strangling her friends, and she was furious with Jonathan because the man was making her reevaluate a life she'd been perfectly content with until he'd come to town.

She was hurting as well. She'd lost two friends, two precious ladies who had enjoyed laughing and reading and discussing politics. But more than that, she'd lost her innocence. Not in the carnal sense of the word; she'd been able to resist Jonathan that much. But she was no longer the ignorant young woman she'd been a month earlier. She'd seen death and known fear, and she'd come face-to-face with her own passionate heart. She wanted Jonathan to understand what she was feeling, to take her in his arms and hold her close, to chase the demons away.

Jonathan held her all right, but it wasn't the way Regina wanted. Her thoughts made her mind wander just long enough for him to reach out and jerk her off her feet. In less than a second she was dangling over his shoulder like a sack of potatoes.

"Put me down!" She pounded his back. "I hate you."

"No, you don't," he said, balancing her weight with a shift of his shoulders. She grunted, then beat at his back again. He reached up with his free hand and planted a hard slap on her wool-covered bottom. "Be still, or we'll both end up with broken necks."

Regina stopped wiggling as he made his way toward the ladder. A turn of her head told her that both Richard Ferguson and Mrs. Chalmers were in the middle of the street, watching the rooftop with amusement, while Jonathan hauled her off it with the grace of a storekeeper hauling sacks of flour out of a wagon. Her muffler was dragging on the roof, sliding across the snowy shingles like a red knitted sleigh. "Put me down," she said a second time, making it a request instead of a demand. "I'll go inside for the night."

"You're going to be inside for more than one night," Jonathan said, realizing that Regina had solved the dilemma for him. If the young lady didn't have the common sense to stay behind locked doors until the killer was caught, then it was his civic and Christian duty to make sure she did. At least that's what he planned on saying if anyone questioned his actions.

But Jonathan didn't think anyone was going to examine his motives too closely. Everyone in town already thought he and Regina were engaged. Mrs. Chalmers was worried. She and Richard Ferguson enjoyed teasing him about the feisty suffragette whenever they had the chance. The male population of Merriam Falls would sleep more soundly knowing that a vulnerable woman would soon be under the protective wing of a man.

"People are watching," Regina balked. "You're the one who's going to end up in jail. It's against the law to assault a lady."

"Hold on," Jonathan said as he started down the ladder. "And you're not a lady. You're a headstrong woman who needs a firm hand."

"What are you going to do?" she asked shakily as he turned around and began to make his way down the wide ladder. She could see the ground. The small row of evergreens alongside the carriage house wall was covered with snow, but its winter sparseness didn't offer any protection if they fell.

Jonathan put one foot on the ladder. It was a very precarious position, so Regina pushed aside the flap of his jacket and gripped the belt holding up his trousers. She held on for dear life, the image of what she must look like forgotten as she found herself perched over the edge of the roof.

"I'm tired of sleepless nights worrying about you," Jonathan said, uncaring if anyone heard him. "You're stubborn, Miss Van Buren. Much too stubborn for your own good."

"My telescope," she said, realizing it was uncovered.

She looked at the tubular instrument pointed toward the main part of town. She'd had time to test its range before Jonathan interrupted her good intentions. If she focused it properly, the telescope gave her an excellent view of every house in Merriam Falls, and an unob-

structed view of the textile mill. She could see all the
way across the Hudson on a clear night, and she was
certain that once Jonathan came to his senses, he'd join
her on the roof.

"I'll have Richard put it right," he said as he made
his way down the ladder, holding onto the wooden rung
with one hand while he held onto Regina with the other.
"Don't worry. I'm going to take care of everything."

Regina didn't like what she was hearing, but there
was nothing she could do about it until she got her feet
on the ground again. When the ladder was finally conquered, and Jonathan was standing in the yard between
the carriage house and the back door to Regina's home,
she waited for him to put her upright and lecture her
until her ears rang, but he didn't.

Instead, he started walking, jostling her insides around
as he moved. The pain in her side was beginning to be
more than a mere discomfort. Her muffler snagged on
a branch and started coming off her head. Holding onto
Jonathan's belt with one hand, Regina tried to jerk it
free, but being carried over a man's shoulder had its
disadvantages, and the muffler ended up on the ground.
Her head bobbed up and down as she struggled to get
free. Another well-aimed slap to her bottom ended the
dispute. She was too well padded to be injured by the
reprimand, but Jonathan's manhandling stung her pride.
Regina pounded him on the back again. "Put me down."

She could hear Lucy laughing and Richard Ferguson's
deep male chuckle as the slushy street came into her
upside-down view.

"I'm not putting you down until you're where I want
you," Jonathan stated, sounding as arrogant as a man
could possibly sound. "Now be still, or I'll dump you
in the middle of the street. Think what the neighbors
will say when they look out their windows and see you
sitting in a puddle of half-melted snow."

By the time he reached the steps to his town house, Regina wasn't worried about the neighbors. She was thinking of how she could murder Jonathan Belmont Parker in front of at least two witnesses and get away with it.

"I'll take care of your telescope," Richard Ferguson called out. "Good night, Miss Van Buren."

"Do calm down," Lucy Chalmers added, giggling the whole time. "Mr. Parker only wants you safe."

Regina lifted her head high enough to give them both a scalding look that said she wouldn't forget they were traitors.

Jonathan started whistling.

She jabbed him in the ribs with her elbow.

He grunted, but the whistling continued.

Bisbee opened the door and greeted his employer as if it were perfectly acceptable for the gentleman of the house to return from the mill with a woman slung over his shoulder.

"Miss Van Buren will be staying for a while," Jonathan announced before he leaned over at the waist and relaxed his hold on the wiggling bundle he'd shanghaied from the rooftop.

Regina felt the floor under her feet.

"A cup of tea is in order, Bisbee." Despite his casual tone, Jonathan agilely avoided the fist Regina swung at his jaw.

It took her a moment to realize she'd missed him by a mile. Her head was spinning right along with the room and her heart was pounding. If it hadn't been for Bisbee's steadfast arm, she would have toppled over like a drunken sailor.

"I think the lady needs to sit down," Jonathan said.

Regina gave him a maddening look. "The lady needs to go home," she said, gritting her teeth so hard, her jaw started hurting. She pointed a shaky finger at Jonathan's handsome face. "If you ever touch me again, I'll—"

"Up you go," Jonathan said as he scooped Regina over his shoulder for the second time in less than ten minutes. While she ranted and raved and pounded at his back like a farmer hammering in a fence post, he turned and gave Bisbee a smile. "Have tea delivered to the second-floor guest room."

Bisbee nodded, holding back a chuckle as he started walking toward the kitchen with a spring in his step that hadn't been there until recently.

While his butler was ordering tea and cakes for their unexpected guest, Jonathan was marching up the main staircase like a conquering hero. He paused at the first landing, midway between floors, to warn Regina that if she didn't calm down, he'd be forced to administer more than a solitary slap to her bottom. She called him a name no decent young lady of her age and breeding should know, then reached for the spindled top of the landing banister.

She hung on with all her strength, but it didn't keep Jonathan from shaking her loose and continuing up the stairs. When he reached the second floor, he turned left, strolling down the balcony hallway. Regina noticed the floor was covered with a patterned red and gold Persian carpet. She caught an upside-down glimpse of several large paintings, and a marble stand that might or might not have had a vase of flowers on top of it.

When they reached the desired door, Jonathan opened it and stepped inside. He kicked the door shut with his foot, then locked it. Regina assumed he put the key in his pocket before he set her on her feet. She was so light-headed, she almost fainted. She swayed, and Jonathan put out his hand.

"Don't touch me!" she snapped. "Don't you dare ever touch me again."

"Sit down before you fall down," Jonathan said, undaunted by her threats. He pulled a delicate-looking chair away from the wall.

Regina sat, but she didn't thank him for offering the chair. She glared up at him. The hair that had once been neatly pinned into a chignon at the nape of her neck was hanging down her shoulders. The large rococo mirror on the opposite wall reflected her appearance. She looked like she'd just been in a brawl. While she contemplated the best way to get past Jonathan and out the door, Regina noticed the room's reflection in the decorative mirror.

Deep shades of rose and pink and gold made the bedroom as feminine as it was expensively furnished. The ceiling panels were painted a light ivory, trimmed in darker wood. The walls were the same color as the ceiling and elegantly decorated with artwork. A painting of fat-cheeked cherubs hung over a rose velvet settee. The bed was definitely French, the spindles tall and elegant. The pink coverlet was fringed with gold braid.

"You can't keep me here," she stated after she'd gained her breath and her flushed cheeks had once again taken on their natural color.

"You'd be surprised what I can do," Jonathan said, wondering if he'd made the biggest mistake of his life. He'd locked himself and Regina inside a room with a very enticing bed less than ten feet away.

"Don't threaten me," she retorted. "You have no right to keep me here."

"I'm protecting the woman I plan to marry," he replied while he walked nonchalantly around the room. "I assure you, it's a natural reaction." His gaze drifted back to her. "I won't let you endanger yourself. No matter how sincere your motives."

There was a sternness to his words that told Regina she would be wasting her breath to try to convince him that he wasn't acting in her best interests. She stood up, growing warm now that she was inside. Jonathan's gaze added to the heat. She wanted to remove her coat, but she was afraid that if she did, she'd be down to her petticoat in less time than it had taken him to carry her around the street. He was looking at her as though she were a temptation he wasn't interested in resisting.

Regina was flattered, but she was also embarrassed and angry. "You think you own me," she accused him in a shaky voice. "But you don't."

"I have no interest in owning you." His eyes gleamed like quicksilver as he stepped closer. "But I am going to marry you. One way or the other."

"I'll never marry you," Regina shouted. "Now let me out of here."

"When I'm ready," he told her.

Bisbee knocked on the door.

Jonathan unlocked the door for the servant, then stepped aside, making sure he stood between Regina and her only means of escape.

"Will there be anything else, sir?" Bisbee asked, turning on a heel of his perfectly polished shoes.

"No," Jonathan told him. "I'll see to Miss Van Buren's comfort. Personally."

Regina bristled, but she didn't say a word until the butler was out the door. Jonathan pocketed the key, then walked to the table and picked up the cup of tea that was poured and waiting. When he held it out to her, she was tempted to slap it out of his hand, but she didn't. Ladies didn't act like hooligans, and she was a lady.

The tea was hot with just the right amount of sugar and cream. Regina took a sip, then sat down, still wearing her coat.

"I'll start a fire," Jonathan said.

Regina wanted to laugh. She was beginning to sweat under the heavy wool, but she wasn't about to admit that it had little to do with the winter garment and everything to do with being locked in a bedroom with the man she'd been dreaming about for weeks.

"I want to go home," she insisted.

Jonathan ignored her request. He concentrated on lighting the small, neatly trimmed logs that were stacked on the hearth. He struck a match, then waited until the crumpled paper had caught. A short time later the fire was crackling, and heat began to reach the corner of the room where Regina was sitting stiffly in the dainty Queen Anne chair.

"Darkness won't cover your intentions for long," Jonathan said as he straightened and turned away from the hearth. "You may be able to spy on the town for a night or two, but eventually someone is going to notice that your telescope isn't pointed at the moon. It's too dangerous."

"I have to do something," Regina said. "I won't stand by while another of my friends is murdered."

When Jonathan looked at her, she felt the sensations start to build again. She couldn't let him seduce her with words this time. "And I won't marry you," she said, her eyes flashing like blue sapphires. "Now, unlock that door and let me go home."

"No."

"You're being rude again. And stubborn and—"

"I'm being sensible," Jonathan said. "Something that you should be as well. Now, take off your coat and relax. Your tea is getting cold."

Regina's self-control broke. She marched over to him with her hand raised, but he caught her wrist in midair and pulled her into his arms. "I'm keeping you where I'll know you'll be safe."

"I'm not safe here," Regina choked out. She wasn't talking about the killer, and they both knew it.

"I won't ravish you," Jonathan whispered. "Even

though I want to." His breath stirred the curls lying against her temples as his hand smoothed her disheveled hair. She shivered in his arms. "I'm going to keep you safe," he added. "I have to."

The last words were whispered so softly, Regina couldn't be sure she'd heard them at all. She looked up at his face. He met her gaze and lowered his head, brushing a kiss across her lips. The warmth of his mouth melted her anger, and she rose on tiptoe.

Jonathan continued the slow, sensual seduction of Regina's senses until she was clinging to his shoulders, but he couldn't let the momentary victory make him forget that she was in real danger. The luxury of having Regina in his arms now didn't guarantee her safety come tomorrow. Knowing that, and knowing that she might hate him for what he was about to do, Jonathan moved aside her coat and let his hands explore every inch of her he could reach.

Regina twisted against him, wanting more of the hungry caresses and hating the clothes that were keeping her from feeling them more intimately. She felt herself being lifted again, but this time she wasn't over Jonathan's shoulder, she was cradled in his arms.

He put her down on the bed.

Knowing he should leave her while he could but not willing to give up the pleasure of having her in his arms, Jonathan followed her down on the bed. He continued kissing her while his hands became bolder, cupping her breasts, then caressing them through the fabric of her dress.

Desire raced through Regina, burning her, making her forget everything but the moment and the warmth of Jonathan's hands. She arched against him as a sensuous whimper escaped her.

Barely able to think, Jonathan had just enough common sense left to tear his mouth away from Regina's.

"I'm not going to seduce you, though God knows I want to." He took a deep breath as he came to his feet. "Get some sleep. We'll talk in the morning."

With that, he was gone.

Regina scampered off the bed, trying to reach the door before the key turned in the lock, but she wasn't fast enough. Pounding on the door, she called her captor every vile name she'd ever heard, but it didn't do any good. Finally, exhausted and angry, she knew she wasn't going anywhere until Jonathan unlocked the door.

Regina moaned softly and stretched her arms over her head. After several blinks of her sleepy blue eyes, she realized where she was. Oh, no! She'd spent the night under Jonathan Parker's roof. If anyone found out! But then, people already knew. Lucy and Mr. Ferguson had seen Jonathan carry her across the street. Of course they knew she hadn't entered the house willingly. But only Bisbee knew she'd been locked in a room all night, and even the butler couldn't be sure that she'd been alone the entire time.

Damn the man!

The next time she saw Jonathan Belmont Parker, she was going to make him regret every wonderful, mind-boggling kiss he'd ever given her.

Fully awake, Regina climbed off the bed, feeling as rumpled and wrinkled as the coverlet she'd slept on. She'd used her coat as a blanket, refusing to turn down the bed. Removing her dress and sleeping in her undergarments hadn't been an option either. Disrobing and crawling under the covers was too much like making herself at home. She shoved her arms into the sleeves of her coat, put on her shoes, and hurried to the door.

It wasn't locked.

With her hair tumbling down her back, Regina

stepped out into the hallway. No one was in sight. Determined to get back to where she belonged, she rushed down the stairs and opened the front door. A gasp of surprise escaped her as she stepped back inside.

Reverend Hayes, who had been in the process of raising the brass knocker to announce his arrival, stood on the opposite side of the threshold, looking just as surprised as Regina. His shocked expression quickly turned to one of disapproval.

"Good morning, Miss Van Buren," he said, putting a great deal of emphasis on the words *morning* and *Miss* as his harsh gaze took in her disheveled appearance.

Regina didn't know what to say.

Bisbee appeared out of nowhere, his black suit neatly pressed, his shirt collar starched to perfection. "Good morning, sir," he greeted the visiting reverend with a distinguished smile. "Mr. Parker is waiting for you in the library."

"I should hope so," Reverend Hayes grunted, giving Regina a censoring look as he stepped past her and into the foyer. "It seems the matter is more urgent than his note inferred."

Without a backward glance the minister followed Bisbee into the library.

Regina sat down on the foyer bench. Her knees were shaking too hard to support her. Having Reverend Hayes see her flee Jonathan's house, looking like she'd been wrestling with the man all night, had only one consequence.

Merriam Falls wasn't the kind of town that turned a blind eye to things of that nature. And Jonathan knew it. *Don't worry, I'll take care of everything.*

He'd taken care of things, all right. He'd put her in a compromising situation of the worst kind, and all he'd done was lock her in a room. He hadn't even touched her! At least not the way the minister thought he had. Virgin or not, she was still ruined.

"Would you care for a cup of coffee?"

Regina looked up to find Bisbee standing in front of her. "I can't live in this town if everyone knows I slept here last night. One word from Reverend Hayes and my boardinghouse will empty out faster than a burning building. And your esteemed employer knows it. I'll lose my reputation and my income. He's trying to force me into marriage."

"Mr. Parker's action may seem unorthodox, Miss Van Buren, but I assure you, he is thinking only—"

"Of himself," Regina spat out.

"On the contrary," Bisbee said with confidence. "Mr. Parker loves you."

Eleven

Love.

As Regina marched across the street with her head held high, she wondered if her definition of love and Jonathan's definition would ever be the same. She had to knock on the door, since Lucy had taken to keeping every entrance to the house locked up tight. Shivering on the outside because the wind was picking up to a fitful tempo, and shaking on the inside because she knew there was only one way out of the situation, Regina's foot tapped the porch floor impatiently. When Lucy opened the door, she stepped inside.

"I'm going to need a bath and a change of clothes," Regina said, pulling her arms out of her coat as she walked toward the staircase. "And a cup of tea." She stopped on the landing. "No. Make that a brandy."

"At this time of the morning?" Lucy looked shocked.

"Why not?" Regina replied with a feigned smile. "It's my wedding day. A little celebration is in order." And little it would be, she thought as she turned and continued up the stairs, leaving Lucy to stare after her.

Jonathan didn't love her. He wanted her, and a legal wife, and a mother for the children he'd decided it was time to produce. But he didn't want love. Love was too complicated. And it wasn't passion.

Passion was losing your mind in a moment of pleasure. It was floating until you could touch the stars and drowning in a sea of sensations at the same time. It was surrendering your body and hoping your mind didn't regret it later.

Love wasn't just a fairy tale, white knights in shining armor rescuing damsels in distress. It was having an investment in another person's heart, and in their soul. It was putting someone before yourself, always wanting their happiness before your own. It was having children and loving them no matter their faults. It was more than most people could give, but that didn't stop Regina from wanting it.

Marriage was supposed to be a combination of love and passion. Two bodies and two souls in balance. Two people who loved and lusted for only each other.

Regina went into her room and sank down on the edge of the bed. Squeezing her eyes closed, she refused to cry. Jonathan Parker, the man who always got what he wanted, the man who always turned failing businesses into successful ones, had won.

One way or the other.

She should have believed him, but she hadn't. She hadn't thought it possible for a man to be both sinner and saint.

But then, what did she know of men? She'd spent her entire life in Merriam Falls, reading and studying about places she'd probably never see, longing for the freedom the world offered only to men. The same freedom that allowed Jonathan to scandalize her reputation while he remained a respectable man. It wasn't fair.

Looking up, Regina saw her reflection in the mirror. No wonder Reverend Hayes had assumed the worst. She looked like she'd . . . It didn't matter. Nothing mattered at the moment but getting her thoughts together. She needed to think, to find some way out of this ridiculous situation. But none came to mind.

When Lucy tapped on the door, Regina called for her

to come in. The older woman had a sympathetic smile on her face. "The tea is nice and hot, and I brought you a blueberry muffin."

"Thank you," Regina replied, getting off the bed and resigning herself to the fact that Jonathan was across the street, gloating and planning their wedding.

"You'll be marrying Mr. Parker, then?" Lucy asked. She set the tray on the dresser, then looked toward the bed. It hadn't been slept in, so there was no work waiting for her idle hands. She poured Regina's tea instead.

"It seems that I don't have much choice," Regina sighed. "He hauled me into his house, then arranged for Reverend Hayes to call bright and early this morning."

"Are you . . . all right?"

"I'm fine. I'm a mess because I slept in my clothes. I want a bath and a little peace and quiet before Mr. Parker calls again. Show him to the parlor when he arrives."

"Very well," Lucy said, turning toward the door. She hesitated, then looked over her shoulder at Regina. "I know you're upset. But I'd bet my blue ribbon apple pie that that man loves you."

Regina smiled, but she didn't have any response worthy of Lucy's faith in the male gender.

She drank her tea while hot water filled the ceramic tub, then stripped out of the plain blue dress she'd been wearing when Jonathan had carted her off the roof, and stepped into the steamy bath. Closing her eyes and leaning her head back, she let the easing warmth of the water surround her. She didn't want to feel the pain invade her heart, but it was impossible to keep it at bay. Jonathan had tricked her, or at least he'd used the current circumstances against her.

She hadn't been exaggerating when she'd told Bisbee that she couldn't continue to live in Merriam Falls once word got out that she'd spent the night in Jonathan's house. As liberal-minded as she was, she lived in a very conservative community. She'd have to go around with a scarlet letter embroidered on her clothing if she wanted to remain an unmarried woman.

As the water lapped at the sides of the tub, Regina stared at the ceiling, counting the events that had led up to her current situation. Jonathan had bought the mill, then rented a room for his foreman, during which time he'd given her every indication that he was attracted to her. She'd responded to the attraction, for which she had no excuse. Hazel had been murdered, and she'd allowed Jonathan to comfort her. Then she'd allowed him to take liberties. Again she had no one to blame but herself. Elisa had been murdered, but this time she'd refused Jonathan's comfort. And still he'd won. Why?

Because she wanted to find the killer and he thought she wasn't capable of doing so without putting herself at risk. It was almost ironic. Didn't the man know she'd been at risk since the day he'd walked into the parlor and stolen her heart?

Wondering why fate had suddenly plagued her with so many things she couldn't control, Regina reached for the sponge and began her bath in earnest. Knowing Reverend Hayes, the minister would insist that she and Jonathan marry immediately.

When a knock sounded on the door less than an hour later, Regina knew Jonathan had arrived. Brush in hand, she opened the door, expecting to find Lucy on the other side.

She'd prepared herself to meet Jonathan in the parlor once she'd dressed in a stern-looking blouse and black skirt. She wasn't prepared to greet him wearing a loose-fitting blue robe with her feet bare and her hair hanging down her back. Annoyed that he thought he could invade her bedroom so easily, she put on an icy veneer and greeted him accordingly. "The parlor is downstairs."

"Are you all right?" he asked, untouched by her cold greeting.

"Should I be?"

"We need to talk," he said, standing in her doorway as if it were his right. There was a glint of approval in his eyes as he took in her appearance.

He was wearing black trousers with a gray-and-white-striped vest under a dove-gray jacket. His coal-black hair was damp from a recent bath, and his face clean shaven. Regina felt a quiver of anticipation in her stomach. He was an incredibly handsome man, dressed for a formal occasion. A wedding. Their wedding.

"We can *talk* in the parlor," she said stiffly. Holding the door to prevent it from opening any farther than it already was, Regina glared at him. "I'll be down as soon as I'm dressed."

Once again his eyes scanned her current attire. When they reached the floor and her bare toes peeking out from beneath the hem of her robe, he smiled. The wicked little expression said he remembered the night on the roof when he'd unbuttoned her dress and seen far more than her naked feet.

"Reverend Hayes is in the parlor," Jonathan announced. "You can talk to me under his watchful eyes and ears or speak to me in private. The choice is yours."

Anger cut Regina to her very soul. Knowing the house was devoid of boarders, she opened the door just enough to confront Jonathan face-to-face. "What choice?" she snapped, keeping her voice low enough to make their conversation private without disguising her temper. "I haven't been given a choice. You're blackmailing me. Tricking me into a marriage you know I don't want."

"I warned you," he said as calmly as if they were discussing the weather instead of the rest of their lives. "Did you actually think I'd sit across the street while you tempted the killer to make you his next victim?"

"Don't use the death of my friends to justify your actions," she replied, her voice trembling from the effort it took to keep from shouting. "You're selfish, manipulating, and—"

"The man you're going to marry."

Regina tried to slam the door in his face, but he was quicker and stronger. He leaned against it with one hand and reached for her with the other. She tried to pull away, but she got tangled in the hem of her robe and stumbled instead. He jerked her against him, supporting her weight with one arm securely wrapped around her waist. The sudden movement loosened her robe even more, revealing the swell of her breasts above the lacy edge of her corset.

She glared up at him. "I don't want to marry you."

"But you will," he said, his eyes gleaming with more than one emotion. "Now, be still and listen. I told Reverend Hayes that I locked you in the guest room. After I told him why, he agreed that it was the safest place for you. Whether or not he believes that you're as chaste now as you were last night isn't important. However, he does agree that a hasty marriage is the best way to avert unsavory gossip."

Something flared in his silver eyes. Regina couldn't be sure if it was lust or triumph. Neither one pleased her.

"You can go downstairs and say your vows with grace and dignity, or you can go kicking and screaming." His gaze settled on the ivory valley between her breasts. "Again, the choice is yours."

The love that had been building for weeks turned into instant hatred when Regina realized he didn't intend to concede an inch on what he considered a logical course of action. But then, why should he? He was getting everything he wanted. She was the one being forced to marry. And she'd be the one forced to live under his roof and under his rules. It went against everything she believed in, against everything she had hoped to gain in her life.

She should have known better than to harbor the hope that Jonathan wasn't like other men, that his softly whispered words and seductive smiles actually meant something.

"I still need to get dressed," she said frigidly. Jonathan might get a wife, but there was no way he was going to get a willing one.

He released her, letting his hand glide slowly from around her waist. "I'll send Mrs. Chalmers up to help you."

Regina's anxiety grew until she thought she'd stumble on her way downstairs. She'd taken more time than usual to dress, debating between a dark blue dress with a fitted bodice and jet beads, and a lighter blue one with ivory trim around the collar and cuffs and a skirt that was fitted in the front but flared out to a small train at the back. The loss of her friends delegated that she wear the more solemn garment, while the ceremony she was about to attend required something more lively. Lucy had solved the dilemma by choosing the light blue, then dutifully buttoning it up the back.

The only thing that kept Regina's knees strong enough to support her was the look in Jonathan's eyes as he waited at the bottom of the staircase. His smile was placid, but his gaze was pure lightning. His silvery eyes glittered with pride and determination as he stood between her and the front door of the boardinghouse.

"You're beautiful," he said, extending his hand.

Regina didn't feel beautiful. She felt beaten and defeated, but she refused to let her future husband see that. Squaring her shoulders, she ignored his outstretched hand. After the events of the last few weeks, her nerves were raw, and her emotions drained. If she spent too much time thinking about the upcoming ceremony, she'd burst into tears. Ironically, she felt very much like she'd felt when Hazel and Elisa had been eulogized. She was numb.

Jonathan took her by the elbow and led her toward the parlor door. "Lucy and Richard will be our witnesses," he told her. His voice softened an octave as he looked down at her. "I'll take very good care of you."

Regina didn't doubt him, but she wasn't impressed by his pledge. Right then all she wanted to do was hold herself together long enough to get the dreaded words spoken. She didn't mind standing in front of Lucy and Richard; in fact, she was glad to count them among her friends. It was the thought of facing Reverend Hayes again that had her hesitating. The man was overbearing and pious on a good day. She could almost hear his mind churning in celebration, another young woman sold into the bondage of marriage, blessed be the event.

She hesitated just outside the doorway.

"What's wrong now?" Jonathan asked.

Regina reached into the pocket of her dress and pulled out her mother's wedding ring. It was a modest gold band, but it symbolized everything Regina knew about love between a man and a woman. She'd debated over the ring more than she had over her dress. Knowing there was no turning back once she said her vows, she wanted to believe that the ring would bring her luck as well as love.

"This was my mother's," she said, giving Jonathan the ring. "I'd like to wear it, if you don't mind."

The sincerity of his smile surprised her. "I'd be honored to put it on your finger."

Feeling frightened and confused, she turned away from his probing gaze and looked at the parlor door.

After placing the ring in his vest pocket, Jonathan opened the door and ushered her inside. As expected, Reverend Hayes was standing across the room, looking very satisfied with himself.

For a moment there was an oppressive silence in the parlor, then Lucy Chalmers smiled and the tension eased from Regina's shoulders enough for her to take a step forward.

With every word spoken, Regina wanted to stop the ceremony, insisting that it was a mockery, but she didn't. Instead, she stood by Jonathan's side, her right hand resting on his arm until the minister asked him to turn and face the bride.

When their eyes met, the minister's voice faded into the background. Her bridegroom's eyes gleamed with victory, but Regina could see something else shining beneath the success. Jonathan's gaze was the same one she'd seen on his face the night he'd joined her on the roof. It was an unspoken promise of things to come.

But there was no turning back from the words he was speaking today, no reprise for either the groom or his bride as Jonathan firmly answered "I will" to the question put to him.

Regina's vows followed. Her voice, starting out grave and serious, gradually turned to a whisper as she recited the vows that would make her Jonathan Parker's legal wife.

Seconds later, Jonathan slipped the gold band on her finger. It felt warm and somehow right, as if the circumstances that had turned her into a married woman had been meant to happen. While the reverend blessed the union of husband and wife, stating that it was unlawful for man to sever that which God had joined together, Regina looked up from the simple gold band circling her finger.

Jonathan's gaze was just as determined as before, but

his expression had changed. He was smiling at her, truly smiling, as though their marriage did indeed give him happiness.

Although the expression on her husband's face was warm and pleasant, and deep inside her heart Regina knew she was falling in love with the man, she couldn't ignore the mockery of the words they had just spoken. Wedding vows represented love and devotion both spiritually and physically, but there was no true love between this bride and groom.

When Reverend Hayes announced that Jonathan could kiss his bride, Regina couldn't stop her natural reaction. She pulled slightly away from her new husband's touch.

The movement was barely visible, but Jonathan saw it. Her rejection turned his pleasant expression to one as hard as steel. Instead of a gentle kiss, he pulled her into his arms and pressed his mouth over hers. The possessive kiss told his bride and everyone else in the room that he was still the man who got whatever he wanted.

A delicious feeling of heat and desire rose up inside Regina, but she fought it, hating herself and the man who was blatantly embarrassing her. When Jonathan finally released her, she barely had time to catch her breath before Lucy was hugging her. The cook's eyes were overflowing with tears as she told Regina to be happy.

Determined to keep her wits if nothing else, Regina forced a smile to her face and hugged Lucy in return. Richard Ferguson gave her a chaste kiss on the cheek before offering his hand in congratulations to the groom.

Reverend Hayes gave her a stern look, then his whiskered face broke into a smile. "Your husband is a good man, Regina," he told her. "Honor him and yourself, and this marriage will last, the way God intended."

There were no civil words to express her feelings at the moment, so Regina gave the minister a brief smile.

Unsure what to do next, she simply stood by her husband's side until he suggested to Mrs. Chalmers that she start packing. He and Regina were to travel to New York City for their honeymoon. The train was scheduled to leave in less than two hours.

Frustrated, irritated, and confused by feelings of entrapment mixed with the joys of a prayer fatefully answered, the bride went upstairs to pack. Lucy's girlish excitement didn't penetrate Regina's numbness as a trunk was pulled from the closet and stuffed with clothing.

"You'll enjoy the city," Lucy chatted. "There's the opera and the theater and ice skating in Central Park."

And a marriage bed waiting for me, Regina silently added. The last few weeks had shaken the foundation of her world, but the emotional upheaval was nothing compared to what she was feeling as she watched Lucy close and lock the trunk. That morning she'd been a free woman, at least as free as any woman could be. Now she was married. Legally and morally bound to a man who had frequently expressed his desire for her. A man who had yet to speak a single word of love.

Feeling like she was walking in a fog, Regina descended the staircase to find Jonathan waiting. There was a good-bye hug from Mrs. Chalmers and another teary blessing for a happy future as Jonathan offered Regina his arm. She took it, but she refused to look at him. Her only thoughts were ones of survival. How was she going to get through the next few hours without turning into an hysterical woman? She fought back the tears that threatened to overflow as she stepped outside the boardinghouse. Regina wanted to look over her shoulder, to regain the past, but it was gone now, forever beyond her reach.

All she had before her was an uncertain future.

Oblivious to the cold snap of the wind and the bright

sunlight reflecting off the snow, Regina felt tears moisten her eyes. She wiped them away before her new husband had a chance to see the effect their marriage was having on her.

Amid the muffled sound of horse's hooves falling on snow and the creaking of harnesses and leather, Jonathan surveyed his bride. It was easy to see that Regina wasn't happy about being married.

"I thought two or three weeks in the city would be nice," he said, breaking the silence that had lingered between them since their wedding vows. "If you prefer, we can take a train south. St. Augustine is a frequent haunt this time of year, and the weather is certainly more pleasant. If not Florida, there's always Charleston or Savannah."

"Traveling south doesn't interest me," Regina replied numbly.

"What does interest you, Mrs. Parker?" He deliberately used her new title. She'd never be *Miss* Van Buren again, so she might as well acclimate herself to it.

"An annulment," she announced angrily. Regina wasn't sure where the idea had come from, but it suited her purposes at the moment. Regardless of her feelings or attraction for Jonathan, she had no desire to be any man's wife.

Her new husband leaned back and smiled. He crossed his legs at the ankles, making himself comfortable before he replied to her request. "An annulment would imply that our marriage never existed because it was never consummated. I assure you, Regina, that will not be the case. I made my intentions clear from the beginning, and I warned you that I'd have you one way or the other. I meant it."

The surety in his voice set a match to Regina's temper. At that moment she didn't care if everyone in town heard her yelling. "I don't want to be your wife," she retorted at the top of her voice. "I won't be your wife."

"You already are," Jonathan said, undaunted by her angry outburst. "Do you really think that the good citizens of Merriam Falls are going to believe that I locked a beautiful woman in a bedroom without joining her there?"

"I don't care what people think," she told him, determined to win the argument. All she had left was her pride. Jonathan had cleverly tricked her out of everything else. "I told you that I didn't want to get married." She took a shaky breath. "I don't have to come back to Merriam Falls after the annulment. I can get a job in the city."

"There won't be a job in the city, because there won't be an annulment," Jonathan said.

He had hoped Regina would eventually resign herself to her new status. But then, they'd been married for only a few hours. He had plenty of time to convince her that he was exactly what she needed. Still, the convincing would be easier if she didn't hate him.

Regina was on the verge of yelling a little louder, when she realized that it wouldn't do any good. Right or wrong, tricked into marriage or its willing victim, Jonathan was in control. If she refused to share his bed, she'd have to undergo a physical examination by a physician to prove that her virginity was intact. No court in the state would believe her otherwise.

The thought of undergoing such an intimate examination was enough to keep her quiet until the carriage arrived at the train depot.

Knowing it would do little good to refuse Jonathan's help as she departed the carriage, Regina gave him her hand. They would be traveling in the private car that was being hitched to the train that very minute. While Jonathan gave orders for Regina's luggage to be added to the baggage car, his wife looked for a familiar face. Other than the porter, there was no one in sight.

Regina entered the Pullman car, unsure what to expect. Dark green curtains were draped over the multiple windows that ran along each side of the private car. Matching green velvet cushions adorned the seats. The car looked more like a parlor than a means of transportation. The carpet and furnishings were as elegant as the ones in Jonathan's home. A small potbellied stove occupied the far corner. Since the train would arrive at Grand Central Station shortly after the dinner hour, a private sleeping car hadn't been added to the train.

Regina removed her hat and gloves, then extended her hands toward the warmth of the small stove. She looked through the window and saw Bisbee giving last-minute orders to the porter before he entered the passenger car. Regina wasn't surprised to see the servant, and a part of her was grateful that he'd be traveling with them to New York. She knew very few people in the vast city, having visited there only a few times, mostly to attend suffrage rallies, and once to do some shopping. She'd been amazed by the number of stores filled with everything from Paris gowns to delicious Swiss chocolates. The gown she'd worn to Jonathan's house the night of Elisa's murder had been purchased in a small, elegant shop on Fourteenth Street. Knowing that she'd become the wife of a very wealthy man, Regina decided she'd indulge in several gowns this time. It was the least she could do to repay Jonathan for his recent behavior.

Underneath her anger, Regina didn't give a whit about Jonathan's money. Her boardinghouse had always offered her a comfortable life, though not an extravagant one. She'd never wanted for food or clothing or shelter. Of course, now she'd have all three, in the most stylish form available, but the knowledge did little to comfort her. The simple life of a small town appealed to her more than the pretentious snobbery of Manhattan and its Knickerbocker families.

As for being married, she'd rather have a husband who truly loved her than one who simply desired to possess her. If only she could convince Jonathan that love was better than passion. She would truly cherish his heart if he offered it, and she'd be more than willing to have hers cherished in return.

While the stove radiated its warmth, Regina watched her new husband board the car. Jonathan immediately removed his coat and hat, setting them aside on the velvet-cushioned sofa. A few minutes later, the engine groaned as though in pain and the train jerked forward, its steel wheels eating up the tracks as it headed east toward the grand city of New York.

"Have you eaten?" Jonathan asked as he inspected the newspapers Bisbee had had the foresight to supply.

"I'm not hungry," Regina replied stiffly. She dreaded the next few hours, confined to the narrow railroad car, almost as much as she dreaded the night to come. Whatever conversation she and Jonathan shared was sure to be argumentative.

Paying her no mind, he walked to a smaller version of the walnut liquor cabinet and opened it. Inside, Regina could see a basket. Jonathan retrieved it, set it on the table, and drew back the linen towel that was covering it.

"We have some fruit," he announced, setting the contents on the table. "And cheese and bread and spiced cakes. And wine, of course."

"What, no champagne?" Regina inquired sharply. "I for one would think you'd want to celebrate."

"We'll have champagne tonight," he replied calmly. "At Delmonico's."

She was about to ask if they'd be staying at one of the city's hotels or if Jonathan had a residence in Manhattan, when her husband sat down beside her, offering her a small wedge of bread and cheese. "You need to eat something."

A retort died on Regina's lips as she looked into his eyes. She wanted to say no to the undeniable intent burning in his eyes, but she couldn't find the words or the strength. Slowly, his head lowered and his lips brushed lightly over hers. It was a mild kiss compared to those they'd shared in the past, a tender kiss that strongly resembled the kiss any husband would give his wife, and its simplicity rocked Regina to her very core.

A strange longing uncurled inside her, and at that moment she knew she was defeated. She cared too deeply for this impossible man to turn her back on their hasty marriage and scream annulment. He was a master, skilled in the art of seduction, and a businessman well trained in persuading investors to part with their money. He was arrogant and demanding and irritating, and she loved him beyond words.

The problem was, he didn't love her. In spite of her increasing interest in passion and adventure, Regina wasn't ready to embark on a voyage that had no destination but the bedroom. She wanted their marriage to be real in every sense of the word. She wanted passionate nights and days filled with laughter and anger and the sounds of children.

In the brief moment that Jonathan's mouth covered hers, Regina realized all of these things. So much so, that when he pulled away, all she could do was stare at him.

Jonathan gave her a questioning look. "Be angry with me if you must," he said. "But know this. I will always take care of you."

She had no doubt that he meant what he was saying. Arrogance aside, her husband was a mature, responsible man. But taking care of a woman and loving her were two different things. If Regina settled for the first without the second, she'd be forever miserable. But if she could find more than passion in her husband, if Jonathan did possess more than mere desire for her, then the bleak future might hold a ray of hope.

If.

If not, she was destined to be just another woman married to just another man, with no hope of ever finding true happiness.

"Do you have a house in the city?" she asked, unable to control her curiosity.

"A town house," Jonathan told her. He returned to the table and cut a wedge of cheese for himself. "On Thirty-fourth Street."

Regina didn't know a lot about Manhattan or its inhabitants, but she knew the Astors lived on Thirty-fourth Street. The neighborhood where Jonathan resided was more than a cluster of expensive homes, it was the center of a social hierarchy with exclusive members who gained entry based upon their pedigree.

"Do you know Mrs. Astor?"

"I've attended one or two of her parties," Jonathan replied casually.

Knowing that Manhattan society centered around fabulous jewels, Paris gowns, Tiffany glass, and ten-course dinners served by liveried servants, it was no small feat for the son of a butcher-shop owner to be invited to the Astor home. Regina also knew that Mrs. Astor and her ladies of society were not advocates of suffrage. It wasn't considered tasteful to support such outrageous legislation, and it certainly wasn't ladylike to parade up and down the street, waving banners and demanding a right the highborn females of Thirty-fourth Street didn't think important. They were more interested in the exclusivity of summers in Newport than in the legal and political independence of their gender.

An awkward silence filled the Pullman car while they ate a meager but tasty lunch of cheese and bread and a mild wine that tasted more like apple cider than spirits. Gradually, Regina began to relax. When the potbellied stove warmed the car to a comfortable temperature, she stood and removed her cloak, grateful that Jonathan realized he didn't need to act the gentleman and help her with the garment. Regina wasn't sure she could abide his touch, at least not then, when their wedding night loomed ahead of her like an uncharted continent.

She sat down and looked out the window. The landscape was a mixture of white snow and brown branches that quickly blurred into nothingness as her mind raced ahead to the night to come. She knew the mechanics of being married, of consummating a marriage, and she'd tasted just enough of passion to know that it could block out the fear of the unknown, but she also knew that no amount of passion could replace love.

Sensing that Jonathan was prepared to handle the situation no matter how she received him, willingly or unwillingly, Regina slowly resigned herself to the fact that when she awoke the next morning she would truly be a married woman. But her acquiescence didn't mean she had to make her seduction an easy one. If Jonathan wanted a willing wife, he was going to have to do more than offer a champagne toast under a Delmonico chandelier to get one.

Twelve

A light drizzle dampened the city streets. Regina was glad to be rid of the hum of metal wheels and the endless silence that had engulfed the private train car for the last several hours. Jonathan, apparently sensing her reluctant mood, had maintained an interest in his newspapers. The few words they had exchanged had been perfunctory ones.

The carriage was filled with shadows, interrupted occasionally by the flash of streetlamps that lined their route. Rested after a long nap on the train and filled with apprehension about the night ahead, Regina sat across from her husband. Like the carriage he used in Merriam Falls, this one was expensively made and more comfortable than most. She looked up from her wrinkled lap to find Jonathan staring at her.

There was something irreconcilable in his gaze, as if he weren't sure if he should continue on his chosen path or instruct the driver to turn the carriage around and take them back to the small town on the banks of the Hudson River. Regina's thoughts were almost as jumbled.

"You'll feel better after you've had a hot bath," Jonathan told her. "I keep a full staff in the city. Bisbee wired ahead, so they're prepared for our arrival."

The encroaching darkness labeled the beginning of social activities in the city, so Regina knew they would have plenty of time for dinner at Delmonico's. It also meant that she had several more hours to maintain a façade of indifference to her husband. Not an easy task, considering she'd like nothing better than for him to wrap his arms around her and hold her close.

They had never spent this much time together without touching each other before. The brief but gentle kiss he'd given her just before leaving Merriam Falls seemed a century old, and she longed for something more to pass between them than stiff silence and politely spoken words.

"A hot bath sounds wonderful," she admitted with a short smile.

Jonathan smiled in return. The expression had its desired effect, and Regina felt some of the tension ease between them. Like it or not, this man had the unique ability to make her feel something deep and real. She should be angry that he'd manipulated her into marriage, and she was, but the anger was quickly being replaced with the excitement of being his bride.

A blush came to her cheeks as she thought about all the things they would share before the sun washed the darkness from the city streets.

Gaslights flickered and wheels clattered on cobblestone as the carriage approached the prestigious row of houses on Thirty-fourth Street. The expensive mansions were little more than large, looming shadows that held no interest for Regina. She was too absorbed in her own thoughts to notice the architecture of the wealthy. When the carriage came to a stop in front of an impressive brownstone with wrought iron banisters and marble steps, her heart skipped several beats.

"We're here," Jonathan said, reaching for the door latch.

He stepped out of the carriage, then turned to offer Regina his hand. She accepted it, praying he wouldn't be able to notice the nervous tremor she couldn't seem to control. Bisbee had come ahead, so he was the one to open the door and formally welcome Regina to her new home. At least it was going to be her home for the next few weeks. Once the honeymoon was over, she was almost certain Jonathan planned on returning to Merriam Falls and the unsolved mysteries that had spurred him into being overprotective in the first place.

A middle-aged woman appeared from the far end of the foyer, wearing a black dress and a starched white apron. She curtsied, then smiled. Bisbee introduced the housekeeper as Mrs. Cameron.

"Molly will be your maid," the housekeeper announced. "If you like, I can have tea served upstairs. Your bath is being drawn now."

"I'll be in the library," Jonathan said, relinquishing his bride into the staff's capable hands. "Our reservations are for eight."

Regina allowed herself to be led upstairs, too nervous to notice more than the most functional things about the town house. Like the house on Whitley Street, it was elegantly decorated. The mahogany banister was as smooth as glass under her hand, and the carpets soft under her feet. So much had happened in the past twenty-four hours, she barely saw the gilded frames that bordered artwork worth a small fortune.

The bedroom the housekeeper escorted her to was decorated in tones of burgundy and white. A cheerful fire blazed in the hearth. Regina's trunk was already resting on the floor at the end of the bed, partially unpacked. The coffee-colored evening gown was spread out on the white bedspread, waiting to be worn to Delmonico's.

There was a dressing room that opened into a bath, where a large ceramic tub was being filled with water. Stream rolled toward the ceiling, and Regina longed to strip away her wrinkled blue dress and soak in the hot, scented water. Gilded mirrors lined the walls, allowing one to view oneself from almost any angle. It was a bit embarrassing for Regina to think about what Jonathan's bath must look like. The man had no shame whatsoever.

Her personal maid was a young girl with curly blond hair and soft blue eyes who smiled the moment Regina stepped into the room. "Pleased to make your acquaintance, Mrs. Parker," the girl said, doing her best to curtsy without falling on her face.

Regina could tell from the girl's awkward actions that she'd probably been recruited from the kitchen to be a lady's maid. Until that night, the Manhattan town house had been a bachelor's residence. Sympathizing with the servant's unexpected plight, Regina smiled. "Thank you, Molly. I'm pleased to make your acquaintance as well."

Seeing a smile and sensing that the new Mrs. Parker didn't have a snobbish bone in her body, Molly relaxed with an audible sigh. "Your bath will be ready in a few minutes."

"First a cup of tea," Regina said. "Then a bath."

Mrs. Cameron hurried Molly downstairs to fetch the tea while she helped Regina out of her wrinkled clothing and into a soft white and pink robe. Once she was resting on a chaise longue with her feet up, Regina noticed a set of ornately decorated double doors on the opposite side of her bedroom. Without being told, she knew they led to Jonathan's room.

Was he relaxing with a brandy before his bath? Or was he already soaking in a steamy tub of water, whistling to himself because he'd finally gotten what he wanted. *Not yet,* Regina corrected her thought. They were husband and wife, but their marriage was little more than a formality until she shared a bed with him.

Sipping her tea, Regina refused to think about what would happen once they'd returned from Delmonico's.

* * *

The private salon that Jonathan had requested was one of Delmonico's best. The room was ablaze with candlelight, the chairs perfectly cushioned in deep maroon velvet, while the silverware gleamed. The setting was almost decadent, but Regina was too preoccupied with being alone with her new husband to think about the salon's decor.

Molly had brushed Regina's waist-length hair until it crackled, then much to Regina's surprise, the young girl styled it into a tasteful array of curls that rested comfortably at the nape of Regina's neck. The coffee-colored gown had been steamed free of wrinkles. Wearing it, along with her mother's pearls and a soft white-mink wrap that had mysteriously appeared in the bedroom while Regina had been soaking in the tub, the new Mrs. Parker drew every male eye in the stylish restaurant.

Unnerved by their entrance, and the admiring glances of men she didn't know or recognize, Regina had allowed Jonathan to escort her into the salon like a lamb being led to slaughter. Once she was seated, she tried to relax. As usual, Jonathan looked irresistibly handsome dressed in a black evening swallow-tailed coat and black trousers. His expression was pleasant, but his eyes made Regina nervous. They were looking at her as if nothing on the restaurant's menu would be more satisfying than the woman he was staring at.

"Relax," he said. "I know you must be hungry."

Actually, Regina was famished. The cup of tea had eased her nervous stomach, leaving it feeling vaguely hollow. If she didn't eat soon, she'd be too weak to walk.

Little more was said until the waiters appeared to serve their dinner. The food was delicious, flavored with delicate sauces. In spite of her apprehension over her new status, Regina enjoyed the meal. Dessert was a light raspberry sorbet that brought a smile to her face when the small silver bowl was placed in front of her.

"Finally," Jonathan chuckled. "I thought I'd never see that smile again."

"I like raspberries," Regina said defensively.

"And I like you," Jonathan countered. The waiters had discreetly made their exit and they were alone.

Regina watched as he pulled a bottle of iced champagne from a silver bucket and popped the cork. The sound echoed in the small room. He filled two flutes with the vivacious wine, then set one in front of her. "A toast," he announced, holding his glass high. "To us."

The simple statement fell short of describing their complicated relationship, but Regina raised her glass just the same. The champagne was the finest money could buy, but she barely tasted it. All she could do was stare at her husband's handsome face. His strong, well-shaped features mesmerized her as his eyes met hers over the rim of the crystal.

An all-encompassing sense of finality seized Regina at that moment, and she realized she truly was bound to this man until her dying breath. Whatever the reasons or manipulations, she was his wife. Soon they'd exchange the privacy of Delmonico's for the intimacy of a bedroom. The anger she'd carried with her since morning melted under Jonathan's soft gaze. It didn't matter that the man deserved contemptuous words. Nor was it of any consequence now that she'd been skillfully tricked into becoming his wife. What mattered was the seething silence building between them, a silence filled with unspoken desire.

Regina lowered her eyes and sipped the champagne. She could do one of two things. She could rant and rave and lock herself in the elegant bedroom on Thirty-fourth Street, or she could willingly become Jonathan Parker's wife in every sense of the word. Either way, her life had become irrevocably entwined with this man. Either way, she still loved him.

Could a heart break more than once? Was it better to go through the embarrassment of an annulment, to gain her freedom, only to love him from afar, or was it better to love him the only way he wanted to be loved—with her body? And in giving her body, dare she hope that one day he might feel what she felt, that inexplicable mingling of their hearts and lives that kept couples smiling into their dotage?

The questions were as complex as the emotions that had become a part of her daily existence since he'd knocked on her front door.

"It's late," Jonathan announced, setting his glass on the table.

The words sounded like a death sentence and a glimpse of heaven simultaneously. Regina felt her resolve beginning to break. Whatever semblance of composure she'd maintained through the meal quickly dissolved as Jonathan walked toward her.

"I'd very much like to kiss my wife," he said, smiling.

Regina hesitated, desperately wanting to fight the pleasure that rushed through her at the thought of one of Jonathan's intoxicating kisses, but she couldn't. Mindless to anything but his silver gaze, she let herself be drawn into the circle of his embrace. His touch was like silken steel, firm but gentle, and very warm.

She looked up at him, knowing more than anything that she wanted the hard pressure of his mouth covering hers. Her skin tingled with an almost electriclike charge as his hands moved slowly up her arms, over the lace of her evening gloves, and on to the heavy satin of her gown, then higher, to the curve of her throat, where there was no cloth to keep her from feeling the heat of his open palm.

With an agonizing slowness, his head lowered until she could feel his breath brushing her lips. They parted, openly inviting him to kiss her. When he did, it was as if she'd somehow miraculously become a falling star spinning out of control. His mouth molded over hers, taking her breath. His tongue teased, probing slowly into her mouth. Regina felt his arms tightening around her, the heat of his body holding her intimately against his stronger one, and the gentle teasing of his tongue. She felt everything so acutely that she wrapped her arms around his neck and clung to him, lest he take the feelings away.

Moments later, unsure of how they'd moved from their place beside the table to the cushioned comfort of the moiré banquette that ran the length of two of the room's four walls, Regina found herself sitting on her husband's lap while he kissed her senseless.

The kisses were long and sweet and painfully arousing. They told Regina things about herself she had come close to admitting but had still held at a distance, because knowing them, acknowledging them, would have been her undoing. But now she didn't have to restrain her emotions, she didn't have to keep a tight rein on what she was feeling. She was Jonathan's wife, and she could kiss him back with all the love she felt inside.

Controlling himself because they were in Delmonico's, not the privacy of his Manhattan town house, Jonathan kissed Regina's throat and the small amount of shoulder the evening gown revealed. His hands smoothed over her waist, then slightly higher, teasing her as he thought about stripping the gown away and touching the firm young breasts encased in a whalebone corset and silk chemise. He made each kiss a promise and a curse, making her twist in his arms, stretching out the torment until they both were shaking. Then, instead of doing what he longed to do, instead of pushing her back on the banquette and raising her skirts, Jonathan removed his wife's hands from around his neck, forcing her to look up at him.

"It's time to go home," he told her.

Regina took a long, slow breath, then nodded.

She was a mass of shaking desire and thrilling tension as Jonathan helped her into the black carriage waiting by the curb. The ride down Fifth Avenue took an eternity. They sat across from each other, but instead of the oppressive silence that had been with them during the trip to the restaurant, the air was charged with a passionate longing that was as tangible as the sound of the wheels on the damp cobblestone streets.

Regina could feel Jonathan watching her. Instinctively, she stared back, as if the darkness applied only to other mortals, mere men and women who couldn't possibly feel what she and her husband were feeling at that moment. And she knew Jonathan was feeling something. Passion, desire, lust. The name wasn't important. The important thing was that this was their wedding night, and soon, very soon, their marriage would be a real one.

Jonathan sat in the carriage, thinking similar thoughts, as the town house on Thirty-fourth Street drew closer. He'd planned Regina's seduction for weeks, from painfully restrained kisses by moonlight to tempting her mind with thoughts of freedom and passion, but he'd never expected to feel what he had been feeling since he'd slipped a gold band on her hand earlier in the day.

He still wanted her. God, how he wanted her. But the wanting was different. Mixed with it was a strange longing to make her completely and utterly happy. To know that whatever he did pleased her before it pleased himself. And beneath that was the knowledge that he had to keep her safe. No matter how distant the small town of Merriam Falls seemed at the moment, Jonathan knew the danger was growing. Whoever was murdering young

suffragettes had to have Regina at the heart of his de-
vious plans. She was the catalyst that kept the other
women interested. Without her the movement would
cease to exist, at least in the sleepy New York hamlet,
and the young ladies of the "literary circle" would return to their hopes of finding a proper young man and
settling down in a lattice-trimmed cottage.

The driving need to protect Regina had been the reason he'd hauled her off the rooftop. Locking her in the
guest room hadn't been on his list of enticing things to
bring her to the altar, but it had worked nevertheless,
and he'd seized the opportunity for fear that another one
might not come his way. His lovely young bride might
think she was safe, but Jonathan knew differently. He
knew at some primal level that the murderer wanted Regina most of all.

He couldn't explain the instinctive feeling any more
than he could explain why he felt the way he did about
the sassy suffragette. She wasn't going to be a pliable
wife, this feisty lady with sapphire eyes and a witty
tongue, but she was going to make his life interesting.

With that in mind, Jonathan pushed thoughts of the
future aside and began concentrating on his wedding
night. He was almost positive that Regina wasn't going
to refuse him outright. She'd returned his kisses in the
salon too eagerly to play the role of an outraged virgin
once they reached the town house. Still, he had to be
careful and patient. The latter was going to be the most
difficult. His body was begging for the pleasure that lay
ahead.

If he wanted to satisfy only his physical desire for
Regina, he'd have carried her upstairs the moment the
carriage stopped in front of the house and appeased his
sexual hunger as quickly as possible. But he wasn't interested in only taking from Regina. He wanted to give
to her as well. He wanted to open the doors of sensual

pleasure. He wanted to slowly unravel the rigid moral cage that surrounded women of their society and teach her that being female could be more wonderful than she'd ever imagined. He wanted to join in that wonder, to discover his own sensuality at the same time, to make love to her totally uninhibited by social mores.

Well-traveled and experienced beyond his years, Jonathan had shared his bed with ladies who considered the sexual arts a woman's domain. They knew just how to taunt and tease a man's body, when to pursue and when to retreat, how to play the enticing game of surrender that made the pleasure well worth the wait. Being a lusty man, and not ashamed of his sexual desires, Jonathan wanted Regina to share in them the same way she now shared his name.

Getting a grip on himself, because he was close to forgetting that a bride deserved a bed with scented sheets and candlelight, Jonathan tried to concentrate on more platonic things.

He wanted her to experience the city to its fullest. They could tour the parks weather permitting, and the art museums, and at night there were theaters and operas, and restaurants where exotic foods were served by people who hadn't yet learned the English language. He wanted her to see the city from the vantage point of the Upper Bay. When the busy harbor was masked by the early serenity of dawn, it was a beautiful sight, one that empowered the viewer.

Jonathan wanted to teach his reluctant bride that sensuality went beyond the bedroom. It pleased all the senses: sight, sound, hearing, taste, and touch. He wanted her to feel the power of living, to know that every morsel of food that passed her mouth could bring pleasure, and that the sound of a foghorn, blown somewhere in the hazy night, could sound as beautiful as a string quartet. He wanted her to laugh for the pure pleasure of it, and to run into his arms because there was no other place she'd rather be.

But most of all, he wanted Regina to trust him. Without her trust, keeping her safe would be impossible. She had to learn that he was a man of instincts, and that those instincts had been tested, making them dependable. With the vivid image of his little sister burning in his mind, Jonathan reached for the door latch as the carriage came to a stop in front of the town house.

Thirteen

Bisbee greeted them at the door, then discreetly disappeared once he'd taken Jonathan's outer coat and Regina's fur wrap. The house was quiet, too quiet for its newest resident. Counting the chimes of a clock sitting on some unknown mantel, Regina tried to convince herself that she wasn't overly apprehensive about the rest of the night. She was a grown woman after all, albeit a virginal one. She was sure there would be a few awkward moments, and perhaps a second or two of pain, then it would be over with. She'd be Jonathan's wife, and perhaps the experience might be as pleasant as she was sure he expected it to be.

Regina wanted to share his confidence, but she couldn't. Her mind might be satisfied with the idea of a marriage based on passionate freedoms, but her heart still wanted love.

Torn between despondency and excitement, Regina turned to find Jonathan smiling at her. "Why don't you go upstairs," he suggested. "I'll be up in a few minutes."

Regina gathered up the voluminous satin of her gown and began walking toward the carpeted staircase that would take her to the second floor. She was tempted to ask if Jonathan was going into his library to have a good stiff drink. She could use one. The champagne she'd sipped at Delmonico's hadn't been enough to fortify her nerves. With each step she took, Regina knew she was getting closer to the moment of truth—the moment when Jonathan's touch would dissolve the last of her resistance, and she'd melt in his arms.

Knowing the inevitability of it all only made the time pass more slowly. Molly popped out of a doorway like a curly haired genie, smiling as she straightened her apron and inquiring if Mrs. Parker had enjoyed her dinner. Regina said that she had, then decided she wasn't up to soothing the young girl's nerves, because her own were close to the edge.

Upon entering her bedroom, she could see that her impromptu lady's maid had already laid out an almost transparent blue peignoir and white nightgown. Not recognizing the garments, Regina frowned. Had Jonathan felt so confident of his ability to trick her into marriage, he'd purchased her trousseau ahead of time, or did the frothy confection belong to a former mistress?

"I helped Mrs. Cameron pick it out," Molly confessed, lifting the short train of the sheer nightgown and letting it slide off her hand like woven raindrops. "I thought it was pretty."

"It is," Regina assured her, almost wishing that she had the excuse of a mistress to bar the door and lock it against the intrusion that was sure to come before the clock chimed the next hour. "What else did you buy?"

"A few dresses and such," Molly admitted, hurrying about the room. She closed the heavy maroon drapes, then scurried to the center of the room to turn down the bed. "Mr. Parker said he'd leave the rest up to you."

"Will you be wantin' another bath?" Molly asked, eager to please.

"No, thank you. But I could use some help with these buttons," Regina replied, offering the young maid her back. Once her gown had been discarded and her corset unlaced, the lady of the house thanked Molly again. "I can't think of anything else you can do for me at the moment. I'll see you in the morning."

"Good night, then," Molly said, dipping into a curtsy that wasn't half as awkward as the first one had been.

Regina waited for the door to close before she sank down on the edge of the bed and stared into a large cheval mirror. It had been an exceedingly long day, and she wanted nothing more than to crawl under the heavy coverlet and sleep until morning.

But brides rarely got a great deal of sleep on their wedding night. Would Jonathan knock on the ornate doors that separated them, announcing his entry, or would he simply stroll into the room and sweep her off her feet? Either way, she had little time.

She unpinned her hair and brushed it until it glowed, then, picking up the thin nightgown, Regina walked into the dressing room and stripped out of her undergarments. When she was wearing nothing but her wedding ring, she slipped the provocative nightgown over her head and looked in one of the half dozen mirrors at her disposal. Studying her own body wasn't something she was comfortable doing. It seemed slightly shameful, but she couldn't help but wonder if her husband would like her garbed in sheer silk and white lace.

"You look lovely," Jonathan said in a low, smooth voice that brought Regina around so fast, she almost stumbled.

She stared at her husband. He was still wearing the black trousers he'd had on earlier in the evening, but the swallow-tailed evening coat was gone, along with the gray brocade vest and white silk shirt. In its place was a burgundy smoking jacket with black velvet lapels. The jacket was loosely sashed at the waist, and slightly open at the top, revealing a wedge of dark chest hair. Her gaze lingered on him for several moments, finally lifting to his face.

Jonathan was inspecting her in much the same way. His eyes lingered on the rosy outline of her nipples, visible through the nightgown, then slowly downward to the shadow between her thighs, and finally to her bare toes.

When he held out his hand, Regina sucked in a long breath, then stepped forward. Their fingertips touched for a brief moment before his hand closed around hers. "Trust me," he said in a husky voice.

"I don't have any choice," Regina replied, saying the first thing that came to mind, then realizing that it wasn't what he'd expected. "I mean . . ."

"You're nervous," he said, feeling her hand trembling. "There's nothing wrong with being nervous."

Regina bit down slightly on her bottom lip and gazed into the silvery depths of his eyes. She felt uncertain and uncomfortable. Nervous. But she didn't like feeling that way. It gave Jonathan an advantage over her, and he'd had more than enough of those already.

"I think another glass of champagne is in order," he said, gently tugging her forward.

On the way across her carpeted bedroom and toward the double doors that led to the masculine suite where their wedding bed was waiting, Regina scooped up the blue robe that complemented her nightgown. A second layer of sheer silk was better than nothing, she thought, but she did not put it on. When Jonathan's gaze swept over her, she felt completely naked.

As Regina let herself be gently coerced to step inside her husband's room, her eyes opened wide. Decorated in rich shades of blue and gold, the room was masculine but comfortable. The bed was huge with four ceiling-tall spindled posts. There was an array of exotic knickknacks on the dark oak mantel. A large overstuffed chair upholstered in blue-and-gray tapestry sat close to the fire. Beside it was a table with stacks of newspapers.

Unaware that Jonathan had released her hand, Regina let her eyes roam around the room. The drapes were a deep royal blue with gold braiding that had been untied so the windows were masked. The painting over the fireplace was a huge canvas framed in rich dark wood inlaid with gold. Whoever had painted the clipper ship had magically captured its grace and speed. She could almost feel the salt spray shooting up from the curling waves and the imaginary wind that had the sails billowed out from the masts.

"It's beautiful," Regina said, so taken by the artist's ability, she forgot for the briefest of moments that it was her wedding night.

"Nothing's more beautiful than you," Jonathan said.

The sight of Regina's body, covered by a fabric so sheer he could have read the headlines of the *Herald* through it, was making it difficult to maintain his self-control. Her unbound hair fell down her back in thick chestnut waves that reached to her waist. When she smiled up at the painting, her entire face glowed. As he poured champagne, Jonathan reminded himself to go slowly. Regina hadn't been the most willing bride, and he didn't want to wake up in the morning to cries that she'd been unfairly seduced.

He turned, holding a champagne glass in each hand.

Their eyes met. The short second they stared at each other seemed like an eternity. Quickly dropping her gaze, Regina realized that it would be ridiculous to put on the robe that was dangling from her right hand. Jonathan would think her a silly schoolgirl if she tried to hide what he'd already seen. Deciding to brave her way through the night the best she could, Regina draped the flimsy robe over the back of the chair before accepting the glass of champagne.

The stunning warmth of his hand as it touched hers started a storm brewing in her body. It was impossible to forget the way he'd kissed her that morning on the train, so tenderly she'd almost cried, and yet how demanding his mouth had been a short time ago at Delmonico's. The contradictions in what this man could make her feel were astonishing.

She was acutely aware of him, the smoldering gaze of his silver eyes, the scent of him that lingered in the room, that distinct blend of bay rum and musky male that she'd associated with him since that night on the roof. Her eyes were drawn to the dark wedge of hair on his upper chest. His skin glowed like bronze in the light of the fire. Though she did her best to hide it, there was no disputing the effect his silent gaze had on her.

"Are you planning on getting me drunk?" she asked quietly, holding on to the champagne glass because she didn't know what else to do with her hands.

"No," he said, smiling like the devil he was. "My intentions are as honorable as any bridegroom's."

He didn't have to say that his intention was to get her into the large four-poster. But then, they were married. He had every right to expect that she'd share it of her own volition.

"Remind me to thank Mrs. Cameron and Molly," he added before she could think of an appropriate response to his baiting remark. "If the remainder of the clothing they purchased is as lovely as the nightgown you're wearing, my money was well spent."

Being reminded that she was practically naked didn't help Regina maintain her façade of indifference to her bridegroom's probing gaze. *You're a passionate woman, Miss Van Buren.* The words haunted her, and deep inside, Regina knew they were true. The truth was in the erratic beating of her heart and in the warm ache that was growing in the center of her body. There was something strangely empowering about knowing Jonathan wanted her.

Was his body aching as well? Did his skin yearn for the caress of her hands, his mouth for the touch of her lips? Why did this man hold such an intangible grip on her?

Regina forced herself to meet his gaze. "Why?"

"Why what?"

"Why me?" Regina clarified the question. "Perhaps if I could understand your reasoning, I might be more amicable to a future as your wife. And don't tell me that you made the choice on impulse, I know you better than you think, and you're not an impulsive man."

"You don't know me as well as you will come morning," Jonathan said teasingly.

His reply was a frown that said Regina was willing to stand there until morning if it took that long to get the answer she wanted.

"Why not you?" he finally replied. "Do you think men actually want to marry boring women? Some of them, perhaps. They feel safer with mild-mannered, predictable wives who will never surprise them. But I've never been a man who plays it safe." He set his glass on the mantel and took a step toward her. "You're irritably stubborn, but you'll never be boring," he said with a smile. "You're young and beautiful. And no, I'm not an impulsive man. When the time came for me to marry, I knew it would be to a woman like you."

"I'm flattered," Regina said. "But that's no answer. There are lots of irritably stubborn women in the world. Ask any man."

"It was your telescope," Jonathan said after a moment.

"My telescope!" Regina's brow wrinkled. "You married me to get my telescope?"

"Not exactly," he chuckled, then closed the gap between them. "We're married. That's all that matters."

The champagne came out of Regina's hand first. The

next second she was being pulled into Jonathan's strong arms. The kiss he gave her wasn't tentative or meant to persuade, it was long and gentle, making the ache inside her body swell until it vibrated from her head to her toes.

Jonathan's palms moved down her back, learning the shape of her, the feminine flare of her hips and the rounded curves of her bottom. When he lifted his head, his eyes were burning with the fire of passion too long denied. "We'll talk in the morning."

Regina started to protest, but he sealed her words with a press of his fingertips across her parted lips. His eyes lowered, fixing his gaze on the bodice of her gown. When Regina glanced down, she flushed with embarrassment. It was impossible to hide her body's reaction to the kiss. The sheer silk of her gown was tight over her breasts, and her nipples were hard.

The next second she was scooped up and cradled against Jonathan's body. She looped her arms around his neck as he walked toward the four-poster.

The short journey from the center of the room to her marriage bed was like a pilgrimage, a rite of passage that Regina knew could be taken only once in her life. How many times since meeting the insufferable Mr. Parker had she daydreamed about being held in his arms? The conclusion of those daydreams had always ended with her thoughts turning vague and the image of his face blurring into an intelligible mystery. No longer. The daydream was reality now.

But the mystery remained.

Jonathan's mouth curved into a faint smile as he placed Regina in the center of the bed. Standing over her, he quickly discarded his smoking jacket, tossing it to the floor. He waited a moment, giving her time to look at him.

Regina's hesitation vanished as she took him in. His

body was silhouetted by firelight and shadows and very, very male. It was like seeing him through the lens of her telescope again. The sleek bulge of his muscles, the thick carpet of coal-black hair, the flat nipples, and the washboard texture of his lower stomach.

When he joined her on the bed, his trousers still on, he stretched out on his side, bracing his weight on one elbow. The tip of his index finger traced the curve of her cheek, then the rim of her lower lip. "Don't be nervous," he said softly. "Or scared. As much as I want you, I won't hurt you or do anything that doesn't give you pleasure. Do you believe me?"

"I'm not scared," she lied.

He laughed a soft little laugh. "No. You're terrified. I can see it in your eyes." His fingertips followed the arch of her brows. "You have very passionate eyes, Mrs. Parker. They tell me what you're thinking. What you're feeling."

What Regina was feeling was an urge to jump out of the bed and open the window. The room seemed overly warm, and she could feel a sheen of perspiration gathering in the valley between her breasts.

"You wanted to talk," Jonathan said, gently arranging wayward strands of chestnut hair over the pillow. "Talk to me now. Tell me what's going on inside that lovely little head of yours."

"I thought my eyes . . ."

He kissed them closed. "Put the thoughts into words. Don't make me guess."

Her body felt like liquid on the inside and cast iron on the outside. Her stomach was clenched so tight, it would be sore in the morning, and she couldn't seem to think of a single word that would come close to describing her dilemma. The best she could do was to let out a soft moan when she felt his mouth moving over the pulse in her neck. His lips were hot and moist and she wanted . . .

"Talk to me," Jonathan said in a compelling whisper. "Tell me what you want."

She sucked in enough air to say, "I want you to kiss me again."

"Where?" he asked, leaning away just enough to make her feel the loss. "Your mouth? You have a beautiful mouth. I like the way your bottom lip trembles when I touch it with my tongue. Or your neck? Do you want me to kiss your neck again? Do you like feeling my breath hot against your skin?"

"Yes." She surprised herself with the admission.

"Yes to your mouth, or to your neck, or to both?"

Regina's hands tightened into fists. She tried to say no, but she couldn't, so she nodded.

Jonathan kissed the tip of her nose instead. "You delight me, Regina Van Buren Parker. And I want to delight you in return. A woman's wedding night doesn't have to be sacrificial. Forget whatever ridiculous rules you've been taught about what ladies should and shouldn't do, and just be a woman. Let your body guide you."

Regina wanted to open her eyes and look at him, but she was afraid she'd find him gloating. "Is that what men do?"

"Spoken like a true suffragette," he chuckled. "Yes. When it comes to pleasures of the flesh, men are most definitely guided by their, uh . . . bodies. To put it more simply, we follow our instincts, just like any other male animal."

"We're not animals." Regina's eyes popped open.

"Sophisticated ones," Jonathan said, shifting his weight until he was lying on his back. He gathered her against him, into the hollow of his arm, easing her closer, until she was lying partially on his chest. "But still animals," he continued. "Males of every species follow their instincts when the time comes to mate. So do the females."

He could sense her wariness and see the doubt in her wide blue eyes. As vocal as she was, he for once had her speechless. "Instincts are funny things," he went on to instruct her in a low voice. "People don't listen to them, but they should. God gave them to us for a reason."

"Just like lions and tigers," Regina said, liking the sound of his voice so much, she wanted to keep him talking. When he was talking to her, she could concentrate on what he was saying instead of the tempting weight of his hand on her hip. It was searing her skin through the thin fabric of her garment.

"Better," Jonathan whispered as his head lifted off the pillow. His let his mouth almost touch her. "People have an appreciation of their senses that's uniquely human."

The words stopped as the chaste meeting of their mouths turned into a real kiss. He tasted like champagne and dreams come true. The kiss was searching, then devouring, as Regina parted her lips. A sweet yearning sang through her body, bringing each of her senses to life. She could feel the touch of his hand, still on her hip, but his fingers were flexing now, softly kneading her skin through the silk. The sound of her heartbeat echoed in her ears, and she could taste the champagne's sweetness. The scent of bay rum teased her nose. Their relaxed pose on the bed left his chest open to exploration, and she couldn't keep her hand from opening, then slowly closing. She felt the crisp hair on his chest weave its way through her fingers. His skin felt warm to the touch, and hard and strong, and totally delightful.

Jonathan stifled a groan as she unintentionally pressed closer to his body. He could feel her heat as the natural cradle of her thighs rested against his hip. "What are your instincts telling you?"

"That I like being kissed," Regina answered, realizing that admitting her desire for him wasn't all that difficult once she had the freedom to touch him. Her hand was resting passively on his chest, but she wanted to move it. She wanted to test the hardness of the male nipples that had beaded to match her own.

"So do I," Jonathan admitted in a husky whisper. His fingertips traced the lacy edge of her nightgown's bodice. "And being touched. Do you like being touched?"

The question was followed by the lazy path of his fingers as they moved lightly over the swell of her breasts. Her eyelids fluttered closed. She sighed out a breath of pleasure that told him the only answer he needed to hear.

His tongue retraced the same path, and Regina drew a deep breath in sensual response. Then his mouth closed over a silk-covered nipple. She couldn't keep her body from arching upward, the sensation was so strong. She stayed arched for several seconds while her very bones seemed to shudder in response to the sucking of his mouth. Wordless sounds came from her throat as he moved her over him, cupping her bottom in his open palms while his mouth drew hungrily on her, first one breast, then the other.

He held her firmly against him. His hips moved under her, rolling suggestively against the center of her body, making her feel things she'd never felt before, making her want things that were still a mystery.

The gown came slowly off her shoulders, aided by Jonathan's agile hands and the gentle pull of his mouth as he licked and teased her breasts until they felt hot and full and heavy. Regina couldn't hold on to her doubts or questions as sensation after sensation exploded inside her. Her bones had liquidized to the point that her body felt limp, lifeless, yet so alive, she could barely breathe.

She could feel Jonathan moving away from her, but his mouth didn't stop its sweet torment. When she felt him again it was really him. No trousers, no cloth of any kind separated their bodies. His legs were almost as hairy as his chest, and she could feel a silky roughness as they moved alongside her own.

The sensations that had her breasts tingling and aching moved deep inside her, so deep that her stomach clenched to keep them there. His mouth teased more and more of her, nibbling at the moist, sucked crowns of her breasts, then pressing kisses across her collarbone and neck, stopping to lick at her ear, then moving to her temple, then down the bridge of her nose until their mouths were fused again.

Regina felt his full weight then, pinning her between his hard body and the feather mattress. A soft, passionate sound escaped her as his hands began to explore more and more of her. Callused fingertips traced her from breast to thigh and back again, learning the texture of her skin while she realized that nothing had ever felt more wonderful in her life.

She wanted to open her eyes and look at him, but the thought of what she'd see kept them closed. Instead, she called up the memory of what he'd looked like that night, standing naked in the tub. Remembering the path the bathwater had taken from his shoulders to his hips, then down long, muscular thighs, was enough to make her breath catch in her throat.

"Do you know how long I've wanted to touch you like this?"

Regina couldn't answer. She was too busy feeling.

"Since the first moment I saw you," Jonathan told her. "Touch me, sweetheart."

Sensual tension had Regina's body so tight, she could

barely breathe, but she slowly raised her hand and stroked Jonathan's bare shoulders. The odd sound it pulled from him made her smile. She repeated the caress, loving the feel of his skin. When her eyes opened, she could see the pleasure on his face.

"I like the way you feel too," she confessed.

"Then touch me some more."

His breath caught when she did as he asked. Smooth, manicured nails brushed across his nipples, making them harden. Then delicate fingers were moving over his skin. Jonathan bit back a curse as he forced himself to endure his bride's hesitant exploration.

A wave of pleasure washed over him as Regina became bolder. The desire vibrating through his body was more than he could handle. He rolled her onto her back and began exploring her again, moving his hands ever so lightly from the roundness of her breasts to the soft concave stomach, down the valley of her hips, like a mapmaker following an uncharted coastline.

Regina abandoned herself to his touch. It was adroit, banishing the last of her shame. She was a canvas, and he was the artist. Every caress was a brush stroke, every lingering touch a dab of color in a sensual portrait of self-discovery.

When his hands moved to her thighs again, she stretched like a cat, begging to be stroked and petted.

"God, you're beautiful," he said, meaning every word.

If Regina had opened her eyes, she would have seen the approval on Jonathan's face. Her body glowed in the firelight, all sleek and subtle. The collection of light brown curls at the junction of her thighs called to him, begging to be explored.

He hoped she was ready. He couldn't last much longer.

"Relax your legs, sweetheart," he said. Her eyelashes fluttered in response to the huskily whispered command.

Back and forth his hands went, slowly easing the tension from her muscles, slowly teaching her that being touched felt too good to refuse.

The next time his hand caressed the curls covering her most intimate secrets, Regina moaned softly and arched her hips.

Jonathan put his hands, palms down, on the insides of her thighs, and drew them slowly down to her knees, then back up, gently forcing her legs to widen. On the upward path, she flinched. "Relax, sweetheart. Trust your instincts."

The words brought down the last wall, and Regina let her legs be parted. Her body felt like it was on fire, but it wasn't going up in flames, it was melting. Jonathan's hands were more magical than his sorcerer gaze. They were skillfully unraveling her. When he touched the very center of her, Regina didn't have the strength even to flinch. Telling herself to mind her own business, she focused on her heart, and all the marvelous feelings that were bombarding her senses.

Jonathan caught an expletive before it escaped his mouth. Damn, but she felt good. She was warm and slick and tight around his fingers as he gently probed and stretched her. He felt the slight trembling when he circled her moist opening, and the instinctive tightening of her stomach muscles as he touched just the right spot.

"Look at me," Jonathan said as he continued exploring her. "Open those beautiful eyes and look at me."

Regina opened her eyes. The fire was no longer crackling flames of light, but soft orange embers that made the room glow. Jonathan was looking down at her, his eyes bright with desire, his face almost taut, his nostrils slightly flared. Her gaze moved over him from his shoulders to his bent knees, down the center of his body, to where the thick covering of chest hair narrowed and circled his navel, then lower still, to where he was so very different from her.

When she saw her own body lying eager and open, she tried to close her legs, but he wouldn't let her.

"Instincts," he whispered just before he took her mouth in a deep, tongue-probing kiss that erased the last doubt from her mind.

After that it was all instinct.

She lifted up when he pressed down. Her hands sought his shoulders as his found her hips. Her tongue teased his when it started to retreat, bringing it back, making the kiss last and last, until she had to pull her mouth away or faint from lack of air. She could feel him pressing against her. He was hot and hard while she was soft and damp, female accommodating male. When he found the entrance to her body and pressed forward, Regina was too hungry for the promise his hands and mouth had been silently pledging to think about denying him what he wanted—what she wanted.

She moved under him, guided by an age-old intuition. When he entered her, their joining was more stretching and fullness than real pain. The texture of it was more than she could imagine. Hardness inside softness, heat inside more heat, steel and velvet and a shared intimacy that stole her breath.

His hips moved, gently pushing him deeper inside her, and Regina's nails bit into his bare shoulders.

"Am I hurting you?"

"No."

He kissed her again as his hands gently guided her body, teaching her how to move with him. He lifted her knees until his lower body was cradled between her thighs, cushioning his hips as they gently moved back and forth.

The rhythm was like dancing, moving when he moved, following his lead, trusting him to guide her. It was physical and emotional at the same time, growing warmer and warmer with each thrust of Jonathan's hips. Instinctively, she followed her senses, riding out the sensual storm, letting nature take its course.

Jonathan lost his patience along with his control. His body was on the edge. It had to have satisfaction. He increased the rhythm of his thrusts, driving deeper and deeper, pushing harder and harder. The silken walls of Regina's body accepted him, caressing him with her response, contracting as if to keep him prisoner, then gently releasing him.

"I can't get enough of you," he mumbled, unaware that he was speaking out loud. Every fiber of his being was straining for satisfaction, reaching for that one maddening moment when a man willingly gave his soul to a woman.

"Don't stop until you do," Regina pleaded.

A quick, hard thrust of Jonathan's hip was his only reply. Ecstasy exploded as Regina jerked in his arms, shuddering with stark pleasure.

Suddenly, the mystery she'd been hoping to solve had an answer.

It was pleasure, pure and simple.

Passion.

Love.

All and everything in one quivering moment of sweet satisfaction.

Regina gave herself to the moment.

"Jonathan." His name came to her lips as her body erupted into tiny quakes that left her feeling completely conquered.

Her husband took her mouth in a long, deep kiss that didn't end until his body tightened, then shivered in a draining moment of surrender.

When he could finally get his breath, Jonathan rolled to his side, taking Regina with him. He held her close, stroking her skin, enjoying the softness of her body resting against his. He wasn't sure what he was feeling as his own body gradually relaxed and his mind started working again. Regina was everything he'd expected and more.

Lying by Jonathan's side, Regina felt the ecstasy slowly leave her. But not the love. It was still burning bright, filling her heart with hope.

Fourteen

Regina's heart finally calmed to an almost steady beat, but she feared it would never be the same again. Her new husband might think passion was an act only of the flesh, but she knew hers had come from deep within her heart. Sharing a bed with Jonathan had been the most incredible experience of her life, and now, afterward, she felt as if she'd never been alive before this night.

He kissed the slope of her shoulder, and she sighed out loud.

Jonathan wanted to ask her what she was thinking now, but something kept him from it. He had known Regina was a passionate woman, and just as he'd expected, she'd given herself passionately once he'd taken her beyond the point of embarrassment. Still, his mind wasn't as satisfied as his body. The discontentment shouldn't be there. He'd just had one of the most shattering climaxes of his life, but . . . He'd told himself that marriage wouldn't tie his heart into knots the way it did some men. He wanted a wife and all the things that came with one, yet he'd fully expected to keep his heart free.

For a moment Jonathan speculated on what he was actually feeling. Satisfied, to be sure, but underneath that satisfaction was a peculiar feeling he couldn't quite name.

Gently, he disengaged Regina from his embrace and left the bed. He finished off the champagne he'd poured earlier, then turned to look at her.

"Would you like a bath?" he asked her, standing in the middle of the room as naked as he'd come into the world and seemingly unashamed of it.

"Yes," Regina replied, holding the coverlet in front of her. Still slightly embarrassed by her own state of undress, she wasn't too shy to look at her husband's body with longing. He was the most beautiful of men, she was sure. And he belonged to her.

At that moment Regina knew she'd do whatever it took to keep Jonathan from straying the way a lot of husbands did. The thought of him sharing his body with another woman was one she refused to let materialize. If he needed passion to keep him happy, then she'd gladly give it. All the passion she was capable of and more.

"I'll run the water," Jonathan told her, surprised by the expression on her face. His newly initiated bride looked like she'd just decided to take on an army single-handedly.

While Jonathan was in the dressing room, Regina left the bed. She felt a slight discomfort but nothing so disquieting that it kept her from hoping she wouldn't be dismissed to her own room once she'd bathed. Ignoring the silk peignoir, she reached for Jonathan's smoking jacket instead. As she slid her arms into it and brought it up to her shoulders, closing it and tying the black velvet sash around her waist, she could smell the imported cigars and the man she had married. The fragrance clung to the brocaded fabric like the bouquet of spring lingered after a May shower, and she smiled.

Jonathan turned off the ornate spigot. There was no French toilet water or scented herbs to add to the bath. This was a man's dressing room, one he'd never shared before. So he simply put a fresh cloth and a bar of soap within his bride's reach. When he saw her standing in the doorway, her hair cascading down her back and shoulders, wearing his smoking jacket and looking as provocative as a woman could possibly look, he sucked in a deep breath.

He was still naked, so there was no hiding the response the sight of her had on him. Remembering it was their wedding night and that his wife was new to the ways of seduction, Jonathan simply assumed that she found his smoking jacket less revealing than the flimsy nightgown he'd removed earlier. She couldn't have any idea that the sight of her long, slender legs was making him ache to spread them again.

Regina took a fortifying breath and stepped into the dressing room. Jonathan had turned up the small gaslight fixture on the wall, so there were no shadows to conceal the details of his body. His legs were long and muscular, lean but strong. There was an athletic ability to his form. She could almost envision him wearing a white cloth around his hips while he ran up and down the hills of some ancient Greek village. The image suited him. His hips were lean as well, joining a hard, flat stomach that gradually widened into a hairy chest. For a moment she wished she could paint like the artist who had created the picture of the clipper ship, sailing across hostile white-capped waves. It would be such a pleasure to capture the image of the man, she thought to herself, to preserve his masculine beauty in bold flesh tones and whirling brush strokes.

"You're staring," Jonathan said, stepping away from the tub.

"Am I?"

"Do you like what you see?"

"Yes," Regina said, unashamed by her thoughts. "You're a beautiful man."

Jonathan couldn't help but smile. Regina's honesty had been one of the things he'd admired from the very beginning of their shaky relationship. And he wasn't above admitting that her words pleased him. "Take off the jacket. I want to look at you too."

The smoking jacket slipped to the floor, but Regina hardly noticed its absence. Jonathan's gaze took away the embarrassment. They were married, and he had been right when he'd told her that marriage offered a woman freedom. Being his wife, she was free to stand before him naked, and free to openly admire him in return.

"Come here," he said, holding out his hand.

She moved to where he stood. The Italian tile covering the floor felt cool under her bare feet. The steam rising from the bathwater warmed the rest of the room, and the heat naturally rising in her body added to the conflicting sensations.

Jonathan devoured her with his eyes as she came closer. Her breasts were high and full, their tips crowned by deep pink nipples that were beginning to pearl in arousal, but not as tightly as they would once he took them into his mouth. The glossy brown hair at the junction of her legs held a sheen of moisture that attested to the passion they had shared a short time earlier. The rest of her body was pure female perfection.

When she was close enough to touch, he smiled. "If I kiss you, the bathwater is going to get cold."

"Will it?" Regina asked in the same teasing way he'd asked her if she liked what she was seeing.

His hand reached out to feather across her shoulder, brushing away her hair. "You have beautiful breasts. Pale and lush. And your nipples are as perfect as any berry. Sweet and ripe for tasting."

No longer a virgin but still very new to the ways of womanhood, Regina blushed from her toes to the roots of her long chestnut hair. The temperature of the bathwater was forgotten as Jonathan wrapped an arm around her waist and pulled her close. She could feel the naked power of his body and the heat of his arousal pressing against her. His hands rested on her hips, pressing her close, but not too tightly.

The tension built between them as he kissed her. Jonathan used his experience to build the sweet anticipation of completion. He could feel her hair brushing against the back of his hands as she twisted to get closer to him. Desire pounded in his blood. He wanted her, deep and hard and fast, but he banked the fires and kept his self-control.

When Jonathan stopped kissing her, it took Regina a moment to clear the sensual haze from her mind and look into his eyes. His gaze was as hungry as her body, hot and blatantly desirous of things to come.

When he took her hand and moved to the stool where he normally sat to remove his shoes and socks, she followed. He sat down, then told her to straddle his lap. Regina hesitated.

"Put your legs on either side of mine," he said with a husky sound to his voice. "I want to kiss your breasts."

Regina did as he asked, albeit with a reluctance that brought a smile to her wicked husband's face. When she was exactly where he wanted her, her legs spread wide, his sex pressed against her moist center, he kissed her again. The kiss was deep and demanding. She was his wife now, and there was no refusing him.

"Put your hands on my shoulders," he commanded softly.

Regina followed his instructions.

He gathered up her hair and smoothed it down the center of her back, leaving her breasts totally exposed. His hands rested on her waist. "Keep your hands on my shoulders and lean back as far as you can."

Once again Regina did as he asked.

Jonathan trailed his mouth from the curve of her neck to the swell of her right breast. He licked her flushed skin, then her nipple. Then he began to suck her in earnest.

The sensation burned through Regina's body like talons of pure fire. They flared in the pit of her stomach, moving outward until she could feel the power of Jonathan's mouth all the way to her fingertips. He wasn't simply sucking her breast, he was feasting on it. His tongue licked and teased, tasting her like the finest of wines. First one breast, then the other. Back and forth his mouth moved, until Regina was twisting on his lap, mindless of the intimate undulation of her hips, mindless of anything but the desperate need her husband was kindling.

Jonathan was just as desperate. Slowly, holding on to her waist to keep her balanced, he began to spread his legs, widening hers even more.

"What are you doing?" Regina asked as Jonathan began to move under her. Her feet couldn't reach the floor as he moved his legs farther and farther apart.

"Opening you," he said. His eyes locked with hers and the intensity of the moment grew. "I want to be inside you again."

Regina couldn't argue with his intentions. She wanted the same thing. But this wasn't a firelit bedroom. They were sitting in the dressing room with the gaslights turned up. She could see him, hard and erect and ready, and she could see herself. Her legs were being slowly spread wider and wider, so he could enter her. It was embarrassing and erotic.

Bracing her hands on his shoulders, she met his gaze again. "You are wicked."

"Yes," Jonathan agreed, adding a devilish smile for emphasis. "I've wanted you too long to be gentlemanly about having you on our wedding night."

He kissed her deep and long, holding her mouth prisoner as his hands wrapped more tightly around her waist, then lifted her. His entry was one long, smooth stroke that buried him to the hilt. Regina's body arched with pleasure, taking him even more fully.

She wanted him as desperately as he seemed to want her. She could feel her muscles tightening, her insides straining to feel what she'd felt before. The strange, delicious ecstasy that had stolen her breath.

"That's it," Jonathan encouraged her as his mouth moved to her breast once again. "Move with me. Take me deep inside you."

He moved in and out of her in slow, deep strokes that made her desire for him build and build. She was open, intimately exposed to his mouth and hands and the deep probing of his sex. In minutes her body was trembling and damp, demanding the same pleasure as his, wanting it so badly, she wasn't aware that she was saying his name over and over. The sensual cadence ended as he pushed deep one last time, and she went soaring, plunging headfirst into the sensual tempest with him.

Eventually, Regina opened her eyes. Her head was resting against Jonathan's sweat-dampened chest. Their bodies were still joined. His hands were cupping her bottom, holding her close as he regained his breath.

"Now we both need a bath," he said, chuckling lightly.

"I can't move," Regina said weakly.

"Then I'll carry you," he announced, coming to his feet as gracefully as a man could when he had a woman's legs wrapped around his waist. "Hold on."

Once they were in the tub, surrounded by warm water, he began bathing her. His soapy hands were gentle, and Regina closed her eyes, sinking back against his chest and enjoying herself far too much not to feel a twinge of guilt over it. This was decadence at its finest, she decided. No wonder married women rarely spoke of what went on behind the doors of their bedrooms. But then, she suspected that few married women experienced what she'd just experienced.

Jonathan Belmont Parker wasn't your average man, so she had to assume that he wasn't an average lover either. He was sophisticated and experienced, and although Regina didn't want to know where her new husband had learned the art of making love, she was grateful that he'd been an adept pupil.

"Are you tired?" Jonathan asked once they were back in bed.

"Exhausted," Regina replied lazily.

"Sleepy?"

"No," she said with a smile. "I'm thirsty."

"Champagne," he said, offering her a glass.

Regina raised her head and took a sip of the now-warm wine. She had no idea what time it was, nor did she care. The fire was crackling again. Jonathan had added several logs to the hearth and the room was comfortable. She was lying naked by his side, her hand resting casually on his chest.

"Is it always like this?" she asked. "Does passion always steal your thoughts?"

"Most of the time," he replied candidly. "If it's real passion, your only thought is the pleasure you're giving and taking. It's a partnership of desire."

Regina silently agreed. She'd certainly been a willing partner so far. She had given Jonathan her body, and in return he'd given her so much pleasure, she was still feeling wonderfully lethargic. There was only one negative element to her wedding night. Jonathan had shared his passion but he wasn't interested in sharing his heart.

An inner chill made the room seem less comfortable for a moment. Regina pressed her face into the hollow of her husband's neck and drank in his scent. She was his wife, and he would take care of her physically and financially, and eventually he'd do the same for their children. He would love the sons and daughters he sired. But would he ever love their mother?

The question wasn't a pleasant one, and it showed on her face.

"What has you brooding?" Jonathan asked. "Do you need your husband to set his champagne aside and tuck you in for the night?"

"No," Regina said, pushing her doubts and fear into a future that could wait until sunlight streamed though the windows. "I need my husband to share his wine. I'm still thirsty."

Something in the way she said it gave Jonathan pause. As always, Regina's eyes gave her away. He could see something in her gaze, a flicker of doubt that made him wonder what she was really thinking. "What's going on in that lovely head of yours?"

"Nothing," Regina said, wishing she could unburden her heart but knowing she didn't dare. Jonathan was a businessman. He dealt in facts and numbers, not emotions.

She lowered her lashes, enjoying her husband's embrace. His lovemaking had made her feel womanly and confident, exposing a part of her personality she had never known existed. Lying by his side, she felt at ease, as if she had been born to be there. But still the doubts plagued her. Passion was an unpredictable emotion. Love an elusive one. Marriage, a good marriage, demanded both. Could one spring from the other, or was she forever doomed to love without ever being truly loved in return?

Jonathan watched as Regina tried to hide her thoughts from him. He didn't like the idea of her keeping them to herself, not after the way she'd responded to him. It was their wedding night, the first of a lifetime of nights they would share the same bed.

He placed the champagne glass to her lips. After Regina took a sip, he set it aside and drew her more snugly into his arms. Her gaze drifted to the painting over the hearth.

"Who's the artist?" she asked sleepily.

"No one of any importance," Jonathan replied while his hand caressed the soft swell of her hip. "Do you like it?"

"Very much."

He was tempted to tell her that he'd painted the clipper ship, but there was more than enough time to divulge his secret hobby. As his hands continued their gentle administration, sliding down the curve of Regina's hip to her silky thigh, then back up, Jonathan decided he would very much like to paint her. Perhaps one day he would.

But for now he was a bridegroom, and his wedding night was still very much in the present. It would be dawn in another three hours.

He lifted her chin until she was meeting his gaze, then smiled. "I want you again," he said in a voice husky with desire. "I want to feel you shivering in my arms again."

Regina closed her eyes, feeling the pressure of his mouth and hands. He pushed her down into the softness of the feather mattress, kissing her all the while. The kisses moved from her mouth to her throat. She felt the rest of her body heating with desire, longing for more and more of his touch. It was addicting, this thing called passion. His mouth moved lower, tasting her breasts and the hard crowns that had already begun to ache. When Regina reached for him, he pulled her hands high above her head and told her to lie perfectly still.

"I want every inch of you satisfied before you fall

asleep," he said, nibbling lightly at her earlobe. "Relax and let me love you."

Tilting his head, he brushed his mouth back and forth, moving from one breast to the next, teasing her thoroughly, rekindling the fire that had been banked once they'd retired to the comfort of the bed. Regina arched under his expert mouth, encouraging him to continue as his mouth moved to the flatness of her stomach. His kisses fell in random patterns as his hands moved to hold her hips in place. His mouth brushed her lightly, stopping to nibble here and there on her tender flesh.

"Please," she moaned, reaching for him.

"Not yet," he told her, returning her hands to their original position, extended over her head, palms up. "Lie still. You're going to like this."

The words sent a new wave of desire rippling through Regina's body. She was shaking on the inside. The touch of his hands sliding leisurely over her hips and stomach added to the anticipation. He moved lower, down the contours of her abdomen, over her hips, licking and kissing his way to the tops of her thighs.

When his fingers began to sift through the nest of curls above her womanhood, Regina stiffened.

"Open your legs, sweetheart."

Regina moved, but not enough to suit her husband. His hands slid to her knees, gently parting her legs until he could lay between them. His access was total now, and he made full use of it, kissing the insides of her thighs, moving higher with each sweep of his mouth until he was tasting the very core of her. His hands moved underneath her then, holding her against his mouth. Regina bit her lip to keep from crying out. Never had she imagined a man doing something so outrageously intimate, or so shockingly wonderful.

"Jonathan!" Regina moaned feverishly. She threw

back her head and arched her body. The pleasure was pulsating deep inside her, intensifying with each caress.

Her hands clenched in the pillows as he explored her at his leisure, sending flames of splintering fire through her body. The fire kept building and building, but Jonathan didn't heed her moan of desperation, he continued his sensual assault until Regina thought she'd die if he didn't do something, anything, to end the sweet torment.

Finally, when she thought she couldn't take another minute of pleasure, the fire exploded like a volcano, and she was tossed upward. There was no controlling her body; it arched and shuddered, then went limp.

But Jonathan wasn't done pleasing her or himself. He came into her in a deep, hard thrust that made her gasp with pleasure. Then the fire started burning again. He had waited as long as he could, holding back until he'd felt her orgasm. Now he was free to find his own fulfillment.

"God, you feel good," he said as he began to move. He took her with a gentle urgency that hadn't been there before, as if an entire future didn't lie before them. His movements were slow, sensual, deliberately controlled to give them both the most pleasure.

In minutes Regina was trembling again, her hips moving in perfect rhythm with his, rising and falling as he pushed deeper and deeper, making the pleasure spiral out of control. When Regina cried out his name, he joined their bodies with one last deep thrust that made the fire burn out of control, consuming them both.

Finally, he eased away from her. He kissed her eyes closed, then smiled, and held her spoon fashion against him. "Good night, Mrs. Parker."

Regina smiled, too exhausted by her husband's lovemaking to protest the arrogance in his voice or the possessive way he'd addressed her. There was no denying

she was his now. His possession had been complete;
there wasn't an inch of her he hadn't touched.

Including her heart.

Passion might have ruled her body, but Regina knew
she could never have given herself so completely, or felt
so right in the giving, if she didn't love Jonathan to
distraction. Snuggling as close as she could to his warm
body, she looked up at the painting. Clipper ships had
soared over the ocean waves, facing the storms and per-
ils of the sea head-on. She'd have to do the same thing
with her future. She was married to Jonathan now, truly
married, and there was no changing her course. All she
could do was sail into the unknown and pray that one
day Jonathan might come to love her.

Fifteen

For the next three weeks, Regina lived in a sensual cocoon. Jonathan surrounded her with enticing sights and sounds, teaching her to appreciate all her senses. They rode in Central Park, wrapped snugly in a blanket while the carriage driver guided an open-air hack through the winter wonderland. They dined at Delmonico's again, but in the main room this time, among the elite of New York society. There were evenings at the opera and lazy mornings curled up in bed while rain washed down on the city.

They spent long hours strolling through the art galleries and museums. They wandered along the boardwalk of South Beach. They spent an entire day at Coney Island. The winter season had closed most of the amusements, but there was still enough going on for Regina to be fascinated. Landing at the steamboat dock on the island's western edge, they started their excursion at Norton's Point, a seedy community known for prizefighting, gambling, and prostitution. Respectable people gave the area a wide berth, but Jonathan wanted Regina to see the entire city, good and bad, so he held tightly to her hand as he escorted her past alehouses and gambling dens.

They ate roasted clams and drank lager beer at Charles Feltman's Ocean Pavilion before touring the chaotic and exhilarating carnival quarter. Jonathan insisted that she ride one of the park's steam-powered merry-go-rounds. The West Brighton carousel was beautiful. The seats were fabulously crafted animals and birds painted in bold colors.

Enchanted by the carousel, Regina adamantly refused to ride the loop-the-loop, a scary roller coaster that tore up and down a giant steel structure. Jonathan was fascinated by the mechanical thrill ride that had been fashioned after the switchback railroads used in coal mines, but he didn't insist on riding it, much to Regina's relief.

He took her shopping at Macy's on the corner of Fourteenth Street and Sixth Avenue. He spent a small fortune on her in the more exclusive shops of Manhattan, insisting that she needed a complete new wardrobe. Within a week of their marriage, she was wearing Worth gowns to dinner. Jonathan gifted her with a sapphire and diamond necklace on the seventh day of their marriage and a matching pair of earrings a week later.

Every day was a new experience for Regina. She discovered that her husband was a connoisseur of exotic foods and wines. He took her into the immigrant neighborhoods of the inner city, where small shops specialized in exclusive European cuisine. They ate lunch at an Irish pub, complete with dark ale and brawny language. An early morning ferry ride to the Upper Bay supplied her with a view of the sprawling city cast in pearl-like light. Every time they stepped outside the door of the Manhattan brownstone, Jonathan taught Regina more about life's small diversities.

The hours they spent inside the house were just as informative. They made love whenever the mood came upon them, and each time, Regina learned that she was indeed a passionate woman. Jonathan taught her to be unashamed of her body and the pleasure it had been created to give and receive. At times he was a generous, thorough lover, making her cry out for completion. At others he was demanding, loving her in feverish bouts of instant passion that left her feeling limp and sated. Every time was different, but they were all very pleasing.

It was after one such session, when a passionate glance had led to even more passionate kisses, that they had their first marital dispute. Regina was recuperating on the divan in the second-floor library. Her face was aglow with satisfaction when she reached for a discarded section of the Brooklyn *Eagle*. She browsed through the newspaper while Jonathan sat next to her, reading the financial section.

When Regina found the small article detailing the arrest of a young New York woman for entering an eating establishment without an escort, she sat upright. The woman had entered the restaurant alone and asked to be served. The proprietor had taken offense to her brazenness and summoned the police, stating that his eatery served spirits and that no decent woman would think to walk through its doors without the benefit of an escort. The police had agreed and the woman had been officially asked to leave the restaurant. She'd resisted, at least verbally, which led to her arrest and a substantial lecture from the judge, who had fined her the sum of twenty dollars for creating a public disturbance.

"What's wrong?" Jonathan asked, seeing Regina's shoulders stiffen.

"This," Regina remarked, shoving the newspaper into his hands. "It's blatant prejudice."

Jonathan read the article, then frowned. "I'd say the lady in question got off lightly," he remarked, folding the newspaper and laying it aside. "I know that section of town. It's near the Tenderloin and totally unsuitable for a woman alone."

"The Tenderloin?"

"Also known as Satan's Circle," Jonathan added.

"The place is littered with saloons, houses of prostitution, gambling dens, and endless pleasure-seekers. Most unsavory. I understand the police inspector has made some progress in cleaning up the area, but he's still got a long way to go before the community's to be recommended."

"Is the community as unsavory as Norton's Point?" Regina asked, suddenly intrigued.

"Norton's Point has its vices," Jonathan told her. "The Tenderloin isn't safe for man or woman, daylight or dark. The police did the lady a favor by arresting her."

"How can you say that?" Regina said with a vengeance. "The woman was arrested and hauled off to jail like a common criminal simply because she wasn't draped on some man's arm. It was an inexcusable display of male authority. The police and the judge used the law to their own advantage instead of applying it fairly to men and women alike. An injustice was done."

Jonathan started looking thoroughly annoyed. In the short time that they'd been married, he'd been able to keep Regina's mind on him and off suffrage. The newspaper article had rekindled an old flame. He didn't like it.

Regina came to her feet and walked to the window overlooking Thirty-fourth Street. She didn't know many people in the city, but she had corresponded with several of the suffrage groups. If ever a deed deserved protesting, this one did. She was thinking of penning a note to one of her lady friends, when Jonathan joined her at the window. One look at her expression and his mood went from bad to worse.

"Whatever scheme you're weaving in that lovely head, forget it," he said sternly. "This is our honeymoon. There will be no letters of protest posted to the courts, no editorials sent to the newspapers, and no street marches."

Jonathan didn't use the word *forbid,* but Regina heard it loud and clear. She was hurt by the knowledge that in spite of his current words and actions, she was no closer to being free than she'd been in Merriam Falls. Realizing an argument would be useless, she excused herself from the library, stating that she planned on taking a bath before dressing for dinner.

Jonathan let her go, frowning even more intensely as the door closed behind her.

Upstairs, Regina paced the bedroom she had yet to sleep in. The more she paced, the angrier she got. If she weren't married to Jonathan, she knew exactly what she'd do. Unfortunately, she was married. If she tried to get involved in any suffrage activities while they were on their honeymoon, the trip would not end happily.

Brooding because he wasn't entirely sure how to turn the day around, Jonathan found himself wandering down the hall toward the suite of rooms he shared with his new wife. He opened the door, fully expecting to find Regina relaxing in a tub of scented water, but what he found was twice as enticing.

His wife was standing near the bed, wearing a red silk robe and brushing her waist-length hair.

"Jonathan! What in the world are you doing?" Regina screeched as he took her by the hand and started dragging her from the room. "I'm not dressed."

"You're perfect," he said over his shoulder as he started marching toward the staircase that led to the third floor of the Manhattan brownstone. "Absolutely perfect."

Regina tried to free herself from her husband's tight grasp. "Where are we going?"

"I want to show you something," Jonathan said, pulling her after him.

"What?

"The attic," he said, dragging her along behind him.

Actually, it wasn't an attic at all. When he opened the door at the top of the narrow staircase, Regina couldn't believe her eyes. Instead of cobwebs and dusty trunks, she saw an artist's flat.

Jonathan let go of her hand.

Regina barely noticed. Gingerly, she stepped into the rectangular room atop the Manhattan town house. The wooden floor felt cool beneath her bare feet. There were several easels holding blank canvases of different sizes. An old wooden table was cluttered with small vases stuffed with paintbrushes. A painter's smock was tossed haphazardly over the back of a black lacquered chair. A small stool sat next to the table. Across the room there was a gold velvet divan trimmed with dark wood. There was a fireplace but no fire. Logs were neatly stacked near the marble hearth, waiting to be used. The room smelled of turpentine and oil paint.

Regina felt like she'd stepped into another world. The anger she'd felt earlier vanished as she strolled the length of the room, gazing at the painted canvases leaning against the walls. Each one was a masterpiece of color and form. She instantly recognized the city of Copenhagen, not because she'd been there, but because Jonathan had painted it so brilliantly. The snow-capped buildings overlooking the Baltic Sea couldn't be anything else but the Danish capital. He'd told her that the city was his favorite. His sentiment showed in his work.

And Regina had no doubt that she was looking at her husband's work. There were watercolors, bright and cheerful and almost alive, and bolder, darker paintings that showed people laboring in fields and working in factories. There was a small canvas that showed a man sitting on a park bench. The painting was more shadows and shapes than a detailed depiction. It was a lonely, heart-wrenching picture, and Regina felt her eyes begin to tear. Then she saw a painting of a steamship moored to a New York dock, and she thought of the painting of the clipper ship in her husband's bedroom. He'd never told her the name of the artist. Until then.

Turning to look at him, she didn't know what to say.

"I want to paint you," Jonathan said without preamble.

"Me?"

"Yes, you."

She watched as Jonathan discarded his vest and began rolling up his sleeves. When he reached for the smock, Regina realized he meant to begin the portrait at that moment.

"I'm wearing a robe," she pointed out, tightening the sash of the ruby red garment.

"I don't want you wearing anything," Jonathan said, stopping to look at her. "I want to paint you in the nude."

Regina stared at him, completely dumbfounded.

"You're beautiful," he said, coming to stand in front of her. "Your body is beautiful. Your hair is beautiful." He reached out and picked up a thick strand of it, letting it slide through his fingers. "I want to paint you wearing nothing but your hair and that lovely ivory skin. Will you let me?"

The question hung in the air like the diffused sunbeams coming through the sloped windows. Regina's immediate response was on the tip of her tongue, but she couldn't get the word out. Saying no now, after Jonathan had just revealed something so wonderfully personal about himself, seemed wrong. It wasn't the thought of being naked in front of him that caused Regina's hesitation. She'd become comfortable with the intimacy of marriage. But this was more than intimacy. She looked at the paintings again.

"Don't be embarrassed," Jonathan said, misunderstanding her reluctance. "The painting is for me."

Any other words and she might have said no, but she couldn't refuse him now. In the few weeks since they'd met, Jonathan had asked her for only one thing. Trust. He was asking her for it again. Did she trust him enough to let him capture her image on canvas?

"I've never posed before," she said shyly.

"It's easy. And boring," he added with a wink. "All you have to do is be still. I'll do all the work."

"How? Where?" She was suddenly breathless.

He looked around the room, his expression pensive. "Standing in front of the window," he finally said. "I like the way the sunlight dances in your hair."

Regina's apprehension built as Jonathan lit a fire to chase the chill from the room. Once the fire was blazing, he turned to her.

"Take off your robe," he said, his voice a low whisper.

Regina's hands went to the sash, then stopped.

"Feeling shy?" There was a slight twinkle in his eye as he joined her in the middle of the room. "I've seen you naked before. As a matter of fact, you've taken to sleeping that way."

"Stop teasing me," Regina rebuked him. "This isn't the same thing, and you know it."

Instead of answering, Jonathan reached out and untied the sash of the red robe. He was smiling as his hands ventured inside. Slowly, the robe slid off Regina's shoulders, down her arms, and onto the floor. He looked at her for the longest time, then, still smiling, he took her hand and led her to the windows that overlooked the park across the street. "Find something interesting to look at," he instructed her as he pushed her hair off her shoulders, leaving her breasts exposed. "There, I think that should do it."

After viewing her from several angles, he decided to paint her in profile. Within minutes he was engrossed in the project.

"Talk to me," Regina finally said. "I feel foolish just standing here."

"All right. But don't move your head," Jonathan told her. "What do you want to talk about?"

"Anything," she replied. "Tell me about your family. What was your mother's name?"

"Miriam."

Your father?"

"My father's name was Albert," Jonathan said as he began to mix paint. "They were normal people."

"Like their son," Regina replied with a glint of humor.

"I'm not that unusual," Jonathan retorted, wondering what his wife actually thought of him. He wasn't in the mood to discuss his family, the words came with too many painful memories. He didn't want to think about Abigail or the grief that had eventually led to his mother's death. It was a bright winter day, and Regina was very much alive. He wanted to put that image on canvas, to preserve it forever. "I'm just a businessman with a flair for making money."

"You're a businessman who paints like a European master."

Jonathan laughed. "I'm flattered, Mrs. Parker."

"Why didn't you tell me?" She turned to look at him. "I'm your wife. Married couples shouldn't have secrets."

"Look out the window," Jonathan scolded her. "And there isn't anything to tell. I enjoy painting. My talent is a matter of opinion, but I'm glad you like my work."

"I do," Regina admitted.

She concentrated her gaze on the park across the street. The small square was squeezed between expensive houses inhabited by some of the richest people in the city. There was nothing warm or welcoming about the structures constructed of brick and mortar with marble steps and wrought iron gates that separated them from the street. The park itself was still clothed in winter. The trees were dark, bare-limbed skeletons against the springlike sky. Small, wispy clouds drifted here and there, but there was no sign that they would darken with another winter storm.

The awkwardness of standing naked in front of a window gradually left her, and Regina found herself thinking of all sorts of things. As her thoughts wandered, she relaxed. Jonathan didn't think himself unusual, but Regina knew she was married to a unique man.

Unlike the stiff, socially conscious people who were his neighbors, Jonathan didn't act as if he'd been dipped in starch. He enjoyed life on a daily basis, and he was teaching Regina to enjoy it as well. Sometimes the things they did were outrageously extravagant, while others were simple things like feeding the pigeons in Central Park. Silently Regina acknowledged that it wasn't the things they did that she enjoyed as much as she enjoyed doing them with Jonathan.

Still, she knew very little about the man she'd married. He could be stern and overly serious when he chose to be. Like this afternoon in the library. She supposed he was within his rights. They were newlyweds. But she sensed that his reasons weren't that selfish. He was obsessed with keeping her safe. Surely the murderer hadn't followed them to the city.

The thought gave her pause as she pondered the possibility out loud.

"There's nothing to worry about," Jonathan reassured her. "We'll confront the issue when we return home. Until then, relax and stop worrying."

"How can I not worry?" Regina asked, wanting to look at him but afraid to move for fear of being scolded again. "Two of my best friends are dead. I think about them every day, and I wonder what news will be awaiting us once we do return home."

"Richard will wire me if anything out of the ordinary happens," Jonathan replied. "So far there hasn't been any bad news."

"I'd like to give the boardinghouse to Lucy," Regina announced unexpectedly. "She's more like family than hired help. I'm sure she's had thoughts of what her future will be since we've married."

"That's a wonderful idea," Jonathan agreed. "I'll have my attorney prepare the papers."

"Thank you." Regina smiled as she continued looking out the window. "How much longer do I have to stand here?"

Jonathan laughed. "Creating a masterpiece takes more than a few minutes. Be patient."

Regina learned a great deal of patience over the next few days. Since the weather was being agreeable, offering bright sunlight for the rest of the week, she spent the better part of each day standing in front of the loft window, completely naked.

Jonathan refused to let her see the painting, draping the canvas in oilcloth before they left the room. When she tried to peek, he swatted her bare bottom, promising dire consequences if she didn't behave herself. Eager to finish the painting, and insisting the house in Merriam Falls didn't have a single room that would serve the purpose as well as his New York City loft, Jonathan postponed their return home. Regina was disappointed, but arguing got her nowhere. Her husband had reached a decision, and being Jonathan Belmont Parker, he wasn't about to change his mind.

During the last week, Regina was amazed to discover how easily she could shed her clothing and assume her place in front of the window. After hour upon hour of posing, she didn't feel the least bit shy. The feeling of being naked no longer embarrassed her. In fact, it gave her an unusual sense of freedom. When she suggested that Jonathan rid himself of his clothing to paint, he laughed, then followed her suggestion with dazzling speed. The portrait was forgotten while they made love on the sofa in front of the fire.

In spite of everything, Regina found herself almost forgiving Jonathan for tricking her into marriage. She couldn't deny that she loved the man, nor could she ignore that she felt a certain contentment in simply being a woman. For the first time in her life, she was willing to let each day arrive and pass on its own merits, to enjoy herself without feeling guilty, and to accept the fact that she couldn't change the world single-handedly. But none of those thoughts changed the past. Hazel and Elisa were dead, and once she and Jonathan returned to Merriam Falls, she was determined to take an active role in bringing their murderer to justice.

Jonathan was waiting for her in the downstairs parlor. The tenderness she saw in his expression wasn't love, but it made her feel cherished and wanted and protected, and she embraced those feelings.

"You look beautiful, as always," Jonathan said, pulling her into his arms and kissing her as though they'd been separated for weeks instead of the few short hours it had taken him to pay a call on his attorney and begin the business of transferring the boardinghouse on Whitley Street to Lucy Chambers. "Are you still eager to leave the city and go home?"

"Molly's been packing all day. I didn't realize I had accumulated so many clothes until we started putting them into trunks. I'm afraid there'll be several. And, yes, I'm eager to go home," Regina confessed.

They dined on roasted turkey, stewed vegetables, and champagne. The conversation was as stimulating as the food. A small group of women had rallied to protest the incident that had been reported in the paper, and Regina was quick to bring the fact to Jonathan's attention, informing him that the judge had been so upset by the protest, he'd taken the back exit of the courthouse and dashed away in a hired hack.

None of the women were arrested, although the newspaper did report that the constable on duty at the city building gave the ladies a stern warning about disrupting the peace.

"I should have been there," Regina told him.

"I'm thankful you weren't," Jonathan said, putting down his napkin and reaching for his wineglass. "I would hate to think that you'd blatantly disobey me."

"What if I did?" Regina challenged him. "Would I find myself locked in another room until you saw fit to unlatch the door and give me back my freedom?"

Jonathan sipped his champagne. When his glass returned to the table, he met her curious gaze with determined silver-gray eyes. "It depends on the disobedience," he said much too calmly for her to think he was making a jest. "I will not allow you to put yourself in danger. Here or anywhere else. You may embrace the concept of suffrage with open arms, but I will not tolerate any activities that could jeopardize your safety."

Regina started to argue, but Jonathan held up his hand, silencing her before she had a chance to speak.

"You're my wife," he said. "It's my responsibility to keep you safe."

Inside, Regina wanted to scream that she didn't want to be a responsibility. She wanted to be loved. On the outside, she stiffened her shoulders and put down her fork. The silver flatware made a ringing sound as it met her gold-trimmed china plate. "I will never understand you," she confessed. "One minute you're treating me like a witless child, the next you're enticing me to pose in the nude. To experience life to its fullest. Am I to be free only when you define the term freedom?"

"You're deliberately twisting my words," Jonathan said. "Suffrage has its dangers. Women are being arrested and kept in jail for weeks on end, not to mention the unsavory treatment they endure while some judge thinks to teach them a lesson. Just because the ladies this morning were scolded, then sent home, doesn't mean it's safe to brazenly march up and down the streets of this city or any other city. And what of Merriam Falls? Do you honestly think the man cares about your personal freedom? Don't be ridiculous, Regina. This isn't an issue of equality, it's a matter of survival."

"I'm not talking about the murders," Regina defended her point of view. "I'm talking about our marriage. About our future together. I don't want to spend the rest of my life asking your permission to be myself."

Jonathan surprised her by saying, "That's understandable. But until the murderer is behind bars, I'll continue to insist that you depend upon me to take care of you. After that, we can discuss the matter again."

Regina wasn't in the mood to compromise, but she wasn't in the mood to argue either. This was the last night of their honeymoon, and she desperately wanted to leave New York feeling good about her marriage.

"Are you ready to retire to the loft?" Jonathan asked, coming to his feet. He reached for the bottle of champagne, then gave her a wicked wink. "We can have dessert upstairs."

The painting was still draped, hidden behind pale oilcloth. Jonathan refilled their champagne glasses as Regina thought of all the hours she'd spent looking out the window. As if drawn there again, she gazed out at the park, but this time the trees were dark shadows against an even darker night. Stars sparkled here and there in the evening sky, and she longed for the peace of the Hudson Valley again and her telescope.

"Are you ready?" Jonathan asked, coming to stand behind her.

Regina could feel the heat of his body pressing ever so gently against hers, and she smiled. "I'm curious. And a little afraid," she admitted, turning to face her husband. "Looking at oneself in the mirror after a bath and looking at a naked portrait aren't the same thing."

"Mirror or canvas, you're beautiful," Jonathan announced, then kissed her gently. "Come."

They walked hand in hand to where the easel was standing. Regina sucked in her breath as Jonathan reached out and carefully raised the oilcloth, letting her see the painting for the first time.

She didn't know what to say. Her husband had captured the sunlight streaming through the window, creating a halo around her body that accentuated each naked curve and plane. Her hair seemed to shimmer with light, while her nipples arched toward the sun, asking for its kiss. There was a spiritual reverence to the painting that brought tears to Regina's eyes.

"It's beautiful."

"You're beautiful," Jonathan said.

Regina raised her head for his kiss. When she looked into his eyes, she could almost imagine it was love making them shine so brightly. Hope flowed through her, filling the void she'd carried around for weeks. His mouth was gentle, seeking her acceptance as his lips pressed warmly against her own.

In awe of her husband's talent and the emotion he'd put into the painting, Regina wondered what Jonathan truly felt for her. Her love for him had overtaken her so quickly, she was still catching her breath. His feelings were still unknown. Their honeymoon was a fragile truce that could be broken at any time, and she feared it would be once they returned to Merriam Falls.

Seeing the painting had renewed Regina's hope. Artists were people who revealed themselves in their work. If her husband shared that trait, then perhaps the painting was his way of telling her that he did care.

"Can I persuade you out of your clothes one more time?" Jonathan asked, folding his arms around her waist.

"I thought the painting was finished." She looked at him and immediately felt the strong male magnetism he always radiated. He was so undeniably handsome.

"It is," he admitted with a devilish grin. "This time my motives are entirely selfish. I want to make love to you."

"Then consider me persuaded," Regina replied, reaching for the onyx studs at the top of his white shirt. "After all, it is our honeymoon."

"Indeed it is," Jonathan agreed. "And I promised you a very special night."

It was. By the time they retired to the comfort of their bed on the second floor, Regina was too exhausted to do more than lay her head on the pillow and drift blissfully off to sleep.

Sixteen

The newlyweds left New York on a bright winter morning. Water dripped from the trees in Central Park and carriage wheels splashed through the puddles along Fifth Avenue. Wanting to arrive in Merriam Falls looking her best, Regina had dressed with the utmost care. She was wearing a traveling suit of light blue wool trimmed with black velvet. The fitted bustle jacket had wide cuffs and onyx buttons. A small hat garnished with tinted feathers sat atop her head, and she carried an ebony-handled parasol trimmed with black Spanish lace.

As they stood on the platform at Grand Central Station, waiting to be ushered into the private car, Regina felt an unexpected bout of nervousness overtake her. All morning she'd been battling the feelings of uncertainty that had seemed to sprout the moment she'd opened her eyes. She was going home, but she'd depart the train in Merriam Falls a married woman. And she'd be expected to act accordingly. Her friends and neighbors would no longer see her as the young lady who ran the boarding-house. She'd be Mrs. Jonathan Parker, the wife of the town's most prosperous businessman.

Regina knew she'd be expected to forsake her suffrage endeavors and fill her time with more matronly activities. Reverend Hayes's wife would no doubt call upon her to head the next charity committee, and she'd be expected to play the role of hostess when Jonathan invited the town banker to dinner. Gradually the excitement and anticipation that her honeymoon had created would fade, and she and Jonathan would begin a routine life. There would be children, if she hadn't already conceived, and then what? The more Regina thought about the day-to-day duties associated with being a wife, the more her doubts increased. She wasn't an actress. She couldn't go on pretending that her husband's lack of affection didn't exist.

It was a sobering thought that kept Regina from noticing the admiring glances she drew from several gentlemen on the platform.

Jonathan noticed them for her. Although he was a possessive man, he wasn't a jealous one. In fact, that morning he felt proud to have Regina standing beside him, looking every inch the lady. Each passing day brought a stronger affirmation that he'd made the right decision in choosing her to be his wife. She was strong-willed, but he found himself liking that more and more. And he certainly had no complaints about her ability to please him in bed. The more he had her, the more he wanted her.

The only doubt that Jonathan did retain was his ability to keep his wife from harm until the murderer of the two Merriam Falls women was apprehended and behind bars. He disliked the idea of having to keep Regina under lock and key, and yet he suspected he would have to do just that to keep her from putting her pretty little nose where it didn't belong.

He intended to continue with his plans to get involved in the investigation of the murders once they returned to Merriam Falls. Until the man was caught, Jonathan planned on keeping Regina as close as possible. The thought appealed to him, but he also realized it was impractical. He had a business to run. Sooner or later the mild argument they'd had in the library would be resurrected. Something would trigger his wife's sense of independence, and when it did, he wouldn't have the excuse of a honeymoon to keep her from dashing out the door and down the road to danger.

Bisbee would keep an eye on her, but Jonathan suspected that the spry Englishman could easily find himself outsmarted if Regina put her mind to it. She was extremely intelligent and excessively stubborn, a precarious combination that was going to test his tolerance.

Once they boarded the train, Jonathan saw to Regina's comfort, then opened the newspaper. While his eyes scanned numerous business articles, his mind remained on his wife. It wouldn't do to let Regina know he was more than overly concerned about returning to Merriam Falls. Nor did he want her to know that he suspected Constable Fowler was doing next to nothing about finding the murderer. The law officer wasn't trained as a detective, and his objectivity was affected by his familiarity with the suspects, which could be any man in town. None of the questions he had asked had turned up any likely candidates. The only thing that linked the murder of the two women was the short time-frame in which the crimes had been committed and the women's common support of suffrage.

Jonathan had considered hiring a Pinkerton agent to investigate, but Merriam Falls was a small town, and a stranger would be noticed immediately, especially if he started asking questions about the two dead women. Since he was certain the murderer was a formal member of the citizenry, a private investigator would serve no purpose but to alert the man to be more careful.

As much as Jonathan disliked admitting it, the best way to apprehend the man would be to bait a trap, and the best bait would be Regina. The idea made his blood run cold. There was no way he was going to use his wife to bring the man out of the shadows. Just the opposite was true. Jonathan would do everything within his power to keep Regina from harm.

If the man wasn't caught, the danger wouldn't go away. It would merely diminish from an immediate threat to one that hovered over them, preventing them from living a normal life. And Jonathan wanted a normal life. It was the reason he'd finally decided to marry and begin a family.

At the thought of a child, he found his eyes drawn to his wife. She was sitting across from him, reading a small volume of poetry. The glance became an appraising look as he studied the small hat cocked jauntily on her head. Her richly colored hair was arranged in stylish curls that brushed her shoulders. His gaze moved from her lovely face downward to the fitted waist of her traveling suit. The odds were in his favor that she was already pregnant. He'd lost track of the number of times he'd made love to her since their wedding night.

Regina glanced up from her book to find Jonathan staring at her. The noisy turning of metal wheels over metal tracks dimmed to nothingness as she met his gaze. As always, it was impossible to ignore the effect he had on her. No words passed between them for several moments. Regina felt a blush of color rise to her cheeks. There was a disturbing possessiveness about her husband's gaze, and her heart seemed to stop as a slow smile came to his face.

"How are you feeling?" he asked, eyeing her warily.

"I feel fine. Why do you ask?"

"No reason in particular," he replied, then smiled the devilish smile that always made her heart do somersaults. "Actually, I was wondering if you might be pregnant."

The volume of poetry closed with a dull thump. "We've never discussed children."

"Not specifically," Jonathan said, "but generally they

go hand in hand with marriage. Are you saying you don't want a family?"

"I'm not saying anything of the sort," Regina replied. "It's just that we've been married only a few weeks. Nor have I forgotten that I was tricked into marrying you," she added with a mutinous tilt to her chin. She hesitated, hoping Jonathan might offer some gesture of apology for manipulating the circumstances to his advantage. When he offered nothing more than another devilish smile, Regina glanced out the window. The landscape rolled by unnoticed while she collected her thoughts. Finally, she looked at Jonathan. "To be truthful with you, I'm not sure how I feel about a family at this point. Eventually, perhaps."

"Eventually has a way of arriving sooner than you expect it to," Jonathan stated, hiding his disappointment. "Or have you forgotten the passionate activities that have kept us occupied these last few weeks?"

"I haven't forgotten." Regina glared at him. "Really, Jonathan, there are times when you try my patience."

"Do tell." A dark brow rose while silver-gray eyes gleamed with amusement.

"Very well," Regina said, setting the book of poetry aside. "Let's discuss children."

"By all means," he replied, spreading his hands wide to let to her know he was willing to listen to whatever she had to say.

"I want a family," Regina stated, unconsciously licking her lips before she continued with her declaration. "But under the circumstances, it would be best to delay having them."

"What circumstances are you referring to?"

Regina glared at him. "You know perfectly well what circumstances I am referring to, Jonathan." Her temper started to burn. "Don't sit there, displaying a gentlemanly calmness that does little to hide your arrogance, sir. You may have manipulated me into marriage, but don't think that that achievement is your final victory. I will not spend the rest of my life dancing at the end of your string."

She had several reasons to be angry with her husband, but Regina knew the real target of her current anger was herself. She'd allowed Jonathan to use her passionate nature against her, and by doing so, she'd walked into his sensual trap. The man might have the decency to display some remorse. But, oh, no, not Jonathan. He was far too used to having his way. If she wasn't already pregnant, she was certain he intended to do everything within his power to correct the oversight.

It wasn't the idea of having Jonathan's child that caused Regina's emotions to surge. It was knowing the child's conception would be a passionate one, not a loving one, that upset her.

Jonathan regarded her pensively, unsure how to verbalize his sudden longing for a child. For a moment he imagined he knew the answer, then realized his formal motives for taking a wife had vanished once he'd introduced himself to the beguiling Miss Van Buren. The simple truth was that he wanted *this* woman to bear his children. So what had changed his mind? Why, suddenly, did the idea of having his seed flourish in her womb, and her womb only, seem like the most important thing in the world? More important, why did having her *want* his children create a challenge like none he'd felt before? She may have been an unwilling bride, but she'd become a willing wife. Their differing viewpoints hadn't kept them from becoming passionate lovers. And yet Regina was holding something back from him. He could sense it now, as he'd sensed it several times since meeting her. Knowing she had reservations, well-guarded secrets that kept her from belonging to him completely, fueled Jonathan's determination to break through her defenses.

He considered his words carefully before speaking. "I have no strings attached to you except those that a lawful marriage always attaches to a woman. And a man," he added. "If you wish to argue, then may I suggest you find a topic worth arguing over."

"I'm not trying to argue," Regina replied politely. "I'm trying to talk to you about a very important subject. Our future together."

"What about our future?" Jonathan asked, wondering if Regina thought she could free herself from the vows they had exchanged. A divorce was out of the question, as was an annulment. If she thought to move back into the boardinghouse, he'd quashed the idea before it had a chance to take root. She was his wife; she was damn well going to live with him.

Regina glanced out the window again, then quickly back at her husband. She'd always prided herself on her forthrightness and honesty. If ever she needed those things to be virtues, it was now. "We are married," she began, then hesitated, "and although there are aspects of our relationship that we both find pleasing, it is still lacking several important qualities."

Jonathan continued looking at her, his silver-gray eyes completely devoid of emotion. God, she wished she knew what he was thinking. It would make confronting him so much easier. She was almost afraid to go on, knowing he wasn't going to like what she was about to say, but she couldn't shut the door once she'd opened it, so she steadied her nerves and said what was on her mind.

"We share a bed, Jonathan, but that's all we share. A marriage should be more than that."

"On the contrary." Jonathan smiled again, looking roguishly handsome. "I have never shared my name with a woman before, nor my home."

"That's just it," Regina said without forethought.

"You let me into your life, but only as far as it pleases you. We talk about politics, but I don't know how you really feel about suffrage, or the other things that are important to me. You're a master at twisting words into an answer that's no answer at all. You tell me that you understand the plight of women, then you forbid me to get involved in their emancipation. You endorse my need for freedom with one hand and take it back with the other." Regina took a deep breath. "You painted me standing naked in front of a window, but you never told me that you were an artist until it suited your purposes. We share a bed, but we're strangers, Jonathan. I don't really know anything about you. How you think, or why you think it. How you feel about me—beyond desiring me, of course. You've made that perfectly clear to everyone. Now you want me to embrace motherhood because it pleases *you* to have a family. What about the things that please me?"

Thinking back, Jonathan could understand Regina's anger. He'd slung her over his shoulder and hauled her into his house in front of anyone who cared to watch, but his motive that particular evening had been to keep her safe. He hadn't seduced her, not completely, until they were legally wed. Still, she was right in blaming him for a certain lack of discretion. But he sensed that her anger was fueled by something else, something much more substantial than mere embarrassment.

Reminding himself that his wife was a romantic at heart, Jonathan carefully weighed his response. If Regina suspected that his feelings ran deeper than those fired by passion, she might do some manipulating of her own. He was too strong a negotiator to forfeit the advantage he now had over her, and he'd be foolish to let her think that he was at her mercy. He did care for her, and it was a genuine fondness. And there was desire, a physical yearning that engulfed him like a raging fire whenever he looked at her, but no love. And love was what Regina wanted. He knew that now. In spite of her modern thinking and fervent need for independence, she wanted to be loved.

It was a perplexing situation, and yet Jonathan found himself liking the idea that Regina might love him. It would explain her current annoyance with him, and the vague feeling that something was lacking from his own life. If she loved him, he could rest knowing that he would always be the most important thing in her life. His silent acknowledgment that he possessed a certain jealousy of her zealousness for suffrage didn't show on his face as he addressed her.

"I'm not a man who intentionally cloaks himself in secrets," he told her. "If I seem mysterious or withdrawn, it is only because sharing the more personal details of my life is as new to me as it is to you. I have never been married before. May I solicit your patience until I overcome the handicap."

Blast the man for being logical and polite, Regina thought to herself. She didn't want logic. She wanted emotion. A burst of anger, or even a lecture, would be preferable to having him reply to her robust confession with little more than congeniality.

"Why do you keep your paintings hidden in the loft in Manhattan?"

Jonathan shrugged his shoulders. "No particular reason, except perhaps their inability to add to my image as a stern businessman." He smiled. "It's hard enough to convince doubting investors of my financial genius without them knowing that I dabble with brushes and paint."

"You think they would see it as a weakness."

"Probably. They may allow themselves to be hauled through exhibits because it's socially acceptable, but few of them give a damn about art. Unless it can bring them a hefty profit."

For some reason, Regina didn't believe him. There was more to Jonathan's reasoning than he was willing to admit to her or to himself. She sensed the same reluctance in him now that she sensed whenever she tried to get him to talk about his family. He was willing to give her details, but he never opened his heart wide enough to reveal his true feelings.

For a man who didn't intentionally cloak himself in secrets, her husband was becoming more mysterious by the day.

"I thought you wanted to discuss children," Jonathan said, reminding her of their original topic. "Does the thought of finding yourself with child distress you?"

"We haven't been married a full month," she said quietly. "Would it be such a terrible thing to wait before opening a nursery?"

"Not terrible," he admitted, masking his feelings behind a wall of politeness. A final shrug of his shoulders came before his final words. "But you should know that I have no plans to employ any method that will keep you from having a child. Nor do I recommend that you take it upon yourself to prevent a pregnancy from happening. Having said that, I suggest we leave the rest to providence."

Although his tone wasn't threatening, Regina heard the resolve in his words and knew she'd be a fool to expand their conversation. As for providence, there was little she could say. She picked up the book of poetry she'd been reading and opened it. A short time later she looked up to find Jonathan engrossed in his newspaper.

The train came to a halt in front of the Merriam Falls depot. Regina looked out the window to see Mrs. Chalmers and Richard Ferguson. A rush of relief filled her as she waited for Jonathan to open the door and help her out of the private car. It felt wonderful to be home, and Regina couldn't wait to fill her lungs with fresh air. The last few hours of the train ride had been filled with a menacing silence that didn't bode well for her future as a married woman. If she wasn't already pregnant, there was little she could do about postponing a future pregnancy. Jonathan was determined to have a family as soon as possible.

Feeling shackled by the wedding ring that adorned her left hand, she stepped down from the Pullman with a feigned smile that turned heartfelt the moment Lucy opened her arms. Running into them, Regina hugged the older woman. "It's good to be home."

"It's good to have you home," Lucy countered with tears in her eyes. "I've missed you something fierce." She pushed Regina slightly away, studying her at arm's length. "You look lovely. It's easy to see that Mr. Parker's been taking good care of you."

Regina smiled, saying nothing.

"Richard," Jonathan said, coming to stand beside Regina as he offered his hand to the mill supervisor. "I expect everything is running smoothly."

"Couldn't be better," Richard replied. "Welcome home."

"Thank you," Jonathan said, letting his arm slide around Regina's waist. He pulled her close. "Shall we take the ladies to the house?"

Lucy and Richard followed in the buggy, while Regina and Jonathan rode in the private carriage that had been waiting for them at the train station. It was a short ride, so Regina didn't feel compelled to make conversation. She wasn't surprised when Bisbee opened the front door of the grand house on Whitley Street. The butler had a knack for being where he was supposed to be at just the right moment. He must have raced in, but the effort didn't show on his staunch British face as he accepted Regina's cloak. "I've arranged for tea to be served," he informed her. "I'll have Mrs. Chalmers wait in the parlor."

"Thank you," Regina said, realizing that she was expected to take a few minutes for herself before formally receiving guests. She'd come home to Merriam Falls, but things were different now. She was the lady of the house, the wife of the town's most prominent citizen, and her actions were expected to reflect that position.

She looked at Jonathan as he peeled off his gloves and tossed them on the foyer table. He gave her a knowing smile, as if to say there was nothing to be nervous about, then informed Bisbee that while the ladies were having tea, he would meet with Mr. Ferguson in the library.

Regina was turning for the stairs, when Jonathan reached out and took her by the arm. He pulled her close, kissed her soundly on the mouth, and then whispered for her not to extend a dinner invitation to Mrs. Chalmers or Richard Ferguson. "We're still newly wed," he reminded her with a gleam in his eye. "You'll have plenty of time to talk to Lucy. She lives just across the street."

A fierce emotion swelled up inside Regina as she watched her husband turn and walk into the library. For a brief moment she considered calling him back to confess that she did indeed love him, and if only he'd open his heart and try to love her in return, she'd be more than willing to fill the house with children. The impulse passed almost immediately, and Regina realized that she was close to falling into another trap. There was no mistaking her husband's true intentions; he'd made them abundantly clear. He wanted a passionate wife and children. He'd gained the first without love, why not the second?

Regina avoided looking at Bisbee as she went up the stairs. She had no idea where her bedroom was, nor did she care. She wanted only to have a few moments to herself. Fortunately, a maid stood by an open door, silently signaling that she was waiting for the new mistress of the house to make her needs known.

Forcing a smile to her face, Regina walked through the open door and into what she assumed was her suite of rooms. The only time she'd seen the upstairs of the large house was the night she'd spied on its occupant with her telescope and again when Jonathan had hauled her up the staircase like a sack of potatoes. Unsure how the rooms lay in relationship to one another, she looked around her.

As expected, her suite was tastefully decorated. The lavish furniture was a dark cherry wood. The draperies and bed coverlet were done in a vibrant shade of blue. A small French-style secretary sat in the corner, while the opposing wall displayed a scallop-backed settee, a small Queen Anne chair, and a delicately made glass-topped table. The maid introduced herself as Annie, then waited for Regina to issue instructions.

Wanting to be alone, Regina thanked the servant for her attendance, unpinned her hat, set it on the table, and then asked for the privacy she'd come upstairs to find. When the door was closed and she was finally alone, Regina sat down on the edge of the bed and wondered if she had the strength to convince Lucy Chalmers that she was indeed happily married. The older woman knew her better than anyone. It wasn't going to be easy to keep her despair a secret, and yet Regina knew that she must. Lucy was bold enough to confront Jonathan and demand that he love his wife if she suspected his feelings were anything less than perfect.

Regina frowned. She had no intention of sharing her distress with anyone. Her husband's lack of real affection was *her* problem, not Lucy's. She'd gotten herself trapped into marriage, and it was up to her to make the best of a bad situation.

Knowing Lucy was waiting downstairs, Regina scanned the room again. There were three doors. One would lead to the dressing room and bath, another to a walk-in closet, and the third, the most elaborately carved, no doubt would open to reveal her husband's bedroom.

Already knowing what the room looked like, she avoided the largest of the three doors and opened the one she hoped led to the dressing area. Luck was with her. Once she'd bathed her face and hands, Regina looked at herself in the mirror. Except for the stylish clothes, she was the same woman who had left Merriam Falls a few weeks past. She was still a firm believer in women's rights, and she still longed for a time when women everywhere could determine their own futures. The only thing that had changed was her name. That, and her current lack of innocence, of course.

But the changes were dramatic ones. She was Mrs. Jonathan Belmont Parker, and she was no longer a naive virgin who thought passion was sweet and gentle. Now, after three weeks in Jonathan's bed, she knew that passion was hot and sweaty and one of the most powerful emotions on earth. It could rob a woman of her ability to think. It could make her a willing prisoner in a man's arms, and if the woman wasn't careful, it could be her undoing.

Determined not to let the physical side of their marriage overshadow the emotional side, Regina walked downstairs and into the parlor. Jonathan might think all he had to do was kiss her to have his way, but he was badly mistaken if he thought she'd forsaken the past for the present. She'd left Merriam Falls and the memories of two murders behind her, but she was home now, and she didn't intend to stop her search for justice until the man who had murdered her friends had a name and a fate that suited his deadly deeds.

"My, but this is all so formal," Lucy said as Regina greeted her in the parlor.

"Don't let the formality stop us from being friends," Regina said. "I've only moved across the street."

"And uptown," Lucy said, smiling. "You won't be needing the income from the boardinghouse to keep you in style."

"No," Regina admitted with a smile. "Which is why I want you to have the house."

Lucy was shaken by the news. She stared at Regina for a long time, then started to cry. "I don't deserve it," she sniffed into a lacy handkerchief she pulled from her dress pocket. "But, thank you," she added. "Thank you so much. It's been my home for so long, I couldn't imagine giving it up."

"And I can only imagine giving it up to you," Regina told her. She gave the housekeeper a long hug. "Now, stop crying and have some tea. We have a lot of catching up to do. Has Constable Fowler made any progress in discovering who might have killed Hazel and Elisa?"

"None that I know of," Lucy confessed, pouring the tea. "In fact, it's like the murders never happened. The Emersons are still grieving, of course. The town's been as quiet as a church these last few weeks." She flashed Regina a smile. "Of course, everyone's speculating about your marriage to Mr. Parker. It was rather sudden."

"I imagine Dorothy Randolph is speculating more than anyone," Regina sighed.

The wife of the previous mill manager was disliked almost as much as her husband. When Jonathan had replaced Stanley Randolph with Richard Ferguson, everyone in town had thought the Randolphs would leave Merriam Falls. Unfortunately, they were still living on Halford Street, waiting until spring, or so Stanley had informed the mail clerk. Until then Dorothy Randolph had free rein to spread gossip from one end of the hamlet to the other.

"Actually, Dorothy thinks it romantic." Lucy laughed. "I heard her telling Mrs. Sturgeon that Mr. Parker had done a noble thing by sweeping you off your feet and down the aisle. It isn't safe for a single woman to be running a boardinghouse, what with all that has been happening lately."

"At least Mrs. Randolph hasn't forgotten that two women were murdered," Regina said. "I can't believe nothing has been discovered, no clues, no idea of who the man might be."

"Nothing that Frank Fowler is talking about," Lucy said. "Tell me about the city. Did you see Mrs. Astor?"

Knowing that her friend was trying to keep the conversation from turning painful, Regina allowed herself to be led into a discussion of what she'd seen and heard in the city. It was almost dark by the time Lucy excused herself and walked across the street, escorted by Richard Ferguson.

Jonathan was still in the library, reading the correspondence that had piled up since leaving town for their honeymoon, and Regina was content to let him remain behind closed doors. She wanted a bath, and some time to herself, before dinner.

Annie was waiting upstairs. "What dress should I have pressed, ma'am?" the maid asked as she looked up from the trunk she was unpacking.

"The green one," Regina answered, thankful the task would take the maid out of the room and downstairs for at least an hour. It was difficult to remember the last time she'd had an hour all to herself. Jonathan had been by her side almost constantly during their honeymoon. She desperately needed time to sort out her thoughts.

Annie nodded, then scooped up the green dress and made her exit.

Regina slumped down on the settee the moment the door closed. Suddenly, she was so exhausted, she could easily have climbed into bed, pulled the coverlet over her head, and slept until morning.

Knowing she didn't have the luxury of avoiding her husband so easily, Regina got undressed and stepped into the tub. The steamy water surrounded her, easing the slight aches and pains that came from a lengthy train ride and endless days of wondering what would happen to their marriage once Jonathan's physical cravings diminished.

By the time she returned to the first floor of the house dressed for dinner, Regina had worked herself into a state of anger mixed with confusion and the knowledge that she was hopelessly in love with a man who may or may not ever love her in return.

As expected, Jonathan was waiting for her. His smile said he approved of the green silk gown and the woman wearing it. He escorted her into the small private dining room they had occupied the night he'd challenged her to admit that she was a woman of passion. Regina's eyes were instantly drawn to the painting over the mantel. Once again the sensuality of the Turkish harem assaulted her senses. But this time she could understand it. The look of contentment on the faces of the women was no longer a mystery. She'd experienced the physical gratification that came from having a man pleasure you from your head to your toes, and she'd felt the pleasure of satisfying a man in return. No matter how much she wanted the emotional side of their marriage to equal the physical one, Regina couldn't deny that Jonathan had been right about one thing. She was a passionate woman.

Her husband took advantage of that passion once they'd retired for the night. He opened the door of their adjoining rooms and strolled to where she was sitting up in bed, reading a book. Without a word he jerked back the covers, picked up Regina, and walked into the room she'd originally viewed through the lens of a German telescope. Once she was exactly where Jonathan wanted her, in his bed, he stripped away her batiste nightgown and made love to her.

They settled into a routine not unlike the one they'd established during their honeymoon.

Regina would sleep late, exhausted by her insatiable husband. She would awaken late in the morning to discover that Jonathan had already left for his office at the mill. Once she'd bathed and dressed, she'd go downstairs, meet with Bisbee to approve the dinner menu, then retire to the back parlor, where she could read, write letters, or share a pot of tea with Lucy in the late afternoon. The weather had turned rainy, and it wasn't suitable for shopping or calling upon neighbors. Still, Regina was determined to visit the constable at the earliest opportunity. She wanted to know what the man was doing to catch the murderer.

Finally the weeklong drizzle and gray haze that had settled over the town was banished by a morning of bright sunshine. Regina looked out the front window of her new home. Her gaze settled longingly on the carriage house across the street. There wasn't a cloud in the sky and the temperature wasn't freezing. Tonight would be a perfect night to watch the stars.

Her eyes moved from the doors of the carriage house to its roof. Her telescope wasn't covered by its customary canvas tarp. In fact, it wasn't there at all. The roof was bare.

Regina called for Bisbee.

The butler appeared with amazing speed, thinking something was amiss.

"Where is my telescope?"

Bisbee gave her a sympathetic smile before informing her that the expensive instrument had been carefully removed from the roof across the street and packed away in the attic.

"May I have the key." Regina held out her hand.

"I'm sorry, madam, but I don't have it," Bisbee replied. "It's on Mr. Parker's watch chain."

Regina held on to her temper. There was no reason to blast poor Bisbee. Jonathan had issued the order to have her telescope locked away.

"Have the carriage brought around," she said stiffly. "I have something to discuss with my husband."

Seventeen

Once they were settled in the carriage, Regina looked at Bisbee. The butler's face was devoid of expression, but his eyes were gleaming with amusement, and she sensed he was looking forward to the upcoming confrontation. Regina wished she shared his enthusiasm. Still angry, she planned on blistering Jonathan's ears once she was in his office, but she had no way of forcing him to hand over the key to the attic.

Suddenly an idea sprang to mind.

"Tell me about the fine art of pickpocketing," she said. "It is something that takes great skill?"

Bisbee smiled. "Well, now, that depends on what you're trying to pilfer. If you're planning on removing a certain key from Mr. Parker's watch chain, I'd warn you against it. Learning to be a proper pickpocket takes years of practice."

"I don't suppose you'd—"

Bisbee shook his head.

Regina let out a frustrated sigh. "I shouldn't have asked. Please accept my apologies."

"None needed," the butler told her.

They rode in silence for another few minutes. It was a brisk day, but the sunshine promised spring wasn't too far away. Regina tried to calm her anger over having her precious telescope locked away, but she couldn't. Jonathan was being unreasonable. There was no earthly reason for him to forbid her the pleasure of using her telescope. And it was a pleasure. One Regina cherished.

When the carriage stopped in front of the mill, Bisbee reached for the door latch, then hesitated. He looked at Regina before speaking. "May I suggest that you try to reason with Mr. Parker."

"What good will it do?" Regina asked. "No matter what I say, he will use the excuse of my safety as justification for his actions."

"He has a right to be concerned," Bisbee said. "The murderer has yet to be caught."

"I understand his concern," Regina admitted. "What I don't understand is his unreasonable fixation with keeping me under his thumb. My telescope could be helpful, if only he'd let me use it."

"Then convince him of the rightness of your idea."

"How?"

"However you think best," Bisbee replied, giving her an impish grin.

Regina refused to blush at the image that popped into her mind. It wasn't proper for a lady to discuss the seduction of her husband with a servant, yet both she and Bisbee knew that's exactly what they'd just done.

Stepping down from the carriage, Regina took a deep breath and decided it would serve Jonathan right to be seduced. He never hesitated to use passion to his advantage. For once, instead of ranting and raving, she'd use her head, and her body, to get her way. It was admittedly shameful, but then, she was Jonathan's wife. If she wanted to seduce him, there was nothing to stop her.

"I have some errands in town," Bisbee informed her. "I shall have the carriage return for you in one hour."

"Thank you."

She proceeded up the walkway that led to the main entrance to the mill. Squaring her shoulders, she opened the door, determined to be the victor in the upcoming confrontation.

Once inside, she smiled approvingly at the newly painted walls and the young brown-eyed man sitting behind a desk. Needing no introduction since everyone in town knew her, the clerk greeted her, then hurried to announce her presence. A few moments later Regina was being ushered inside her husband's private office.

Like the outer rooms, the walls were freshly painted. A dark green carpet covered the once bare floor and thick drapes framed the windows. Bookshelves had been added, along with a liquor cabinet and a comfortable leather sofa. Jonathan rose from behind his desk as Regina entered the room. Nothing was said until the clerk closed the door.

"To what do I owe this pleasure?" Jonathan asked as he walked around the desk.

"It was too nice a day to stay inside," she said, smiling at him. "Am I intruding?"

"Never," he told her, leaning down to place a light kiss against her mouth. He gave her a curious look, then smiled. "If you plan on shopping in town, I can escort you."

Regina shook her head, then began to take off her gloves. Slowly, remembering the way Jonathan had teased her one night during their honeymoon, she put her gloves in the pocket of her cloak. Holding his gaze, she unfastened the garment, then let it slide off her shoulders and onto the carpet.

Her husband's expression took on a surprised look when she unpinned her hat and tossed it aside.

"I don't want to go shopping," Regina said, amazed that her voice wasn't shaky. She'd never seduced a man before. Actually, it was quite exciting. "I have more clothes than I'll ever wear. Don't you agree?"

Jonathan smiled. "I couldn't agree more."

When he reached for her, Regina stepped back.

He stopped and stared while she undid the small pearl buttons on the collar of her silk blouse. When he could see the lace trim of her chemise, she smiled. "Please don't let me disturb you," she said softly. "Why don't you sit down and continue your work."

Jonathan wasn't sure what his lovely wife had in mind, but if she wanted him to sit down, he'd gladly sit. He returned to his desk while she walked around his office, stopping to glide her fingers over the leather binding of a book before turning to look at him once again. Her strides were graceful as she moved toward him, not stopping until she was standing beside his leather chair. When she bent down and kissed him, Jonathan felt his body respond.

He pulled her down on his lap and kissed her too.

Regina broke the kiss, drawing back to meet his blazing eyes. She knew Jonathan well enough by then to realize that if she let him take control of the situation, she'd be the one seduced, and in record time. Enjoying the feeling of being in charge, Regina resisted his tightening embrace. "I'm very angry with you," she announced.

"Angry?"

Regina maintained a bland expression while she moved on her husband's lap, making herself more comfortable and causing him to grimace as her hips rubbed against his aroused body. "I've been informed that my telescope is behind locked doors and that you have the only key."

"Is that why you're here? Do you think you can convince me to give you the key?"

Regina shrugged nonchalantly. "I considered picking your pocket, but Bisbee told me I didn't have enough experience to get away with it."

Jonathan laughed. "At least you're honest."

"Of course I'm honest," Regina stated. "Married people shouldn't have secrets. And they shouldn't be unreasonable with each other."

"I'm not being unreasonable. I'm being practical," Jonathan defended himself as he reached for the buttons his wife had neglected to unfasten.

Regina pushed his hands away. "You are being unreasonable. There is no earthly reason why I can't enjoy my telescope. If I happen to see something that will benefit Constable Fowler's investigation, then so be it."

"That's what I'm afraid of," Jonathan told her. He pushed aside the collar of her blouse and kissed her bared throat. Her skin was soft and warm and smelled of scented soap. His hands tightened around her waist. "You're too emotionally involved to be objective about what you may or may not see."

"Of course I'm emotionally involved," Regina protested, deliberately wiggling on his lap. "Hazel and Elisa were my friends. There's nothing to be objective about. I want the man caught and hung from the highest tree."

Before Jonathan could come up with another *reasonable* excuse to keep her and her telescope under lock and key, Regina kissed him again. Her mouth slid slowly over his, her tongue darted out to tease, then withdrew before Jonathan could take advantage of her willingness. Her eyes held his as her hands moved to the buttons of his shirt, just above his vest. Slowly, deliberately, she unfastened one, then another. She smiled as she parted the garment to reveal his chest. Jonathan flinched as her nails found his nipples, raking over them with just enough force to make them harden.

Lost in the power and wonderment of actually being the aggressor, Regina kissed her husband again. This time she didn't retreat when he tried to deepen the kiss. She gave herself to the moment.

Jonathan wedged his hand between them and began

unfastening buttons. He was relieved to discover she wasn't wearing a corset. Once his hands were cupping her breasts, he groaned deep in his chest.

Regina curled her fingers into the thick hair on his chest and pulled. The next thing she knew, she was being lifted off his lap, only to be put down again, but this time her legs were straddling his hips and his hands were sliding intimately up the insides of her legs. Her skirt and petticoats were bunched up around her waist as Jonathan's hand moved closer and closer to the warm center of her body. He found the slit in her drawers, ventured beyond it, and felt the enticing warmth of his wife's body welcoming the intrusion. His fingers stroked and tease until she was squirming to get closer.

"You could spy with me," Regina whispered as she concentrated on the small patch of skin just below her husband's right ear. "Admit it. It's the best chance we have of catching the murderer."

"You're impossibly stubborn," Jonathan said half-heartedly. A raving need had taken over his body, and all he could think about was satisfying it. "God, you feel so good."

Regina heard the mumbled endearments that followed, and smiled.

His mouth sought hers again and all pretense slipped away. Their tongues matched in wild abandonment, while Jonathan did his best to remember that his scheming little wife meant to seduce him into letting her have her way.

Unfortunately, she was right. Her idea of using the telescope had merit, and he couldn't dispute that they might just stumble across something of interest, but he refused to let her think he was giving her full rein to go man hunting. His impetuous wife was far too eager for him to feel completely comfortable about trusting her to do what she was told.

"I'm right and you know it," Regina said, managing to say the words at the same time her body began to throb with pleasure. "We can watch the town together," she suggested as the feelings began to tighten and twist inside her. "The roof has more than enough room for two."

Jonathan kissed her again, cutting off any further comment.

While his hands continued their artful enticement, hers found the buttons of his trousers. Once he was free of restriction, she explored him just as thoroughly as he was exploring her.

"I taught you too well." He lifted her again.

Regina gasped softly as she felt him enter her body.

Jonathan pushed into her very slowly. "You always feel so warm," he groaned.

"You feel hot," she told him. "Hot and hard and wonderful."

He was deep inside her now, stretching her, filling her, becoming a part of her. Unable to think about seduction now that the act had begun, Regina began to move. Jonathan's hands rested on her hips, guiding her, restraining her when she would move too fast. "You are incredible," he said in a husky whisper. "Incredibly beautiful and incredibly bold."

"If I'm bold, it's because you like me this way," she rebuked him between kisses.

Their bodies moved in unison, Jonathan lifting his hips as Regina pressed down. He could feel the tiny shudders that preceded her climax, and thrust hard, filling her completely. He held her close and covered her mouth, masking the sound of her release as her nails dug into his shoulders. Her whole body trembled. Simultaneously, Jonathan unleashed his own self-control and joined her. With a muffled sound, he felt his own climax race through his body.

A few moments later he opened his eyes and looked at his wife.

Regina was smiling, her gaze softened by the physical satisfaction he'd given her and her own sense of victory.

"Are you going to seduce me every time we disagree about something?"

"Are we having a disagreement?" Regina asked, resting her head on his shoulder. They were still joined, and she moved seductively against him, enjoying the closeness as much as the pleasure she'd just experienced.

"You are not to take one peek through that telescope unless I am with you," he said firmly. "Not a single peek. Do you understand."

"Yes, darling, I understand."

Later that afternoon Regina supervised while Bisbee and two other servants carried her precious telescope onto the roof of her new home. Delighted that the sunshine had cleared the flat portion of the roof of rain, she hovered over the fragile instrument like a hen over a nest of new chicks. Once the telescope was mounted on its tripod, she rushed forward to begin the delicate art of focusing the lens. The lack of foliage on the trees that normally shaded the house in summer helped the alignment, but Regina wasn't satisfied until she could see the entire village of Merriam Falls as easily as she could swing the telescope to the left or right.

"I can't wait until dark," she told Bisbee. "I know we'll discover something if we watch closely enough."

"I hope your efforts are fruitful," the butler replied. "The sooner the man is apprehended, the better."

"Do you have any suspects in mind?" Regina asked, eager to hear what Bisbee thought of the men he'd met in Merriam Falls.

"No one in particular. However, one doesn't have to

look far to find several candidates. The town isn't bubbling over with men who support the emancipation of women."

"I doubt there's one to be found within a hundred miles," Regina sighed. "I thought my husband might be the first, but he's as prudish as Reverend Hayes about some things."

"I'm sure Mr. Parker's horizons can be broadened once this unsavory situation is put to rest."

"I certainly hope so. I hate to think what our marriage will be like if he insists on remaining pigheaded."

Bisbee smiled. "Mr. Parker can be obstinate on occasion. But he has only your best interest at heart."

Regina gave him a skeptical glance. Bisbee had once told her that Jonathan loved her, but she'd heard nothing from her husband to confirm that statement. "I'll try to be optimistic about the future," she said more cheerfully.

"That's the spirit," Bisbee remarked as he began covering the telescope with the canvas tarp that would protect it from the weather. "You're an independent woman. Daring and outspoken and just what Mr. Parker needs to keep him on his toes. I daresay, the two of you will have a long and amicable marriage."

Regina wasn't so sure she agreed with the Englishman, but she didn't want to discuss her relationship with Jonathan in more detail. For the moment, she was too happy about having freed her telescope from the attic.

Realizing it was getting late, she reluctantly left the roof via a narrow door that led directly to the attic. Then she retired to her room for a leisurely bath before dinner.

Jonathan returned home to find his wife waiting in the parlor. She was wearing a modest gown of cranberry silk with long, fitted sleeves and tiny ribbon rosettes decorating the hemline. Her hair was pulled back from her face and secured with pearl-studded combs purchased in New York City. She set aside the book she'd been reading, and smiled.

Regina realized that no matter how many times she saw her husband, she never tired of the sight of him. With his tall, agile body and his handsome face, his entrance into a room always caused her heart to skip a beat. She also realized that no matter how many times she told herself to keep their relationship in perspective, her heart filled with hope whenever he looked at her the way he was looking at her then.

"Hello," he said, thinking she looked unusually beautiful. Her skin was glowing and her eyes sparkled. For all intents and purposes, she looked like a woman in love. Jonathan cherished the thought as he walked across the room and helped himself to a brandy.

"Hello," Regina said, feeling suddenly shy. It came as a surprise, considering she'd intentionally seduced the man that very afternoon. She should greet him with more than a solitary word, but she couldn't think of anything else to say.

Fortunately, Jonathan broke the fragile silence, slumping onto the sofa across from her with a weary sigh. "I'm afraid I have to go out after dinner. Hopefully, I won't be too late. I know you're eager to do some stargazing."

"Out? Where?"

"A town meeting," Jonathan told her. "Frank Fowler issued the invitation as I was leaving the mill. It seems a meeting is held every three months."

"I'd almost forgotten," Regina remarked. "I'll go with you."

"I'm not sure that's wise," her husband replied. "The main topic is bound to be the murders of Hazel Glum and Elisa Emerson. I don't want you upset."

Regina brushed an imaginary bit of lint from her

sleeve, then looked at her husband. The truce they had reached that afternoon, or at least the truce she'd imagined them reaching, was a thing of the past. Once again Jonathan was trying to exile her to the role of parlor-sitter and bed-warmer. "You mean you don't want me disagreeing with the esteemed elders of Merriam Falls when they insist that everything that can be done to find the murderer is being done."

"Something like that."

Regina left her seat and walked to the bellpull hanging in the corner of the room. She gave the brocaded strip of fabric a firm tug, then waited for Bisbee to make an appearance. When the butler arrived, she politely asked that dinner be served as quickly as possible. Turning back to her husband, she smiled. "If I recall, Mayor Gaston calls the meeting to order at precisely eight o'clock."

"So I was told," Jonathan remarked dryly.

The church was filled to capacity, but Regina was disappointed to discover that she and Lucy Chalmers were the only women in attendance. Her best friend was seated beside Richard Ferguson. Jonathan led her to the same pew, midway down the aisle. Mayor Gaston was seated on the podium next to Reverend Hayes and David Quinlan. All three men looked surprised to see her, and Regina gave them a cursory smile as Jonathan helped her remove her cloak.

Mayor Gaston was a tall, heavy man with silver hair and a ruddy complexion. He was far from attractive. His eyes were small and pouched, and his nose was too flat. His political clout was limited by his passive personality, and it constantly amazed Regina that he'd been elected to the office for two consecutive terms. Still, he seemed a fair man, one willing to hear both sides of a story before passing judgment.

The meeting was called to order. The first issue to be discussed was the expansion of the train depot. Built more than twenty years before, the shingled platform was in dire need of renovation. Funds were budgeted for a new roof once the weather permitted the work to begin. Several less significant items were discussed before the more controversial topics were brought to the attention of the citizens.

Mayor Gaston looked to the rear of the room, where Frank Fowler was sitting, before he tapped his gavel lightly on the pulpit. "I've been asked by the constable to extend the curfew on the ladies of the town. No one here needs to be reminded of the dreadful events that plagued us earlier this winter. I for one am in favor of keeping our ladies safe. However, my authority to enforce the curfew will lapse at the end of the week. Therefore, I am calling for a show of hands to extend the curfew until such time as Constable Fowler feels it is safe for our women to once again walk the streets without fear of retribution."

Every male hand in the church was raised.

Regina wasn't surprised, nor did she disagree with the vote. But she wasn't about to let the matter stop there. Standing up, she looked toward the podium, then over her shoulder to where Frank Fowler was sitting. "I would like to know what is being done to find the murderer," she said in a clear voice that echoed off the paneled walls of the small church. "A curfew is all well and good, but it won't satisfy justice."

"I'm still investigating the murders," Constable Fowler said, coming to his feet and his own defense. "I can't discuss the details in a public forum."

Regina was on the verge of the rebuking the law enforcement officer, when Jonathan stood up and did it for her.

"We are all aware that specific details might benefit the murderer if they are discussed openly," Jonathan said to the room at large, "but it would help to know if anything of value has been discovered. Are you near to making an arrest?"

"No," Fowler admitted. "There's the possibility that whoever killed Hazel and Elisa isn't in town any longer."

"You still think it was a stranger." Regina turned to look at the man entrusted with the welfare of the town. "It doesn't make sense," she continued. "If a stranger had been in town, someone would have noticed him."

"Not necessarily," Fowler replied with a bite in his voice. He didn't like being called on the carpet by a woman, and it showed on his face. "Mr. Parker is new in town. The murders didn't happen until he bought the mill and moved here."

"That's the most absurd thing I've ever heard!" Regina shouted.

She looked at Jonathan. He seemed undaunted by the vicious accusation. She wasn't sure which man she wanted to bash first, the man she'd married or the thickheaded constable.

"Enough," Mayor Gaston called from the pulpit. "Please, *ladies* and gentlemen. We're here to discuss issues that apply to all citizens of Merriam Falls." He looked at Jonathan, who resumed his seat. "Please, accept our apologies, Mr. Parker."

Jonathan reached up and gave Regina's hand a jerk. Her bottom hit the walnut pew with a soft thump. She tried to free herself while several men muffled their laughter, but her husband only gripped her hand more tightly. Matters got worse when Lucy laid a hand on her other arm and whispered for her to sit still before she got her herself in more trouble.

"No apology is necessary," Jonathan told the mayor. "Constable Fowler was only pointing out the obvious. I am a newcomer to Merriam Falls, but my wife was born here, and I plan on raising my children here. I want the man caught as much as any of you do."

Jonathan's reference to children only made Regina's temper burn higher. How dare the man treat her so shabbily, and in front of the whole town. *I plan on raising my children here.* If she wasn't already pregnant, Jonathan would be lucky to ever have children. If he tried to enter her room tonight, he'd find the door locked. And it would stay locked until he cured himself of being an arrogant ass.

The mayor adjourned the meeting, then asked Reverend Hayes to lead everyone in prayer. The pious minister gave Regina a scalding look before he requested that everyone bow their heads.

Jonathan was still holding Regina's hand. She tried once again to free herself, but it was a wasted effort. Her husband didn't release her until he opened the carriage door and shoved her inside.

Jonathan didn't think he'd ever been more furious.

"I can't believe—"

"We won't discuss this until we are home," Jonathan said, cutting off her words.

Regina could hear the fury in his voice. Equally angry, she sat stiffly on the cushioned carriage seat, counting the seconds until she could unleash her temper. She'd warned Jonathan that a wedding ceremony wasn't going to turn her into a docile female. What did the man expect?

Somehow sensing the urgency of the evening, the driver deposited them in front of the house on Whitley Street in record time. Jonathan helped Regina down, then ushered her inside, where Bisbee was waiting.

"We'll be in the library," Jonathan told the butler. "See that we aren't disturbed."

Taking Regina's arm, he escorted her into the library, then closed the door. He towered over her as she took a deep breath. "I've done everything within my power to keep you safe," he told her. "What did you think you'd accomplish by insulting Frank Fowler in front of the whole town?"

"I didn't insult him," Regina countered.

Jonathan clenched his fists. "Yes, you did. And you intentionally drew attention to yourself."

Regina's hands went to her hips. "The man named you as a suspect in the murder of two women!"

"He was reacting to *my* wife," Jonathan said angrily. "What did you expect him to do? Smile while you called him incompetent?"

He walked to the liquor cabinet and poured himself a drink. At that precise moment he desperately wanted to exercise his legal right to beat some sense into the woman. He swallowed the whiskey in one gulp, then turned on his wife. "You've done everything you can to make yourself the next victim. Every time I turn my back, you're up to something. You've convinced me to let you spy on people, but even that doesn't satisfy you. What more must I do to make you realize that this isn't some political game? You could be in serious danger."

"You're not being fair." Regina's anger flared. "Those women were my friends."

"Your life could be at risk! Do you think getting yourself killed will serve justice any better than Frank Fowler is trying to serve it?"

He couldn't shake the image of her lovely body lying on the cold ground, her throat bruised, her face lifeless. It sent a trembling chill through him along with an overwhelming fear that he would never be able to protect her. If anything happen to Regina, he would never forgive himself.

Regina took a deep breath. Arguing with Jonathan would accomplish nothing. Although she could understand his concern, it stung her pride to think that she needed a man to take care of her. She looked around the room. She'd seen it before, of course, the night she'd spied on her future husband and several times since then, but only from a distance as she walked across the foyer on her way to the dining room. The library was her husband's domain, the room where he conducted his business, the place where he retired when he wanted to be alone.

Her attention was drawn to the painting over the fireplace. Unlike the rest of the room, it sang with color. The young girl seemed almost alive, her smile brilliant, her movements fluid.

Regina knew instinctively that Jonathan was the artist. Yet, the painting seemed out of place in the otherwise masculine room.

"Who is she?" Regina asked.

Jonathan seemed taken aback by the question. He poured himself another drink. There was a strange sadness in his silvery eyes as he turned to look at the painting. The melancholy quality of his gaze made Regina uneasy. Had she stumbled upon another of her husband's secrets?

Setting the drink aside without tasting its contents, Jonathan walked toward the fireplace. He stared up at the painting for a long while. "Abigail," he finally said. "She was my sister."

His admission stunned Regina. He'd never mentioned having a sister. And since he'd used the past tense in identifying her, Regina knew she was dead. But when? And how?

When she didn't respond, Jonathan said, "She was

very young when she died." He took a hard breath, then turned to look at Regina. "She was killed. We were playing outside my father's shop. I was a young boy myself and easily distracted. Abigail must have wandered into the street. I heard her scream, but it was too late. By the time I reached her . . . it doesn't matter now. She's dead. My mother never got over it." He turned back to the painting, as if the sight of it somehow renewed his own grief. "Her health started failing after that. My father did what he could, but Mother locked herself away in a world where my sister was still alive."

As his voice trailed off to a deafening silence, Regina felt her heart aching. For the first time since meeting Jonathan, she saw him for what he was. A lonely man who had carried the blame for his sister's death since he was a little boy. Her heart went out to him, and she wished she could think of something to say that would comfort him. But no words came to mind.

Like her, he had no family left. At least she had pleasant memories of her childhood and her parents. Her anger over his previous behavior evaporated as she walked toward him.

The silence was broken by the loud ticking of the grandfather clock in the foyer. Regina watched as her husband stood with his back to the room, staring up at the painting he'd created as a memorial to his sister. Realizing that she'd finally discovered the real reason behind Jonathan's obsessive need to keep her safe, Regina reached out and placed her hand on his back. She could feel the tension in his body, coiled and ready to explode.

Jonathan stood rigidly under the faint pressure of her hand.

"You can't blame yourself for your sister's death," she said softly. "It was an accident."

"I was supposed to be watching her," he confessed

in a shaky voice. "I shouldn't have been playing hide-and-seek in the alley."

Regina felt tears pool in her eyes. "You were just a child yourself. All children play games, Jonathan."

He felt himself begin to shake on the inside. He'd never told anyone about Abigail. The memory was too painful. "Mother trusted me to take care of her, but I was too busy to notice that she'd wandered into the street."

"It was an accident," Regina whispered. "You can't blame yourself."

Her hand felt warm against his back, and Jonathan wanted that warmth to envelop him, to block out the dark shadows that had invaded his mind the day Abigail had been killed. Shadows that had somehow become a part of him. Turning abruptly, he drew her into his arms and buried his face in the curve of her neck. He nestled his mouth against warm skin and breathed in her scent.

Regina wrapped her arms around him and held him close. He hugged her more tightly, and she felt an answering response in her own body. She knew at that instant that Jonathan *needed* to be loved. "Don't grieve anymore," she whispered. "And don't worry about me."

Jonathan was aware that he'd divulged another part of himself, but the finally told secret seemed to have freed him somehow. He held Regina for a long time, feeling wave after wave of emotion sweep through him. Joy, pain, despair, and a strange, unnamed exultation.

His wife felt warm and alive in his arms. He could feel the heat of her body pressing intimately against his, but instead of passion, he felt a deep longing that centered in his heart. He was shocked at how much she meant to him, how deeply she'd rooted herself in his life.

He grasped her shoulders and forced her to meet his

gaze. "Promise me that you won't do anything foolish," he said. "Promise me."

"I promise," Regina whispered, cradling his face in her hands. She rose up on tiptoe and covered his mouth with her own.

The kiss was meant to be comforting, but it soon exploded with the passion they always stirred in each other. Their tongues mated, while soft sounds escaped from Regina's throat. Jonathan wanted to take her upstairs, to make love to her in the feathery comfort of the big bed, but the need he felt was too strong. Too powerful.

He sank to the carpet, taking her with him. When she was lying beneath him, he rained kisses on her face while his hands molded themselves to the curves of her breasts. Regina moaned his name.

"I won't let anything happen to you," he whispered urgently. "I vow that no matter what, I'll keep you safe."

Regina clutched at his shoulders, kissing him back. She felt his hand reaching for the hem of her dress, then pulling it up. Seconds later he was freeing himself from the confines of his own clothing and plunging deep inside her. He tried to be gentle, but Regina didn't want him to be. She wanted him out of control, unable to hide his need from her, unable to keep any more secrets.

When he finally collapsed, shuddering with the violent conclusion of their lovemaking, she held him close, caressing him. His expression softened as he looked at her. "I can't seem to control myself where you're concerned. And, heaven knows, I can't control you."

"Then stop trying," she said softly but vehemently. She longed to confess the love in her heart, but she didn't want Jonathan to think it more pity than affection. "We will find the man, and the danger will pass. Until then, I promise to be careful."

Later that night, while Jonathan held his sleeping

wife, he was assaulted by the sensations she evoked in him. So many sensations, so many feelings. He tried to shake them off, to sleep, but they refused to be chased away. He'd lost the battle he'd been waging since the day he'd knocked on her door and invaded her life. His plan to select, woo, and eventually win an interesting bride had backfired on him. Somewhere along the way, he'd fallen hopelessly in love with a passionate suffragette.

Eighteen

Jonathan awoke early the next morning as was his habit. He turned onto his side and looked at the woman sleeping peacefully beside him. The woman he loved.

Calmer now that the night had passed, he could sort out his feelings, define them more carefully. But how did one define love? It was a rash emotion, reckless in its nature, but more powerful than anything he'd ever felt. Even in the light of early day, with passion satisfied, it rushed through his veins like fire.

Regina hadn't wanted to marry him, yet she'd bent to convention and done the right thing. She hadn't wanted to admit her passionate nature, but on their wedding night she'd surrendered with a fierce sweetness that had stolen his breath. He stirred something inside her, something warm and wild and purely feminine, just as she stirred something inside him. Could he dare hope that she might love him? Was he overly confident to think that her heart had warmed to his attention the way her body warmed to his touch?

Did he dare reveal the feelings he'd only just come to understand?

Perhaps in time, when the danger had passed. Perhaps then he could tell her how he felt, how much she meant to him. Until then he had to keep her safe. She could be carrying his child. And he desperately wanted a child with her, a combination of their souls and beings, a confirmation of the love he felt for her.

He decided that a second honeymoon was in order. He'd seduced Regina in New York City. When the weather warmed, he'd take her someplace exotic, and he wouldn't hold back his feelings. He'd tell her that he loved her so much his heart would never be his own again.

Regina moaned softly when he bent to kiss her, a murmured whisper that was his name. It brought a smile to Jonathan's face, and he was tempted to wake her. Instead, he kissed her again, a light pressing of his mouth against her cheek, before leaving the bed.

It was several hours before Regina opened her eyes. She stretched lazily, then smiled. For the first time since Jonathan had slipped her mother's wedding ring on her hand, Regina felt truly married. Last night had been a revelation. Jonathan had turned to her in his moment of need, and then, later, snuggled next to each other in bed, he'd talked to her. Really talked. He'd held her close in the dark and told her about growing up in New York City, about his parents, and the sister he had lost. Some of the memories had been painful, some bittersweet, and some had brought a smile to his face.

Her husband had finally shared more than passion with her; he'd shared a part of himself.

Regina left the bed and walked to the window that overlooked the backyard of the house. Bramwell was sleeping on the marble windowsill, a habit he'd taken up since being transported across the street and introduced to his new home. He blinked as Regina's hand stroked him from head to tail, then he began purring to let her know he enjoyed the attention. She continued petting the large cat while she looked out the window at the new day. The trees were still bare of leaves and the ground was a damp clump of earth and dead grass, but spring was on its way. She could feel it in the bright blaze of sunshine that warmed the windowpanes. Scooping up Bramwell and cradling the cat against her chest, Regina's mind wandered back to the previous night and the enormity of its events.

She'd learned a great deal about her husband in the last twenty-four hours. His desire for children, for one. She was hurt by his unwillingness to talk to her before, but she could understand why he wanted a family. In his own way, Jonathan needed children to make up for the lack of his own childhood. Circumstances had matured him well beyond his years. He needed children to bring laughter and fun and games back into his life.

Regina looked down at her flat stomach. Was she pregnant? Suddenly the possibility didn't seem so distasteful.

If she was, Jonathan's vow to keep her safe would turn into a crusade. She'd be lucky to get a breath of fresh air as long as the murderer was free. The thought gave Regina pause, but she decided not to worry until she had something to worry about. For the moment, she wanted to luxuriate in the hope that she and Jonathan had bridged a very important gap in their marriage.

By the time Jonathan returned home that evening, Regina was so eager to see him, she was pacing the parlor.

A strange tingle of excitement raced through her body as their gazes met and held. His eyes softened, and in some ascetic way, Regina realized he was trying to tell her that he felt the same way she did, that this day was in fact the first day of their marriage. They both hesitated, silent, one standing in the middle of the room, the other poised in the doorway. The tension between them stretched taut, and seconds seemed like hours, like an eternity.

"I missed you today," she said simply, moving gracefully into his arms.

"I'm glad," he replied. A mysterious expression lightened his face as he lowered his head and pressed his mouth over hers.

Seconds ticked by as they enjoyed a long, thoroughly satisfying kiss, but reality came back to Regina as her husband released her and she remembered that she'd requested Bisbee to serve dinner early again. "The sky is as clear as glass this evening," she said, smiling at him.

Jonathan laughed. "I see there's to be no relaxing in front of the fire tonight." He glanced toward the hearth, his expression changing the moment he saw Abigail's painting hanging over the mantel.

"I had Bisbee move it this morning," Regina told him. "It's too bright and beautiful to be hidden away in the library."

Jonathan's surprised expression slowly changed into an approving one. "And what of my mantel? It is to be dull and blank?"

"No," Regina told him, relieved that he no longer felt the need to keep his past to himself. "I took the liberty of ordering one of the paintings from the town house in New York. It's to be crated and shipped by train."

"Ahhh." He winked at her. "Then my library wall is to be graced with beauty. If I can't lure a business investor into my lair with the promise of wealth and power, I'm sure a glimpse of my lovely wife can entice him for me."

"Not that painting!" Regina slapped at his arm. "The clipper ship. It's majestic and powerful and perfectly suited for a gentleman's library."

"I prefer my most recent work of art," he teased, pulling her back into his arms. "I think I'll turn one of the upstairs guest rooms into a private library. Of course, the servants will be shocked when they clean. Imagine their faces when they see the lady of the house posed so brazenly."

"Don't you dare," Regina chided him. "That painting will remain in the loft on Thirty-fourth Street, under lock and key. I can't believe you talked me into posing for it."

Jonathan kissed her again. "As I recall, it was a very pleasant conversation."

They stepped onto the roof hand in hand. Regina breathed in the crisp night air, loving its freshness. She looked around, always amazed by the beauty of the night. A smile came to her face as she saw the bench Bisbee had brought up and placed by the telescope. A bottle of brandy, two glasses, and a thick wool comforter were waiting on the walnut seat. "I must thank Bisbee," she told her husband. "He's always seeing to our comfort."

Jonathan agreed as he closed the attic door. Like Regina, he was mesmerized by the night. Above the tree line, the sky seemed to explode with stars. Their crystalline light flickered, frayed, and thinned out into the infinite darkness. The moon hung huge and silver, while long, wispy clouds floated across its glowing surface. The air was cold but not unbearable, and if you listened carefully, you could hear the water of the Hudson River lapping at the shoreline.

"Whom do you want to spy on first?" he asked Regina as he uncovered the telescope and removed the metal cap that protected the lens.

"We're not spying, we're investigating."

"Call it whatever you want," Jonathan replied, "but remember, we're going to see things that are none of our business. Everyone has secrets."

His words made Regina pause. She had no intention of poking her nose in where it didn't belong, but Jonathan was right. They were bound to see things they shouldn't, personal, private things that didn't concern them. Still, she couldn't forego the possibility that they might discover something that could help unmask the murderer.

Once she'd checked the telescope to make sure it was still in focus, she sat down, covered her lap with the blanket, and began her search. As expected, most of the town's residents were indoors. She looked toward the train depot first. A thick triangle of light advanced from the small office window and onto the porch, curling over the wooden edge and onto the ground. The depot was closed, of course, and there was no one in sight. Slowly, Regina inched the long tube of the telescope to the right, north along Gardner Street, toward the town square. It was after nine o'clock and she was surprised to find a light burning in Frank Fowler's office.

She held the telescope steady, and in a few minutes she was rewarded with the appearance of the constable himself. He moved in front of the first-floor window, coat in hand. The lights dimmed to nothingness. Regina waited, holding her breath, until the front door of the city building opened and the constable stepped outside.

"What do you see?" Jonathan asked, uncorking the brandy bottle.

"The constable," Regina said, keeping her voice down and advising her husband to do the same. Sounds seemed to travel twice their normal distance in the dark. "He's making his nightly rounds."

"An admirable task," Jonathan remarked before taking a sip of brandy. He sat beside his wife, surprised that he was eager to have his turn at the telescope. "Tell me what you see."

"He's walking along Gardner Street, stopping to check the doors of the shops there to make sure they're locked. He's almost to the depot. He'll probably go home from there. His house is just around the corner."

But Frank Fowler didn't go home. Instead of walking east on Lowry Street to the modest home he shared with his wife and daughter, he headed for the local tavern.

"He's going into McKinley's," Regina announced.

Jonathan chuckled. "Don't sound so shocked. Just because the man's a law officer doesn't mean he can't enjoy a beer now and again. Why are you watching Fowler of all people?"

"If he can suspect you, I can suspect him," Regina replied rigidly.

Jonathan was surprised by her loyalty, then warmed by it. The feisty, outspoken lady had come to his defense last night, albeit inappropriately. She'd accepted her role as his wife. Now all he had to do was win her heart.

It wouldn't be an easy task either. Regina was proud and stubborn and far too intelligent to be won easily. Her seduction had been aided by her own passionate curiosity to discover life's many secrets, but she'd guard her heart well.

He was still amazed that he'd fallen so completely in love. It wasn't a comfortable emotion, at least not yet, but Jonathan knew it was a lasting one. He couldn't imagine his life without Regina. His mind had wandered all day, his thoughts jumping ahead to the future. There would be children and eventually grandchildren.

"What's happening?" he asked as Regina continued looking into the telescope.

"Nothing," she mumbled.

"Let me have a look-see," he said, gently maneuvering her away from the lens so he could have a try.

He squinted into the narrow opening and saw the white-and-blue lettered sign above the entrance to McKinley's tavern. Knowing men and their fondness for spirits, Jonathan moved on to another part of town. It could be hours before Fowler exited the tavern.

A few seconds later, Regina saw her husband smile. "What is it?"

"A courting ritual," Jonathan chuckled, leaning away from the lens so she could look through it. "If I've ever seen a woman wanting to be kissed good night, it's Emily Fowler."

Regina peered through the lens. David Quinlan was apparently escorting Emily home after an evening in town. The couple was standing outside the wrought iron gate that opened into the small front yard of the Fowler home. David's back was to her, but Regina had a clear view of Emily's face. She did have an anticipating look about her. But if she was waiting for a kiss, she could be waiting a long time. David wasn't even holding her hand.

"I can't imagine what she sees in him," Regina remarked.

"You really don't like the man, do you?"

She shrugged her shoulders. "It's not that I dislike him, it's just that . . . I'm not sure what it is. A feeling, I suppose. He's so serious all the time. I don't think I've ever seen him smile."

"Seminary students are a serious lot," Jonathan replied. "Just be thankful he isn't planning on taking over the parish."

"Perish the thought."

She watched the couple for several more minutes. Whatever was being said between them was being said mainly by David. Emily was looking at him with dutiful brown eyes and nodding her head, agreeing with his every word.

A few minutes later, David opened the gate and escorted Emily to the front door of her home. Regina held her breath, wondering if he would indeed kiss her good night. When he leaned down and placed a very short, very chaste kiss on her forehead, Regina wondered if

Mr. Quinlan was as serious about Emily as the young lady was about him.

Once Emily was inside the house, David Quinlan made his way toward the church. The Reverend and Mrs. Hayes resided in the parish house that adjoined the church property. David took his meals with the minister and his wife, but he lived in a small suite of rooms at the rear of the church building. Regina watched him while he unlocked the door to his living quarters and stepped inside.

"Anything interesting?" Jonathan asked, grateful that Bisbee had stocked the rooftop with brandy and a warm blanket. Regina seemed intent on studying every inch of Merriam Falls.

"Nothing so far," she told him. "But I'm not giving up. Sooner or later, I'm going to see something."

"Here," Jonathan said, holding out his brandy glass. "Have a sip of this while I do some spying."

The next hour was spent taking turns at the telescope. Frank Fowler finally left McKinley's, staggering just a bit as he walked home. Except for the occasional barking of a dog and deep hoot of a night owl, the town was as quiet as a tomb. Smoke billowed from the chimneys, and parlor lights dimmed as people retired for the night.

Jonathan called a halt to the evening despite Regina's protests. "Everyone's in bed," he told her. "Weather permitting, we can try again tomorrow night."

Reluctantly, Regina agreed. She went inside, disappointed, but confident that her idea was still the best one available.

Over the course of the next week, Regina was amazed at what she discovered about the residents of Merriam Falls. Frank Fowler spent more time at McKinley's tavern than he did at home. David Quinlan was courting Emily, if one could call short walks and male-dominated conversation courting. Mrs. Alden's cat had given birth to a litter of kittens that resembled Bramwell.

The most surprising thing Regina discovered was Reverend Hayes's fondness for whiskey. The sanctimonious minister wrote his blistering Sunday sermons with a bottle of spirits sitting on his desk.

"I wonder what secrets we'll unveil tonight," Jonathan said as they stepped onto the roof. "Are you sure you want to do this? Seeing Reverend Hayes consume a bottle of imported whiskey upset you so badly, you didn't sleep for hours."

"He's a minister! A man of God," Regina retorted. "And he acts so damned self-righteous. I'm tempted—"

"To do nothing," Jonathan said in a firm voice. "I warned you that you'd see things you weren't going to like. If you insist on spying on people, then you'll have to learn to be objective about what you see. No one's perfect."

Surprising or not, nothing she'd seen so far had shed any light on the murderer.

With so much on her mind, Regina was growing more anxious by the day. She was still convinced that her telescope would reveal something important, but she had to admit that she had hoped for better results than she'd gotten so far. Other than Reverend Hayes and his infatuation with imported whiskey, she hadn't seen anything that supplied a motive for murder.

Regina was putting the telescope into focus, a nightly task that usually took ten to fifteen minutes, when she gasped in surprise.

"What is it?" Jonathan asked.

Regina couldn't speak. She pointed at the boardinghouse across the street, then looked at her husband.

Jonathan took control of the telescope and stared through it. A few seconds later, he began to laugh.

Swinging the telescope around, he said, "I think we'll concentrate on the north end of town tonight."

"You'll have to speak with the man," Regina said once she'd recovered. "You're his employer. And Lucy is my friend. I won't have her shamed."

Jonathan shook his head. "I thought you were a free thinking woman. Besides, Lucy is old enough to know what she's doing."

What Lucy had been doing or, more precisely, what she and Richard Ferguson had been doing was enough to make Regina blush. Passionate as she might be, it was still embarrassing to see other people indulging in their own pleasure. "That's beside the point," she stammered. "If the man has any real affection for her, he'll propose marriage. Immediately."

Jonathan didn't remark one way or the other until Regina poked him in the ribs with her elbow. "I'm his employer, not his father," he grunted.

"You're the one who moved him into my boarding-house."

"It's Lucy's boardinghouse now. She can do whatever she wants in it."

"Don't be rude," Regina snapped. "I insist you talk to the man."

"And tell him what? That we accidentally watched him making love to Lucy."

"We didn't watch," Regina said, still flustered over what little she had actually seen. "And that's not the point. The point is, I don't want Lucy's heart broken. If the man is a gentleman, he'll marry her."

Jonathan let out a frustrated sign. If he didn't say something to Richard, Regina would, and she wouldn't be tactful about it. "Very well. I'll *talk* to him tomorrow."

Nineteen

A few days later Lucy came rushing across the street to inform Regina that she was officially engaged to be married. The older woman held out her hand to show her friend the small ruby-and-gold ring Richard Ferguson had gifted her with the previous evening.

"You look so happy," Regina said, thankful her husband's discussion with his manager had brought about the desired results.

"I am," Lucy chimed, all smiles. "After Henry died, I never thought to marry again. But Richard is a good man. With his job at the mill, and the boardinghouse, we'll have a good life."

"I'm glad," Regina said, hugging her friend. "Now, let's have some tea. We have a lot to do. I want to give you an engagement party. Is it going to be a spring wedding?"

"We haven't decided," Lucy told her. She followed Regina into the parlor. "I suppose it would be best to wait until the weather is more agreeable. But you don't have to give us a party. My goodness, you've already given me a house."

"I want to give you a party," Regina insisted. "Besides, why have this big house if I can't put it to good use?"

"You're right," Lucy agreed. "You've been back from

your honeymoon almost a month now. People should see how happy you are."

Regina did her best not to frown, but Lucy knew her too well.

"You are happy, aren't you?"

"I'm not sure," Regina confessed with a sigh. She poured the tea the maid had just brought, then handed a cup to Lucy. "Jonathan's an attentive husband and an excellent provider. The house is lovely, and . . . I think I may be pregnant."

"Oh, how wonderful!" Lucy smiled as Regina stood up and began to pace the room. "A child." She sighed loudly. "Oh, it will be grand having a baby to take care of."

Regina scowled out the window. A few moments later Lucy came up behind her and patted her on the shoulder. "You're nervous and anxious. That's to be expected," she added. "You'll feel better once the newness of the idea wears off."

"That's not it," Regina sighed. "It's Jonathan. I'm going to have his child and I don't even know how he feels about me."

Lucy urged her back toward the chairs. Once Regina was sitting down with her hands folded in her lap, her friend smiled. "The man loves you," she stated with conviction. "Everyone who sees you together can see it as plain as day. He'll be a wonderful father, and you'll be a wonderful mother. Stop worrying."

Regina wiped away a tear. "Everyone *thinks* Jonathan loves me, but he's never told me how he feels. I know he cares for me in some way, and he worries, but that isn't love."

"How do you feel about him?" Lucy inquired patiently.

"I . . . I love him," Regina admitted.

"Have you told him that?"

Regina shook her head. "I'm afraid to. I'm already wrapped around his little finger," she said. "It's shameful to admit, but I can't seem to refuse him anything."

"From what I've seen, he's as wrapped around your finger as you are around his," Lucy told her. "The man adores you. The only thing he won't let you do is put yourself in danger."

"When he finds out about the baby, he'll be even worse." Regina chewed her lip for a moment, then frowned. "I feel like the murderer is holding me hostage in my own home. I long to call a meeting of the Merriam Falls Literary Circle, but I can't for fear of putting another woman in danger. It isn't fair. The man is walking around as free as a bird, and we're all cooped up in our houses, afraid to go out at night. I feel like I'm smothering."

"Try to concentrate on the good things," Lucy said. "You have a wonderful husband and a baby on the way. All this trouble will pass, and you and Jonathan will have your whole lives in front of you. Be happy."

Regina wished it were that easy. She was feeling the strain of keeping her feelings hidden. She woke every morning, elated to be sleeping next to the man she loved, and worried that he'd never open his heart wide enough for her to gain entry. Her relationship with Jonathan was more relaxed, but she was still in the dark when it came to knowing how he felt about her. The restlessness she'd felt since the murders had increased tenfold in the last few days. Regina didn't *think* she was pregnant; she was *certain* she was pregnant. And she hadn't been exaggerating when she'd said that Jonathan's mother-hen attitude would become unbearable once he found out she was going to have a baby. She felt like a ball of tangled emotions, happy one moment, depressed the next.

Determined not to dampen Lucy's happiness, Regina turned the discussion toward the upcoming party. The more she thought about it, the more she realized she was allowing the murderer to intimidate her. It wasn't fair for the women of Merriam Falls to live in fear, but they'd been doing it just the same, letting the unnamed man win. Well, it was time they stopped.

Regina decided to make Lucy's engagement party bigger and better than any party the small town had ever seen. In the meantime, she'd issue an invitation to several of her old friends to come by for tea. And she'd start going into the village every day. With the party, there'd be lots of shopping to do. It would give her an opportunity to renew her relationship with the people in town.

It was time to come out of hiding.

"Hello," Regina greeted Emily Fowler later in the week. The two women met on the sidewalk in front of the post office. Regina was dressed in a dark green suit with gold braid around the collar and cuffs. "It's good to see you again, Emily."

"Oh, yes," the younger woman exclaimed, then smiled. She lowered her voice slightly. "We've all been eager to see you again. I understand Mr. Parker took you to New York City for your honeymoon."

"Why don't we have lunch and I'll tell you all about it," Regina suggested.

A gentle wind was blowing off the Hudson. The day wasn't overly cold. The sun was shining cheerfully as the two women made their way toward Hartley's Eatery, the only restaurant in town. Once they were seated at a corner table, Bisbee excused himself, assuring Regina that he would return in one hour to escort her while she shopped.

"Mr. Parker's butler seems very attentive," Emily remarked.

"Bisbee is that," Regina replied, not bothering to explain why the servant was acting like a shadow. "He's English, you know, and very dedicated."

"How exciting it must be," the constable's daughter exclaimed. "Who would have imagined that you'd go from running a boardinghouse to being the wife of the richest man in Merriam Falls." Envious eyes surveyed the fashionable cut of Regina's suit. "Marriage brings about a lot of changes."

Regina got the impression that Emily was talking about more than financial changes. Unfortunately, one of the prevailing attitudes of their times was to expect young women to go to their marriage beds totally ignorant. "Marriage isn't exactly what I expected," she responded candidly. "It can change the way you think about things. There's another person to consider, after all."

"Of course," Emily agreed. "David thinks marriage is the most serious step two people can take. He insists that to enter into matrimony without seeking God's guidance is a sin."

Then I'm a sinner, Regina thought to herself. *I barely had time to change my clothes.*

She wasn't offended by the young lady's remark, knowing the girl hadn't meant to be cruel. One of Emily's most endearing qualities was her lack of malice. There wasn't a mean bone in her body. She saw the best in everyone.

The waitress returned to the table, suggesting the daily special. Regina scanned the menu. She really wasn't all that hungry considering her condition, which she'd always heard caused a woman to eat for two.

Emily ordered a sandwich and a cup of hot tea.

Folding her menu and setting it aside, Regina did likewise.

"I understand you and Mr. Quinlan are still keeping

company," Regina said once the waitress had taken their order.

"He calls on a regular basis," Emily admitted, then blushed to the roots of her hair. "Mother is sure he's going to propose."

"Will you say yes?"

Surprisingly, the younger woman hesitated. "I'm not sure. I like David. He's very refined and very well educated. He hopes to take over a parish near Syracuse this fall. Reverend Hayes wrote him a sterling letter of recommendation."

Pretending not to know that the associate pastor was also far from affectionate, Regina offered Emily a light smile. "And you're not sure if you're up to being a minister's wife?"

"Something like that," Emily admitted. "I believe in what he's doing. Choosing a holy vocation requires a lot of discipline. But David's so serious."

"Most ministers are."

Emily chose not to comment. Instead, she talked about the various social functions she and David had recently attended, and the changes that were being implemented at the mill. "Father agrees with the workers," Emily announced. "The new equipment your husband has had installed makes their work so much easier. He's improved the heating system, and I heard that he's planning a summer picnic for the employees. Mr. Rutherford would never have done something like that."

"Jonathan's a very generous man," Regina said, grateful that she hadn't been tricked into marrying a penny-pincher. "He's still very concerned about the safety of the women who work at the mill."

Emily sighed in agreement. "I know. Father is at his wit's end. I get so depressed when I think about the murders. David and I called on Elisa's family last week.

It broke my heart to see how Mrs. Emerson is grieving. She's aged years in only a few weeks."

Regina thought of what Jonathan had told her of his own mother. *Her health started failing after that. My father did what he could, but Mother locked herself away in a world where my sister was still alive.*

Like Emily, Regina's heart ached for the families of the two murdered women. She longed to be able to give them the solace that the man who had killed their daughters would soon face justice, but there was nothing to tell. All she could do was continue to sit on the rooftop and watch the town, hoping that sooner or later the murderer would to do something to make himself known.

"Have you heard the news?" Regina said once the waitress had served their food. "Mr. Ferguson proposed marriage to Lucy Chalmers. I'm having an engagement party for them the first Saturday in April. Please extend the invitation to your parents, and Mr. Quinlan, of course."

The idea of a party delighted Emily. She began talking about dresses and weddings and how spring would surely bring the town out of mourning.

Bisbee appeared in the doorway of the restaurant right on schedule, and Regina excused herself, insisting that Emily come to tea the next afternoon.

After an afternoon of shopping, Regina and her English escort returned to the house on Whitley Street. She was delighted to find that her husband had decided to work in the library rather than in his office at the mill.

She walked to where he was seated and placed a quick kiss on his cheek. "Thank you."

"For what?" he asked, moving his chair back and pulling her down on his lap before she could step out of reach. He kissed her leisurely. "That's better," he said once her mouth was red and swollen. "Wives of fifty years kiss their husbands on the cheek. We're still new-lyweds."

The idea of being married to Jonathan for fifty years was enough to make Regina's head spin. She was still acclimating herself to being married, period.

"What are you thanking me for?" her husband asked again. "I know you've been shopping. Did you buy something outrageously expensive?"

"In Merriam Falls?" Regina laughed. "No. Lucy showed me her engagement ring. I wanted to thank you for talking to Mr. Ferguson. I've never seen Lucy happier."

Jonathan gave her a lopsided smile, then confessed. "Actually, I didn't do much talking. I mentioned that he was doing a fine job at the mill and that he didn't have to worry about being replaced. Richard did the rest. He'd already bought the ring. In fact, he proposed to Lucy the very night we saw them. You might say they were celebrating."

"I'm glad to know that he truly loves her," Regina said, feeling sad that she couldn't say the same thing about her own husband. "Lucy deserves to be happy."

"Everyone does," Jonathan said, kissing her again.

As always, it was almost impossible for Regina to think clearly when her husband was kissing her. She rested her weight more fully against him and enjoyed the sensation of his hands rubbing up and down her back. At times like this, she could almost believe that Jonathan did love her. His touch was both gentle and arousing, and he looked content, as if he'd like nothing better than for her to remain in his arms forever.

But contentment and physical satisfaction weren't love. At moments like this, Regina's love was a combination of bittersweet longing and a heartfelt hope that the love she felt for him wasn't in vain.

Between kisses, Regina realized she hadn't discussed

the party with her husband. He was just beginning to nibble on her earlobe when she told him.

"That's nice," he mumbled. "But it would be a hell of lot nicer if you closed the door."

Regina laughed. "You're insatiable."

"And I plan on being insatiable for a long time to come." He grinned. "Now, close and lock the door and come back as quickly as possible. I'm hungry for the taste of you."

On her way back to the desk, Regina unbuttoned her suit jacket. She was in the process of returning to her husband's lap when he shook his head and stood. His hands went around her waist, and she found herself being lifted and set on the edge of the desk, facing his chair. He caressed her cheek, then smiled as his other hand began to lift the hem of her skirt. Gently, his mouth covered hers, sealing a protest that Regina had no intention of uttering.

She accepted the touch of his hand on her leg as he slowly made his way past the edge of her gartered stockings. Her hands clutched the hair at the nape of his neck as he inched his way to the center of her body. Soon both his hands were beneath her skirt.

Desire swept through Regina. She needed Jonathan in a way she didn't understand, but the need went as deep as her soul. Sighing, she pressed closer to him. His hands moved gently, teasing her sensitive flesh through the thin cotton of her undergarments, moving closer and closer to the part of her that ached to feel his fingers probe and penetrate.

"Spread your legs, sweetheart," he whispered against her throat.

Regina's legs parted while her body trembled with anticipation.

Her husband undid the buttons on his trousers, smiling all the while. When he joined their bodies, he was still smiling.

Regina clutched his shoulders, barely able to contain a moan of pleasure. It was at moments like this that she forgot all her doubts and fears. There was only the passion and the intensifying pleasure that came with it. Her body belonged completely to Jonathan, but she didn't feel controlled or manipulated when he possessed her like this. She felt wonderful. Feminine and cherished and powerful, a strange combination to be sure, but one Regina enjoyed experiencing.

Jonathan moved slowly and deep, pushing into her hot channel, then holding himself there while his mouth took hers in a long, demanding kiss that left her gasping for breath. His hands cupped her bottom, holding her snugly against him. "You feel so damn good," he said. "Hot and wet. It's all I can do to keep from exploding the second I'm inside you."

The silence of the library was filled by soft moans, male and female, as they moved together, each straining for the ultimate completion that would leave their hearts racing and their bodies weak. When it came, Regina felt almost faint.

Jonathan held her in his arms for a long time. When he finally pulled away, he smiled down at her. "As much as I'd like to work at home every day, I'd never accomplish anything. You're too distracting."

"It wasn't my idea to shut the door," Regina told him as she straightened her clothing. "I only wanted to say thank you."

"You did," her husband replied, giving her a wicked wink. "Now go plan your party. Invite as many people as you want. If you need more help, send for the servants in New York."

"I think I can manage with the ones we have here,"

Regina said, inching herself off the desk only to discover that her legs were still weak.

Her husband steadied her with a hand around her waist. "Are you all right?"

"I'm fine," she told him, knowing that her weakness was a combination of sexual satisfaction and pregnancy. But she wasn't ready to tell Jonathan about the baby. She was still getting used to the idea herself.

For the next two weeks, Regina divided her time between party preparations and spying. Jonathan joined her every night, taking his turn at the telescope. While she gazed through the lens, he talked to her, telling her about the improvements he was making at the mill and the new business ventures he was considering.

"It's getting late, and you have a party tomorrow," Jonathan said, calling a halt to the night's rooftop activities.

"Just a few more minutes," Regina said, returning to her surveillance of Stanley Randolph. The previous mill manager was spending a lot of time at McKinley's tavern lately. She'd never particularly liked the man, mostly because of the way he'd treated the women who worked at the mill, as if they were little more than horses hitched to a wagon. Fortunately, her husband didn't tolerate similar attitudes in his current managers. "What do you think about Stanley Randolph?"

"Nothing much," he told her. "Which is why he's no longer employed at the mill. Why? Do you think he might be the murderer?"

"I'm not sure," Regina said. "He's certainly not an advocate of suffrage. In fact, he did his best to have Hazel fired after he read the article she wrote for the paper. He told Mr. Rutherford that she was a trouble-maker."

"That doesn't mean he killed her."

"Then who did?" Regina asked, growing weary of watching without seeing anything substantial.

"It's late and you're getting tired," Jonathan said, capping the telescope.

"I'm getting frustrated," she admitted. "We have to do something to bring the murderer into the open."

"Stop right there," Jonathan told her. "You're not going to be the bait in a trap that could get you killed."

Regina would have argued, but she had a baby to think about now, a baby who was growing inside her womb and making her increasingly nauseated every morning. Jonathan was an early riser, so he hadn't witnessed her morning discomfort, but sooner or later he was bound to notice her increasing waistline.

Surprised that his wife wasn't arguing with him, Jonathan gave her a skeptical look. He became more suspicious when she folded the lap blanket, then reached for the canvas cover that protected her telescope. Getting Regina off the roof and into the house usually took a good hour. Tonight she was obeying him without hesitation. Something was definitely wrong.

His skepticism continued once they were inside. Strongly suspecting that Regina was on the verge of doing something dangerous, he reiterated that she wasn't to provoke the murderer by calling attention to herself.

"I promised I'd be careful," she told him. "Now, stop frowning and come to bed. My feet are cold."

Jonathan laughed.

Regina was finally beginning to sound like a wife.

Being a dutiful husband, he stripped out of his clothes and got into bed beside her. An hour later, after he'd warmed more than her feet, they slept.

* * *

The following evening was a smashing success. With Bisbee's gentlemanly supervision, the house had been waxed and polished from top to bottom. The large dining room was filled with people. Lucy Chalmers and her future husband were all smiles as a large three-tiered cake was wheeled into the room. Jonathan stood at the head of the table, champagne glass in hand, as he proposed a toast to the couple's future happiness.

Regina sat at the opposite end of the table. She was pleased that the guests seemed to be enjoying themselves. Even Reverend Hayes was smiling, but then, he'd consumed several glasses of wine during dinner. Midway down the table, Emily Fowler was seated across from David Quinlan. The young minister was engaged in conversation with the mayor, while several other guests talked about the upcoming wedding. Frank Fowler had complimented her on the menu, seemingly putting the incident at the town meeting behind them.

Wearing a royal blue dress that everyone correctly assumed was a Paris original, Regina looked as happily married as she hoped Lucy Chalmers would one day be. But on the inside she was worried that if she didn't get out of the crowded room, she'd faint dead away. Her gown required a corset, which she hadn't laced too tightly, but in spite of that, she felt an overwhelming need for fresh air. It would be another half hour before Jonathan invited their male guests to join him in the library, while she ushered the female ones into the parlor. Gritting her teeth behind a forced smile, Regina prayed she could last that long.

If she fainted now, Jonathan would come running from the other end of the table, while Dr. Rumley fetched his bag from the foyer. Her secret would be out in a matter of seconds.

Taking small sips of water, Regina told herself she was being foolish. Sooner or later she would have to tell Jonathan about the baby. Why was she waiting to share the news with him? Could she possibly think it might change the way he felt about her? No. A man who felt no love for his wife wouldn't begin to love her just because her womb had accepted his seed. Jonathan wanted children, but he wasn't going to turn over his heart the moment he found out that he'd sired one. Then why?

Because I want to be as happy about this baby as Jonathan will be, she admitted to herself as Richard Ferguson began to cut the cake. *I want him to love me as much as he's going to love our child. I'm jealous, and I can't help it.*

Taking another small sip of water, Regina reminded herself that she was the hostess for the evening, and a hostess didn't run away from her own table. Somehow she managed to keep smiling, and finally, blessedly, Jonathan stood up, calling an unofficial end to the delicious meal.

"Gentlemen, please feel free to join me in the library."

Taking a deep breath, Regina allowed Richard Ferguson to help her away from the table. Lucy joined her a few moments later, and a procession of female guests moved across the foyer and into the parlor. The room wasn't as large as the dining room, but it did feel somewhat cooler. Coffee was served by two of the housemaids, while the room buzzed with female chatter.

"Your home is beautiful," the mayor's wife remarked. "And the artwork is exceptionally lovely."

"Yes," Regina agreed, wishing she could tell everyone that Jonathan had painted most of the canvases that decorated the walls. "My husband enjoys art as much as I do."

Pleased that she wasn't the center of attention, Regina unselfishly allowed Lucy to dominate the room and the conversation. She also realized that the majority of the women guests had felt cheated by not being able to attend a wedding for herself and Jonathan. They saw Lucy's upcoming nuptials as an end to the mourning that had settled over the town after the murder of Hazel Glum and Elisa Emerson.

Regina didn't feel nauseated any longer, but she did feel overly warm. Underneath her dress, her skin was damp with perspiration. Being discreet, she made her way toward the door.

Once she was outside the parlor, Regina went in search of a room where she could open the window and let in the cold March air. The library door was open just wide enough for Jonathan to see her pass if she walked toward the back of the house. That left the second floor. Unfortunately, several guests were standing on the balcony that overlooked the foyer, chatting away while their hostess felt another attack of nausea. Reverend Hayes was one of them. He gave her a condescending smile, the only kind he knew how to bestow upon a woman, as Regina made her way toward the foyer servants' entrance under the grand staircase.

Once she was behind the closed door, looking up at three flights of stairs, Regina wondered if she could make it to the second floor without fainting. Holding on to the banister with one hand, she gathered up the voluminous folds of her dress and climbed the stairs. When she reached the second-floor landing, she stopped to take a deep breath. Another flight of steps would take her to the third floor; from there she could make her way to the roof and some precious privacy.

Her stomach fluttered nervously as she climbed the last few steps. Regina held on to the image of stepping onto the roof and the blast of cold night air that would quickly relieve her current state of distress. She could make it. Only a few more steps, she told herself as she twisted the brass knob on the attic door.

The moment she stepped outside, Regina felt better. She took long, deep breaths while the wind cooled her feverish skin. It had rained earlier in the evening, and the damp rooftop gleamed in the moonlight. She leaned against the door for a few moments, savoring the cold night air and the blessed feeling of freedom. Jonathan was right, she thought as a small smile lit her face. She was a creature of the night.

Regaining some portion of her composure, Regina stepped forward. The sky was as dark as pitch, with only a few random stars showing through the thick layer of clouds that promised more rain before morning. The moon was waning and shrouded by more clouds, leaving only a minuscule stream of moonlight to brighten the earth below it.

The sound of the door creaking closed behind her stopped Regina halfway across the roof. She turned, expecting to see her husband, who would no doubt chastise her for leaving their guests. But it wasn't Jonathan standing in front of the attic door.

It was David Quinlan.

Regina stood as still as stone, the wind biting at her face. The moment her eyes fell upon the young minister, she knew he was the one who had murdered two of her dearest friends. His amber eyes glowed in the darkness and his face was contorted with anger.

Nothing was said as the realization of danger soaked into Regina's very bones. She could scream, but her body seemed numb, unable to respond to anything but the thoughts racing through her head.

"Miss Van Buren," David said, his voice low and thick with sarcasm.

"Mrs. Parker," she corrected him, her voice shaky but found. Her eyes frantically searched for a way around him, but the flat portion of the roof was limited, and he was standing directly in front of the only door. She was trapped.

"You've made a mockery of your vows the same way you've made a mockery of your womanhood," he snarled. "You're a Jezebel, Miss Van Buren. A harlot who uses instruments of Babylon." He looked at the telescope. "The stars don't control your destiny, God does. And you've turned your back on him."

Regina knew explaining the differences between astrology and astronomy was useless. David Quinlan couldn't be sane. No sane man would think the way he was thinking, or look at her with such blatant hatred, as if she'd brought a plague upon the town.

"I'm no Jezebel," she said. She needed time. Surely someone would miss her soon and come looking. She had to keep him talking. "Hazel and Elisa weren't Jezebels either."

"They worshiped you," he told her. "You infected them with your modern ideas. You blinded them to the role God had preordained for them to play in his kingdom the same way you're trying to blind my sweet Emily. I won't have her soul tainted by your filthy ideas of equality," he said, his voice flat and unfeeling.

Regina stared at him, hearing the hatred, and suddenly understanding it. David was a man obsessed. To him, Christianity wasn't based on love or God's ability to forgive, it was an unobtainable perfection. A faultless contest of behavior that couldn't tolerate any form of disobedience. She pitied him at the same time she knew he was truly mad.

He moved toward her. His face blank, his gaze determined. His hands were clenched at his sides, the same hands that had strangled the life from Hazel and Elisa.

"God's wrath is mighty and just," he said.

Tears blurred Regina's eyes as she stepped backward,

but there was nowhere to go. She was only a few feet away from the edge of the roof.

"They'll find your body in a few hours and think you fell off the roof. It's slippery," he added, his mouth twisting into a perverted smile.

He lurched toward her, gripping her by the shoulders. His face was completely distorted now, his mouth curved into a sardonic grin as he turned her around so she could see the edge of the roof and the darkness that hid the ground below.

"You won't get away with another murder," she cried, twisting to get free. A new kind of nausea swept through her body as he laughed low in his chest. She was drenched in the cold sweat of fear. A thousand thoughts raced through her head—Jonathan, her baby, a future that could never be.

"I will," Quinlan assured her mockingly. "Everyone in town knows your appetite for the unconventional. They won't find it strange that you left the party and made your way to the roof."

Gathering her strength, Regina did her best to break free of his steely grasp, but she wasn't strong enough to overcome the energy of a madman. And David Quinlan was truly mad. He pushed her forward while her feet slid over the damp roof. She was sliding nearer and nearer to the edge, when a roar of outrage sliced the air.

"Damn you to hell!" Jonathan shouted as he hurled himself toward Quinlan. He gripped David's shoulder, his clawlike fingers biting into muscle and bone.

Regina used that moment to break free, taking only a single step before she collapsed on the roof, shaking all over.

Beside her, the two men fought. Quinlan and Jonathan were well matched, both tall and lean, but the young minister had the strength of insanity on his side. He lunged at Jonathan, knocking him flat on his back. His fists began to smash and batter in a furious flood of blows.

Regina screamed, but she wasn't aware of it. She could see the cruel set of Quinlan's lips and the fury in his eyes, and now she feared for her husband.

Jonathan's right fist connected with Quinlan's ribs. He used the split second of pain to his advantage, rolling to his side. Within moments their positions were reversed, and it was Jonathan pounding his fists into the other man's face.

Then the roof seemed to overflow with people. Frank Fowler came barging through the small attic door, almost tearing it off its hinges. It took the constable several minutes to get Jonathan off the young minister, who was grunting Bible verses between punches that had his nose and mouth bleeding. As Jonathan was pulled to his feet, Quinlan followed, totally out of control. He exploded with a fist to the constable's jaw that left the bigger man staggering on the edge of the roof. For a moment Fowler tottered on the brink of disaster, his arms flailing.

Regina reached for Jonathan at the same moment he grabbed for the constable. Her fingers fell short, but Jonathan was able to catch hold of Fowler's jacket and pull him back. Before either man could catch their breath, Quinlan was at them again, trying to plow his way past them to get his hands on Regina.

Jonathan turned on the man like a prizefighter, his right fist hooking under Quinlan's jaw. The young minister was momentarily lifted off his feet. When he regained his footing, he was poised at the edge of the roof, his arms swinging wide in search of a nonexistent handhold. Then he swayed backward over the edge, a frightening scream escaping his throat as he fell to the rain-soaked ground.

Jonathan gathered Regina into his arms, holding her so tightly, she feared for a moment that he might break her ribs. "I'm fine," she mumbled, shaking with the desperate realization that her life and the life of their child had come close to ending. "I'm fine."

Jonathan continued to hold her, rocking her back and forth. His face was as pale as the moonlight, his chest heaving from the fight and the soul-chilling fear that Regina could have been killed.

He wanted to tell his wife that he loved her, but his mouth was too dry. His whole body felt like it was on fire, first with the hatred that had spread through his blood when he'd seen Quinlan getting ready to push Regina off the roof, now with a trembling kind of relief that made him feel as weak as a kitten.

Clinging together, Jonathan unable to speak, Regina mumbling words of comfort, neither one of them paid any attention to the men who had gathered on the roof. Mayor Gaston listened while the constable told him what he'd seen and heard. Reverend Hayes was struck speechless by the news that a man who had professed to be caring and devoted to Christianity had actually been a murderer. Richard Ferguson barred the door, keeping the women who had followed him up the stairs confined to the attic.

"I think we should get the lady inside," Bisbee said, touching his employer's shoulder.

Jonathan raised his head. Regina was looking at him, her face streaked with tears, her lips quivering from cold and fright.

"I almost lost you," he whispered fervently, trembling with the words.

"But you didn't," she said, a faint smile brightening her face and eyes. The party guests were forgotten as she decided it was time to tell Jonathan how she felt. The reality that death could come at any time made her realize she couldn't hold her feelings inside a minute longer. She wanted her husband to know that he was loved. "Bisbee's right. I'm cold. Let's go inside."

Completely blind to what was going on around them, Jonathan lifted Regina and carried her off the roof. Bisbee made a path for them, insisting that all was well and requesting that the guests take themselves back to the first floor, where something more substantial than champagne was being served for those who felt the need.

Frank Fowler was already on his way downstairs; someone had to take charge of David Quinlan's body. His wife comforted Emily while the rest of the guests took advantage of Bisbee's invitation.

When they reached the privacy of their bedroom, Jonathan kicked the door closed behind him, holding Regina in his arms as he sank down on the feather mattress.

"It's over," she reassured him. Her husband was still shaking like a sapling in a storm. She rubbed her hands up and down his arms while she snuggled closer to his chest. "I'm safe," she kept repeating. "Quinlan's dead. No one is going to hurt me now."

Jonathan looked at her, his eyes glazed with tears. "I love you," he said for the first time. "I love you so much."

He kissed her long and hard.

"I didn't plan on falling in love with you," he said after several long kisses. He stretched out on the bed, pulling her down on top of him. His fingers began to work on the tiny row of buttons at the back of her dress while she reached for his tie. "I wanted a young, healthy, passionate woman who could give me spirited children, but I didn't plan on losing my heart in the process." He kissed her again. By the time he was done, her dress was around her waist and his hands were cupping her breasts. He gave her a wicked smile. "Actually, I didn't lose it. You stole it. You and your sapphire eyes and your stubborn ways. Look at me," he growled. "My hair's turning gray and it's all because of you. I'm shaking on the inside, and I need a whiskey so bad, I'd almost go back on that godforsaken rooftop to get one. And all because I can't imagine a future without you in it."

He took a quick breath, then smiled. "Don't ask me to explain it. I can't. I shouldn't enjoy the company of a stubborn woman who insists that men are ignorant and selfish and domineering, but I do. The sound of your voice pleases me. When you smile, my heart smiles with you. Everything about you pleases me."

"You please me too," Regina said. She kissed him, then smiled. "I love you."

Jonathan held her close. "When I saw Quinlan go up the stairs, I saw something in his eyes. I'm not sure what it was, but the hair on the back of my neck stood up. Then the mayor waylaid me in the hall. He must have thought me the madman. I pushed him aside and ran up the steps. It's my fault," he added impatiently. "You were right about Quinlan, but I was too busy worrying about you to see the man for what he was."

"No one could see inside his soul. And, no," Regina said, forcing Jonathan to look at her, "it isn't your fault. You didn't poison Quinlan's heart and mind."

Her lips found his in a kiss of deep affection and reassurance. Gradually, he relaxed. "I was frightened," Regina admitted softly. "I don't think I've been more scared. All I could think about was dying before I could tell you how much I love you."

"You can tell me every day for the rest of our lives," Jonathan replied, knowing he'd never love anyone as much as he loved this woman.

"I will," his wife assured him, then shivered in his arms as the image of David Quinlan's face flashed before her eyes. "He was insane," she whispered.

"Shhh, don't think about," Jonathan said, reassuring her now. "The town will get over the shock and everything will return to normal."

"Not everything," she replied, thinking about the changes that would soon take place in their own lives.

"What in the hell were you doing on the roof?" Jonathan asked as his fingertips teased the pink crowns of her breasts.

"I needed some fresh air," Regina replied, calm and content now that she knew she was loved. She made quick work of the buttons on his vest and shirt, then began teasing his nipples with her fingernails. "I don't know why people call it morning sickness. Not when it makes you dizzy at ten in the evening."

Jonathan went still for a moment, then quickly rolled over, pinning her gently beneath him. "You're pregnant!"

Regina laughed with pure joy. "Yes." She turned her attention to getting his clothes off as quickly as he was trying to rid her of the satin dress. "We have guests," she said, suddenly remembering the house full of people.

"Bisbee will see them to the door," Jonathan said, tossing her petticoats up and out of his way. His hand settled tenderly over her still-flat stomach as a smile came to his face. "Are you sure?"

"Yes. In a few months I'll be waddling around the house like a plump goose. Will you still think I'm young and passionate?"

"There'll be no waddling up to the roof," Jonathan told her, regaining his arrogance. "And no suffrage rallies. Not until my son is born."

Regina didn't argue. She was too busy being kissed breathless.

It was much later before she had the energy to speak. "What if it's a girl?"

The room was dark, the covers pulled snugly around

them since Jonathan hadn't taken the time to light a fire. Her husband ran his hands over her body, measuring her from knee to hip, then letting his touch rest gently over the spot where their child was growing. "It doesn't matter if we have a dozen daughters." He grimaced, then laughed as Regina bashed him with a pillow. "I'll love them just as much as I love their mother."

"By the time they're grown, they'll have the right to vote," Regina announced proudly. "I'll make sure of it."

Jonathan groaned as he buried his face in the curve of her throat.

"I didn't want to love you either," she confessed while her hands explored his body. "You didn't steal my heart, you seduced it, but the result is the same. I can't imagine life without you either."

"Then it's settled," Jonathan told her. "We'll spend the rest of our lives gazing at stars and making babies."

"And painting, and signing suffrage petitions, and loving each other."

"Especially loving each other," Jonathan agreed as his wife slid her leg over his hip, then sat up, straddling him. "On second thought, I think I'd rather have sons. Daughters usually follow in their mother's footsteps. One passionate woman in this family is more than enough."

"There's never enough passion," Regina told him, then spent the rest of the night proving it.

Epilogue

"Papa, Papa. Come quick!"

Jonathan stood up as his son Matthew came running into the library. "What is it?"

"Abby," the little boy said, mixing his sister's name with a gasp for air. "She's stuck up a tree."

Jonathan stifled a groan as he headed for the door. Regina had given him four wonderful sons and one precocious daughter. Abigail Elizabeth Parker was five years old, as pretty as her mother, and full of the devil.

He followed the boy through the house and out the back door, nodding to Bisbee as the elderly Englishman came around the corner, carrying a ladder. Stopping under the branches of a sprawling oak, Jonathan smiled up at the cherub-faced little female who was perched on a limb a good twelve feet above the ground. "What do you think you're doing, young lady?" he asked, using the fatherly voice that usually scared her three older brothers into immediate obedience.

Abby smiled down at her father. "Seeing how high I can go."

Jonathan removed his coat and handed it to Bisbee. Once the ladder was in place, he told Abigail to sit still. "Papa's coming to get you. Don't be afraid."

"I'm not afraid," she chimed. "I like it up here."

Jonathan cursed under his breath. "I'm going to spank

her this time," he assured Bisbee. "Wait and see if I don't."

Bisbee nodded, knowing full well his employer wasn't going to do anything of the sort. Little Abby would wrap any male in the household around her finger with one look from her silvery eyes, and her father was no exception.

"Oh, my!" Regina said, coming outside, followed by their second son, Richard. She'd been in the nursery with the newest addition to their family, a healthy three-month-old little boy named Benjamin. Her gaze went up the ladder to the branch where her daughter was sitting. The hem of Abby's dress was torn and her white stockings were covered with dirt.

"What in the world is she doing up a tree?" Regina asked.

"She's seeing how high she can go," Jonathan said, looking over his shoulder. "This is all your fault."

"My fault!"

"You're the one who keeps telling her she can go as far as she wants in life," he grumbled. "The next time you attend a suffrage rally, my daughter stays home."

"I said as *far* as she wants, not as *high* as she wants," Regina replied. "Now, stop complaining and get her down before she falls."

"I won't fall," Abby assured them. Swinging her feet back and forth, she looked down at her mother. "Papa will rescue me."

"I've lost count of the times," Jonathan grumbled out loud. When he reached the thick limb where his daughter was perched like a tiny bird, he scooped her up and went down the ladder. Once he was standing on solid ground again, he dusted off his hands and pointed toward the back door. "Up to your room, young lady. Now."

Abby nodded, thanked Bisbee for fetching the ladder,

then scampered past her mother and brothers and into the house.

"See these gray hairs." Jonathan pointed at his temple. "Every one of them is named Abigail."

Regina laughed. "Oh, I think a few of them are named Richard, Edward, and Matthew. After three rowdy sons, you thought raising a little girl would be easy."

Richard and Matthew shrugged their shoulders and went on their way. Rescuing their little sister was a daily event. So was listening to their parents argue. Both of them had often wondered how two people who never agreed on anything could spend so much time kissing and hugging and smiling at each other. Bisbee said it was perfectly normal, so the boys didn't worry about it.

Jonathan looked at his wife. She was still as beautiful as the day he'd met her, despite the fact that she'd given him five children in twelve years. Her face glowed with love and her eyes still sparkled with life.

"Boys are supposed to climb trees. It's natural. Little girls should—"

"Don't say it," Regina warned him.

Jonathan passed the ladder to Bisbee, then looked toward the top of the house. He'd made a few renovations over the years. The attic was now an artist's loft with slanted windows that caught the morning sun. It opened onto a glass conservatory complete with potted plants and crank-out windows that could be opened whenever his wife wanted to use her telescope.

"There's a lunar eclipse tonight," Regina said, wrapping her arms around his neck and giving the hair at the nape of his neck a little jerk. "Want to watch it with me?"

"With or without our clothes?"

Always unpredictable, the last time his wife had invited him to gaze at the stars, he'd opened the conservatory door to find her dressed in nothing but moonlight. Thinking about the results of that evening brought a smile to his face. "Is it time to feed Benjamin?" he asked. "I can't finish the painting without him."

Regina laughed. The first painting she'd posed for was still in New York. She'd made Jonathan promise to keep it under lock and key until their children were old enough to appreciate its artistic value. The painting she was posing for now wasn't as risqué, but like the first one, it couldn't be displayed in the parlor of their Merriam Falls home. Her husband's newest creation was a portrait of her nursing their youngest son. She'd been posing for it for the last several weeks, with Benjamin's help, of course.

"One day I'll be able to say no to you," she replied, knowing she was loved and cherished, and reveling in the freedom that allowed her to pass those feelings on to her children.

"Bring our son up to the studio," Jonathan said, smiling the devilish smile that his wife couldn't resist. "I'll be waiting."